LAST
DAYS

Other Fiction by Joyce Carol Oates

LAST DAYS

Stories

JOYCE CAROL OATES

E. P. Dutton, Inc.   New York

"The Witness" originally appeared in *Antaeus* (Spring 1983).

"Last Days" originally appeared in *Michigan Quarterly Review* (Summer 1983).

"Funland" was published in a limited edition by William Ewert (Concord, New Hampshire), July 1983.

"The Man Whom Women Adored" originally appeared in *North American Review* (March 1981), and was reprinted in *Prize Stories 1982: The O. Henry Awards.*

"Night. Sleep. Death. The Stars." originally appeared in *Queen's Quarterly* (Autumn 1983).

"Ich Bin Ein Berliner" originally appeared in *Esquire* (December 1982).

"Détente" originally appeared in *The Southern Review* (July 1981), and was reprinted in *Pushcart Prize VII: Best of the Small Presses 1982–1983 Edition, Vol. 7.*

"My Warszawa: 1980" originally appeared in *Kenyon Review* (Fall 1981), and was reprinted under the title "My Warszawa" in *Prize Stories 1983: The O. Henry Awards.*

"Old Budapest" originally appeared in *Kenyon Review* (Fall 1983).

"Lamb of Abyssalia" was published in a limited edition by Pomegranate Press (Cambridge, Massachusetts), 1979.

"Our Wall" originally appeared in *Partisan Review* (Spring 1982).

Published in the United States by E. P. Dutton, Inc.,
2 Park Avenue, New York, N.Y. 10016

Library of Congress Cataloging in Publication Data

Oates, Joyce Carol, 1938–
Last days.

I. Title.
PS3565.A8L37   1984   813'.54   84-1591
ISBN: 0-525-24248-1

Published simultaneously in Canada by
Fitzhenry & Whiteside Limited, Toronto
COBE

DESIGNED BY EARL TIDWELL

10 9 8 7 6 5 4 3 2
First Edition

for William Abrahams—
to whom American short story writers
owe an ongoing debt of gratitude and affection—

CONTENTS

LAST
DAYS

THE
WITNESS

My father lies on top of the bedspread, the pillows propped up crooked behind him, the seashell ashtray on his chest, smoking, leafing through the Bible, staring smiling out the window. "The Holy Ghost has departed me," he sometimes says. I am running light as air across the roofs on Main Street. Threading my way through the flapping laundry, around the television antennae. One of the neighbor women calls out to me. Be careful, you're going to trip yourself and fall, you're going to *hurt yourself*, but already I'm a mile away, five miles away, running so lightly I only need to come to earth to bounce up again, springy, my toes like a monkey's toes, my hair flying.

You don't know what you're saying, my mother tells me. Her eyes are puffy from crying. Her lips look chapped—all the lipstick has been wiped off. You're dreaming with your eyes open: you're a liar.

I was running away from home but not for the first time. I had taken $3.87 from the secret place in my mother's stockings-and-underwear drawer in the bureau. Beneath the sheet of old

3

Christmas wrapping paper. I was running, flying, galloping. No one could catch me. No one saw me. Mrs. Howard hanging her laundry, old sour-breathed Mr. Ledbetter on the first floor landing, Whoa, horsey! Where are you going so fast? Do you live in this building?

Why do they always talk in loud joking voices. And make swipes at my hair because of the curls. But I have learned to duck and keep on running. . . .

You tell such lies, my sister Irene says. But of course she's jealous.

It is many years ago, too many to calculate. Below Waterman Park where you're not supposed to go alone the man with the coat slung over his shoulder is speaking softly and angrily to the woman in the peasant blouse, but I can't hear, I have pressed the palms of my hands against my ears. I am not to blame, I am only eleven years old.

It is the last summer we will be living above Harders Shoes on Main Street, Main Street at the corner of Mohigan, a few weeks before the fire, before everything is changed. "What is going to happen?" my mother's sister from Trenton asked. "He isn't dangerous, is he?—I mean, you or the girls—" My mother didn't answer at first. Maybe she knew I was listening behind the door. Then she made a sound I couldn't decipher, a laugh, a thin tired snorting kind of laugh. She said: "Not the girls, he's crazy about the girls."

I am running away from them, from the apartment on Main Street. Irene and me sharing a bed, Momma on the sofa in the living room, my father in the "large" bedroom. Was he dangerous? No. Yes maybe. Of course not. Sometimes love for us brimmed in his eyes. Sometimes he had to wipe at his eyes, ashamed, with the back of his hand.

I am running away to Waterman Park. My father shuffles the cards for a game of gin rummy, then changes his mind, lets the cards fall onto the floor, a cascade like water falling, with almost no sound. He isn't drunk but he isn't friendly right now. His feet are bare and bluish-white and the nail of the big toe on the injured foot is that queer plum color, and grown very thick: maybe a quarter-inch thick.

He reaches for the Bible, he reaches for a fresh pack of cigarettes.
He says: "Get out of here. Shut the door. I've had enough of you
spying on me—all of you." His voice is low and murmuring, he
doesn't sound angry. He never does.

It is an afternoon in late August. Warm muggy motionless air. I
am running up the dim-lit stairs to the roof, the three bills and the
coins are in my pocket, no one will know where I've gone. My
mother is at work, my sister is at a friend's house, my father is lying
on top of the bedspread, smiling, not smiling, staring out the window. The bedspread is scorched in several places from his cigarettes.

I slam outside, letting the door strike against the asphalt siding,
not taking time to close it. The tarry roof is quivering with heat. It
is our last summer. The four-room apartment above the shoe store.
The sandstone building. Main Street at Mohigan. Momma
worked days at the hospital out East End Avenue, Irene was fourteen and in tenth grade at the high school. My father went out
sometimes in the evening. Then he wouldn't come home until two
or three in the morning, or much later, eight o'clock, but we
wouldn't see him, he'd go into the bathroom and lock the door.
But most of the time he didn't go out. They were quarreling once
and I overheard my mother say, Why don't you leave, then, go
back to Isle Royale and live alone the rest of your life—go to
Alaska for Christ's sake, and my father said without raising his
voice: Where? Where can I go? I'm here. I'm in my skin. Here. This
is it.

He is lying against the crooked pillows, there are tufts of dark
hair on the joints of his toes, the air in the bedroom is stale and
smells of tobacco smoke, whisky, sweat, unwashed clothes. The last
time it rained, my father didn't close the window, so the mattress
got soaked and the wallpaper got stained but the air was fresh.
What does it mean, stupid Irene asked, —the Holy Ghost "departed"? What does it mean? Is it something like God, or Jesus
Christ—? Will we be all right?

I am running across the roof of our building. Running, flying,
my arms outstretched. No one can catch me. No one can see me. A
woman is hanging up laundry in the heat, clothespins and nylon
cord and a wicker basket filled with damp clothes, she calls after

me but I don't hear, I am already past the chimneys, jumping across to the next building, no one knows my name. One building and then another and another. The air is wavy with heat. There are expanses of soft tar. There are plyboard strips to walk on. Loose bricks, stacks of asphalt siding, beer cans, yellowed newspapers. Last spring a boy held me out over the edge of the roof, he wanted to make me cry but I wouldn't, he wanted to make me beg him but I wouldn't, and afterward when they let me go and I ran I heard him say, She runs like a deer—which makes me proud. A deer or a light-footed horse or a cheetah. Running springing up into the air. My hair flying, my arms outstretched. You're dreaming with your eyes open, my mother says. But I'm not asleep. I'm not in bed. It's daytime and I'm running across the roofs above Main Street, jumping six feet at a stretch, ten feet, twelve, high up into the air, and when I come down it doesn't hurt my feet, I feel nothing at all, no more than a deer or a horse or a cheetah would, not looking to the left or right.

Once some of us climbed down the fire escape here and went into an opened window into a corridor, but we couldn't figure out where we were. An old fat woman in a bathrobe chased us back out. You're the ones, she said, I'm going to call the police, but we climbed back out and ran across the roof laughing. We didn't take anything. But we were blamed. Irene told my mother. Some kids had stolen somebody's mail including a check, so we were blamed but it wasn't our fault, I didn't even know who had done it. We should burn the building down, I said. The whole damn row of buildings down. See how they like it then.

I am eleven years old, I have stopped growing, the school nurse says I must bruise easily. What are these marks on the backs of your legs? And I was so ashamed, when the nurse made us all take off our shoes and socks, and my feet weren't clean. Don't cry, one of the girls said. But I wasn't crying.

Clothespoles and television antennae and pigeons, and pigeon droppings all over. Which is why you can't run up here barefoot. That, and the hot tar. The hot asphalt. It makes me dizzy to look over the edge, the girls are always saying, but we're only five floors up, the buildings along Main Street aren't very high, nothing like the Wolcott Building where we played in the elevators: fifteen floors not counting the basement. Is someone calling after me? Is it

Momma shouting my name? I am running downstairs now, in the
dark. I know which building this is, at the far end of the block, I'll
come out on the street between the La Mode Women's Fashions
and Dutch Boy Paint & Paper.

Whoa, little horsey! old Mr. Ledbetter says.

Don't you touch me, I whisper. And duck under his arm.

Why did I go all the way out to Waterman Park, they will ask me
afterward. Was I crazy, to take the bus three miles alone, to go out
there by myself. . . . The woman stumbling in the grass, in the high
grass along the canal bank, wasn't anyone I knew. I really didn't
look. I shut my eyes, I pressed my hands against my ears. She was
Momma's age maybe. She had hair the color of Aunt June's—dark
brown that looked maroon, like she'd dunked it in purple ink. The
red scarf around her neck was one of those filmy chiffon scarfs
Irene bought at Woolworth's. You tied them around your neck
just for the looks of it. Or around your head if your hair was up in
curlers.

Once when they were fighting and Irene was at the roller rink
with her boy friend I ran away to my uncle's and aunt's house
across town—that was a long time ago, the summer before. My
aunt hid me in the bathroom where my little cousins couldn't peek
at me. She washed my face, and brushed my hair except for the
snarls, and hugged me, and said not to cry. She asked about my
father. Wasn't he seeing that doctor any more, wasn't he seeing *any*
doctor? She asked about my mother—"Why doesn't she ever give
me a call? I miss her"—but I didn't know how to answer. I told her
I wanted to live at her house. I wasn't going back home. I made her
promise not to telephone my mother and say I was there.

She let me make popcorn for myself and my little cousins. I
melted butter in a tin measuring cup on the stove. But I shook too
much salt on the popcorn—I wasn't used to her salt shaker.

She promised not to call my mother but she must have called
because my mother and father both came to get me, in a car bor-
rowed from the people who lived next door. I ran to hide under the
stairs. I wasn't crying but I was afraid. When they pulled me out I
told Aunt June I hated her and wished she was dead. So Momma
slapped me. I knew she would slap me. I didn't care, I wasn't crying. I wish I could close my eyes and see Aunt June's face but I

can't. I mean, the way she was then. So many years ago. The house on Ingleside Avenue, the red-brick fake siding, my youngest cousin still in diapers. She wasn't as pretty as my mother. But she was pretty. She was just a young woman, wasn't she?—maybe twenty-six, twenty-seven years old. A mole on her cheek, the maroon-gleaming hair in a pageboy, crimson lipstick, her eyebrows penciled in like Elizabeth Taylor's—too heavy and dark for her narrow face. I can't see her now. There isn't any young woman there. I open my eyes and see an angry old woman staring right through me. Her scalp shows through her thin white hair and her eyes are badly bloodshot. She can't talk now because of the throat cancer—because of the operation. She's angry at me because I am still alive. Because I told her I hated her that day, and wished she was dead. But I never meant it. God will forgive me. Unless God is angry too.

I am running inside the store windows, one after another after another. And in the windows of cars parked at the curb. The lady shoppers are annoyed with me but I don't pay any attention to them, I don't even look at them, no one knows my name. The window of the jewelry store, and the window of the discount drug store, and the long wide windows of Woolworth's, a shadow-girl running, weightless, quick as a deer. My father says it's no point in going back to Isle Royale to work for the National Parks Service, it's no point going back to visit my grandparents in the northern peninsula, or looking for a job, or taking up his church work again (after he was discharged from the hospital he'd gone around door-to-door with the Bible for a few months but I don't know all that happened—Momma won't tell us): it's no point going anywhere because all spots are the same identical spot in God's mind and he was perfectly happy where he was. But I wanted to take the bus out to Waterman Park because I loved it there. Because I was so happy the times we went there.

Except once. But I didn't tell anyone.

That time, at the Jaycees' picnic, Momma and Aunt June took us all out. I won first prize in the ten-to-twelve-year-old foot race, and was given a silver dollar, and a boy named Pat I knew from school, he was in seventh grade, asked me if he could see it. He said he'd never seen a real silver dollar before. So I showed it to him.

Can I hold it? he said. I didn't want to give it to him, I said, Why?—you can see it. No, he said, coming closer, I just want to hold it for a second. I had it in my hand. Come on, he said, let's see, and I didn't want to but I held it up, and he snatched it out of my fingers and ran away behind the refreshment-and-restrooms building with the little tower on top. I cried but didn't tell anyone, not even Irene. I told her I lost the silver dollar. "Then that's double bad luck," she said.

My father says he's proud of his little girl. Proud of both his little girls. But he doesn't want to talk because his head starts to ache and because there isn't anything to say he hasn't said already. Also the light hurts his eyes. Also my voice hurts his ears. "If I had it in me to love anyone I would love you," he says, shaking his cigarette ash in the ashtray, "but you know the Holy Ghost saw fit to depart from me leaving just this husk and whited sepulchre, and I can't lift a finger in rebellion. 'The Spirit bloweth where it will.' Do you know what that means? *That means everything.*"

My mother begins to cry. Short ugly sobs like hiccups. My father turns away as if the sight disgusts him. But he doesn't say anything. He isn't angry. He never gets angry any longer.

"I don't want to taste blood," he says. "Not ever again."

The black bus driver doesn't seem to think it's strange that I have climbed up into the bus by myself, dropped two nickels into the fare box, gone to sit by one of the windows at the rear of the bus. My heart is beating like crazy. There is a queer sensation in the pit of my stomach. To be riding the bus alone! Out to the park alone! But I don't have my bathing suit. I won't be able to swim in the pool. Two Sundays before, Irene and I went out with a carload of kids, the mother of one of Irene's girl friends drove us out, we swam all afternoon in the pool and had a picnic lunch before coming back home. But now I'm alone. Now I'm going to be alone for the rest of my life.

The seashell ashtray is a souvenir of Tampa, Florida. At its center a miniature mermaid has been fashioned partly out of creamy pink shells, her coiled fish tail glittering prettily, her blue eyes blank and staring. She has seaweed hair that hides her breasts. She is very shapely. But no one admires her any longer, she's been discolored with tobacco, ashes, grime from my father's fingers. No one sees her any longer.

The ashtray sits on my father's chest or abdomen, rising gently, falling. Gradually it becomes filled with ashes and then the ashes are dumped into a wastebasket. I can see my father's crinkly chest hair through his undershirt, curly-red going gray. And under his arms. I can remember how his hair used to grow close about his temples, and in warm weather it would curl damp on his forehead. But now he is going bald. His eyes are a strange pale pebble-color, not blue and not gray, but lighter than his skin. Why is his forehead so creased?—and the cheeks too. He is always thinking. He frowns, makes faces, runs his nicotine-stained forefinger hard across his front teeth. "I don't trust myself out there," he has said. He means out the window, out on the street. Anywhere outside. "I don't want to taste blood ever again."

He smokes Camels. The bed and the floor are littered with cellophane wrappers and those little red cellophane strips. The brand of whisky varies, why can't I remember the labels on the bottles, why are they so much less distinct than the cigarettes . . . ?

Sometimes we play gin rummy for pennies but whoever wins has to put the pennies back in the "kitty"—in a cigar box. Sometimes we play checkers, Parcheesi, or one of the games with dice that Irene is crazy about. The three of us shaking the dice in a little black cardboard cup that got soft and damp from our hands, hooting with laughter, exclaiming, while rain hammered against the window a few feet from the bed, and the air in the room was close and stale and cozy and secret. Only the three of us. My mother never played even when she wasn't at work.

My father had a disability pension but something had gone wrong, or hadn't been completed, so the checks never came. My father and mother quarreled about this but my father explained to Irene and me that it was better to go without than to crawl. "They want to make a man crawl," he said. "But the Spirit of the Lord is infused with too much pride for that." So he lies on top of the bedspread smoking his cigarettes and drinking his whisky, at peace. Sometimes he will flick through the newspaper or something I bring home from school, but mainly he reads the Bible. He reads a verse or a page at a time, then leafs through to another section and reads there, his lips working, his forehead sharply creased. Anything he discovers in the Bible is important. But then it is important too to close the book, and open it again at another place, and read any verse his eye happens upon. It is the most important thing in life. It *is* life. But all the verses are of equal importance.

What is going to happen? Momma's older sister from Trenton asked.

I don't know, Momma said.

I mean—isn't he dangerous? If he was arrested for trying to kill that guy, whoever it was—

That won't happen again, Momma said.

How do you know it won't happen again?

Because it won't.

How do you know, for Christ's sake?

I don't know, Momma said. Go ask him yourself.

He might hurt you or the girls—

Not the girls, Momma said flatly. He's crazy about the girls.

There are a half-dozen scorch marks on the bedspread, a long narrow one on the pillow case. My father says he wasn't asleep but somehow the cigarette slipped from his fingers. He wasn't asleep, the light was on, he'd been studying the Bible. Once at four in the morning he had to beat out a little fire with his hands and he burnt himself so that tears ran down his cheeks from the pain, and my mother screamed at him, screamed and yanked and pulled at the bedclothes, tearing the sheets off the bed, throwing the pillows on the floor. Irene was too frightened to see what was wrong, she just lay there not moving in bed, but I ran out in my nightgown, and there was my mother sobbing and my father with his hands cupped in a strange way, the fingers bent like claws, trying to comfort *her*. "It wasn't anything," he said. "It was just an accident. Calm down. Calm down. God only meant it as a warning."

At Waterman Park there is sometimes a crippled man who isn't a beggar, a man with funny mottled skin, nothing but stumps for thighs, rolling himself around on a wooden platform with skate wheels attached. He wears gloves so his hands won't be hurt. I never look at him. My eyes dart to him but then lift over his head. Momma says it's rude to stare at a cripple but that isn't why I don't look at him.

This afternoon he's here—pushing himself on his little wooden platform around the wading pool where the small children are splashing and trying to swim. His shoulder and arm muscles are all bunched, his neck is thick as my father's, in spite of the heat he is wearing a felt cap. He pushes himself slowly along the pavement. His movements are precise and rhythmic and unhurried. If you make the mistake of looking into his face you see that one of the eyes is milky and staring off into the air. But the other eye is fixed onto you.

Why did you go out to Waterman Park alone, they will ask. All the way out there alone. You little brat. You liar.

Were you testing God's love for you, my father will ask. But you should know better. You should know that He loves you in any case. You can't injure His love. You can't increase it. You can't even test it.

I am running through the sloshing chlorinated water at the shallow end of the swimming pool, making my way around the other children. I am running barefoot up to my knees in the water, giggling as if someone is chasing me. The skirt of my dress is wet, my underpants are splashed. I want to laugh and shout and scream and kick, pummeling my arms, making a windmill of my arms. I collide with a little girl of six or seven and her head is dunked underwater but it isn't my fault, I keep on running. Someone shouts behind me but I keep on running, waving my arms, squealing as if I am being chased.

I am swinging on one of the swings, kicking myself higher, higher. The sky is empty and very blue. I am stretching my legs as straight as they will go. No one is pushing me. No one calls out to warn me that I am going too high, that I'm being reckless. Suppose I jump off?—and let the swing fly backward?—suppose it strikes the boy swinging beside me? That happened once when I was a little girl. My grandfather was pushing me then and he scolded me. But now no one is watching, no one knows where I am. I can jump off the swing and let it fly back, I can do anything I want.

My head is ringing, my throat feels very dry. I am climbing up the slide, clambering up like a monkey, clowning around. At the top I am going to jump right off. I've done it before, it isn't dangerous, but the soles of my feet will tingle. I don't want to lose my balance and fall by accident. I feel lightheaded all of a sudden. So I go down the slide the way you're supposed to, pushing myself down, the hot metal makes my skin stick, I hear myself whimpering aloud in pain, it's a mistake to be here, something is going to happen, I am going to be punished. . . . Then I'm safe on the ground again, springing up on my heels. I haven't been burnt. I don't give a damn what happens.

"Moving your hand, see: this is God," my father says, raising his hand slowly in front of his face. "But then—" and here he whips his head around and pretends to be spying on his other hand, halfway behind his back. "—here's God too. All sides. All points. Do you know what that means?" He pauses to look at me. His smile is gentle. *"That means everything."*

The ice cream cone is melting, chocolate ice cream running down my forearm to my elbow. It's very sweet but hasn't any taste. My throat is aching from all the dust. Suddenly I am angry—suddenly I feel sick to my stomach. I let the ice cream cone drop onto the grass. Something is wrong but I don't know what it is. I don't know how to name it.

I am very excited, but I don't know where to run. I can run and run and run. I'll never get tired or hungry, I can run forever. Jumping into the air, leaping, landing on my toes and springing up again, who will stop me?—who knows where I am? Momma wiped her eyes with her knuckles and pushed past me, she didn't care that I was peeking in on them, she didn't scold. Behind her my father was saying, "I love you, you know that. I love you first last and always." He spoke quietly, he never raises his voice.

Can you fall asleep with your eyes open? I wonder. I have been standing staring at some pigeons picking in the garbage. Five, six, seven of them. Beautiful wings, tail feathers. Pebble-colored eyes. The beaks picking, striking, never making a mistake. But if one pigeon comes too close to another it's chased away. The pigeons are actually very angry—you wouldn't want them to peck at your outstretched hand. You wouldn't want them to peck at your eyes.

Can you see things when you're awake? I wonder. Like dreams. Like wisps and bits of dreams. But with your eyes open.

There is a snapshot in blurred blazing color of my father and a red fox, taken up at Isle Royale on the lake, when he worked for the government for eight months. My father is wearing a blue nylon Windbreaker and a wool cap, he's squatting, grinning at the camera, and the fox is only a few yards away, his slender snout turned three-quarters toward my father. It looks as if the fox is grinning too. My father is very handsome but the visor of the cap cuts across his eyes making a dark shadow. Whoever took the picture faced the sun too directly, the scene is over-exposed, blazing with light. "Your father had to get away for a while but it doesn't mean he stopped loving us," Momma explained. She explained this to everyone she met.

The program my father was hired for had something to do with charting the movements and patterns of behavior of timber wolves. Whether their population was stable or not. Whether their prey—deer, moose, rabbits—was stable. At first he loved the work because of the solitude, the silence, for weeks on end. Then the work began to sicken him: he had to examine the part-devoured carcasses of animals, he had to take photographs, keep records. He still limped from the accident at the foundry and the cold weather—sometimes it was 30° below zero, not counting the wind-chill—made the injury worse. So he came home. "I never stopped loving you," he said. "Did you stop loving me?"

I can hear the crippled man grunt as he pulls himself along on his wooden platform, but I don't look up. If I don't see him he can't see me. The pigeons are still pecking in the garbage, squabbling over a hot-dog bun. Rushing at one another with their wings outstretched. Is it still the same time, hasn't anything changed?— the sun will never move in the sky.

Dear God I am so afraid of what is going to happen. Dear God forgive me my sins. Help me to be a good girl.

Momma keeps saying: "Things are getting better now, the worst is over."

Momma keeps saying, pouring some whisky for herself while she's talking on the telephone: "He needs me. He loves me. I love *him*. It isn't the way you think."

A boy of about seventeen is crouched in the rose garden, taking photographs of a bride and her new husband, everyone is smiling, laughing, calling out, maybe they're a little drunk. If I was behind the married couple I could get in the picture but I'm on the wrong side, behind the photographer, peeking through a trellis. There are five middle-aged women in the wedding party, all dressed up, corsages on their shoulders, hats with pretty straw brims, but only three men. No one pays any attention to me. The bride in her long white beautiful dress, with her lace veil hanging down over her back, smiles toward me but doesn't see me. I can roll my eyes and stick out my tongue like I'm choking, it won't make any difference.

I am a snorting horse, a moose with its head lowered, galloping along the path, kicking up gravel. The hell with them staring at me—I don't give a damn. The North Pole is in one direction, the Equator in another, but there isn't anywhere to go that isn't God.

Now I am running along the edge of the park, an angry little heart is beating in the center of my forehead. You aren't supposed to climb down, the signs say Warning, pebbles and rocks and hunks of dried mud are coming loose, you can hurt yourself falling, my hand is scraped and bleeding a little but there isn't much pain, the sensation is mainly numb, the dust will clot the bleeding and make it stop. I am singing at the top of my lungs. Singing and laughing. I will never go back home again: I will live in the park forever.

Did you stop loving me? someone whispers. . . . loving me, loving me?

I am all hooves and wings and flashing antlers. Scaly rippling sides.

Then suddenly I see them: a man and a woman down by the canal: but I've seen them before, those two, on the canal bank in the high grass, and there isn't anything I can do to stop it.

The man is jerking the woman along, his fingers are closed around her bare upper arm. She is already crying. She shouldn't cry, it makes him all the more angry, they don't like tears. I know he's going to kill her but I can't get away. I can't stop it.

His blue coat is slung over his right shoulder, his trousers are streaked with dust. He is wearing a necktie made of some shiny silvery material. His hair is no color at all—trimmed short—standing up stiff and straight as a brush. He has a pig's snout, his face is red and mottled. His voice isn't raised but you can tell he's very angry.

The woman isn't pretty. Her lips are too thick and blubbery. She has a double chin that wobbles as he pulls her along, I can't stand to look at her, hair dyed maroon and teased out around her head like straw, filmy red scarf around her neck, high heels that make her stagger in the grass. She is wearing one of those off-the-shoulder blouses with the elastic neck, they're in Sears' window, Mexican or Spanish they're supposed to be, and a red cotton skirt with a black elastic belt, cinching her waist in tight so that her fat hips bulge, and her fat breasts. When the worst of it begins I am crouched down hiding, my eyes are shut tight and my hands are pressed over my ears. I don't hear her screaming, I don't hear the thuds, the blows. I don't hear a thing.

I hadn't been asleep. But when I opened my eyes I was in the park again, in the rose garden again, crouching behind the trellis. It was still daylight. Maybe no time had passed. Children were still playing in the pool, my head felt very strange but I wasn't bleeding anywhere so maybe everything was all right. The roses were very beautiful, I hadn't looked at them before. The wedding party had gone.

I knew it was later because I was so hungry. The sun had shifted in the sky.

I started crying and couldn't stop.

A woman in yellow shorts came by, another woman joined her, a patrolman, a small staring crowd. My knees had given out and I was sitting on the grass. I was afraid of wetting myself and soiling my underpants but I couldn't stop crying. The woman was lying on her back, her skirt was pulled up, her thick pale lardy flesh exposed. One high-heeled shoe had been twisted off her foot but the strap was still attached to her ankle. I didn't see any blood. I didn't hear anything. The man's necktie had flapped over his shoulder as he ran away but I didn't really see it, I wasn't watching. I was crouched down behind a pile of rocks hiding with my hands pressed against my ears. My heart beat so hard in my chest I knew it was going to burst.

They were asking me what was wrong but I couldn't answer. Was I sick? Had I hurt myself? Had someone hurt me? I couldn't get my breath to answer. Had I fallen off the slide? A woman told the patrolman she had seen me on the playground earlier, I had been acting "strangely." It was her opinion that I was lost. More people drifted by. Children staring. Was I lost? Where were my parents? Were they at the park? What was my name?

I was shivering so hard the policeman took a beach towel from one of the women and wrapped it around me. He said I'd be all right now, nothing bad would happen. But my teeth kept chattering. I couldn't get my breath.

It's hysteria, the policeman said, you see it all the time. He wore sunglasses with very dark green lenses. His voice was kindly, he wasn't scolding.

In the ambulance going to the hospital I did soil my underpants. But nobody said a word about it afterward.

After the accident at the foundry when two men on my father's shift were killed, and my father was hospitalized, the "great silence" came over him more and more often.

He would be lying in bed. Or walking with a cane along the corridor. Or joking with the nurses. Or staring out the window over the parking lot. ("Sometimes it was the way the sunlight flashed on a windshield: simple as that," he says.) There would be a pressure in his ears, and a deafening roar, and then silence. Just—silence.

He couldn't hear anything. He couldn't swallow or blink. Nothing had changed around him but it was all at a distance because he was in God's mind. He could hear God's thoughts, which were identical with his own. "There is the first half of my life," he says, "and then the second. I'm in the second now. I was in it all the time but I didn't know. God had been with me all the time but I didn't know. You think you're alone—that makes you happy when you're a kid—I mean, you can get away with anything, do anything, right? But God is with you all the time. You're not free. Even the thought of it, being free, it's God's thought in your head. Whatever you think or do, God has got there first. So you can't make mistakes. Even the warnings He sends you aren't mistakes."

Sometimes when it snows—when it has been snowing for days on end, as it has this winter—I stand at the window and hear the silence all around me. I know it will swallow me up someday the way it did my father.

But even this thought—isn't it God's? Of course it is.

In the hospital I started to tell them about the woman by the canal, what the man had done to her, but my words were garbled and I couldn't get my breath. If I closed my eyes I could see her but when I opened them I couldn't remember what I was saying. There was blood on the lower part of her jaw. There was blood, a widening circle of blood, on her blouse.

He had killed her. Then he'd run away. But not light on his feet, not leaping and prancing. He hadn't any hooves or wings. The blood had splashed onto his shirt. I hated them both—they were so ugly.

"You never saw anything," my mother tells me, whispering, leaning over the bed, giving me a secret shake. "You mind your own business!"

Someone was sent out to search by the canal but of course there wasn't any body, there wasn't any evidence of blood or struggle. A single high-heeled shoe was found in the grass.

"She makes things up," my mother says, not looking at me.

Later, after a woman was reported missing, they dragged the canal but never found any body. By then I was back home (I'd only been in the hospital overnight, in the children's ward), by then school had started.

"You just tell them you don't remember," my mother says. "Tell them you don't know. Anyway you made it all up—didn't you?" My father's door has been closed against me for a long time. If I press my ear against it I can hear him singing and humming to himself, sometimes Irene and one of her girl friends are in there with him, playing gin rummy, or shaking the dice until they rattle in the old cardboard cup. The three of them laugh together, I think they must want me to hear. "Anyway you made it up," my mother says, lighting a cigarette, staring at me, "didn't you?"

She has never said anything about the $3.87 from her bureau drawer. Which means I didn't take it—which means that nothing has happened. But my father's door is closed against me for eleven days. I am chipping at the plaster in the wall beside my bed with a safety pin, to mark each day.

LAST
DAYS

... the Scourge of G–d. But perhaps he is born too late? A Messiah at any hour. For a while he is "into" Holocaust literature, for a while it is Wittgenstein who obsesses him ("Whereof we cannot speak, thereof we must be silent"—or words to that effect: Saul is too excited to get them 100% accurate), for a few unfortunate weeks in his senior year of college it is Kant's Categorical Imperative: "Do you realize," Saul says heatedly to his friends and to whoever will listen, even to his offended father at long distance, "—that whatever we do or say or *think*, it should be a moral imperative for *all of humanity*? Our slightest whim or action—a transcendental law for *all time*?" The semester of his first (official, recorded, historic) breakdown. Six frenzied mock-frothing-at-the-mouth hours in the infirmary.

Saul Morgenstern, the Wrath of G–d. The apple of G–d's eye. He rips the letter to shreds from the Rhodes Foundation, throws the pieces like confetti into the air. He walks away from the "minimum security" mental hospital at Fort Spear, Michigan. Not five weeks later he takes a lumbering exhaust-spewing bus, a wide-shouldered big-assed bus (Saul's own "surreal" images, he has

taken to writing poetry feverishly in his last days) to Toledo, to buy
a $15 pistol for $78.24 at the Liberty Pawnshop, from a clerk whose
gold-rimmed innocently round eyeglasses resemble his own, and
whose swarthy good looks (so Saul imagines) mirror his in an *almost*
Semitic way. The Ohio laws governing the sale of rifles, handguns,
and bullets are much friendlier than the laws of neighboring states.
If you are a former convict or a former mental patient, if you are
visibly agitated and "in the wings of" the hottest event of your life
(so Saul has been gleefully warning his friends for weeks) you will
not be turned away. "No doubt about it," says the youngish stoop-
shouldered gentleman with the gold-rimmed glasses, Saul's smirk-
ing twin, "—a gun is your best friend these days. Of course I am
speaking of an emergency. Have you ever found yourself caught up
in the confusing flurry of an emergency?" Saul was turning the
pistol over and over in his icy fingers. He hadn't counted on the
object having such weight; such gravity. ("There is physicality
here in all its surprising abruptness," he tells himself. For a brief
while Wittgenstein's disciples toyed with the idea of calling his philosophy "physicalism" or a word to that effect: selling it to Stalin
perhaps: but Stalin had been unimpressed, probably had his mind
on other things.) He hadn't counted on so much reality though he
was the proud author of two articles on the subject of current "academic shibboleths" published precociously in *The New Republic*,
and a one-hundred-sixty-five-page seminar paper on the subject of
Buber, Existentialism, Structuralism, Post-Structuralism, and the
Holocaust as Text, a paper generally acclaimed as brilliant among
Morgenstern's circle, though intemperately rejected as "unaccept-
able as either scholarship or poetry" by that Professor W—— who
had best remain nameless, as Saul is "contemplating" graphic revenge. Saul's fingers are shaking. He pays no heed. Nor does the
pawnbroker's clerk. It is a workday like any other, a Tuesday perhaps. It is ordinary life "sliced" in a perfectly ordinary way. Saul
could photograph with his eyes the crowded interior of the Liberty
Pawnshop on Seventh Street, downtown Toledo, or is it Day-
ton?—the affable clerk bent smiling over the badly scarified glass
counter, he has an unfailing "photographic memory" ("what a
great device for cheating," his envious freshman-dorm roommate
little Sammy Frankel said, Sammy set like a wind-up toy for medical school and a million-dollar practice: contemptible little Jew-

boy, Saul called him)—but why trouble to immerse himself in
what is, after all, only *statistical* reality? (The police report will describe a Colt New Police model .32-caliber revolver, its original
five-inch barrel sawed off to two, for pocket convenience; the usual
six-shot cylinder. A weapon manufactured twenty-five years ago.
Commonly sold over (and under) the counter. So badly in need of
oiling, "surprising that it worked at all," one of the police will say.)
Saul has been staring for some uncomfortable seconds at the
amazing *object* in his hands, and his eyes, though customarily
"dark, piercing, or brooding," have gone as blank and round and
empty as his glasses. The clerk breathes warmly onto Saul's hands.
He squints up companionably at him. "This material is chrome, if
you are wondering," he says, "—that, zinc. A fine gun. The very
best for emergencies. And if you had maybe a secret pocket sewed
into your coat, I don't mean any big deal, or maybe you have one
already?—it would be absolutely safe. And the price is right." Saul
stares at the gun and the left corner of his mouth begins to twitch.
Because he has seen this gun before, he has seen the scratched glass
counter before, his own nail-bitten winter-reddened hands, the
clerk's amiable ghostly reflection observing him from out of the
glass. The forbidden thought arises: the Messiah has come and
gone. Saul Morgenstern is too late. But "Right-o," Saul says in his
deep bass voice, the most manly of voices, to deflect the clerk from
suspicion. It is really a very ordinary very *routine* sort of morning.
Rabbi Reuben Engelman is always telling Saul that it is the *routine*
of life, the "happy dailiness" in which Faith and Practice are
"wed," that constitutes the real challenge. Saul defeats the hypo-
critical old windbag with one loud slam of his hand on the desk
top. And afterward re-enacts the scene for his table of undergraduate disciples in the student union cafeteria. ("I'm the Zen hand,
the single Zen hand, that pounds and pounds and pounds my enemies to dust," he shouts. Saul Morgenstern the Scourge of G–d.
Saul Morgenstern who rejected a Rhodes Scholarship. So forceful
in the smoky interior of the Union, so Biblical, with his deep voice
and flashing eyes and lustrous black wiry kinky hairs that curl
from out of his clothes . . . no wonder the little WASP girls slit their
eyes at him.) Now he turns the pistol in his fingers. Murmurs,
"Right-o," while he tries to remember precisely why he is here.
Murmurs, "But can't I 'jew you down' a few bucks, I have doubts

that this thing is worth $85. . . ." Several minutes of animated conversation. Saul says laughingly that he doesn't intend to kill his father: Ernest Morgenstern isn't worth killing: that kind of sloppy *personal* behavior ("acting out" the shrinks call it) has no class. The pawnbroker's clerk agrees. Or hasn't precisely heard. Saul turns the empty cylinder, sights along the barrel, licks his numbed lips, asks the clerk if he'd had any member or members of his family lost in the Holocaust, makes the comment (mildly, even sadly, smiling) that the family is a vanishing animal in the United States, doomed to extinction. "That's right," the clerk says agreeably. Saul stares blinking at him and sees that he isn't a twin at all, he's a morose ugly man in his late thirties, going bald, a queer sagging to one eyelid. He's an informant, probably. The pawnshop is monitored. ". . . a target like Kissinger," Saul is saying, ". . . from the point of view of the Jewish community. But of course it's too late. Years too late. I was only a high school kid then, I didn't know shit. Also I've always been a pacifist. Even when my father struck me in the face and cracked my nose—I didn't strike back." "That's right," the clerk says. He is making an unconscious "wringing" gesture with his hands. Pontius Pilate. Naturally. "David Gridlock" (the name on the purchase slip) files the image away for future reference. He has become feverishly interested in poetry lately; he begins to wonder if his real talent doesn't lie in that direction, and not in the direction of somber meticulous mirthless scholarship. . . . Also, he hasn't yet settled upon the absolute sequence of events, to be enacted in the synagogue next Sabbath: whether, after performing the assassination, he will then commit suicide by firing a single bullet, calmly, into the base of his skull; or whether he will allow himself to be captured by his enemies and led away. At the moment he leans toward the former. But, if the latter, he will want to immerse himself in poetry. And certain images are so "haunting," so "clustering." . . . The bargain is made, the price is right, Saul pays in cash, that is, "David Gridlock" pays unhesitatingly in cash, though he wonders if he is being cheated—being so bookish, so obviously not a man of the world. The price of the bullets too is suspiciously high. But what can he do?—he plays it safe, buys three dozen.

Freddy C——, Dale S——, Sol M—— discuss the problem of Morgenstern endlessly. "Frankly I'm afraid of him," says Freddy.

LAST DAYS   23

"Also very exhausted. I wish he'd kill himself soon." But this isn't
serious talk, this is sorrow, despair, cowardice. Vera R—— (by
simple and insignificant happenstance a niece of Mrs. Morgenstern's oldest sister-in-law) becomes emotional, sometimes very
angry, when the others say such things. ". . . how do you think we'll
all feel, if . . ." she says in a low trembling voice. Of course they
agree. They absolutely agree. And the fact that Saul has been
going about claiming his former housemates have cheated him of
"six months' rent" and "invaluable rare books" cannot fail to add
to their uneasiness. Denise E—— has tried to make contact with
Saul's former psychiatrists (Dr. Ritchie at the hospital, Dr. Mermelstein in the city) but since she is afraid of telling the gentlemen
who she is, and hasn't been able to finish typing out a fifteen-page
letter chronicling Saul's behavior in the past several months, her
efforts have been unsuccessful. (Afterward, Denise will tell at least
one reporter that Dr. Ritchie was "flippant" and "hurried" on the
telephone, and told her that "if Saul's hostility was acted out, it
would most likely be directed only against himself." This statement Dr. Ritchie has denied having made.) Dale thinks the police
should be called and if Saul shows up at the house again he will
call them himself. Sol thinks the parents should be told ("but they
know all about it, don't they"), the hospital's administration
should be told ("but they don't give a damn"), Saul's former professors at the university, Saul's former friends. . . . But maybe it's
wisest not to get involved. Not to get involved officially. For Saul
has already threatened to sue everyone from the Governor of the
state on down to his former housemates at 18332 Twenty-third
Street if any terminology hinting at his "mental condition" is
made public. He has told Rose P—— (herself not altogether stable) that certain betrayers of his trust will soon "regret the day of
their birth" as the inhabitants of the cities of Hiroshima, Berlin,
and Pompeii regretted theirs. Rose P—— thinks Saul is probably a
saint. If he could be rooted in the earth somehow, brought into
contact with his sensual primitive fundamental self . . . "It's ideas
and thinking and books that have made him sick," she says in a
passionate reedy voice, which makes Dale explode nervously, "For
Christ's sake Saul doesn't think at *all* these days, he's given up
thinking for the past six months, he can't even sit still to *read* unless
he's on medication," and Vera says over and over, ". . . if he's

really dangerous and does something, and ... how do you think we'll feel. ..." However, it *is* a free country. Even if Saul has some sort of "infectious malaise" as Rose thinks, a "psychic virus" picked up out of the air of America. Even if he drives without a driving license. (His license has been suspended for ninety days.) Even if as rumor has it he has bought a gun. And probably he *is* a saint, Rose says, are there saints in the Jewish religion ... ? Rose makes a nuisance of herself hanging out around school, dropping in at the house on Twenty-third all hours of the night, hinting clumsily that she and Saul are "devoted lovers." The others will refute her angrily, saying that Saul hadn't ever made love to a girl, he basically detested girls, but Rose, ferret-faced little Rose, will make her grubby claim now and forever. After all she often accompanies Saul on his nocturnal wanderings about the city and at the Eastland Hills Shopping Mall where he sings so that his rich vibrating voice (a baritone voice?) echoes. He sings fearlessly, lustily, even in the library stacks, even in the Chippewa Tavern where the younger workers from the Chrysler plant hang out, even in the maze-like undulations of Abbey Farms, the "luxury custom-homes" development where the Morgensterns bought a house before the husband divorced the wife—easily worth one-half million dollars in today's inflated market: he isn't shy. Singing Leporello, singing Don Giovanni, singing sweet German lyrics by Schubert, shifting raucously into the sleaziest of Janis Joplin, while his spaced-out girl trots after him clapping until her palms burn. She loves him, she's crazy about him, why isn't her adoration enough to save him, why didn't he (if Fate and Karma pulled him in that direction) propose that they die together, snug in his Volkswagen overlooking the lake, while the snow dreamily falls and covers them up ... ? Rose P—— who wants to convert to Judaism, "the most orthodox kind." Rose P—— who is the only person, apart from Saul's mother, to notice that his right eye is just perceptibly darker—a darker greeny-brown—than his left. Rose P—— at whose tremulous bosom Saul had once cocked and fired a forefinger, chuckling, in front of five or six embarrassed friends. Rose P—— whom Saul succeeded in "breaking down" by reading her harrowing selections from such Holocaust literature as *Survivors of Auschwitz, Voices of the Deathcamp, In the Ghettos of Warsaw and Lodz,* and *After the Apocalypse.* Rose P—— to whom he confessed on the eve of the assassination/suicide, "The real thing is, God's curse on me is, *I was born too late. All the suffering is over—all the memoirs have been written. Every breath of Saul's has been breathed by someone else.*"

His senior year, Saul is editor-in-chief of the student newspaper and works on the average of fifty hours a week. He is known for his generosity. He is known for his "biting" sarcasm. He is locally famous for having published articles in *The New Republic* that bravely criticize the university from which he will graduate. An editorial on academicians who have "prostituted" themselves for federal grant money appeared on the Op-Ed page of the *New York Times*, and impressed even Mr. Morgenstern (at that time living on East Seventy-sixth Street with his second and very young, or at any rate youthful, wife and her eleven-year-old son). He discovers that he doesn't require sleep as other people do. He runs for miles in the still dry winter night (temperatures as low as 5°, breath steaming, heart a wondrous unstoppable fist that opens and closes, opens and closes, absolutely triumphant—why for Christ's sake had he ever worried about his health, frightened himself that he had cancer of the rectum when it was only bleeding hemorrhoids)—he chins himself on railings, impresses those credulous WASP girls by climbing over walls, not minding the iron spikes and broken glass scattered about, he *is* invulnerable on certain days, and strong as an ox besides. He gorges on non-kosher food and never feels a tinge of nausea. He sits at the rear of the Adath Israel Synagogue, that "eye-stopping eye-sore" that Rabbi Reuben Engelman dreamt up out of his shameless materialistic dreams, before (and after) the murder/suicide lavishly featured in national magazines—Saul sits quietly as any sweet little brainwashed Jew-boy, a yarmulke on his head, taking notes in his loose-leaf journal on the fixtures, the fur coats, the "masks of cunning and deceit" on all sides. He even takes notes in a shorthand of his own invention when Rabbi Engelman delivers his rousing patriotic take-pride-in-America-and-don't-look-back sermons. Sometimes he chuckles, but quietly. No one appears to notice.

No psychiatrist can help him because he's too smart—he knows the Freudian crap, the jargon, inside and out. His I.Q. has been measured at 168. Perhaps it is 186. No one at the hospital dares approach him *on his own terms* because his problems aren't trivial and personal: his problems have to do with life and death, G–d

and man, the special destiny of the Jews, the contrasting fates of
Vessels of Grace and Vessels of Wrath. ("For twenty-two years I
was a Vessel of Grace," Saul says with a bitter lopsided grin,
"—and then I realized that was the wrong category.") Dr. Ritchie
is an idiot, Dr. Mermelstein a homosexual sadist, Professor W——
who handed back his paper covered in red ink is an impostor, a
crook. "David Gridlock" was born one drizzly December afternoon
while Saul ran panting through the hospital woods, his parrot-
green canvas jacket unzipped and his tongue lolling, borne along
on waves of elation so powerful, so exquisite, he knew they were the
province of G–d: except of course he didn't believe in such superstitious crap. He never had, in fact. Even at his Bar Mitzvah, in
fact, reading his prayers and singing his chants with as much solemn assurance as if he'd been doing it all his young life. ("If I were
G–d," Saul tells his nervous housemates Freddy and Dale, "I
would bless you all and suck away your oxygen and that would be
that—before you had a chance to wake up and ruin everything. Of
course I mean 'you' in a generic sense," he explains.)

The psychiatrists, the psychologists, the therapists, the self-
appointed do-gooders, certain meddlesome members of the Morgenstern family . . . no one is qualified to give advice to *him*. He
baffles Mermelstein with a recitation from Kafka which he asks
him to identify ("If we are possessed by the Devil it cannot be by
one, for then we should live quietly, as with God, in unity, without
contradiction . . . always sure of the man behind us"), he shocks a
former philosophy professor at Ann Arbor by a late-night visit
meant to "hammer out" the problem of Wittgenstein ("Is it true
that 'what can be said at all can be said clearly, and what we cannot talk about we must pass over in silence'?—and how is this to be
reconciled with the philosopher's compulsive homosexual promis-
cuity?" —delivered in a ringing triumphant voice), he dismays his
father with an unannounced appearance in New York during
spring break ("Van Gogh cut off his ear with a razor blade for
atonement," he tells his angry bewildered father, "—if I castrated
myself would that please you and the new Mrs. Morgenstern?"), he
works long fevered idle hallucinatory hours on a prose-poem tenta-
tively titled "Last Days" (". . . At the age of twenty-three I see that
everything is falling in place at last and that there was no secret to
its meaning all along, except that Saul Morgenstern 'saw through

a glass darkly' "). He wakes in alarm, and sometimes in a sweating rage, with the conviction that he will be, *he cannot avoid being*, a belated Messiah. It is very late in the twentieth century. The sacrificial act has already been performed. Every syllable of his speech has been recorded on tape, even the gunshots, even the idiot screams of the congregation: and pirated (no doubt) for the local radio stations.

"I'm starving! Dying of hunger!" Saul accuses his mother when he chances to appear at the house on Sussex Drive. "I can't breathe," he accuses his housemates, who foul the air with their cigarettes, their solemn mirthless clichés, the unwashed heat of their bodies. Dale S—— will remember an "uncannily lucid" conversation with Saul on the subject of the Holocaust and its significance for all of human history, past and future. The face of absolute evil, the anonymity of sin, Hitler as the Anti-Messiah, the "Final Solution" being the pollution of every cubic foot of oxygen—hence Saul's choking, his coughing spells. (Which certain of his acquaintances, grown less indulgent with time, saw as shabbily theatrical. "He was faking," they say. "He was always faking. Except—of course—at the end. But only at the *very* end.")

He graduates with highest honors, he is the only Rhodes Scholar named this year in the state of Michigan, he will study history, politics, religion at Oxford: but sickness intervenes. Now he practices firing his Colt New Police pistol into a pile of stacked newspapers and magazines in the basement of his mother's (no longer his parents') custom-made house on Sussex Drive. His mother is away for the afternoon, fortunately. At the Club. At the hospital visiting an aged ailing female relative. "I cannot understand you, Saul," Mrs. Morgenstern has said many times. Sometimes she blinks tears out of her eyes, sometimes she stands somber and stoic, not to be "broken down" (in Saul's own words) by the non-negotiable presence of her son. Her name is Barbara, she is altogether American, assimilated. She bears very little resemblance to her dignified son except for the shade of her eyes—a queer muddy-green—sometimes enlivened with thought, sometimes merely muddy. Saul loves her, he readily admits, but he cannot bear her: not her voice which is so painfully *sympathetic*, not her touch which burns, not the faintest whiff of her expensive lethal perfume. All this he explains patiently to Rabbi Engelman in the rabbi's handsome paneled library in his home. All this he explains to Freddy, to Sol, to Vera, to Dr. Ritchie, to the contemptible Mermelstein, to passengers on the Greyhound bus returning from Toledo, to anyone who will listen: for, after all, as Saul reasons, isn't it the story of our (collective) lives? Stunning in its transparency, irrefutable as a mathematical equation, how can it be resisted—? Pulling the trigger, shocked and gratified by the simple loud *noise* of the explosion, Saul knows for the first time that though everyone is lying to him, everyone has agreed to "humor" him at least to his face, it no longer matters *to him* what they think.

Still, in his last days, he makes many telephone calls. He will become famous for his telephone calls.

Lying sleepless in his rumpled bed on the third floor (rear) of the "boarding house" at 3831 Railroad Avenue, a half-mile from the squalid southerly fringes of the university campus, some eleven miles south and east of the Adath Israel Synagogue on the Hamilton Expressway . . . Lying sleepless by day and night, "David Gridlock" plotting his revenge which will take the form of simple atonement. It isn't the sickish terror of insomnia that overcomes him. He has long been adjusted to insomnia. It's the bed rumpled and smelling of someone else's heated thoughts, someone else's turbulent nights, *before Saul lies in it.* It's the soiled sheets, the indentation of a stranger's head on the pillow, stray hairs, curly and dark but not his own. The unflushed toilet in the hall. Waste, foul and sickening and *not his own.* His fear is of being unoriginal, accused of plagiarism, exposed, ridiculed, cast aside as ordinary: "What's so special about *you*, that you have the right to persecute *me*?" Mr. Morgenstern shouts. As editor-in-chief of the student newspaper he *knocks himself out*, rewrites slovenly half-assed copy, his head buzzing with coffee, cigarettes, amphetamines. Often he hears the half-scolding half-awed exclamation: "Saul, don't knock yourself out!" And again, "Saul, why do you knock yourself out over this?—you don't even get academic credit." It is his responsibility to write three or four editorials a week. Provocative "controversial" pieces. The undemocratic nature of fraternities and sororities, discrimination even by self-styled liberals, *de facto* segregation . . . that sort of thing. One of his editorials is a passionate attack upon prejudice. He is actually moved as he types it out, very moved, agitated, close to tears. For the principle is—*can* human

nature be changed, after all; what in fact is "human nature," that
it might be "changed"; what hope is there after so many centuries . . . ? A bold editorial, Saul thinks. An attack. A frontal as-
sault. And then comes a prissy sarcastic letter from a graduate
student in engineering, *engineering* of all contemptible subjects, ignoring the thrust of Saul's editorial and accusing him of plagiarism. Plagiarism!—with reference to a (famous) essay by Sartre on
anti-Semitism which Saul has never read, or cannot remember
having read, G–d as his witness. Fortunately Saul can get rid of the
letter before anyone sees it. . . . Then again, not long ago, in his
"Issues in Contemporary Thought" seminar, for which Saul wrote
a fifty-page paper embellished with clever footnotes, he is accused
of "not having adequately acknowledged" his sources: whole paragraphs, it seems, in the language of Camus, certain insights from
Camus's "Reflections on the Guillotine" ("Capital punishment
throughout history has always been a religious punishment. . . .
The real judgment is not pronounced in this world but in the
next. . . . Religious values are the only ones on which the death
penalty can be based. . . ."), turns of phrase appropriated from
Buber and Tillich: *which Saul has never read, or cannot remember having
read.* The mortification, then, of pleading his case with the professor. Of uttering the truth in so shaky and childish a voice, it is
transformed into a falsehood. I am innocent, Saul says, how can I
prove my innocence, have I been born too late, have all the words
been used, has all the oxygen been breathed . . . ? His heart pounds
with the shame of it, the oppression, the humiliation not to be
borne. Better to die, Saul instructs Saul, than to crawl like a dog
into someone else's sheets, stare helplessly into the toilet at someone else's shit.

In general, however, he is happy; almost euphoric. He shakes the
hands of strangers, helps derelicts across the wide windy streets,
helps push a car out of an icy snowbank. He never exaggerates because there isn't the need. "Around me," he boasts, "the world itself exaggerates." In any case he knows the importance of
maintaining a certain level of energy in his bloodstream, maintaining a certain gut strength. He's bookish but no fool. He's suffered the ignominy of electro-convulsive shock treatments but he
has always bounced back. In his loose-leaf journal he writes as
clearly as possible so that, after his death, he won't be misunder-

stood as he was misunderstood in life. *Around the hero all things turn into tragedy; around the demigod, into a satyr-play; around Morgenstern— clumsy farce.* The freshness of the insight and the vigor of its language excite him. Death promises not to be painful at all.

In the crappy little room on Railroad Avenue he finds himself thinking of Fort Spear and the long dazed fluorescent-lit corridors, the fenced-in woods through which he ran with the intention of making his heart burst; but when he was in the hospital he thought of the house on Sussex Drive, the Abbey Farms sub-division, Rabbi Engelman and his wife Tillie seated in the living room, Mrs. Morgenstern serving them coffee and weeping. In one place he thinks of another. In one time-zone he yearns for another. Hence the frantic letter-writing, the telephone calls.... His father in Manhattan, Moses Goldhand at the University of Chicago, Professor Fox at the University of Michigan who had had such "high hopes" for him as a Rhodes Scholar, Vera R—— who "perhaps unconsciously" betrayed him, Dr. Ritchie the homosexual-charlatan, Dr. Mermelstein whom he will soon expose. It is a preposterous and almost unsayable fact that both his parents, united after years of bitter disagreement, conspired to so misrepresent facts to a Probate Court judge that Saul was "committed" to a state hospital: this truth must be acknowledged, turned fearlessly in the fingers like a rare poisonous insect, a lurid glaring jewel of an insect, *this truth the son cannot shirk.* "Rabbi," Saul says in a boy's abrupt voice, "I think I need help. It isn't that I feel sick or weak or anything ... I feel too strong."

Saul's clothes don't exactly fit though he dresses with fussy self-consciousness: his Englishy tweed jacket with the leather patches at the elbows and the buttons covered in leather; his handsome silk tie, a tasteful dark red; his black silk-and-cotton socks, the very best quality. "He took pride in his appearance," says Rose P——, "and why shouldn't he—? He was so beautiful sometimes, you could see his soul shining in his eyes." Vera R—— says, "Well—he was a little vain, I suppose, when I first met him. He said something strange once: that if he'd been able to sing, if he'd gone on the stage, his life would have been peaceful and dedicated to beauty." The girls adore him, his disciples in the coffee shop applaud, Morgenstern the Scourge of G–d with his wiry curly black hair, his Semitic nose and eyes, the gold-rimmed glasses that give him so perplexed and scholarly and teacherly a look—one of those skinny dark-browed anarchists of Old Russia, a student out of Dostoyevsky, prepared to give his life in the rebellion against tyranny. But lately his clothes have grown so baggy he wonders if in fact they are *his*. Perhaps his housemates have hatched a cruel prank, sneaking into his new room, substituting someone else's clothes for his. Suddenly it seems very plausible. A Jew's worst enemy is another Jew, right? The swastikas scrawled on his poster of Freud with cigar (taped to the door of his library carrel) were doubtless the work of other Jews envious of Saul's success at the university and with WASP females in particular. Sol M——, for instance. The Frank kid, what is his name, his physician-father hangs out with Rockefeller. . . .

"Rabbi," Saul says, "I think I need help. People are insulting me behind my back. It hasn't been the same since Fort Spear, since my parents turned me in, I mean they gave me the highest dosage of drugs there, the highest legal dosage, and I lost count of how many shock treatments, which I believe are against the state law—I'm seeing a lawyer in the morning—I'm not going to let any of this rest—but from you I need help, they have begun calling me the 'worst kind of Jew,' *will you please tell them to stop?*"

He pays $78 in cash for two weeks in the boarding house (the flophouse) on slummy Railroad Avenue though he knows secretly that he won't be there that long. He won't be anywhere that long. Carefully he arranges a selection of his most cherished books, certain newspaper and magazine clippings, a slightly wrinkled but still dramatic poster-photograph of Ché Guevara ("Ché Guevara!" Freddy C—— will exclaim, "—I mean, since when, Ché Guevara and Saul Morgenstern?"), and the typed and heavily annotated manuscript of "Last Days." But the clean white dime-store envelope containing his denunciation speech is kept in the left pocket of his tweed coat. In the right pocket, the pistol. Its compact weight has become assimilated to his own in recent days: he rarely needs to think of it any longer.

His friends, his former friends, the frightened housemates, certain university acquaintances and gossipers—they debate the existence of the pistol, which no one has ever seen. Some are certain that Saul has a gun ("He keeps his elbow pressed against his pocket in a way, you know there's something dangerous there"), others are

equally certain that he is lying ("All he wants is for us to talk about
him—always to talk about *him*"), a few believe that his carefully
stylized "crazy behavior" is the real thing and that he should be
considered dangerous ("Maybe he was kidding around at first but
now he's lost control—you can smell a really weird odor on him").
An unidentified young woman tells one of the campus security police that there is going to be trouble unless a certain "graduate student in history" is taken into custody, but she professes not to know
his name, and refuses to give any further information. Mrs. Morgenstern telephones her former husband and leaves a message with
his maid which is never returned: possibly because (so Mrs. Morgenstern says, she is renowned for always putting the best face on
things) the maid spoke with a heavy Hispanic accent, and probably had not understood the message.

Saul aka "David Gridlock" jogs through the Abbey Farms sub-
division one chill Sunday morning, wishing to see it with uncon-
taminated (i.e., an anthropologist's) eyes. Essex Drive, Queens
Lane, Drakes Center, Pemberton Circle, Shropshire Way, Sussex
Drive. . . . An exemplary Jewish neighborhood, Saul thinks, panting, laughing silently, a real kike fantasy, all these English names,
all the undulations of the lanes, ways, roads, drives, not a street
among them, not a hint of urban origins. He runs, he swings his
arms, he forgets not to breathe through his opened mouth, the
fierce sunlight pours into him and swells him with energy, his very
brain is tumescent, he realizes suddenly that he will live forever: a
bullet from his own gun cannot stop him. Drakes Center and
Shropshire and here is Sussex Drive and here is 18 Sussex . . . a
custom-made house like all the rest . . . built by the same developer
. . . dreamt up by the same architect. Saul "sees" for the first time
since the Morgensterns bought the house eleven years before that
18 Sussex is . . . a remodeled barn: that all the houses in Abbey
Farms are remodeled barns: made of wood specially treated to look
"weathered," even slightly "rotted"; with narrow vertical windows
designed to give the illusion of having been "cut out" of obdurate
barn walls. He begins to laugh aloud as he runs. Perhaps he will
succumb to a fit of laughing, wheezing, asthmatic choking, he
can't help himself, it *is* hilariously funny, he will have to add a
footnote to "Last Days," a sly dig at Abbey Farms the "restricted
residential community" a few miles from Adath Israel, the private

and domestic expression of that Jewish essence of which (he is straining for the most muscular but also the most mocking syntax) Adath Israel is the public and cultural expression. English lanes and circles and ways, gaunt gray-weathered Andrew Wyeth barns, hexagonal and octagonal "classic" shapes, rough unpainted fences, even "split-rail" fences, even mock-silos with orange-red aluminum roofs adjacent to garages. . . . Disneyland! Fantasy land! Kike heaven! Saul jogs along the deserted wintry streets, his breath steaming, his lips and tongue going numb. "I will go until I am stopped," he thinks, elated, "—and I never am stopped. G–d be praised."

The Last Will & Testament of Saul Morgenstern: . . . *as I cannot and will not continue to live in this abomination of hypocrisy I will make you an outright present of my life to satisfy your bloodlust. As for my worldly goods . . . if it should be discovered that the debts lodged against me are fraudulent and I should possess after all some wealth I direct that it be given to the Lubavitcher Hasidim and not a penny to those who have betrayed me. My books, papers, personal possessions etc. to be burnt and scattered with my body.*

Saul's car breaks down en route to Adath Israel but he has learned to be affable (i.e., fatalistic) enough, he doesn't waste precious minutes shaking his fist at the skies, why despair when it's only a few minutes after eleven and in his tweed coat and red necktie and glinting gold-rimmed glasses he's an excellent candidate to be picked up and offered a ride by a passing motorist . . . ? In any case he is only about four miles south of the synagogue, on the Hamilton Expressway. And a weightless sensation pulses through him. *He cannot fail, he has entered History.*

A certain Judge Marvin McL——of the Probate Court receives a letter from Dr. Harold A——, the Director of the Fort Spear State Hospital, explaining that Mr. Saul Morgenstern, having left the hospital on "unauthorized leave," was now being granted the status of "convalescent" as he had initiated "therapy of a private nature" outside the hospital, with a certain Dr. Aaron Mermelstein, and had made a "reasonable adjustment" there. This, a bitter triumph for the forces of Justice after long haggling, begging, whispered pleading, the defiant restraint of the injured party to scream aloud the circumstances of his degradation. Mrs. Morgenstern is particularly alarmed to see that he's grown so skinny—a

weight loss of fifteen pounds in two weeks—does this mean that her
boy is *eluding her in the flesh?* Vera R—— is also "alarmed" and
"shocked" when by accident she encounters Saul in the university
library, he looks so sallow, so "old," "not himself." . . . Speaking
idly but lucidly in the coffee shop he reads to her selected passages
from "Last Days," explaining the principles of desecration (DE-
(reversal) + (CON)SECRATE): these principles necessary in order
that G–d be summoned back to the community. First, there is the
desecration of the SABBATH, the holiest day of the week; then,
the desecration of the SYNAGOGUE, the holiest place; if possible,
the desecration of the BIMAH, the most sacred place in the synagogue; the desecration of the HOLINESS OF THE RABBI; the
desecration of the PUBLIC RITUAL. . . . ("By which I mean that
a 'counter-ritual' is performed not only in view of the members of
the congregation, and by extension all the Jews of the world, but
the entire world of non- and anti-Jews itself," Saul says.) Vera R——
confesses that her underlying instinct was simply to escape her old
(former) (doomed) (depressing) friend. She "maybe" told three or
four people about the conversation. In truth she didn't take it altogether seriously because Saul had been talking along such lines for
months and didn't know whether Suicide to him meant an actual
act or a metaphor (as in one of his favorite expressions, "the suicidal drift of our generation . . ."), you didn't know whether an elaborate exegesis of the principles of desecration was something he
had dreamt up himself or appropriated from one of his masters,
Buber, say, or Eliade. And in any case, says Vera R——, he spoke
in so calm and low-keyed and even *fatigued* a voice, it didn't seem
that anything urgent was being pressed upon her. He said too as
she was leaving that he probably wouldn't be seeing her again—he
had been accepted as a tutorial student at the Jung Institute in
Zurich and would be leaving the first of March.

Saul walks as many as eight or nine miles in the falling snow, in
the cruel swirling winds. A "living snowman": hatless, gloveless,
wearing only his shoes, lightweight socks. Is he cold? Are his teeth
chattering? His skin is so hot that snow melts and runs down his
cheeks in rivulets like tears. He arrives as if against his will at his
married sister's house in Bay Ridge: ". . . with no explanation, just
walking in and announcing he was starving, he hadn't eaten all
day, I'd better prepare him something to eat or he'd collapse. Della

and I were both terrified, he walked in without knocking or ringing
the doorbell, we thought it was a madman at first. . . ." He arrives
at the university library from which he has been barred by an "ex-
ecutive order" of the provost: he only wants to test the thorough-
ness of the security police. (The doors are unguarded. The
librarians don't recognize him. No one "sees" him, in fact.) He arrives at Flanagans on Fifteenth Street where he sits with a group of
(former) friends and acquaintances, a long rowdy table that shifts
as the hours pass (from approximately nine in the evening to one-
thirty in the morning), being most crowded and friendly around
eleven. In the dim light he insists upon reading passages from an
"obscene" and "outrageous" book titled *The Fallacy of the "Final
Solution"*—"some book by a writer no one had ever heard of, Saul
claimed he'd stolen it from the bookstore, the thesis being that the
Holocaust had never occurred, it was only 'public relations' on
the part of the Jews. . . . The book *was* fairly outrageous but when I
asked Saul why didn't he just throw it away, who gives a damn
about a nut like that, he didn't even seem to hear me, he just
looked through me, then went back to the book, leafing and paging
through it. . . . He said that someone had told him not to pollute
his spiritual energy with sick people, it might have been a professor
or a rabbi, or his father, Saul was never very clear who it was, only
that he'd said in rebuttal, 'but it's *sick people* we have got to help.' "
He is radiant with certainty, his eyes shine, his hands no longer
shake. He says: "Some of the Holocaust survivors believed that
simple survival was resistance but what does that mean for us . . . ?
Simple survival is defeat now. It's succumbing to the enemy." No
one argues, no one even questions him. Perhaps no one hears.

Saul arrives at the synagogue just as Rabbi Engelman is con-
cluding his sermon. He has been sleeping a stuporous "David
Gridlock" sleep for forty-eight hours. Reverently he puts a yarmulke on his head, unobtrusively he enters the sanctuary at the
rear (left), makes his way along the aisle at the far left, walking
slowly, calling little or no attention to himself. He takes his seat in
the same pew with members of his mother's family but doesn't
catch sight of his mother or sister at first. He has heard the sermon
before and has no need to hear it again. All the words have been
spoken, *all* the words, Saul clutches this excruciating truth to his
chest and belly, a clawing beast, clawing and tearing and pulling

at his guts, and sits slightly hunched over. He is breathing shallowly through his mouth. The pistol is comfortable in his pocket along with five or six Smith & Wesson cartridges. The speech in the envelope has been carefully prepared, typed, proof-read. *I make this congregation a present of my life, before you can take it from me.*

The pawnbroker's assistant in Toledo will not remember him.

After the first breakdown in Ann Arbor his father said: You've been poisoned by books. (Saul had just read a passage from Kafka, in a high ringing accusing voice, and thrown the book down on a table.) According to friends who remember Saul's anecdote he shouted triumphantly in the (angry? frightened?) man's face: What should I have been poisoned by—*you?*

The room is dimly and vaguely oval. There are no windows. There are queer and somehow frightening indentations in the walls. . . . When Saul approaches the wall it shrinks away. He knows he must escape because his oxygen supply is diminishing but there are no windows, no doors, no actual walls. . . . Suddenly he sees his own body lying at the front of the synagogue. His arms and legs are outspread, he is vomiting blood. Is he "conscious" or "unconscious," is he "in terrible pain" or "beyond pain" . . . ? The commotion is distracting, the place is a madhouse, screams, wails, a stampede in the aisles, where is his mother . . . ? It is the dying rabbi the congregation mourns but Saul can't see where he has fallen. One shot in the side of the neck, the second in the upper left arm, the third into the left eye and into the brain. . . . Abruptly the image dissolves and Saul finds himself in an unfamiliar dark that isn't dark enough. The ghostly outline of his single window disturbs his sleep, a mottled patch of light from the street that falls slantwise across his ceiling. . . .

Once Saul confided in his closest friend Freddy C—— (who later betrayed him) that he was "afraid." "Afraid of what?" Freddy asked. "Just afraid," said Saul. After a long uneasy moment Freddy said, blinking and staring at his feet, "Well—I guess I am too." But now Saul isn't at all afraid because the Sabbath services are always taped and everything he says will be preserved for the record. His elegant speech of denunciation won't be distorted or mangled or misquoted. And he is well-informed enough to know that the crucial area of the brain is at the base of the skull, he won't fail to fire directly into it, he has always been something of a physical coward but this lies in the province of abstract logic. In "Last Days" he puzzles over the fact that in life *as it is actually lived* we feel very little genuine emotion: it is after an event, perhaps even years afterward, when we "remember," that we imagine we also "feel." *Hence an episode as it is actually lived (performed) may be without any emotion whatsoever.*

The elder of the two cantors has opened a prayerbook at the lectern and Rabbi Engelman has returned to his seat when Saul reasons that it is time to make his move. Lithe and unhesitating, though still somewhat hunched over, he rises and comes forward with the pistol in his hand. If he has worried that his voice won't be forced enough, that it will turn shrill at the climactic moment, he was mistaken—it is vibrant and manly beyond his most intoxicated dreams.

All who are gathered here this morning . . . an outrage and an abomination . . . a betrayal of the sacred heritage of . . . Deceit, worship of false gods, mendacity, hypocrisy . . . I alone raise my voice in protest . . . I alone utter the forbidden thought. . . . Did the Jews of Europe bring upon themselves the cruel justice of the Holocaust. . . . Do the Jews of the "New World" bring upon themselves . . .

He runs in the stinging swirling snow to hail the Greyhound bus as it is pulling away from the curb. He runs through the woods at dawn, in his green Windbreaker, not minding how the branches of trees and bushes claw against his face. ("Don't be so faint-hearted, time is running out," he says when he meets one of his numberless girls in a coffee shop on State Street and she professes shock at his bleeding forehead and cheeks. "Don't you know we're in the *last days* of this era—?") He's exhausted, he wants to press his face against his mother's breasts and burrow in deep, deep. He's exuberant, trotting out to I-95 by way of the back fields of the Fort Spear hospital grounds, an illicit $15 snug in his pocket. Who can stop him? What is the magic word that can stop him?

To the dazed congregation it must look as if Rabbi Engelman is welcoming him on the bimah. As if the performance has been rehearsed. "I know this young man," the rabbi says in a high stern courageous voice. "I know this young man and I trust him," he says, raising his voice to be heard over the murmurs, the isolated screams, the faint falling incredulous cries. Saul bounds up the steps to the bimah, to the sacred place, pistol raised like a scepter.

He smiles calmly into a blur of light, a pulsing radiance in which no single face can be discerned. Why had he ever imagined fear, why had he ever imagined failure? He belongs to history now. Every syllable will be taped and preserved. "I know this young man and I trust him," the rabbi is saying, insisting. "I don't fear him. Please do as he says. Please do not anger him. Of course we are willing to listen to him, of course he may have the lectern and the microphone and our undivided attention. . . ."

The surrender of one generation to another, Saul thinks. The aged battered wolf, king of the pack, baring his throat to the fangs of the next king. "Thank you, Rabbi Engelman," he says in a strong formal voice.

He takes his speech of denunciation out of his pocket and begins to read.

Dale S——, though not present at Adath Israel this morning, will write an article called "The Enigma of Saul Morgenstern, Sacrificial Assassin," to be published in late May in the Sunday supplement of the larger of the two newspapers: a controversial piece that draws so much attention Dale is led to think (mistakenly, as it turns out) that he might have a career in journalism of a glamorous sort. Freddy C—— will revise a doctoral dissertation on the subject of "American assassinations" in which Saul Morgenstern is eventually relegated to a lengthy footnote—a reasonably well-received academic study published by Oxford University Press. Sol M—— tries for months to organize his thoughts on the subject of Morgenstern (did he despise Morgenstern from the very first, did he envy him his brash crazy style, did he think that "basically" Morgenstern was correct, did he think that in fact Morgenstern was insane?)—and eventually fails: *there is too much to say.* Denise E——, though on the periphery of Saul's "circle," writes an overlong impressionistic piece for the university paper, "The Tragedy of a Lost Soul." Rose P—— will stubbornly revise a short story over the years, presenting it in various awkward forms to writing workshops in the university's extension school, and rejecting all criticism with the angry rejoinder, "but it happened like this, *it happened exactly like this.*" Saul Morgenstern assassinated Rabbi Engelman of Adath Israel Congregation in full view of eight hundred people by shooting him point blank, three times: the fatal shot entering the brain through the left eye, at a slightly upward angle.

Without hesitating he then turned the gun against himself, pressing the barrel just behind his right ear, and pulled the trigger. The impact of the blow sent him staggering backward. His legs spun beneath him, his wet shoes skidded, he fell heavily and never rose again. A witness cited in Rose's story says Saul Morgenstern "stood on tiptoe" when he pulled the trigger. His expression was tight and strained but "radiant." He fell about ten feet from the dying rabbi. His head was nearly touching the base of the Ark. A blood-tinted foam with bits of white matter began to seep from the wound in his head, and, dying, he started helplessly to vomit. At first he vomited bile and blood, and then just blood, a thick flow of blood, a powerful hemorrhage. . . . He was vomiting as he died. (But Rose P—— wasn't a witness. She isn't Jewish, she never was Saul's lover, she must have read about the assassination-suicide in the newspaper, like everyone else.)

Saul Morgenstern, the Scourge of G–d. His style is outrage tinged with irony and humor. "Black Humor" perhaps but humor nonetheless. He is a marvelous talker, a tireless spinner of anecdotes, tall tales, moral parables. With enviable agility he climbs the steps to the "sacred" space before the congregation. With a burst of extraordinary energy he hauls himself over a six-foot wall (littered with broken bottles, it is afterward claimed) while his friends stand gaping and staring. He risks death, he defies death, knowing himself immortal. The entire performance is being taped. Not a syllable, not a wince, will be lost. He has penciled in last-minute corrections in his fastidious hand, the manuscript awaits its public, he can hear beforehand the envious remarks of his friends and acquaintances and professors. Am I the Messiah, he wonders, with so many eyes upon me?—standing erect at the lectern, the pistol in one hand and the microphone in the other.

FUNLAND

Eugene Ehrhart was driving his eight-year-old daughter Wendy up to Juniper Springs, on the Hudson, one bright cold morning in early December. The hospital wasn't located in the village of Juniper Springs but a few miles north, near Lake Mohawk. Wendy's mother had been there since mid-April and somehow eight terrible months had passed and Wendy hadn't seen her. There had been complications, misunderstandings, unanticipated setbacks. Even so, when Ehrhart brought up the subject of a visit his daughter had responded strangely, and, he thought, somewhat unfeelingly. With no perceptible alteration in her expression she had raised gray doubting eyes to his, and adjusted her glasses in a gesture appropriated from him—pushing at the bridge with one brusque forefinger—and said: "Will Mommy come out to the car, or will I have to go in?—I hate hospitals."

The child's voice was low and hoarse but every word was startlingly clear. She didn't offer her father even a meager flash of enthusiasm, not even the stingiest of smiles, and sometimes he resented it, that he, the only adult male in the family, was required to do all the smiling. It corroded his soul.

But he smiled sunnily and said they would be guided by whatever happened—whatever worked out. That autumn he was in the habit of saying vaguely, "Whatever works out for all of us . . ." and then humming under his breath. He was not a nervous person by nature, none of the Ehrharts were, but the tragedy in April, and subsequent complications in his domestic life, had undermined him.

In June, partly to celebrate Wendy's eighth birthday, Ehrhart had planned a visit to Juniper Springs but it had been canceled at the last minute, for reasons that couldn't be explained to a child. Again, in early September, a visit had been scheduled and Wendy had even bought her mother a touching little gift out of her own allowance, from the dime store—three tiny, fuzzy, bulbous cactus plants in a bright green plastic pot—but again the trip had been canceled. Ehrhart did not want to explain the details to his daughter, that would have been an act of pointless cruelty against his wife, so he had said it was "doctor's orders." Not Wendy's mother's fault, and not theirs.

Wendy had cried for a while, in her room, in her bed, with the door "locked" against him (not really locked, of course, but fixed shut with string, rubber bands, and Scotch tape), and Ehrhart had not disturbed her. Let her cry, he thought, let her purge and heal herself. Though he had long ago lost the confidence of his family's Lutheran faith he retained a certain optimism regarding the soul's natural ability to heal by way of its own efforts.

What did Wendy know about hospitals? he wondered. Had she seen something alarming on television, when he wasn't home; had one of the children in her class frightened her? He knew it was most prudent not to ask, however, since that might disturb her, and, in any case, she couldn't be relied upon to tell the truth. "If Mommy feels strong enough maybe she'll want to come outside into the fresh air," he said reasonably, "and if she doesn't maybe you'll change your mind and want to go in. Why don't we see how things work out? Isn't that the best tactic? We shouldn't make decisions twenty-four hours ahead of time."

When Ehrhart had brought the subject up Wendy was staring into the aquarium, which had become scummy again. Sometimes the cleaning woman neglected to take care of it, or cleaned it carelessly, and the task then fell to Wendy, since Ehrhart simply hadn't time to waste on the fish, much as he admired their delicate, near-transparent beauty, and the restful motions of their swimming. Of eight tropical fish only three remained alive, which was a pity, they *were* exquisite little things, but since Mrs. Ehrhart's accident a great deal in the household had become neglected. Wendy peered into the green-tinted water, her glasses nearly touching the aquarium's side, and Ehrhart could see her gaze darting about—mimicking the motions of a black-striped angelfish even as it followed the motions. He said: "I suppose we should put them out of their misery, before they die. It would be a kindness, to give them peace right away, instead of . . ." But Wendy pretended not to hear and Ehrhart let the matter drop. It was altogether likely the three remaining fish would be dead anyway when they returned from their trip.

In the morning, just before they left the house, the telephone rang and it was Ehrhart's mother-in-law calling from Darien. Ehrhart explained that he couldn't talk at the moment, he and Wendy were driving over into New Jersey, to Fair Hills, where they were going to spend the weekend with friends of his. (He supplied a name—the altogether convincing name of "the Novaks"—but his mother-in-law asked for no details. She had become intimidated in recent years by Ehrhart's assured manner and even by his courtly, breezy, mock-flirtatious behavior to her.) Naturally she asked to speak with her granddaughter. "Of course," Ehrhart said at once. He cupped his hand over the mouthpiece. He waited. Wendy was struggling with her down-quilted parka, trying to get the zipper in place, he could see her down the length of the hall, by the front closet, but she hadn't much awareness of him at the moment.

After a beat of some ten seconds Ehrhart told his mother-in-law in a voice that communicated both embarrassment and the effort to disguise embarrassment: "I'm sorry, she's being a little stubborn this morning—you know how she is—I'm *very* sorry—maybe I can get her to telephone *you* this afternoon—do you plan on being home?"

On the Palisades Parkway Ehrhart was careful to drive precisely at the speed limit, since he didn't want to attract any attention from the highway patrol. Also, there were occasional snaky ripplings of ice across the pavement that might have been dangerous. Beside him, Wendy made a show of not troubling to glance out the window when Ehrhart exclaimed over the beauty of the river, and the granite cliffs, and the winter trees: she kept her nose buried in a book. (It was something from the school library called *A Little French Ballerina*. He had skimmed it—he skimmed all his daughter's books—and it seemed harmless enough.) Only when he turned off the Parkway to stop at a roadside restaurant did she look up with any expression of interest. "This isn't some ratty old tavern or something, is it?" she said, though she could see clearly enough that it wasn't. There was even a "scenic overlook" promontory nearby, with a view of the Hudson and the cliff on the opposite shore.

In the restaurant, Ehrhart used the men's room, and sent Wendy into the ladies' room, and the two of them sat companionably at a rough-hewn table made of pine logs and unfinished pine, in which innumerable customers had carved or burnt or inked in their initials. Though it wasn't yet noon Ehrhart ordered a stein of beer. Wendy wanted a chickenburger with French fries and cole slaw, and afterward a chocolate marshmallow sundae, and he allowed her to order everything though he knew she wouldn't be able to eat more than a few mouthfuls of each—she was spoiled rotten, he was nearly as much to blame as her mother, but this wasn't the time to impose discipline. Ehrhart himself hadn't any appetite, he rarely did these days, and made an effort to eat a sizable and nutritious meal once a day, at dinner. So he ordered nothing at all. That way, he would save money too.

Wendy had been defiant enough to bring *A Little French Ballerina* into the restaurant with her, but Ehrhart closed it, and set it aside, and she did not protest. She pouted for a few minutes; puffed out her cheeks in that particularly ugly piggish way Ehrhart disliked; then began to chatter about school, her teacher Miss Flanders, her classmates Janey, Barbara Ann, Laurie, a birthday party or was it a Christmas party. . . . Ehrhart's attention wandered. He knew that Wendy did not always tell the truth: she resembled her mother that way. Once he had caught her out in a fib that hadn't seemed important at the time (she claimed that the little dyed rabbit muff he'd given her the previous Christmas had been "stolen" but he knew very well it had simply been "lost") but, my God, how the child argued, and shouted, and wept angry tears, and *insisted*—! Another time there had been a most suspicious mix-up involving a party one of her classmates was having, to which little Wendy Ehrhart either *was*, or *was not*, invited: she claimed she *was*, but didn't want to go because she disliked the girl who was having the party; Ehrhart gradually realized she *was not*, and her contempt was sheer bravado, pitiful of course (for do children of six and seven persecute one another socially? and deliberately?), but annoying too, and certainly alarming. "I don't like little girls who tell lies," Ehrhart had told her calmly. And *that* mild statement had set off a tantrum of tears and rage that had ended in a sound spanking, and father and daughter both exhausted with weeping. . . .

Wendy might have sensed the drift of his thought, for her chatter had acquired a sharp nervous edge. He studied her face; a pity she was so plain, with her small snubbed nose and somewhat sallow cheeks, and those curiously adult pebble-gray eyes, the whites so unnaturally white they gave her a look of perpetual apprehension. . . . Wendy was telling him about a program she'd seen on television, a documentary on some kind of dreadful disease (children aging into adults and then into withered old crones?—he doubted anything like this was possible) and while he loved her for this innocent childish babble he understood it was a strategy for *not* talking about her mother, while of course she was secretly thinking about her mother all the time. He said: "Your glasses are smudged, you'd better clean them. But not on the napkin, that will only smear the lenses worse, don't you have a fresh Kleenex?—well here's one now for God's sake *use* it."

Without the transparent pink glasses her face looked smaller and more vulnerable. Her eyelashes weren't thick like most children's—in fact the eyelids looked a little grainy, flaky—and sometimes Ehrhart was convinced her left eye had a cast. The eyeball seemed always about to drift off to the side, as if something were tugging it, and of course in her infancy Wendy's eyes had been quite a problem (would she be crosseyed, would an operation be necessary, would she be *blind* . . . ?) and Ehrhart suspected that his wife had never entirely forgiven Wendy for not being perfect.

He had knocked gently on the door. He had knocked more forcibly. Receiving no answer, not even a drunken murmur of alarm or intimidation or anger, he had pushed open the door (it wasn't locked, *that* meant something) and saw her there in the bathtub. Naked, bluish-gray, her breasts just perceptibly floating, the knobby bones at her shoulders prominent, the collar-bone, the skeletal arm. . . . Her eyes were unevenly closed. It looked as if she were winking lewdly at him. But the eye showed only a crescent of white.

"Let me check your glasses to see if they're really clean," Ehrhart said calmly. He was smiling again so that Wendy could have no cause for fearing him. "And then: back on the road with no further delay!"

The responsibility of bringing new life into the world. The responsibility of propagating (1) the species (2) your lineage (3) yourself.

Eugene Ehrhart sat in his office at the second floor, rear, of Jerome A. Andrews & Associates (Commercial Residential Industrial Farm Insurance), at his massive glass-topped desk, staring sightlessly at the accumulation of letters and orders and bills and invoices that lay scattered before him. He was not thinking of his wife, he was not even thinking of the responsibility of his daughter. He half-closed his eyes and saw again the pew with its faded wine-colored cushion, he felt the solid weight of the hymnal in his hand, he breathed in deeply the comforting odor of dust and sanctity. "God have mercy, God have mercy," was his frightened mindless prayer. As a boy Ehrhart had rarely prayed for any positive boon but only for freedom from God's wrath, which, he supposed, he deserved. "Dear God help me to be good," he begged.

He had long ago lost his childish terror of God's judgment but he often felt that someone might be closely observing him. For what purpose, whether out of motiveless cruelty, or mere idleness, he could not have said. It was ironic then that his wife accused him of spying on her. When he denied it she grew the more vehement. "I can't breathe if you're always watching me," she said. "I'm trapped in your head. I'm suffocating." To elude him she grew gaunt, secretive, cunning. She acquired the deathly austerity of a Modigliani female, all vertical lines, sloping bones, empty passionless eyes. In an erotic dream that shaded helplessly into nightmare he seized hold of her body, he tried frantically to penetrate it, only to discover that it was a corpse: and this horror, many months before the accident in the bathtub.

He sat dazed in his office, at his desk, absorbed in his work. Hour upon hour. His work. He had always been praised for his industry at Jerome A. Andrews & Associates and he knew they were watching him closely now for symptoms of incompetency and breakdown. He was one of the junior associates, it wouldn't be a simple task to force him into resignation, yet he had to maintain his vigilance. He made telephone calls, he gave his secretaries work to do, he stayed late at the office and contemplated the future. It distressed him to find important correspondence doodled on, torn, crumpled; it frightened him to realize he'd been drawing cartoon figures for a half-hour, with no clear knowledge of what he did. (Ehrhart had been told he had "genuine talent" for cartoons, and should "pursue a career in commercial art," by a high school teacher, many years ago. He resented it, that life had hurtled him in so different a direction.)

He covered sheets of paper with angry zigzag lines, question marks, exclamation points, comic strip symbols for profanity, funny no-holds-barred "obscene" representations of the female body which (he realized with a guilty smile) he had better shred, for fear someone might discover them in his wastebasket. And trot about spreading tales.

The responsibility of bringing new life into the world weighed heavily on his shoulders. He was making plans, he was meditating. Something had begun to form at the back of his mind (the back of his *skull*, actually: he could feel it like a tumor growing by microscopic grains day by day) but he hadn't any intention of hurrying it. He didn't believe in forcing Fate.

The situation with his daughter was becoming urgent. Which grim-humored but perceptive philosopher had it been, Ehrhart had perused a snippet of the old German's wisdom in the *Reader's Digest* just the other day, the gist of it being that if human reproduction depended upon man's rational faculty the world's population would die off within a century.... Ehrhart laughed aloud, it *was* a droll thought. And altogether convincing.

His wife, emaciated, all blue veins and hollows, her flaky scalp showing lewd through her thin hair, lay slumped in the bathtub in the scum-gray cold water. Ehrhart's big gentle hands cradled her head. What remedy, what solution? Was she still breathing? Should he very gently force her head into the water and put her out of her misery? His scalding tears fell into the scummy water. He counted and resented them, every one.

As for Wendy, she had been at school at the time. But due home within the hour.

Ehrhart skimmed magazines in the waiting rooms of specialists: psychiatrists, neurologists, endocrinologists, gastroenterologists, pediatricians. He acquired the rudiments of a new vocabulary. He felt his horizons broaden. He wasn't bitter. In a lavatory he embarrassed one of his colleagues by pointing at himself in the mirror and saying: "There's the happiest man I know."

In one of the glossier medical journals, squeezed in between enormous multi-colored ads for pharmaceuticals of every species, Ehrhart discovered an article about defective births and their effect upon parents. Evidently it was the case that (contrary to widespread popular belief) parents love their defective babies *almost as if they were normal.* Mothers want to nurse and cuddle these babies. Even if the baby has died, they want to *see* and *fondle* the baby. A doctor reported that he found it "amazing" and "touching" that parents would contrive to find a single attractive feature in their baby, and focus on it, often to the exclusion of other factors. Even badly deformed infants. Even infants suffering from Down's syndrome. They recognize "normal" features in the baby: it has its father's eyes, for instance, its mother's nose, a familial bone structure. The doctor said that many parents do not, or cannot, "see" deformities in their young which the rest of the world sees.

Ehrhart was greatly moved by this article. He may have wept secretly.

He no longer believed in sin but very often he felt sinful. He *did* believe in redemption but was uncertain how it might be pursued. "There's the happiest little girl in the world!" he had said, pointing at Wendy's reflection in the mirror. "You'd better believe it!" But of course he was only joking and Wendy wasn't frightened.

Wendy made a mess with her melting ice cream sundae, and Ehrhart felt the need to discipline her, and afterward, at the cashier's counter, his hands shook so badly as he paid his bill, he tried to explain: "My little girl isn't well. Her mother died last spring, and . . . and she isn't making a very rapid recovery." Wendy had slammed out of the restaurant sobbing and could now be observed running hard across the icy pavement of the parking lot to Ehrhart's car. But naturally the car was locked. "I'm sorry," Ehrhart

told the cashier, whose white-powdered face now registered a gratifying sympathy. "Sometimes she loses all control of herself and
even a spanking won't help."

Ehrhart exited from the Palisades and drove north along a smaller
highway, near the river. He kept his speed limit stable because
there was no need to hurry, hadn't they all the time in the world?
Wendy soon sobbed herself to sleep and lay as far from her father
as she could, her head nestled between the edge of the seat and
the door. Ehrhart was grateful for the quiet. The peace. The solitude. He ran a slow surprised hand over the stubble on his jaws,
which was perplexing because he had shaved only a few hours
before.

The child was headstrong, the child was becoming a pathologi-
cal liar like the mother, and she was always coming down with
colds. At certain privileged moments like the present one she was
almost pretty, however: her hair was reddish-blond and wavy, like
Ehrhart's as a child: her nose was so cutely snubbed; her mouth
delicate as a rosebud. If only she wasn't naughty thinking her secret thoughts and scratching at herself and picking her nose. She
told fibs about her father to the cleaning woman, and to her
teacher, probably to her classmates and to *their* mothers, and flew
into a tantrum when she was caught. She'd told fibs about Ehrhart
to Ehrhart's wife but he had put a stop to that, and so had Ehrhart's wife: she had locked Wendy in the clothes closet to discipline
her. Later, when she told Ehrhart that "Mommy wasn't well" and
"Mommy was sick all day" and "Mommy had a fight with somebody on the telephone" he had been slow to believe her, or even to
listen to her. In such cases, a pediatrician had told him, it was wisest not to encourage the child to fantasize.

She was acquiring unfortunate habits—not bathing frequently
enough, not changing her underclothes. She wore soiled panties
and her little white t-shirt to bed, night after night, under her pajamas: and she didn't change her pajamas, either. She didn't
brush her teeth, didn't keep her fingernails clean. He hadn't the
heart to chastise her. His wife had failed and he would fail. "Look
at this," Ehrhart's wife said. Her face had gone dead white and she
was making gagging motions, as if she were about to vomit. Ehrhart examined the evidence: an expensive hardcover illustrated

copy of *Little Women,* given to Wendy by her grandmother, whose
pages were badly soiled and stained and even clotted. Wendy had
picked her nose and evidently wiped it on the book, it *was* a dis-
gusting spectacle, Ehrhart had thrown the book into the trash
without another word.

Perhaps it would be a kindness, a simple human kindness, Ehrhart thought, watching his daughter, if, by accident, her head or
arm moved with sufficient force to open the car door. . . . But probably that couldn't happen, logistics argued against it, it would only
arouse suspicion.

In any case it was unreasonable to worry, Ehrhart told himself.
Misplaced anxiety simply drains you of energy. The child was *perfectly* safe.

They had overshot Juniper Springs by fifteen or twenty miles but
Ehrhart was in no hurry to turn back. Perhaps he could bribe his
spoiled daughter into behaving if he promised to visit West Point
on the way back, or one of the castle-museums along the Hudson,
or that amusement park or arcade he'd noticed advertised in Lake
Mohawk. Though there'd be hell to pay if he promised her MEL'S
FUNLAND and it was closed for the season.

The Hudson River had begun to fascinate him. He could drive
along its high cold banks forever. Mist rose in delicate pale strips
from the water, the waves were choppy, very dark, heaving, mean.
Saw-toothed patches of ice had formed along its banks and phan-
tom rainbows, almost invisible, played on all sides. The water
would be freezing. The shock of it alone would be enough to kill, to
provide a merciful death.

Ehrhart's foot pressed nervously against the accelerator. His excitement was such, he had better drive more slowly, so he let his
speed drop until the driver behind him sounded his horn. "I can't
breathe with you spying on me," Ehrhart's wife had said angrily.
But then she had begun to plead. He hated her cowering, cringing,
pretending to be in terror of his temper. He preferred her rage because his own did not then seem inappropriate.

The water would close companionably over their heads, Ehrhart
thought. A somber grave. Father and daughter united. He wondered if the doors and the windows of the car (it was a new-model
Buick Skylark) were tight enough to form a sealed capsule—sealed,

that is, for a few minutes. Two, three, five, ten? Would it be most pragmatic to open his window beforehand, or would those final minutes between them be precious? He wondered if any reliable studies on the subject had been published.

He drove on at the speed limit. He wasn't to be hurried by anyone rudely sounding his horn or by truckers swerving out to pass. The sun was now slanting in the afternoon sky, pale and winking, shading into dusk, because the shortest day of the year was approaching.

The awkward angle of Wendy's head resting against the door made Ehrhart think again of his wife, his poor spiteful wife, lying in the bathtub, sprawled across the untidy ash-littered bed, hugging the baby in her naked arms and rocking slowly from side to side as if she were alone. "You are doing this to spite me, aren't you," he said. She had lost weight, her fine dark hair came out in brushfuls, she must have recalled how, in the early intoxicating days of their love, he had squeezed and kneaded her buttocks, her thighs, her breasts, in a half-sobbing ecstasy of worship. "You are taking your revenge, *aren't* you," Ehrhart said.

She was leaning over the aquarium that was Ehrhart's gift to the household, and the gently agitated water, rich with undersea plants, cast a greenish light across her face. She was a woman he'd never seen before, no longer pretty, stark and grave and austerely beautiful, with gray-green eyes like washed glass. "We can't live like this! You poison everything you touch!" Ehrhart began shouting suddenly.

Now Wendy hiccuped in her sleep and woke up. For a few minutes she seemed badly confused. Ehrhart's heart was beating rapidly but he showed none of the anger he felt, he teased her for being a lazybones, and for missing the magnificent scenery. On one side of the Hudson the rocky cliffs had turned an icy bluish-gray, on the other they were sun-bronzed, so noble and exhilarating a sight that Ehrhart regretted not having brought along the camera. Wendy blinked and stared. She fixed her glasses firmly in place against the bridge of her nose. "Where are we, Daddy?" she asked in a faint voice.

He joked that they were halfway to Alaska. Then he said that they had bypassed Juniper Falls and would have to double back. But they were going to stop at Lake Mohawk first because she'd been a good girl since lunchtime and there was a nice surprise there for good little girls.

It took Ehrhart nearly an hour to locate MEL'S FUNLAND at Lake Mohawk, and then he was disappointed it wasn't a real amusement park but an arcade, housed in a shabby stucco building with a neon marquee in front. The "A" had burnt out of the crimson neon tubing. Wendy read aloud in a drawling tone: *"Mel's Funl'nd.* Here we are, *Mel's Funl'nd.* What a ratty old stinky old place!"

Still, it turned out there were rides in operation, for small children, as well as a crowded bingo game, and a row of noisy bleeping video games, and a sharpshooter's range featuring silhouetted targets of bears, antlered animals, and helmeted men. There was a "Baby Animal Zoo," there was a miniature golf course patronized by rowdy drunken teenagers, there was a bright-lit refreshment booth that sold beer as well as soft drinks and food. Ehrhart felt conspicuous in his camel's-hair coat and white silk scarf but he thought the cavernous old building had something agreeable about it, and it didn't fail to please him that, though she didn't let on, Wendy had been roused from her sulk. Under ordinary circumstances the din of amplified rock music and the rancid mingled odors of hot dogs, tobacco, animal excrement, and people in close quarters would have offended Ehrhart, but tonight even the squealing of small children had a curious comforting effect. "Why, this is how people live," Ehrhart thought expansively. He was dazed with his own sense of well-being. He felt he could lay his hand on the heads of strangers and bless them.

He bought himself a bottle of beer and quickly drained it. Wendy was too excited about taking a ride on the miniature merry-go-round to want anything to eat or drink, so Ehrhart bought a ticket for her, bought a half-dozen tickets, what the hell, she was just a child and might as well be indulged in childish things. For an eight-year-old with a high I.Q. she was behaving like a much younger child but he wasn't going to take offense. "Peace and quiet is the first priority," he said with a laughing sigh to a woman in a simulated leopard skin coat, who was watching her daughter on the merry-go-round as well. "Don't we all know it," the woman responded at once. Her pretty plump face was lavishly powdered and her red lips had been shaped in an old-fashioned cupid's bow that was surprisingly attractive.

This is how America lives, Ehrhart thought, looking around with a slow dazed smile. He wasn't one to pass judgment.

Wendy had clambered onto a palomino pony that moved up and down as the merry-go-round turned, in an uncoordinated motion that was sometimes jerky and sometimes languorous. It was a dream creature with bared grinning teeth and a mane and tail made of bristling synthetic hair. Only about one-third of the animals were occupied. There were horses, big cats, camels, a swan "boat" for tiny children.

They forget everything, Ehrhart thought, shaking his head in wonderment. Children. God bless them.

Two young mothers, and one youngish father rode the creaking contraption, with their toddler-age children, so Ehrhart thought what the hell, and bought himself a ticket, and clambered aboard, behind Wendy on her bucking palomino. He was a child at heart, wasn't everyone a child at heart? It was necessary to see things in proportion.

Wendy cast a pale frightened glance over her shoulder but Ehrhart only grinned and waved at her. He wasn't going to embarrass her. The atmosphere was too light-hearted, the mood too festive. He chose a flatfooted comical donkey to sit on since his weight might have broken one of the livelier animals. A little boy riding a black horse with a broken foreleg pointed at Ehrhart and giggled, but Ehrhart only grinned and waved at him in return. He felt he could bless everyone in sight.

The beer had gone to his head. He clapped his hands as if to rouse the slumberous donkey, he shouted "Giddyup!" in a ringing voice. Wendy, on the animal just ahead, fell in with the game and slapped her horse's reins against his neck, and kicked her heels hard against his sides, and screamed "Giddyup! Giddyup!"

Round and round they went. The amplified music blared overhead. There was the red-lipped woman in the leopard skin coat, there was the ticket seller's booth, there, a scant yard in front of Ehrhart, his sweet little daughter in the blue parka, squealing with childish laughter. Whatever happens, Ehrhart thought. They might drive south to Disneyland in Orlando, Florida, over the holidays. They might take one of those muleteam rides in the Grand Canyon.

Wendy is a little princess thundering along on her palomino pony. Lunging muscular legs, graceful neck, mane and tail rippling in the wind, hooves complete with genuine horse shoes. . . . By contrast Daddy's donkey is nailed to the floor. He will never overtake her. But Daddy doesn't mind. Daddy is feeling very content. Daddy has all the time in the world.

THE MAN
WHOM WOMEN
ADORED

The rumor was that he had died—had died of something sudden and catastrophic, like a coronary thrombosis or a stroke—or had it been a beating, in a disreputable part of the city?—but clearly the rumor was false; for there William appeared, unsteady on his feet, in the slanted acrid sunshine of early October, crossing Broadway at Fourteenth Street. He might have been drunk. He was certainly unwell. With that elegant and slightly self-mocking gesture of his hand I remembered so distinctly he waved back traffic. The driver of a delivery van angrily sounded his horn, the driver of a low-slung rusted taxi edged forward, his fender brushing against William's thigh. I stared—I wanted to cry out a warning—for certainly he *could* be injured—but in the next moment William had maneuvered himself out of danger.

Was this derelict William? He had aged a great deal and his hair had at last gone white. But it was a coarse, sallow white, unclean. His face too was soiled, smudged: a mass of wrinkles, like a crushed glove: but the lips, and even the slightly swollen nose, still had that peculiar sculpted beauty. He wore a shapeless flopping overcoat that was clearly not an overcoat from his former life—he had prob-

ably bought it at one of the venders' stalls on Fourteenth Street—
and he walked with that dream-like precision of the drunken or the
very old, his eyes fastened to the pavement at his feet, as if it were a
narrow strip above an abyss, dangerous to navigate. His lips
twitched, he must have been talking to himself, arguing, cajoling,
explaining. I wanted to call out his name but I said nothing. I
backed away. Turned away. I avoided him by ducking around a
parked car and crossing the street through traffic.

I thought he called my name, I seem to have heard my name,
but I didn't look back.

Do you know, I said, once, not at all bitterly (for I watched myself:
and I was rarely bitter), you are a man whom women adore?

William laughed, surprised and pleased. Of course he must have
known he was a man women adored; but he had never heard the
thought so succinctly expressed. He looked at me as if, for the first
time, I had to be taken seriously.

That was long ago, of course. Many years. Both William and I
have changed a great deal since then.

When I first heard the rumor of his death I had a vision of a
gravesite around which numerous women in black stood in pos-
tures of mourning, not joined by their common loss but further
isolated by it. And degraded too: for there is something degrading
in such abject surrender.

I was not one of the mourners. I never mourn anyone I outlive—that is, anyone whose attraction for me I outlive.

In the beginning, William once told me, frankly and amiably
enough, it was perfectly natural that everyone adored him. He was
the youngest of six children; he had almost died of a throat infection as an infant. His family was genteel and all the soft luxurious
emotions—love, tenderness, sentiment—were highly prized by
them, the women especially. At the present time emotions are examined with a sort of amusement, held in the palm like exotic,
possibly dangerous insects, but at the time of William's babyhood
emotions welled up from sources believed to be sacred, when they
were not demonic. William cried a great deal as a child and he was
never made to feel ashamed of his tears. He was hugged, he was
cherished. He was certainly the center of the universe.

His father was a partner in one of the oldest brokerage houses in New York City. His mother's family owned, among other things, iron ore deposits along the St. Lawrence River. William's parents lived with their six handsome children in an Edwardian mansion on Fifth Avenue; in their employ were nursemaids, serving girls, a cook, a chauffeur, an English butler, and other servants. It was the 1920's and everything lay ahead.

I begged William to show me photographs from his childhood. You don't seem real to me, I said. You don't seem weighed down by history, not even personal history.

(Because of his extraordinary charm, I think. His uncommonly handsome face, his graceful manners, his sense of self.)

We were intimate at that time. But not genuinely close. I had no right to make demands but he complied, after a while, and seemed as struck as I by the packets of old photographs he brought me one Sunday—"Baby William," "William at the age of 3½," "William on his first pony"—William with his pale curls, his smile that was ethereal and pouting by turns, his rather round, thick-lashed eyes, his charming little velvet suits and ruffled shirts. William, and never Billy.

There was something legendary about the child in those sepia-tinted photographs, as if he knew very well what was his due, what his beauty required; and knew too that he would never have to insist upon it. The immense calm of *being* loved, and having to do very little *loving*. (After William left me that Sunday I discovered a snapshot left behind, which I must have slipped out of the pile, must have stolen, half-consciously. William at the age of 8. Unsmiling, even a little melancholy. But very striking. A child to be cherished. If William noticed that this photograph was missing when he returned home, he never mentioned it to me. He always forgave small sins committed through love of *him*.)

Between the ages of nine and fourteen William sang in an Episcopal boys' choir good enough to travel about the Northeast. He discovered that he loved music—loved singing—loved the "religious atmosphere." Describing himself as a choirboy he meant to be amusing, but in fact his voice deepened with a kind of awe, as if he had been a witness to those stately processions and not a participant. How handsome the boys were—all the boys! William had worn a long velvet robe of a deep burnished wine color; his pale blond curls had been brushed off his forehead; the expression of his gray-blue eyes was grave and demure. Angelic, everyone said. Of course they fussed over him in the family, the women especially, but he saw how, as the boys filed out the center aisle of the church, into the sunshine, the congregation—men and women both— stared at him. It seemed as if he were walking in a dream through their odd rapt faces. They looked at all the boys but they certainly looked at *him*, week after week. Quite openly, not at all rudely, but as if it were altogether natural. Of course some smiled—some were friends of the family. But others simply stared. William met their gazes shyly and his cheeks burned and his breath went shallow. What did it mean, to be so admired! So *contemplated.* When the procession of choirboys marched out of the church, clean out of the church and into the ordinary daylight, when it appeared they were only boys after all, despite their long robes and carefully combed hair, William felt a keen disappointment. Was this it? Was this all? Had he imagined everything?

He loved the choir, he said. Even the rehearsals, even the choir-master's peevish demands.

William was sent to his father's schools—Lawrenceville and Yale—and at the age of twenty-six he married the heiress to a meat-packing fortune out of Kansas City, whom he had met in Manhattan. Within a few years he was unfaithful to her. (Technically, that is. For of course he had been unfaithful to his young wife immediately after the wedding. There are smiles which, quickly and covertly exchanged, are consummate acts of adultery; there are even occasions when the refusal to smile, the fixing of a solemn stare, is dramatically adulterous.) Women so adored William, how could he keep himself from them? He sensed too an implicit approval from certain older men, like his own father. And surely there was enough of William for everyone—his spirit was magnanimous as a Sunday buffet.

But it really began, he told me in a voice that trembled with emotion (and so many years afterward!), when a cousin of his wife's, an ordinarily pretty girl of twenty-eight, unmarried, from Missouri, came east to visit, to see their infant daughter. For some reason William and not his wife led the girl into the nursery. It was a hazy April afternoon, a breeze stirred the gauzy white curtains, the girl placed her cold, nervous fingers on the back of William's

neck as he bent over the crib—and it was really the case, the girl
maintained for years, that she had been unable to help herself. It
happened, it simply happened, no one was to blame.

"Did you love her?" I asked.

"Oh—*love!*" William said.

"But if she was the first—"

"She loved enough for both of us," he said flatly.

The first time I saw William, he was pointed out to me at a large
gathering. It was a reception held in the newly-opened wing of a
museum. There he is, an acquaintance said, there, do you see?—
that man? (My acquaintance was the former lover of a woman
who had been, as they said, "involved" with William for a brief period of time. His voice was coarse with an indeterminate emotion—jealousy, bitterness, a curious masculine pride.)

We became acquainted that evening. There was an exchange of
telephone numbers. William was struck by the fact—or the postu-
late—that I was an "artist" of sorts myself. "It must be very difficult to write," he said, "I mean to write about serious things, to
give the kind of depth to consciousness that it really has. . . . I
mean, in my own head I am going in ten directions at once, even as
I stand here, but in literature or art there's a wonderful single-
mindedness that allows you to go deeply into . . . into the soul. Isn't
that true?"

His enthusiasm was gratifying—it was intoxicating. We are always intoxicated with the danger of being overvalued.

So I became acquainted with William, who was already legendary in his own circle and who was moving out, in this phase of his
life, into wider, more experimental circles. He had money, a great
deal of money, for the acquisition of art by "unknown contemporaries"; he bought books, including high-priced limited editions;
he would want, eventually, to help finance an off-Broadway play.
Talking with him I felt the power of his own enchantment: I was
buoyed up by his intensity, his marvelous gift for exaggeration.
How could I resist summoning him to me, though I was hardly the
kind of young woman who "summons" men—! He had my number and did not telephone. I had his number, and did.

His eyes were a wonderful keen gray-blue, widely spaced in his
strong face, rather deeply socketed. His nose was straight, and
long, with a Roman bridge. Though he was only in his late thirties
at the time of our initial acquaintance (we were to see each other

intermittently for years—William was always "rediscovering" me)
he did give the air of being older: there was something patriarchal
about him, an authority graced with kindness, affection, an interest in detail. He was filled with questions about "craft" as well as
"art"—he was dizzily flattering! Does a writer *feel* things more
deeply than the average person, William wanted to know, and is it
dangerous?—is it exhilarating?—or merely an aspect of one's professional skill?

"Suppose you were to write about me someday," he said shyly.
"And I read it. And then—"

"Yes?"

"And then—well—well I would *know*."

He never spoke of his wife to me, and of course he never spoke of
his other women. (It was fairly common knowledge that he had a
mistress—and the word "mistress" is not inappropriate—who lived
in one of the brownstones William's family owned, on West Eleventh Street.) Sometimes he alluded to his children: they were "expensive" children. His curiosity about my own life, my solitude,
my eccentric working hours, my bouts of despair that could shift so
abruptly into hours of fierce airy energy, struck me as unnervingly
impersonal. He was interrogating me, he was learning from me, yet
I was not very real to him. He might have thought my "art" protected me—I could not be injured like his other women.

He had a habit, not so annoying as it sounds, of humming tunes
under his breath. Cole Porter, Hoagy Carmichael, Rodgers and
Hammerstein—that sort of thing. His smile could be melancholy,
and then it could shift and dazzle you with—with the very fact, the
impact, of good spirits—of sheer simple happiness. He liked to
laugh, he liked to tell anecdotes. His stories were never original but
they were wonderfully entertaining. At school and for a year in
college he had wrestled and played football, and in the war he
was said to have had a "distinguished" record; though he rarely
spoke of that aspect of his past, as if sensing that it did not exactly
represent him, I sensed in him the absolute calm that comes of a
masculinity that has been put to the test and has not failed. Now
he was freed of *that*, now he could give himself over simply to being
adored. And the adoration, of course, had to come from women.

Sometimes he said, speculatively: "I might have been a priest,
you know. An archbishop . . ."

I understood his meaning. I said: "But you would have been an

Episcopal priest, you wouldn't have had to take a vow of celibacy."

"I *would* have taken a vow of celibacy," William laughed.

Evidently he had wanted to enter the seminary as a boy. His father was disappointed but would not have opposed him; his mother was quite enthusiastic. But when the choir sang the Apostles' Creed in their high, thin, hauntingly beautiful voices, William's eyes flooded with tears because as he sang so winningly of his beliefs he knew he did *not* believe—it was impossible.

Certainly there might be God—that was reasonable enough—a presence called "God" that inhabited the universe without passion—floating through it, bodiless as cigarette smoke in a closed room—that might be true: but this presence had never taken on the contours of a personality, in William's experience. The Bible was strident and terrifying but not very convincing. As the years passed "God" became more and more abstract, more general. William shocked the chaplain at Lawrenceville by asking whether "God" wasn't a fancy word for "whatever happens." In any case God snagged on nothing immediate in William's life.

By the age of sixteen his belief had faded; and of course he had given up the choir long before.

I was sick, and William came to see me. As I lay on a sofa reeking and parchment-colored with jaundice this extraordinary man in his three-piece tailor-made suit bounded about raising windows, straightening the clutter of my life, making an attempt with a sponge—which was filthy—to clean my sink and cupboard counters. He hummed songs from *Porgy and Bess,* he whistled "Old Buttermilk Sky" so energetically one knew he had never listened to the lyrics. Though he was in his mid-forties at the time and beginning to put on *some* weight he was as airy and light on his feet as a Chagall lover.

Had he been my lover, years before? He seemed not to remember. Though of course he was gravely considerate now, even courtly. He *might* have been a former husband.

He told me about his boyhood, and about the choir. He confessed that his success as an adult, and his personal happiness (for of course William was happy—no matter that he had caused so much grief) did not mean as much to him as those hours in church. If only he could explain—! The boys' voices lifting—the organ filling the immense church with its remarkable sound—the priest in his vestments—the sanction of the Church itself—the dizzying air of drama, meaning, intensity—

"Do you understand?" he asked, apologetically. "I'm afraid you can't understand."

But of course I did.

His second wife was said to be a gifted but erratic horsewoman, small-boned, quick and nervous and very beautiful; she brought with her, to the marriage, two young children and a $1.5 million estate in Far Hills, New Jersey. She was thirty-one and "shaky" from the experience of her first marriage, or at any rate from the protracted experience of adultery with William, which she could not have foreseen, with confidence, would develop into marriage. The divorce was mildly scandalous but did not come before a judge.

William was thirty-six years old. He loved the country, he claimed to be discovering "domestic life." (There were more than a dozen servants and groundsmen employed at the Far Hills estate.) He journeyed to the city only once a week, staying from Monday through Thursday; then he returned to the country where he cultivated a small vegetable garden and learned, with some difficulty, to bake bread. He took riding lessons at his wife's insistence so that he would be able to accompany her, eventually, on her daily rides.

But the rumors began again. There were always rumors. William this, William that. Of course he could not be blamed: women approached him: even the most gracious, the most genteel women: it was claimed they could not help themselves.

Oddly, as William grew older, and must have become less "attractive" in the usual sense of the word, the love women bore him began to acquire an increasingly desperate tone. There were scenes, there were threats, one or two attempts at suicide. A shouting match in the cocktail lounge of the Far Hills Hunt Club; a drunken street scuffle in mid-town Manhattan with the husband of a well-known actress. There was even a rumor, especially injurious because the subject was so petty, that William had put pressure on the membership committee of the Hunt Club by way of an older member's wife to get an acquaintance and *his* attractive young wife admitted to the Club. When the nomination was blackballed William was furious.

Shortly after this incident William's wife had an accident while riding, and badly smashed her right kneecap. She spent a long time in the hospital. After her recovery the two of them left for a protracted vacation—it had always been William's fancy to "travel around the world"—to Japan, to India and Ceylon—where both husband and wife became interested in Buddhism. They bought Buddhist art, took hundreds of color photographs, attended Buddhist ceremonies. It was said that they took instructions in Buddhism with a renowned teacher.

But William's wife grew ill with an intestinal disorder, so they cut their vacation short and returned to the States. She sold her horses one by one; there was talk for a while of selling much of the estate; then something happened, and William moved away to an apartment in the city—a legal separation was arranged. (I saw a photograph of William's second wife once, in a newspaper. Perhaps she had aged, perhaps the photograph was poor, but she did not strike me as unusually beautiful.)

Buddhism was one of the subjects William loved to talk about. He had memorized passages from certain sacred texts, which he loved to recite in his rich dramatic voice. *When the mind is disturbed it will strive to become conscious of the existence of an external world and will thus betray the imperfection of its inner condition. But as all infinite merits in fact constitute the one mind which, perfect in itself, has no need of seeking after any external things. . . .* These were the words of Asvaghosha, a Sanskrit philosopher; William was not absolutely certain of the pronunciation of his name.

But then he loved to talk about so many things. It gave him joy simply to talk, to hear his own voice, to gauge its effect upon others. He gossiped, he recounted the plots of novels that had "struck" him, he worried aloud about the international economic scene, he criticized restaurants and nightclubs, he knew amazing little stories about government officials, exiled royalty, fashion models. Once he telephoned me simply to talk about the "extraordinary" writings of a Frenchwoman named Anna de Noailles of whom I had never heard. As he spoke I could imagine his handsome face lined with thought . . . *thought,* not worry, of the most noble sort.

He began to see me again, with more regularity. Much had gone wrong in my life and he saw it as his mission to "rouse me from despair." He loved to speak, in long rambling charming monologues, of "serious" issues—God, immortality, the soul, how to live. These were genuine issues; they were more important than anything else in life; yet no one knew the first thing about them.

William did not fall in love with me, even then, though my wretchedness, and my obvious need for him, must have been a temptation. (As he grew older these temptations were to become more difficult to resist.) But I think he was in love with—he was fascinated by—my apparent intimacy with these "serious" matters. I was a writer, after all. Not only a writer but a woman willing to live a spartan, severe, even monastic life in the service of my "art"; it was no exaggeration to say that I never went for an hour in those years without thinking of certain solemn, marvelous, slightly outlandish "questions"—the riddle of death, the paradox of our yearning for immortality encased in our mortal flesh, and so on, and so forth. I was not only willing to sacrifice myself for my art but in fact was doing so, and quite visibly.

Other women who had adored William had certainly been serious enough in their adoration of him, but they hadn't really been serious *women*—they were not obsessed with such matters. It is possible that William, though he loved them, might have believed that they deserved their misery, for wasn't it absurd of them— wasn't it an aspect of their vanity—that they should *presume* his love for them would be permanent? Sometimes he recounted anonymous incidents of a dismayingly petty nature, and we burst into mutual laughter; for wounded feelings, grief, jealousy, even rage *were* amusing. Another time he told me of scenes he'd had with his second wife near the end of their marriage: the poor woman had stopped accusing him of infidelity and had begun to claim that men were pursuing *her.* William would listen to her tales, and force himself to say, And—? Yes—? What happened—? with an air of startled and irritated possessiveness that indicated he still loved her. She would conclude her stories by saying in a small neutral voice: —Then I told him I couldn't see him again, I told him I was in love with my husband.

William sighed and laughed and rubbed his face brusquely. The great haunting philosophical questions—how are they to be linked, to be yoked, to such painfully *physical* moments? His life

was becoming a riddle. He could not solve it. It seemed to him re-
peatedly that the women he adored in his imagination were betrayed by their counterparts in the real world. Self-pitying tears,
unconscious vulgar expressions, banal or ignorant remarks . . . the
mistaken notion that passionate jealousy would flatter him. . . .
"You're a writer," William said to me, "you must have thought
about these things deeply, so perhaps you could explain: why does
everything fail?"

His question angered me. That he should assume that *everything*
failed—! *Everything*, when he meant of course only *women*; not even
women so much as *adoration*. I said impatiently that it isn't the role
of the writer, or of any artist for that matter, to *explain*.

"It isn't?" William asked with great seriousness. "Oh I see. Then
what is—?"

At that time I was just recovering from a long illness. Not a
"medical" illness but an illness just the same. I was grateful to be
alive, and resented William's tone. I said: "Well—first we survive.
And suggest pathways."

William stared. He was silent for a long moment. It was clear
that he admired me, and his admiration was always flattering; but
it could not last. He stared, and nodded, and repeated: "I see. Yes.
First we survive. Yes."

He was under the enchantment, or was it the curse?—of his own
being. Which was one of the reasons I telephoned him a few
months later, though I knew I should not be interfering with his
life (he had married again, a third time, and was living on East
Seventy-second Street, in an apartment overlooking the river).

He was in his early fifties now. He had gone through a period of
intense revulsion for his work—for everything to do with finances,
with money itself—but had come through. It was said that he was
"happily" married at last.

I called him, though there had been a tacit agreement, on my
part, that I would not bother him, and I heard his voice register
surprise and disappointment and courtly patience and finally concern as I explained as frankly and calmly as possible that I only
wanted to see him, to talk with him, one more time. . . . I did not
break down. There were no tears. He took a cab to my apartment;
I hadn't needed to beg. And somehow it happened, I am not cer-

tain how or why, that by the time he arrived I had dropped off into a profound stuporous sleep, from which I had to be awakened with great effort on William's part. (Poor William! He guessed, correctly, that I had taken a dozen or more sleeping pills, washed down with vodka. That I had *wanted* and had *not wanted* to die in his arms.)

So it happened that William saved my life. He shook me awake, shouting, and hauled me to my feet, and forced me to vomit, and afterward made black coffee which he forced me to drink. He was stern, he was furious, there was nothing loving about him, and I was angry at him for saving me, and then, a few minutes later, hysterical with gratitude. Stop, stop, shut up, he said, I've had enough of you.

But he gave me a considerable sum of money—considerable from my point of view, I mean—enough for several months' rent—and I had reason to think he paid the superintendent of the building to watch me, to do a little amateur spying. He wouldn't have wanted one of his women to die on him.

He telephoned frequently, to see how I was. In a voice meant to be encouraging he assured me that my behavior was nothing more than eccentric. He had been reading about certain "temperamental" artists lately—Gustav Klimt and Egon Schiele. (He sent me an excellent reproduction of Schiele's *Girl in Black Stockings*, saying that the figure had reminded him of me!—a statement I took to be preposterous.) "Such spells, such moods," William said, "are probably quite normal for your nature and your genius."

"Genius?" I inquired mildly.

"You have to do these things," William said slowly. "I think I understand."

"But your other women do them too," I said. "Don't they? Haven't they?"

"My other women—?" he said.

"Don't you have other women?" I asked.

"Of course not," he said. "I'm happily married now."

A few weeks later it occurred to me to test William's friendship by asking for more money. Just a little more. A loan. And he did not disappoint me though I think he was hurt. (His voice registered hurt. I had called him at his office on Bank Street.)

"I'll send you a money order," he said. "But that will have to be the end. Do you understand?"

"Of course I understand," I said softly.

He was about to hang up, then changed his mind and asked my opinion of—what had it been?—a new sculpture exhibit, a new "difficult" novel? We talked for a few minutes. Again he was about to hang up. Then he happened to mention, as if incidentally, that he was having difficulties with his new wife after all. He loved her very much, he said. But for some reason he couldn't seem to make her happy.

"Do you know what she said last week?" he asked in a puzzled voice.

"No. What did she say?" I asked.

"She said—If you leave me and go to any of them, any one of them, ever again, I won't be here when you get back."

I slapped my hand over the receiver to hide my laughter.

I said, "Then you mustn't ever leave her again."

He said, "I know."

"You *mustn't* ever leave her again."

"I know," he said, his voice rising. "I know."

As William grew older and his life became more unpleasantly complicated—there were problems with his grown children, there were problems with his family's business—it happened that the women who adored him were more and more distant from his social world, and more desperate. And, except for a thirty-seven-year-old actress ("Anne-Marie"), they were getting younger.

He was still a striking man, of course. His silver-blond hair receded gracefully on a brow that was imposing; his cheeks were ruddy, as if with exuberant good health. His lips were so sharply cut as to suggest sculpture. It was not an exaggeration to say that he was a beautiful man, for his age at least, maneuvering himself about like an athlete past his prime but still in superb condition.

His wife had been an artist of some sort—or perhaps a designer or an interior decorator. It was said that she had given up both her marriage and her job for William. She loved him passionately, with a young girl's caprice. (She was in fact forty-two years old.) She could not shake off the notion—which was hardly so far-fetched as observers thought—that William's love for her began to diminish as soon as they were married and he had "saved" her from her former husband. Their quarrels were tempestuous and exciting. William had to shout her down, and then comfort her. Help me, why don't you help *me*, he whispered, but of course she did not hear, or if she heard she did not understand.

In this marriage, William declared, he rediscovered "romance"—he and his wife met for drinks in little unknown bars, saw 6 P.M. showings of foreign films, held hands in the dark, strolled along the busy avenues, stopped for dinner impulsively in restaurants they had never seen before, and often could not find again. He was very happy. His wife was a woman with whom he might discuss Shakespeare (whose complete plays he meant to read, one by one) and even Schopenhauer (whose *World as Will and Idea* he was trying to read at last—he'd heard so much about it for decades), or the latest bankruptcy scandal on Wall Street, or the mysterious meditative nature of bread-baking. (William was trying to bake his own bread again, on the weekends. It was all he seemed to retain from his Buddhist period.) Everyone said that it was obvious his wife adored him.

It was a happy time. Yet friends were disappearing from his life.

Invitations went unanswered, calls were unreturned. An old classmate from Lawrenceville, a corporation lawyer whom William saw for lunch two or three times a month died suddenly of a heart attack, on an early train from Greenwich. One of his old Yale suite-mates lost a great deal of money in real estate speculation in Long Island and committed suicide—shot himself in the head. Other friends and acquaintances drifted away because, it turned out, they belonged to William's ex-wives rather than to William, or because, remarried themselves, they found it difficult to interest their wives in their old connections. And it seemed too that William was beginning to drink too much in company, and his "charm" and "high seriousness" were becoming tiresome.

He was obsessed with the same old topics. How to live—what is love—why are we on earth. The "meaning" of death. But his voice often slurred and he was developing the habit of nervously squeezing his listeners' arms for emphasis.

A mild heart attack at the age of fifty-six. So unexpected! And unjust, for William *had* been dieting, he *had* been exercising and watching his weight. (He had joined an impressive new health club on Lexington Avenue where he swam for a vigorous half-hour before taking a cab down to work.) In his doctor's office he spoke resentfully; his face grew coarse; he knew he had been unjustly treated. His wife was blackmailing him emotionally, he said. Women had always blackmailed him. He couldn't control it. . . . Couldn't understand. . . .

The heart attack had been dangerously mild. William insisted for days that it had been nothing more than indigestion—only his wife's tears had forced him to make an appointment with his doctor.

He had said to her, irritably, Well—you can't expect me to live forever just for *you!*

The women were younger, scruffier, less clearly defined. One was a "psychiatric nurse" in her early twenties who was unable or unwilling to say exactly where she had trained, or where she had been employed (when William was introduced to her, by way of a friend of a friend, she was living on unemployment insurance and sleeping most of the day). Another was a "therapy assistant" who worked three or four times a week at a "clinic" in the West Forties, near the river. She was often vacant-eyed, her smile had no focus, her sentences trailed off into silence. A pretty girl, William thought, but mysteriously soiled; smudged; as if a playful giant had picked her up and smeared her with his thumb. The "psychiatric nurse" called herself Inez, the "therapy assistant" called herself Bonnie, a girl by the name of Kim Starr who struck up a conversation with William one mild June day in Washington Square was a former "ballerina." The girls had nothing in common but their youth, their vague blurry soiled prettiness, and their interest in William.

Meeting him for a very late lunch at the Oyster Bar—it was after three—one of the girls snatched up William's hand and kissed it. "You in that expensive suit—it's tailor-made, isn't it?—and your shoes!—and your fingernails manicured—and that scent— did you just shave?—oh I love you, love you—I mean it—I wouldn't lie—I'm *crazy* about you, William—" the girl cried.

Inez, Bonnie, Kim. And later the young step-daughter of a business acquaintance named Deborah. William made it a point to telephone the girls several times a week from his Bank Street office, careful that no one should eavesdrop. (The place was in disarray. The outer office was being used for storage, there was an old carpet, stiff with dirt, rolled and tied and set on end in the corridor outside William's door, that had been there for weeks.) In his address book with the worn black cover William had scribbled down two and sometimes even three telephone numbers for each of the girls, but it often happened that they were not available at those numbers. Strangers picked up the phones, shouting Yes? Hello? Who is—? Their accents were harshly foreign.

William had not forgotten me entirely. Every few months he called, took me out for a drink, squeezed my hands in his and assured me that I was lovely as always. And how was my work going? And my life?

He was happy, he said. Though after two or three drinks he would complain mildly about his wife. She had completely redecorated their apartment, had even knocked out a wall, you can imagine the inconvenience—and the expense!—yet her moods were more capricious than ever. She imagined he had a mistress. She was even jealous of his former wives, and of his grown children. (It maddened her that William should continue to loan money to his children, or give it to them outright, when his own financial problems were becoming so serious.) "I will soon be sixty years old," William said with an elegant, helpless gesture, "and I assure you I know nothing—not the first thing about love and marriage and children and how to live one's life—"

It was my strategy that day to speak lightly. I said: "Too many women have loved you."

"What?" he asked, cupping his hand to his ear. "—Love? Oh, that!"

In a dark gold-flecked mirror I spied upon the two of us, seated at a pretentious little pedestal table of simulated marble. William had become an aging gentleman with hair that looked white; I was a woman with a shadowed face.

The lounge was disagreeably noisy. New customers were continually filing past our table.

"I suppose you're going to write a story about me someday," William said, raising his voice. He was both accusing and affectionate. "And if you do—I wonder: do I dare read it, or not?"

* * *

It was not long after this meeting that William happened upon Deborah, the eighteen-year-old daughter of a business acquaintance. Though in fact she was the man's step-daughter.

She was walking north on Seventh Avenue, near Eighth Street, with her arm around the waist of a slender, swarthy-skinned young man in a white shirt. She was obviously drunk, or high on drugs. She nuzzled the young man's neck, giggling, and staggering around him; it seemed awkward, it seemed rude, that the young man didn't trouble to slide his arm around *her*. William stared in amazement. He had last seen this girl at her parents' summer cottage in East Hampton, years ago. Deborah must have been no more than thirteen or fourteen at the time, yet he remembered her face distinctly. —Deborah, William whispered. Here? Like this?

On the street that day she was wearing clumsy high-heeled shoes with open toes, and jeans that fit her slim body tightly; her red-brown hair tumbled past her shoulders, snarled and matted; her pale skin was freckled as William remembered. She was wearing theatrically red lipstick but the lipstick had smeared onto her face.

William followed the couple for a block or two, and saw that they were not getting along well. Deborah's mood had changed; now she was pushing and slapping at the young man, who slapped her right back. Passersby stared at them. William came hesitantly forward. He called her name and she ignored him. She was saying something in a low rapid furious voice to the young man.

"Deborah—?"

Finally she turned and saw him. It was astonishing, it was miraculous, the stages of her *seeing* him. At first her gaze merely swung onto him, as if he were an intruder, a stranger; and then her expression sharpened; and then softened; and it was clear from the change of light in her eyes that she recognized him.

"You're— You're— Oh Jesus I can't think of your name—"

She staggered forward, she clutched at his arm.

"Oh Jesus I can't think of your name but I *know* you—"

William tried to tell her but she was too excited, too high, to hear. Her voice was all exclamation, her eyes were glittering, he could smell the odor of dried perspiration on her body. It was certainly Deborah, his friend's step-daughter; they knew each other and their behavior on the street—for now Deborah was hugging him, she had thrown her arms around his neck wildly—was really not so extraordinary as it might appear. William's face flushed scarlet and he did not know what to do with his hands.

"Oh I *know* you—I *know* you—" the girl wept.

One terrible night the telephone rang in the apartment on East Seventy-second Street. And William knew from his wife's voice, and her expression as she called him to the phone, that this was Deborah at last.

It was many months later. The start of November. William had given Deborah his home number but begged her not to call unless it was an emergency.

She was not very coherent on the phone. There were voices— they might have been angry, they might have been merely festive—behind her.

"Yes? Deborah? What is it? What are you saying?"

"—in trouble," she said, "I think I'm in—"

"Deborah? Where are you?"

"I'm in bad trouble," she said, "I'm in bad trouble—"

He asked her what was happening, how could he get to her, but she kept repeating that she was in trouble, in bad trouble, until she began giggling, and the phone must have been taken from her, and slammed down.

William's heart was pounding in his chest. He had to sit—had to grope for a chair. It was a long time before he heard his wife's questions. "One of your girls, wasn't it, another one of your girls, *wasn't it*, don't lie, don't you dare lie to me—!"

He did not answer her. He did not really hear her. He was waiting for the telephone to ring again but of course it did not ring and he sat beside it for several hours, numbed, in a trance of sheer despair, too upset even to heave himself to his feet and go to the liquor cabinet.

Near dawn he tried the door to the bedroom but his wife had locked it against him. So he slept, fully clothed, his shoes on, on a leather couch in the room he called his study.

The calls came infrequently that winter, though William was always prepared for them, and bitterly disappointed to hear the wrong voice. His wife laughed: "Oh, wasn't that the girl—? Oh what a pity!"

"There is no girl," William said. And then, befuddled, licking his lips: "She's the daughter of an old friend. The step-daughter."

"What old friend?" his wife asked. "You haven't any friends."

Sometimes he wandered about the apartment at night, lingering in the doorway of his study. It was alarming, the vividness with which he could recall the girl. He had escorted her along the street that day, he had taken her uptown in a cab, and once in the cab they had fallen upon each other hungrily—the girl had clutched at him, kissing him, and he had responded with a convulsive frenzy he had not known—he really had *not* known—he was capable of making. Though it was possible (as he thought afterward) that he had merely succumbed to the girl's passion.

He took her to a hotel on Seventh Avenue. Not one of the better hotels—because he hadn't much cash with him that day, and didn't care to use his credit card; and because, in a better hotel, the girl's noisy exuberance might have attracted attention.

Her arms were like steel bands around his neck and back. She screamed, she wept, she rolled her head from side to side, in a transport of passion—so clearly unfeigned!—that excited him more violently than he had been excited in many years.

And then, afterward, she had not wanted him to move from her.

"No, no," she said hoarsely, angrily, "no, I want you there, I want you *there*, I'll kill you if you leave—"

So he lay on top of her, vastly flattered, sweating, his heart hammering in his chest, his thoughts racing so crazily they were colored paper streamers, razor-thin strips of confetti.

"Don't you leave me don't you ever leave me or I'll kill you—I swear I'll kill you—" the girl shouted.

She clutched at him. Her young slender body was rancid with sweat.

"No—no—no— Don't leave me—"

But his heart, his heart!—hammering so violently. He could not get his breath. Her arms which had seemed so thin were in fact hard with muscle—hard with the violence of her frenzied need.

But of course he had to shift his body from hers. It was impossible for him to make love to her again so quickly; he could not penetrate her again; his penis had shrunken, had gone limp. . . . Fortunately she grunted and pushed him from her and fell asleep suddenly. She fell into a thin twitching feverish sleep that excluded him.

He lay beside her for a long time, his pulses racing. She was so young—so extraordinarily young! *That* did amaze him. The bodies of young women, young girls, which they inhabit so unthinkingly—the smooth unlined flesh of the thighs, the belly—the small hard lovely breasts—

My love, William whispered, close to tears. My sweet little love.

She gave him her telephone number. But she must have made a mistake, jotting it down so hurriedly on a scrap of paper; for when he called a woman answered, speaking in a querulous Spanish-accented voice, she knew no one named Deborah, knew nothing about Deborah, what was the number he had dialed?

Fortunately William had given her *his* number. Both at the office (where he preferred her to call) and at home. And she did call—she did call—always very late at night—always in a strange mood: she was gay, she was exhilarated, she was panicked, she was very, very tired. William was so pleased, so flattered, that he refrained from asking her exactly what it was she wanted from him.

William's marriage came to an end one snowy night in February.

This was the night Deborah called for the last time, and summoned him to her.

Her voice was shrill and terrified and clear: "Could you come get me right away?" she said. "There are some people here—some men—some very strange men—"

"Deborah? What is it? Where are you?" William cried.

"Oh William I'm so afraid—oh can you help me— William—"

It was a measure of her terror, that her voice was now so clear. Despite the noise in the background he could hear her words distinctly.

"What is it?" William said, "what is happening?—where are you?"

"Oh William could you come get me—come in a cab— Oh please, please—"

"Deborah, dear, tell me where you are— Can you tell me where you are—"

His hands shook so badly, he could barely write down the address. And then it wasn't a complete address—just the intersection of two streets in the warehouse district, near the river.

"Deborah," he whispered, "Deborah— I'll be there immediately— Deborah?"

But the line was dead. She had replaced the phone, or someone had taken it from her.

So William dressed, William prepared to leave, though his wife—in her nightgown, looking stunned and haggard—was trying to dissuade him. There was even some foolishness—a humiliating scuffle of sorts—at the hall closet. His wife was nearly crying. "Where are you going! What on earth do you think you're doing! It's two in the morning, it's bitter cold, how can you *think* of going out in your condition—"

On the icy street he ran, vigorous, frightened, shouting for a cab, waving his arms. It *was* bitter cold though he did not register the fact for some time.

It took him ten or fifteen minutes to get a cab, over on Fifth Avenue. By then he was shivering convulsively and his face and exposed hands ached with the cold.

And then, on the street again, he found himself hurrying along one block of darkened warehouses after another. The streets were poorly lit here; it was very hard to see. He rubbed his hands together, he muttered to himself, what would be wisest to do, what should he have done, should he have telephoned the police. . . . He dare not call her name: she might be held captive: her tormentors would be alerted.

Ice had formed curiously humped and coiled shapes on the sidewalk, upon which thin dry patches of snow lay. It was dangerous to walk so fast—the soles of his shoes were slippery—he had forgotten his overshoes—he had forgotten his gloves. A very cold wind was blowing from the river. He stared, looked from side to side, bewildered, why were there so many blank featureless doors?—windowless buildings? Loading ramps, immense sliding garage doors, an air of utter solitude, silence. No one lived here, surely. He would never find her here.

He ran from one side of the street to the other, panting, whimpering. If only he saw a crack of light— If only there was a doorway that might lead up into a loft— Piles of debris had been heaped in the gutters, and ice had formed over them. An uninhabited place. Blank featureless pitiless buildings.

"Deborah," he cried. "Deborah—?"

He could hear himself panting. And his heart, could he hear his heart as well?—queer clipped arrhythmic beating—now rapid, now slow—a hiccuping sensation—no pain but sudden surprising airiness.

Far up the street William saw, suddenly, figures on a stoop. They were just leaving a building, were they? He stared at them for a long moment before he had the sense to shout at them.

"Wait," he cried, hurrying forward, "you there, *you*—wait— don't let that door swing shut—wait—don't let it lock—"

Three or four figures. Young people, probably. They ignored him, they strode away in the other direction.

"Wait," he cried, "oh please wait—"

He stumbled forward, whimpering with the cold. His breath was alarmingly loud. He had forgotten his gloves, he had forgotten his overshoes. He could not remember—exactly—the girl's name. She was the daughter of a friend. An old friend. She would know him, of course, when she saw him. If only they had not let the door swing shut— But then perhaps it had not *locked*—

It was locked, he seized the knob and tugged at it, crying, "Open up! You in there! *You!* I know you're listening!" He pounded on the door. Fist over fist, whimpering with the pain, on that blank ungiving door.

"Open up, do you hear? I know you're in there! I know what you're doing to her! I insist—"

They must have been listening to him, in frightened silence. For he heard no sound. No sound at all.

The building was a warehouse. There were enormous sliding doors made of corrugated aluminum or tin; there was a loading ramp upon which ice had formed in serpent-like coils. He could see no windows though the building was four stories high, at least. A blank featureless pitiless facade.

William's shouts echoed faintly in the streets, among the high buildings. It was remarkable, the silence in this part of the city.

"Open up!" he cried, his face now wet with tears. "I know you're in there, all of you— I've come for her— You can't deny me— She's in there and I know what you're doing, I know, but I won't let you—I've come to take her away—"

He pounded on the door until there was no more sensation in his fists.

* * *

One day William appeared at my door. I had heard rumors of his
death—he had been renting a room by the week in a hotel on West
Forty-seventh Street, he had been found dead in the room, or col-
lapsed in the street?—or had he died in the hospital? Obviously the
rumors were false.

It was a fact, however, that he had been eased out of his partnership in the family business. But without putting up much of a defense.

A fact too, that his marriage was over.

He had not wanted to talk about these misfortunes, however. He
wanted only to talk about general things, "serious" things, the old
issues of life and death and the immortality of the soul and how to
live one's life. . . . He was inquisitive about me: had I accomplished
what I wanted, was I happy, did I regret living alone? (For now, at
my age, it was too late. Quite clearly too late.)

We talked. Beneath William's words I could hear him pleading
with me, silently. Do you still adore me? he was asking.

I had not much time for him that day. It was late afternoon, I
was on my way out. I pitied him because the enchantment was
over—one could see that at a single glance, the poor man looked so
battered, so hopeful—but I had not much patience for him. None
of us do, once the enchantment ends.

Do you still adore me, do women still dream of me? William was
pleading, his watery eyes fixed upon me, his fingers (which were
surprisingly dirty) plucking at the hem of his suit coat. Though of
course he said nothing of the sort: he was asking about my life, my
work.

I explained that I had to leave.

He walked alongside me for a block or two, before he tired. And
finally he did ask, as he had been meaning to ask all along, touching my arm: "Will you write about me, do you think?—someday—?"

NIGHT.
SLEEP.
DEATH.
THE STARS.

Again this morning *though I prayed hard to God otherwise* it is snowing. It began around four-thirty when I first woke up to look out our bedroom window and now, hours later, it is still snowing. Great soft wet clumps the size of blossoms. *And tomorrow is Easter Sunday. And the girls will be angry.* Fist-sized clumps of snow, so silent. So slow. Falling in the woods, in the overgrown fields, in the old cow pasture where the rail fences are down. Falling and turning to lacy filigree in the trees out back. In all that underbrush Jonathan hadn't finished clearing last fall. *It is very beautiful probably, a benison of God. It is serene and comforting at least* and all in silence. Therefore I dread the girls waking.

Holy Saturday and tomorrow is Easter and this morning it is snowing again. So soft and wet. Like cherry blossoms. Like tufts of cotton batting. Falling and melting in the weedy stubble. In the ruin of the old barn, in the rotted roof, in the stone foundation where snakes nest. Falling and dissolving in little pocks and kisses in the forbidden pond. (Which is really a lake, in my secret opinion. Because it is so long and narrow and still and dark. And deep. At the other end—fifteen feet deep, or more. My thinking is, a *pond* must be *round*; and much smaller. For it has a *round sound* to its name: *pond*. And it is *small-sounding*. *Pond*. A lily pond, a goldfish pond. A pond you can easily walk around. But Jonathan's people call the lake the pond, giving it no other name as if it weren't significant, or did not possess beauty, *which God knows it does despite its treachery*. The pond, they call it. The pond, say the little girls, though the deep end is forbidden to them and they must not play there or take out the boat. Jonathan's people lived here for one hundred years, he said, before they sold off most of the acreage, and there was always a pond or a watering hole for the cattle, always that water, and no name for it except *pond*.)

Jonathan will be irritated because I make too much out of everything. But snow is wrong in April. It is out of place on Holy Saturday. No one can get warmed. I mean warmed through and through—to the bone marrow. So we don't have to wear layers of sweaters and sometimes gloves in the house. And two pairs of woolen stockings. If tomorrow is Easter Sunday and it is already April 14 then snow is out of place. And freezing temperatures every night. My step-daughters in their Easter dresses and shoes and coats will be blaming me. Driving to church (which is nine miles and the car heater doesn't work)—and sitting through the services—and driving home again. And there is to be an Easter egg hunt in Rookes Corners on the hill behind the Volunteer Fire Company building and if I take them they will be wet and cold and shivering and sniffing and complaining, and if it's canceled they will be furious with me.

But the snow is very beautiful, falling so slowly and silently as it does. Like delicate white lace, like flowers, like cherry or lotus blossoms, falling and melting and disappearing. *Praise God, for I do not mean to give offense.*

II

At first the girls asked Jonathan, so I couldn't hear, *When is our real Mommy coming back?*—I might be in the kitchen, or just coming up the cellar stairs, or just entering the room. (In warm months I never wear shoes. And I walk gracefully, I've been told, for a girl my size—never slamming down hard on my heels.) Sometimes he would hug them and whisper some answer or other, that I could never hear, and sometimes he would be angry, and scold them for asking such stupid questions when they knew the answer. Little Gillian cried all the time, those first months, as if her heart was breaking. And always wiped her nose on her blouse.

Vicky, and Niall, and Gillian. Eight, and seven, and five years old. My step-daughters. My inherited daughters. Whom I love more than my own life. Whom I will protect with my own life.

But lately they have invented a game of asking *When is our real Mommy coming back?* when they know I can overhear. If they are feeling reckless enough—if it has been raining or snowing all day and they are eager for excitement—they will ask Daddy, and risk being slapped (and sometimes slapped hard—so that I feel the sting in my own face); but most of the time they ask the question of their dolls, or their stuffed animals, or someone's photograph in a magazine, or the wall, or the window, or the air, or one another. So that I can hear. And be hurt.

You know I am your real Mommy now, I tell them quietly. When I can trust my voice. When the quivering in the air goes away. You know, I tell them. You know how we are living now. You know what Daddy has said.

Sometimes they are sorry. And Niall will come hug me around the knees, and poor little Gillian. But Vicky never. Little Victoria. Her Mommy's special girl. Her Mommy-that-ran-away's special girl. Vicky can be sorry for her nastiness and afraid of being punished, and Vicky can even cry, but she never says a word of apology, *she is hard, hard as nails inside, hard as her own selfish mother who ran away,* crying without making a sound, just big hot splashing tears running down her face, and no sobs as in a normal child, no panting for breath, her skin all slack and white and her eyes the ugly gray color of pebbles. These eyes are always wide open staring at me. *You are not our Mommy.*

Sometimes she has made me so confused that my voice has risen after all, without my intending it. And my heart is leaping and straining, and my fingers twitch with wanting to take hold of something. And the air feels strange all around me—quivering and dislodged. And my cheeks are wet though I haven't been crying and will not cry.

You know I am your real Mommy now.

III

Vicky, and Niall, and Gillian. My inherited daughters. *My daughters who love me and must mind me.* A lady at church, a lady in her late sixties perhaps, took me aside one day and assured me it was a miracle, they looked *like my own daughters,* the oldest one especially, such fine hearty coloring and strong bones. And so pretty! The three of them, so pretty!

I must have blushed crimson, the way I do when I'm pleased and surprised, my face just burned, and I was afraid I might cry. *When people are nice for no reason* you are always in danger of crying.

May the Lord God bless you, I told this lady. You are one of His good people.

IV

Scattered throughout the three stories of the farmhouse I have found secret things about which I should not speak. To profane the dead is wrong *whether of necessity or not.*

For instance, certain snapshots. Scrunched at the very back of the "junk" drawer in the kitchen. Wrinkled and folded over. Here is Jonathan my husband fifteen or twenty pounds lighter, standing in the sunshine with a girl, both of them in t-shirts and jeans, both squinting and smiling at the camera, Jonathan without a beard, Jonathan looking boyish and happy *without me* and *before ever setting eyes upon me.* And the girl is almost his height, like me. Tall and red-haired and very pretty. Praise God, she *is* pretty. I do not contest it. Meredith, was her strange name—an ugly name to say aloud. Meant for a man. Not right for a married woman and a mother.

Tall and thin and red-haired, the hair loose and curly on her shoulders, parted in the center of her head. The forehead showing a little bump, or a ridge of bone. In another snapshot you can see how anemic she is. Freckles scattered across her face and forearms, like a young girl, squinting, showing small white teeth, one of the canine teeth protruding. Meredith, I whisper aloud, and the quick thought comes to me: *It is wrong to profane the dead.*

She has not died but has done worse—she has run off. So it was necessary for Jonathan to divorce her, and it is not immoral for us to be married, married in flesh and in spirit, *one flesh and one spirit,* and living in this house *which is Jonathan's house by inheritance.* And nothing of hers.

These snapshots, these secret things, I realize it is wisest to rip up and flush away in the toilet, lest the girls discover them. (For all evidence of Jonathan's first wife has been cleaned away, according to Jonathan. So that nothing remains behind to confuse his girls. So that nothing ugly might turn up.) And other secret things—a soiled red scarf in some silky material, one frayed suede glove, recipes typed out on little cards and kept loose in one of the kitchen drawers—all these it is wisest to destroy, to clear the air.

Once I asked Jonathan, If she came back would you take her back, and he only laughed, so I said, Would you take her back and make me leave, like I wasn't any real wife of yours, like I was only your whore, and this roused him to actual wrath, *which I was a fool not to foresee,* as he had said so many times how he was bringing his temper under control. So he grabbed hold of my shoulders, and shook me hard, hard like I deserved, and shouted certain truths at me which were necessary to be voiced, as I had forgot God's intentions, and spoke out of spite and small-mindedness.

Because I am Jonathan's wife now, and the girls' true mother, and *no force on earth can change that fact.*

V

Oh, yes, where did your wife run off to?—why did she run off?—she must be pretty silly, to run off from *you!*

This was the sort of thing I said to Jonathan, which I can hardly believe now, when we first met, when he came around to the Windmill Diner where I worked, or we went out in the evening. Because I was so happy and light-hearted. Because I didn't know who Jonathan was, and only guessed from his way of talking and his vocabulary how educated he was, how intelligent. O dear God, all the funny crazy things I said, all the times I fell into fits of giggling, you wouldn't believe it!—Elizabeta flirting and blushing and having the time of her life.

You're not twenty-three years old! Jonathan said, staring and grinning. Why, you're just a big baby. You're a big grownup blownup sweetheart of a baby. You can't be more than twelve in your heart—don't fib!

I was four months out of the county hospital then and doing

well. Doing better than anyone back home expected. I lived by myself in a nice clean room and waited tables at the Windmill Diner and took my prescription to get it refilled every Saturday morning on schedule, to ward away evil thoughts, and there was no trouble in the slightest, not the slightest bit of trouble. And waitressing in the diner isn't really hard because you don't have to walk far. In addition to the counter there are only five tables, each seating four people. And I liked my work, I praised God *each and every heartbeat for my freedom,* so I smiled a lot and laughed, which men always appreciate, and they gave me such generous tips, sometimes I felt tears rush into my eyes.

Why, you're just a baby! Jonathan said laughing, grabbing my loose heavy breasts in both his hands, and squeezing, and squeezing—don't you pretend to me you're a grownup woman, I know them inside and out, honey I know all about them, *I've had enough of them for life.*

And one time I asked him, I was crying about something I have forgot now, some silly little trifling thing, I asked him, Why did he want to marry beneath him, why did he want to marry *me,* and he just grunted and laughed and said, Because I love you: only you. And I said, Even with me telling you about the hospital, and how I sinned so terrible trying to take my own life, and how they took my baby away from me, and pretended it was dead, and Jonathan framed my face in his hands and said, I love *you,* only *you,* and all that is past, and nothing of the past is going to happen again, *because I decree it.* Do you understand, "decree"—?

Praise God, I understood, O yes I understood, though it was never a word I would say for myself, or write down, nonetheless I understood it at once, and *have never forgot that sacred moment.*

VI

As for one of the secret things I have thought wisest to rip up and flush down the toilet—I can't believe anyone would use a recipe like this, which I found in one of the drawers, on an old yellowed card, neatly typed and some words underlined in red; so I halfway wonder whether it is a joke. (And what if I cooked it up for Jonathan and the girls, the way *she* must have done!)

BEER-BATTERED BLOSSOMS

Flour—5 tablespoons
Beer—½ cup
Zucchini Blossoms—12
Vegetable Oil & Seasoned Salt

Mix FLOUR & BEER for batter—dip ZUCCHINI BLOSSOMS
to coat w/ batter—fry in OIL until GOLDEN BROWN—turn
& brown other side—drain on PAPER TOWELS—season w/
SALT.
    SERVE HOT. YUM.

(N.B. Most of the male blossoms on the zucchini plants
can be used; but leave enough for GOOD POLLINATION. &
HARVEST BEFORE FROST KILLS.)

How strange it is, how it makes my head start to flood, too many
thoughts all at once, reading these typed-out words to myself in the
kitchen, and *hearing her voice* inside my own. There are things here I
don't understand in a recipe or otherwise, things that are maybe a
joke, such as *male blossoms*, which I have never heard of, and also
frying food in beer. But Jonathan would be furious if I ask him.
None of your spying and poking around, 'Lizabeta, he says. *Drive
your cart over the bones of the dead.*

Ripped in pieces and flushed down the toilet with the other
things of hers. God be praised, it has not snowed or frozen over for
eight days running and the girls have been easy to manage, and Vicky
has smiled.

VII

Jonathan's curly black beard and the curly wisps of hair around
his ears and collar are shining in the sunlight, he showered and
shampooed his hair this morning, in readiness for the day in St.
Paul. (Where he will use the public library for certain research—
"cultural-anthropological" research—having to do with his book.)
He has taken his lunch, he doesn't want to risk eating food carelessly handled, when I feed him so "superbly" (as he says) and his
health is being restored. But because he will be in the city *for approximately ten hours* there may be danger.

Now it is May, and warm, and once he is gone the girls will want to do forbidden things, and will sneak out to do them *if I turn my back.* For instance, they will want to play in the barn, and the old chicken coop, and the silo. And certainly in the pond. (Once the three of them dragged the old rowboat out and tried to maneuver it like a raft!—using sticks for poles. And Jonathan only realized they were in danger when *a terrible freezing fear went through him* as he sat at his desk in the attic. And then he ran to the window and saw.)

Sailing, sailing!—sailing! the girls sing out, now that the weather has changed and Easter is past. Why can't we go sailing on the pond!

But they don't say such things so that their Daddy can hear. It is only Elizabeta they torment.

Why do they want to do forbidden things?—O dear God, when there are so many healthy things to do? Jonathan says he can't patrol the place like a storm trooper, and he can't keep watch from his attic study, *he must trust me for something.* And of course he can.

All the outbuildings—except the garage and the tool shed, which Jonathan built himself out of prefabricated materials from Sears—are forbidden for play, because they are rotted through and might cave in at any time. Also, the girls might cut themselves on broken glass, twisted nails, and the like. (Vicky once had a serious infection from a splinter, Jonathan told me. In the days of "Meredith," he told me, with a thin stretching of his lips. The good old days gone by.) In the foundation of the hay barn and in the silo especially there are rats, and snakes too, maybe poisonous snakes, you can't be sure. These are all off-limits. These are wicked places. The girls know.

Most dangerous of all is the pond.

The pond is most dangerous because it is most attractive.

At its shallow end the muck is filthy and germ-infested from the droppings of cows over many years. If you walk in it it sucks at your feet—maybe it is quicksand—maybe it would pull a human being down. At its deeper end where the banks of cattails and marsh grass grow its stillness is deceptive because *there are things beneath the surface* to pull you down. Also, the bottom is much deeper than you might think, and it's filthy black muck at that end too, a child could drown there in a matter of minutes if she fell in. (In fact a little boy once drowned in the pond, Jonathan says. A long time ago. A hundred years ago. When Jonathan's family first came over from Norway and settled in. He doesn't know the details but the details don't matter, all that matters is *the pond is forbidden*.)

The girls must be watched every minute, says Jonathan, and disciplined if they are naughty.

They are good girls, they're not *really* naughty, I tell him.

Yes, they are good girls, they are our girls, Jonathan says at once, but you mustn't be deceived, and you mustn't give in to them out of kind-heartedness. For instance, if they beg you to take them out in the rowboat yourself. Sometimes, Jonathan says, framing my face in his hands, and staring hard and long at me— sometimes you are too kind-hearted. You know where that can lead.

So, at this very minute, the girls are playing by themselves in the side yard, in safety. And all is well. And I am watching them through the circle window on the stairs *which is a strange wonderful secret kind of window* I wish I could describe, it is round in itself, but with oval panes of glass, old wavy glass, set in like spokes, divided by narrow leaded strips. It is a kind of eyeball set in the wall and when I look through it I can see the girls in the side yard, and the silo, and much of the pond, and I know for some reason that *no one can see me*. It is as if the window on the stairway landing went one way only. O it is difficult to explain!

VIII

She's asleep! How can she sleep so long!
She isn't asleep—she's pretending!
Her eye is open, she can see us—
Her eye is all *white*—
She's dead! She's dead! She's dead!
My step-daughters, my little girls, are crouched at the side of the bed, and I can see them, I can reach out and touch them, but I can't move, my arm is too heavy to move, my eyelids are too heavy to open. Jonathan is gone and I am so lonely, so heavy-lonely, I take my pill and sleep on top of the eiderdown spread, without undressing, just my skirt unbuttoned at the waist where it is too tight. It is only ten o'clock in the morning but the shadows in the bedroom are strange.
She's drunk, isn't she.

She's sick and going to die.

Hey, she can hear us—she's looking right at us!

She *can't* hear, she's asleep.

She's looking right at you, stupid.

No she isn't, she's blind. She's *dead.*

My step-daughters, my sweet little girls, giggling and whispering by the bed. I am dreaming of a boat too—a lovely shining boat painted white, with white sails—and the girls are with me in the boat, we are all sitting together, the girls just in front of me, and my arms around them all to hold them safe, to hug them and feel their warmth. The sun is bright and warm, the wind is calm, but strong, making the sails bell out, and the little boat move across the lake.

I hate her, says Niall, starting to cry—why does she sleep all the time Daddy's gone?—I wish she would die!—I wish she would go away!

Be quiet, says Vicky, giving her sister a hard pinch, she can hear everything you say. She's wide awake. She's listening.

I hate her, Niall is whispering. I wish she would go away. *I wish Mommy would come back.*

I'm going to tell Daddy how long she sleeps, says Vicky.

Is she sick? Is she going to die? Where will he take her? little Gillian starts to cry, her fingers jammed in her mouth. *Mommy, Mommy—*

Be still! Stop that!

Mommy—

But the wind is pushing us along in the shining white boat. Across the dark lake. The cattails and marsh grasses and scrub willow catch at us but can't stop us. Elizabeta sits in the prow of the boat in her full pleated skirt hugging her sweet girls close, to protect them from harm and to rejoice in their warmth. *Praise God for these blessings. Praise God that the boat sets sail and cannot be stopped.*

IX

When she was disciplined she slapped and kicked and provoked her mother all the more, and then her nose started to bleed, and the bedclothes were filthy, and the sobbing! sobbing! sobbing! in every corner of the room. No wonder the air quivers so and won't

let me rest. No wonder there is something more to be found, something nasty and secret, to be ripped up if it is small enough and
flushed down the toilet. Or something lying beneath the surface of
the water, in the black mud, *that you try to row quickly over* but fail,
because the oars are caught.

Why can't you sit still, for God's sake, Jonathan says, bringing
his magazine down flat on the table, making a slapping noise that
frightens the four of us, why can't you sit in one place and stop
fussing?

I feel my face turning hot and try to apologize. And try to explain, how maybe I could try again with the tub in the bathroom
upstairs, the old tub, the fixtures all stained and rusted, the drain
especially, maybe I should try again with the kitchen cleanser and
the aluminum scrub pads. Because I hate to sit idle at 8:20 P.M.
Because I hate to have it said by anyone that my house isn't clean.

Jonathan is staring at me. I can see that I have displeased him,
and in front of the girls too. They are all staring at me. Vicky's eyes
are cold and hard and hating and wishing harm.

Why can't you sit still, Jonathan says, trying to keep his voice
low, why are you always jumping up and down? Even your eyes—
the way you keep looking around—what are you looking for, what
in Christ's name do you *see*? And thinking! Always thinking! I
know you're thinking!—I can feel your thoughts.

I'm sorry, I tell Jonathan.

And I am sorry. My heart is broken, I am so sorry to have displeased him, and in front of the girls too.

Now Jonathan is angry and has cause to be angry. He throws his
magazine down and begins walking around, bumping into furniture, talking, waving his hands, pretending to laugh, speaking of
some fat dumb cow named Elizabeta, who can't sit still and is always fidgeting, or rolling her eyes, or licking her lips, or smacking
her lips, or turning her lips inside out (these things are said to make
the girls laugh, and they do laugh, Vicky especially, laughing,
laughing, shrieking with laughter), stuffed into her clothes like a
fat ripe sausage, ready to burst out of her clothes, a face like a pie,
flat and round and plump like a pie, a cherry pie, some of the
cherry filling dribbling out (O how the girls howl and shriek and of
course it is funny, it is very amusing, Jonathan paces and prowls
and says these things in a low wild tricky voice like someone on

television, *you should laugh because it is so funny*), fat dumb sweet Elizabeta, baby-fine hair, so blond and pretty, fat and dumb and blond and pretty, *his* Elizabeta, and no one is going to take her away.

Upstairs in our bed Jonathan loves and loves and *loves* me, O it is so powerful and strange, he likes to pinch and to burrow, to kiss hard, to bite, to knead my skin, my flesh, *man and wife in one flesh*, praise God for His benison. At first he teases, still angry, in singsong, It isn't *your* house and it *can't be made clean*, it isn't *your* house and it *can't be made clean*, a singsong like a nursery rhyme, pinching and biting, O dear God I must not show hurt, for it will displease him, and then he forgets, and then he is saying things under his breath, things not for me to hear, murmuring, and moaning, and laughing to himself, wife, wifey-wife, *wife wife wife*, over and over so it isn't a word but only a sound. And behind my eyelids something moves. My eyes are shut tight, tight, and my eyelids are turning red. It isn't fire but sunlight. I think the sun is shining on water, on the pond, the lake, the pond, the deep dark still lake, the pond with its secrets, on the surface of the water there are tiny ripples and air bubbles and insects jumping and scuttling, water spiders, tiny flies, dragonflies, and the sun shining broken in the water, and our boat is caught in the cattails, *O dear God let us sail over, let us come to no harm*, but she has reached up to stop us, her fingers are part eaten away, I can see them gripping the oar, the forefinger is almost gone but the thumb holds fast, O God she has the strength of the Evil One, she has the strength that has drained out of me, the red-winged blackbirds are shrieking, something is splashing in the water, struggling and splashing, her arms are flailing, her long red hair is soaked and straight and falls straight from her head showing the curve of the skull and the ridge of bone in the brow, her mouth is open sucking for air, for life, for air to shout, she is blaming me but I am not to blame, the oar is raised, the oar is brought down hard on her head, she screams and sinks, she is sinking, drowning, her fingers clutch at the side of the boat but haven't any strength now, she is sinking into the muck at the bottom of the pond, *God have pity, God have mercy, I am sinful but I am not to blame, God forgive us we know not what we do.*

Black sucking mud is her proper grave for she is evil and cruel and hard, hard of heart, not like sweet Elizabeta. So Jonathan seems to be whispering. So he confides in me, his wife, squirming and wriggling in ecstasy, gripping me tight, my thighs and my buttocks, my neck, so tight, slamming all his love into me, that I dare not cry out this time and displease him.

X

Can we look for pretty stones, the girls beg, when Jonathan is away in the city. Come with us, they say, pulling at my limp arms. Down by the pond. Down by the shallow end.

In the July sunshine, in midday heat. Tiny bubbles rising to the surface of the water. Nothing can happen! What on earth can happen! And of course they are right for *a special dispensation lies across the land.*

A suntanned little girl with blond flyaway curls poking about in the pebbles at the shore, looking for pretty stones. My own, my precious Gillian! And Niall in her pink cotton shorts, her soiled white Minnie Mouse t-shirt, stooped over, frowning and intent upon her search, Niall, my second-born, my sweet child. And here is Vicky!—loud brash husky Vicky!—big-boned like her mother, clumsy and slow to smile, but she *will smile*, she *has smiled*, praise God for Your kindnesses.

After they have collected the pretty stones they bring them to the pump and I help them with the cleaning-up. Three very muddy little girls! Squealing and splashing and shoving one another under the gushing water. And Elizabeta is wet too. And the rusted old pump handle shrieks, being forced up and down, up and down. *O thank you dear God my baby is not dead but gone away. And three sweet girl-babies have come to take his place.*

XI

One summer night when we can't sleep because it is so hot and airless, and the bedclothes are damp, and the cicadas are singing shrill and crazy, and the moon is crazy-bright, Jonathan gets out his old book of maps of the United States, his Rand McNally Road Guide, which he has owned for ten years, to show me the "peregrinations of his soul," from Evanston, Illinois to Riverside, California to Vancouver, British Columbia (which is in Canada), to Hamilton, New York to Athens, Ohio to the place where he lives now, where he lives with his family, settled down here in Minnesota west and north of St. Paul where there is nothing on the map except Rookes Corners, which is twelve miles away.

Some of the pages are bent and torn and mended with cellophane tape. Others are missing. (The states of Oregon and Washington. All of Texas.) Along the highway leading west from Bismarck, North Dakota to Helena, Montana and Sandpoint, Idaho someone has printed in a tiny hand *Why? why? why? why? why?* I know without asking that this is Meredith's work and though it might strike you as a joke of some kind it is really not funny. *Why? why? why?* the drowned woman is whispering and cursing up through the bedsprings of our hundred-year-old bed. I turn past the maps of the Dakotas, Montana, and Idaho as fast as possible but Jonathan isn't watching.

The peregrinations of a soul, Jonathan says, pulling at his beard in a way he has, so that heat seems to shake loose from it—a soul that has learned the ways of the world not wisely, but too well.

It is because he has an "X-ray intellect," that the academic world has shut him out. Because he has never stooped to flattery and ass-kissing. Because, even as an undergraduate at the University of Minnesota, when he was sixteen years old, he was *heralded as a genius and praised to the skies by all his professors.*

But Jonathan is far from finished, he says. At the age of thirty-six, far from finished! O yes O yes O yes.

That morning I discovered more evidence of *her:* a needlepoint cushion, covered in cobwebs and filth, hidden in the cellar, in one of the nastiest corners. Someone had thrown it there. Someone had stuffed it into a crevice in the stone foundation.

She had worked so hard at the needlepoint—you could see that, how slow and patient she had been. The design was complicated, blacks and reds and grays and yellows and blues, and so faded you could barely read the legend. *Night. Death. Sleep. The Stars.*

I was frightened because when I said the words to myself they were in her voice and what if her voice remained in my head, after I had destroyed the cushion? I dared not destroy it but hid it in the crevice where it had been.

Jonathan buries his face in my neck, against my breasts. He is so tired. He is so angry. He tries to love but can't, he tries and tries but can't, it has happened so often lately, and who is to blame? It is the moon shining so queer through the curtains. It is the cicadas singing so shrilly. And Meredith brushing her long red hair, standing naked a few yards away, Meredith, beautiful Meredith, so thin, the knobs of her backbone showing white, knobs of sharp bones at her pelvis too, one morning I discovered her hairbrush in one of the bureau drawers, the bristles soiled, long red hairs entwined in them, and Jonathan's wiry black hairs too, man and wife in one flesh before Elizabeta was born. When they took my baby out of my arms they were careful to say it was not my fault he had died and *truly it was not my fault* but God saw fit to punish me just the same, *Thy will be done on Earth as it is in Heaven Amen.*

Jonathan does not know about the needlepoint cushion and the hairbrush and the other secret things but he is angry just the same. He has cause to be angry. He has cause to be disgusted. Biting and sobbing and kneading Elizabeta's floppy big breasts. He wants to love but can't!—he needs to love but can't! It is the fault of the moon shining so bright, it is the moths and gnats in the bed, it is sweaty Elizabeta with her unshaved underarms and legs, and her forehead no longer a girl's smooth forehead, and her ugly mouth stretched wide, Elizabeta thinking her private thoughts, never any peace, never any let-up, thinking thinking thinking forbidden things, and giving off cow-heat, big meaty pocked thighs, look at the dents and nicks and creases and broken veins in the lardy flesh, look at the bruises, fat flabby flaccid thing, giant fetus, half-woman and half-embryo, a great overgrown sweaty lardy baby, not a brain in its noggin, and mine, all mine, Jonathan says, so loud I am afraid the girls will be awakened, and run into our room, all mine, Jonathan says, laughing, sobbing, slamming against me so hard our flesh slaps and stings, slick with sweat, rough as sandpaper, tiny hairs catching and tearing, *mine, mine, mine.*

XII

A small hand is drawing the sheet away. Slowly it is being drawn away. I am awake and see but I can't move. Mommy. Mommy. My eyes roll out of focus like they do when you sleep but I can see everything that is happening but I can't move. Mommy. O

Mommy. The sheet is drawn away and my left breast is exposed. A
finger touches the nipple—pokes at the sore nipple—and I can't
move though I am awake, *I am awake and watching.*

Then the girls burst into giggling and run away, pushing and
shoving at one another, out of the bedroom, down the stairs. Nasty
wild clamoring like horses. Thumping their feet on the stairs to
make the old house shake. I am alone in the shining white boat. I
am lying on the bottom of the boat, unable to move, blinking at
the waterstained sky overhead. Mommy, O Mommy, the little girl
whispers, I love you Mommy, don't die Mommy, and she cuddles
into my arms and burrows against me and we hug and hug and
never let each other go.

XIII

Jonathan has gone away to the city for three days. But he was to
telephone and he hasn't and now it is four days-going-on-five. *O
dear God, let nothing be amiss, bless and keep him Amen.*

Jonathan has gone away "for experimental purposes" which I
do not understand. The girls cried and pulled at his hands but I
was not allowed to cry and my eyelids were red and raw. I whispered in his ear how good he is, how it is a benison of God and un-
deserved by me, our marriage, and his trust in me, to make me the
mother of his babies.

Yes, says Jonathan, framing my face in his hands and squeezing
and squeezing, and staring at me without smiling, yes it is a benison of God. I trust you with my life and with theirs.

After he drove away I went upstairs to lie down because I felt so
weak and my head was like crockery wobbling on my neck and my
sweet girls cuddled and napped with me all morning and all afternoon. I am not asleep now but the air is so quiet and still it is like a
dream and the girls who are playing and splashing nearby are
making no noise at all, like a dream, though I *am* awake, and leaning over the side of the boat to look at the strange face there. Pale
and quivering with pale hair and dark staring eyes. It is forbidden,
and very hot in the sun. It is August and the pond gives off a queer
hot stench at the shallow end especially because things are rotting
in it. There are dragonflies everywhere, and tiny stinging black
flies, and mosquitoes, and frogs. A coiled-up garter snake that

crawls through the grass when Vicky walks nearby. And her shrieks and screams, you would think she is being killed!

It is August and a bad time, a hard time, the girls are asking Where is Daddy, when is he coming home, why did he go away, Gillian is starting to cry, they are tugging at my arms, making my limp arms twitch, burrowing against my breasts. I make them their favorite pancakes—buckwheat pancakes and waffles both—and we have apple cobbler and fresh peaches and the jelly doughnuts sprinkled with confectioner's sugar which we love, our favorite doughnuts, a dozen doughnuts gobbled down in one afternoon, the girls' faces smeared with sugar, and mine too, we lick our lips greedily and are ready for more, and no tears, no tears, *do not provoke God's wrath, praise Him in all things great and small.*

Sometimes, says Jonathan, he knows in his heart why he was born and why certain things were done to him and what he must do, in return; other times, he says, he looks in his heart and *there is nothing residing there and never was.* And when he is not in the same room with someone he cannot remember them and cannot believe in them and has no love to spare for them.

Each word of his by itself I can hear and shape with my lips and say aloud and comprehend, but all the words together make my head flood, I cannot repeat them and cannot comprehend them, and cannot explain to the girls. Where is he, is he mad at us, is he gone where Mommy went, when will he come back, they are asking, begging, dear God do not let Vicky begin shouting, do not let her provoke Your wrath, restore my Jonathan to me and all will be well.

I am waiting at this moment for him to telephone and *all will be well.*

XIV

We have pushed off from shore in the shining white boat. Elizabeta and her babies, her girls. Elizabeta is wearing an old floppy-brimmed hat she found in the attic, pale yellow, with lavender cloth flowers sewed to the band, and a chiffon scarf to tie beneath the chin. Elizabeta, rowing, is startled by the way muscles in her shoulders and upper arms have come to life.

We have pushed off from shore at last. It is August. Or another time. The boat snags and turns in circles and the girls squeal in excitement and have to be hushed. Elizabeta and her girls, sailing across the wide shoreless lake. It is false to say that the bottom is deep because there is no bottom at all. You cannot see any bottom. Sailing away! Vicky shouts, so that the veins bulge in her slender neck, sailing away and never coming back!

OUR
WALL

ICH BIN
EIN
BERLINER

As the younger brother, indeed the only sibling, of a "notorious" deceased, I have frequently been interviewed: but I will give no more interviews. It was thought indiscreet of me to say certain things. Such as, the advantage of being a younger brother is that one generally *outlives*. Such as, the advantage of being younger is that one eventually becomes *elder*. Such as, the distinction between *suicide* and *murder* might be overrated.

When I flew to Berlin the first time, to "claim" my brother's body and arrange to ship it back home, a disagreeably public flurry attended my departure. Now, a year later, nearly a year later, approaching the exact anniversary of his death, my journey to make other claims goes unreported. *Some things can only be performed in secret,* I seem to recall my brother saying—*or not at all.*

Did you anticipate his death, I ask one of my brother's acquaintances, shouting to make my voice heard over the din in the Flash Point Discothek on the Kurfurstenstrasse—did he seem, well, you know—suicidal?

Here is Rudi, young and shaggily blond and very much a Berliner, a sullen boyishness about his features, a prettily evoked *brutal aura*, not to be taken altogether seriously, a manner of fashion, costume (tight scarlet velour shirt unbuttoned to mid-chest, tighter blue jeans, cattleman's boots that come to mid-calf), sheer style, a thug who is in fact a university student, a male prostitute who is in fact only a waiter at the Flash Point, costumed like the other waiters, male and female. His embarrassment is good manners as well as surprise, his pretense of not having exactly heard is to be attributed to the deafening rock music, and not to the thin timbre of my American voice. So he hunches forward, and cups his ear, and asks me to repeat my question, and the ruddy flush overtakes his throat and face in a most becoming way, and then he says, not altogether willing to bring his luminous steely-gray gaze up to mine: Did I anticipate your brother's death, his death in particular, in those weeks?—no, I would say *no*—but did I anticipate Death—that is another question, Sir—to which the answer is *yes I think so, yes maybe, yes, who knows?* Sniffing loud enough for me to hear over the noise, releasing a *soupçon*, not altogether disagreeable, of cologne and hearty male sweat and an unidentified acrid-sweet drug, though perhaps it is only the odor of grief, though perhaps it is only the odor of fear, for who am I, after all, making inquiries about *that particular death* once again, who am I pretending to be *a younger brother of the deceased . . .* ? To win my heart, perhaps, he wipes at his nose with the cuff of his velvety scarlet sleeve, and says in a voice blurred by the din on all sides, or by his own internal agitation: Who can know, who can be sure of these things?—premonitions—anticipating suicide—death? That same day your brother walked into their bullets another friend of mine died, a friend of twelve years, our mothers had known each other since they were schoolgirls, she was my age exactly, she was found in a telephone booth in the Pankstrasse station, a stupid death, a death I hate her for. . . . I had knowledge of *some death* about to happen, *someone's death*, but I cannot pretend now, so long afterward, to know whose it would be. She died, this friend of mine, of an accident so stupid, I would like to grab hold of her to stop her, to hurt her, he says angrily, making a gesture toward one forearm with the fingers of the other, gripping a ghost-syringe: so that I cannot help but wince, that death is too sad, too ugly, more ridiculous perhaps than my brother's.

I know, I tell Rudi, by way of consoling him, I understand, I say to him, drawing back from his harsh acrid panting breath, —it's so hard to forgive them. So difficult to forget.

Afterward, in my sanitized bunker of a hotel room, I wondered whether I should be angry that the Berliner Rudi had deflected my "line of questioning" so skillfully; and imposed his somewhat sordid grief upon my own.

That other death, after all, might be judged contemptible. But my brother's death might be judged—or so certain persons have argued, in both prose and poetry—heroic.

The danger of being an American in Europe (West no less than East): your casual remarks, even your facial expressions, may be interpreted as Allegorical.

No matter if you are of the tribe of (1) tourist-Americans, or (2) professional-Americans. *You must watch your tongue.*

Thus I assure them, as if there were any conceivable doubt: Of course I know how he died. Everyone knows how he died. *Time*, after all, reported on the number of bullets, and the general condition of "vital organs." In fact I have memorized the official reports issued by both sets of police, on both sides of the Wall, I have memorized the documented facts, the testimonies under oath, the protestations of regret from "high-ranking officials" of both governments: I often murmur to myself, I can't quite imagine why, that masterpiece of *scolding*, and *commiseration*, from the German Democratic Republic. (Where drugs are blamed, unofficially. Where some vague notion of "American hippie of the Sixties" has coinage: though in fact my brother, seventeen years old in 1965, held himself marvelously aloof from that climate of behavior: because he hoped for a more aristocratic destiny.)

Of course I know how he died, I tell young Mr. G—— (the seemingly helpful State Department lackey, of junior rank, who worked closely with Amerika Haus, and with visiting Fulbright fellows at the Free University)—but *how*, my friend, doesn't translate into *why*.

A beat of some seconds. An uncongenial silence, Teutonic rather than American, decidedly "foreign," not chummy. Then he says with a just perceptible glance at his wristwatch, As you know your brother became very interested in certain subjects—Berlin now, Berlin in the Forties, Berlin in the Thirties. Berlin when it became *Berlin*, in 1920—and he became very interested in Germany, and the Germanys, and the Reich, and the Republic, and of course the Wall—and so he neglected his work at the University—he disappointed quite a few of us—and gradually the fixation increased, the obsessive thoughts, conversations with him became difficult, he might be said to have become *disturbed*, and it enraged him that other people were people *less disturbed*, less *morbid*. But all this, the youngish Mr. G—— said in his accentless foreign service English—you certainly know.

Politely I inquire: How would you define *morbid*, in this context? A *morbid interest* in Berlin, and in German history, and in the Wall—?

Any interest at all, he says, amiably enough, though with no semblance of a smile—any interest at all, pursued beyond a certain point, in this particular context.

Midnight on the Hardenbergstrasse. Tourist-gaiety, tourist-euphoria, a little frenzy is good for the soul. Automobiles, taxis, the usual amplified music. It is America. But no it is Berlin. West Berlin. Germany. But no it is America. No? Yes? America? But with such strong accents?

Everyone a tourist here, in this part of the city, in this part of Europe. We are Westerners in the East. An oasis of sparkling West in the glum barbed-wire East. Everyone infected with tourist-gaiety, everyone strolling tonight on the Hardenbergstrasse, linked arms, "wild" young people with spiky dyed hair, well-fed gentlemen in tailored clothes, solitary "foreigners" like myself. Look: the radiant Mercedes-Benz cross, rotating nobly overhead! A sacred vision beamed over the Wall into the shadowy East.

But why not content oneself in the surfaces of life. After all.

Why *must* the head pull away from the body? There are so many lively bodies here . . . here on the Hardenbergstrasse.

For the record, I am not a Berliner.
Nor can I be called a tourist.
And I am not an *American*—in the allegorical sense.
The Wall, for instance. It interested my unfortunate brother to

the point of obsession but it holds no (apparent) interest for these packs of people, German and foreign, nor does it hold any interest for me *save as a point of geographical information.* I am not an obsessive personality; *the morbid* I find merely commonplace.

What is the Wall but a dotted line on my tourist map?—my glossy much-folded tourist map, courtesy of the Deutsche Bank Berlin? It's even difficult to locate that dotted line, tiny pale blue dots, aswim in a typographical picnic of livelier colors. (I have added a "tourist attraction site" of my own, in red ink, at that point in the Pankow district, where the Wall borders the Reinickendorf district, where my brother died. On "Eastern" soil.)

What is the Wall but a distant fantasy, an irrelevant fact?—here on the Hardenbergstrasse at midnight. Sauna Paradies, the New Crazy Shock Revue ("Herren Als Damen"), the Weingarten family restaurant, not at all like Times Square, not America, simple frank robust good-natured Germanic spirits, altogether healthy, a tonic dose of the pagan. Why did my scholarly brother seek out morbid diversions, why did he betray his commitment to American optimism, why do his former students at the Free University still protect him, *even from his own brother.* I wonder what sort of "research" he did, those last six or seven weeks.

The Flash Point Discothek again, where I had best not return so soon. Would not want to embarrass, or alarm, or annoy, or intimidate—or, most of all—bore, dear shag-haired Rudi.

Perhaps his research took him to the Internationale Spitzengirls Salon, and to the Cabaret Chez Nous, and the Big Eden Peep Show, and the Chalet Noir. Non-Stop-Sex-Shop. Drugged teenaged girls, very pretty. But skeletal-thin. Something has happened to the robust Aryan mammalian form.

Lounging about the much-photographed tourist attraction, the bombed and never-repaired Kaiser Wilhelm Church (forever a monument, a luridly visible monument, to their suicidal zeal and our zealous bombs), here are very young girls, such familiar girls, skin-tight blue jeans, silky shorts, halter tops, spiky dyed hair, eyes outlined in hopeful circus colors, sit with us a while, have you change, have you dollar, bitte Deutsch marks, cigarette please Sir, thank you, you are very kind.

Did you know my brother, I ask, supplying the name, but they are too young and too recent, memory fades swiftly in this part of the world.

Courteous, though. The blank smooth foreheads crinkling in a pretense of solemn thought.

Nein, I think. No. Sorry, *no.*

Why are there so many shoes for sale in West Berlin, I ask the girls, why marvelous gleaming pyramids of shoes, show windows brilliantly illuminated all hours of the night, stores like cathedrals?—but meaning no harm, jocose sort of chatter, friendly American passing the time, no danger. X-Rated Playtime, Colonel Sanders Kentucky Fried Chicken, I move on to prescribed tourist pleasures, baby prostitutes in platform open-toed shoes, robust singing in beer gardens, Old World charm, marching songs, Salon Massage ("Boys & Girls All"), a floorshow called "Welcome to Hell" in helpful English.

All in the spirit of jest.

My research brings me back to festive Kantstrasse. Three-thirty in the morning. Odors of grease-fried foods, spilled beer, the companionable blare of American acid rock, ruddy thug-faces cruising in their Mercedes, pigs' snouts, small blinking beady eyes, but I am being unfair, am I being unfair?—I am reporting what I see and failing to alter a syllable.

Among the debris in his room, photographs of this very street. This kiosk where the History of the Wall (as seen from the West) is on perpetual display in the usual tourist-languages. His photographs of their photographs of the Brandenburg Gate, and Checkpoint Charlie, and the dying eighteen-year-old Peter Fechter, many years dead.

Obviously, the martyred youth gave my brother the idea. The inspiration. The goad.

He was shot down—Peter Fechter, that is—on 17 August 1962. As all the Free World knows, or should know. Shot down by East Berlin guards at the foot of the Wall, and allowed to bleed to death for a long, a very long, a famously long time.

He is bleeding to death still: you can see the snaky black blood on the pavement. Propaganda hero, amid the neon traffic, the outdoor cafés, X-Rated Kino, summer strollers licking fat ice cream cones, business as usual. Granted you die only once: but how long does it take?

Photographs of my brother were taken too, of course. But by then he was already dead.

He was interested, I surmise, morbidly interested, in the origins of Berlin, in the early thirteenth century; and in the history of the Prussian eagle, and the terrible triumph of Napoleon, and the founding of the German Empire, and Kaiser Wilhelm II, and the Thousand-Year Reich, and the Berlin blockade, and the erection, *at last*, of the Wall, in 1961. When my brother was in the eighth grade at St. Ursula's on Gratiot Avenue in Detroit and I was in fourth grade in the same school which is still in session though the nuns do not look like nuns any longer.

How peculiar, that he was older than I in those days. And now seems younger. And soon *will* be younger.

Imagine the surprise of the East Berlin guards, I find myself saying to Mr. G—— whom I have coerced into having a drink with me at the well-lit Weingarten—that any East Berliner, at this point in history, would approach the Wall on foot. Just walking. Maybe swaying a little—staggering—d'you think? Because he must have been drunk—euphoric—with the daring of it. The theatrics. Because the bullets can't have hurt, there were so many.

Time of death 4:25 A.M., 17 June 1981, said to be a fairly cold northern European night.

Mr. G—— has heard it all before, Mr. G—— yearns for a respite from West Berlin, a respite from Germany, from history. Doubtless he is very much moved by my brother's silly death but he cannot avoid yawning behind his hand and glancing covertly at his watch. Clearly we aren't chums, the foreign service has refined his American weaknesses from him, we share a common language but no common memory, my last name—my brother's last name—is a distinct embarrassment to him: an "international incident," after all—!

Suicide is the triumph of the will over biology, don't you think, I ask him, but he mistakes my twitchy sardonic smile for the first signs of weeping. And explains nervously that he must get home.

Was it a drunken prank, was it an exploit for publicity's sake (he had published a few poems, translated from English into German by one of his colleagues at the Free University: he was therefore a "poet" and a problematic character known as a Leftist sympathizer); was it a simple mistake; was it a heroic political gesture; was it—just suicide?

In any case the member of his family who had to fly to Berlin to "claim" the body, and arrange to ship it back home, was most inconvenienced. And finds it very hard to forgive suicide as a *witty gesture.*

(It should be mentioned that I have been personally affected by none of this. My temperament is not morbid; I celebrate health; I celebrate clarity. If it amuses me to indulge in certain philosophical speculations, that is only because I presume they are of general—which is to say, allegorical—interest.)

N.B. Since West Berlin is a walled city in the East, an escape from "East" to "West" might involve an attempt to scale the Wall in an *easterly direction.*

The "escape" from the Pankow district to the populous Reinickendorf district, however, would have been ordinary enough—from East to "West."

Is a certain crisis in history past? There are fewer escapes by way of the river now—fewer drownings, bullet-riddled bodies. Landmines detonated along the great stretch of the border between the two Germanys are apt to be set off, these days, by such innocent creatures as hares, deer, stray dogs, etc. *The Wall is forever,* my brother scrawled across one of the letters he never sent.

I am about to leave, my curiosity hasn't been satisfied but rather numbed, the Wall may be forever but I have no interest in it: as I said, my temperament is not naturally morbid.

I am about to leave but here is a box of his *personal effects*—loose papers, crumpled letters, dog-eared paperback books. In my sealed hotel room I lie upon my bed and examine the evidence, my eyes begin to smart from so much print, orange Penguin spines, exclamation points and question marks in red ballpoint ink, perhaps this person was not my brother after all but a stranger whose passion would embarrass me.

The Wall is forever, he wrote, but nothing is forever.

Here is a paperback edition of *Beyond the Pleasure Principle* with passages underscored on every page. *A drive is an urge inherent in organic life to restore an earlier state of being,* one must imagine the dead man striding purposefully forward to his death, ignoring the shouted commands in German, *the aim of all life is death,* substantiating the State Department's suspicions of Leftist sympathizing and general morbidity, hadn't one of his terse little poems been an elegy for the "martyred" Meinhof who hanged herself in her prison cell?—*Sadism is in fact a death instinct which, under the influence of the narcissistic libido, has been forced away from the ego,* rumors suggested he must have been in contact with East German agitators, rumors hinted he might have been a spy, what are the journalistic terms—dupe, pawn? All very teasing, all very enigmatic, which doesn't solve the problem of why he died, why by that particular method, *Our views have from the very first been dualistic, and today they are even more definitely dualistic than before—now that we describe the opposition as being, not between ego-instincts and sexual instincts, but between life instincts and death instincts.*

I shall burn his *personal effects*—not excluding as many pages of his books as I have the patience to tear out—in a tidy little funeral pyre in the aluminum wastebasket close at hand. Thus, all evidence is erased. Thus, even the offensive smoke is whirled and sucked out of the room, by the wonderfully efficient German ventilation system.

I shall fly from West Berlin to Frankfurt (by special *air access route*) to New York City to home, my flight leaves at 11:25 A.M., in the meantime I am too restless to stay in one place, in the meantime I must walk quickly in case I am being followed, it occurs to me that the traffic-clogged streets along which I hurry, in the very center of West Berlin, do not, from the Soviet perspective, exist—in a manner of speaking.

"West Berlin" is thus a trope; a way of speaking; a fiction.

Yet if West Berlin does not exist, from the perspective of the East, the Wall—at which I am now staring—does not exist, from the perspective of the Allies. (The Allies being the United States, the United Kingdom, and France. For it is still World War II here.)

The Wall disappoints, it hasn't the terror of heaped-up rock, the Gothic look of centuries, no boulders dragged out of fields by the bleeding hands of peasants, all very smooth and monotonous and modern, it might be said to be in good taste, gray concrete, approximately fifteen feet high, resistant of subtlety and poetic embellishment, a matter of statistics, isolating, as the guide books say, some 480 kilometers of the 880 kilometers of Greater Berlin, a matter of facts that cannot contend with its presence.

There is even some doubt about its existence. For, as a consequence of an old decree granting powers of sovereignty to the "victors"—by which is meant the Allies—the city is under the jurisdiction of those who conquered the Nazis, and, in support of the legal fact, an armed patrol consisting of one American soldier, one British soldier, and one French soldier drives over into "East" Berlin each day, on a routine mission, and their passage is never impeded by any Wall.

Thus, the Wall does not exist: and West Berlin does not exist: and, by logical extension, "East" Berlin does not exist.

A sort of bombed-out wasteland here, a zone of abandoned houses, weedy paper-strewn vacant lots, ancient billboards, posters in tatters, even a few stripped hulks of cars. As one nears the Wall the curious thing is, history is left behind. There is nothing here to indicate what year this might be, which language might be spoken if there were anyone at hand to speak. . . .

"Gretel" with the silver eyelids and kinked lavender hair and long skinny dead-white legs, giggling, squirming, certain it is all a joke and I am a very funny gentleman indeed, knows me, I insist, despite the jolly confusion of languages, *far more intimately than my brother did*: which is to say, far more intimately than any brother could. Handsome brute of a girl!—face shaped like a shovel, enormous smiling teeth, pancake makeup in skillful layers of beige, beige-rose, and ivory, those amazing slow-blinking silver eyelids, each eyelash fastidiously painted black, and curled. No wasteful coy motions—no morbid tendencies. I find myself shivering at her Berliner accent. It really *is* a remarkable accent. The quintessence of German? The quintessence. Of German. Ah German! Speak to me, I beg her, speak, tell me a riddle, a joke, a story, a legend, scold, tease, punish, anything you will: *Speak to me in Berliner.*

No, we were not intimate. It doesn't count. It was only one aspect of my research.

═══

The anniversary of his birth is approaching. 17 June.

An error: I meant to say, the anniversary of his death is approaching. 17 June. —I shall have returned to the States by then. Don't you think? At the hotel they evinced surprise—it seemed quite sincere—that I had decided to extend my stay for another week.

"Surprise" is rendered more convincing in a foreign accent.

"Surprise," "regret," "suspicion"—the usual. More convincing in a foreign accent in which primary tones are emphasized and subtleties are cheerily abandoned. *Speak to me in Berliner,* I beg.

Arabesques of light that glitter like a massive snake's scales along the Hardenbergstrasse.... Is this all? Is *this* a political gesture?

I am standing in that street or in another shouting after two German girls who have passed me by, bitches, sluts, pigs, cunts, I shouted, krauts I shouted, I'll make you regret laughing at me!—laughing at an American!

My brother's wallet contained only a few Deutsch marks when his body was found. Snapshots of home, of childhood?—gone. Identification?—gone. He had thrown away his passport but it was later discovered in some very ordinary place—a trash container in a railway station. He had thrown away *being American,* it seems, preparatory to throwing away *being human,* preparatory to throwing away *being alive.* I hate him for that logic.

How dare they laugh at an American, how dare they unlock the door of my room in my absence and investigate my belongings and the findings of my research?—a violation so skillfully performed, *they have left no trace except an unmistakable disturbance of the air.*

My hotel room in the Berliner Hospice: a sealed capsule, a bunker, ventilated by a ceaselessly humming mechanism, which might from time to time emit its own subtle gases, and which causes everything to vibrate in a most disagreeable, though hardly perceptible, manner. (Consider my hands. So finely trembling. My inner organs—they too vibrate, and have begun to grow exhausted with the strain. A foreign pulsebeat is evident, a hard thrusting sexual rhythm, not my own, an infection from without: Gretel and Rudi and the others whom my research must encompass.)

The doorknobs should be remarked upon: they are unusually small, perhaps five inches in circumference, solid steel, very difficult to turn, particularly if your hand is damp, or weak, or shaking. And the telephone?—I cannot think it might be trusted.

A ludicrous fate, to die locked in a windowless bathroom in a sealed hotel room, my invaluable passport only a few yards away, and the telephone too: but the door will not open because the doorknob will not turn. Help help I cry, bitte, danke I cry absurdly, O help, I know you are listening, is the doorknob riveted in place?—are the poisonous gases being filtered in?

... Of course we have not forgotten your brother, yes we remain concerned, yes it is a tragedy, we spoke of little else here at the Institute for weeks, but you must understand that a year has passed, or nearly, and naturally we have other matters to concern ourselves with, there are new developments, new crises, the young Germans' hatred of our current administration is unfortunate, their demonstrations against nuclear power, there are invariably new problems, and yes, new tragedies, but of course we have not forgotten your brother, please do not take offense, no the Berlin police are certainly not watching you, no you are not in danger, yes I must admit we would advise you to return home, yes it is generally believed your brother had been emotionally disturbed for some time before the accident, no I couldn't offer any particular reason, he spoke to me a few times about the claustrophobic atmosphere here, but this is a common reaction, not just among visiting Americans but among Berliners too, the younger Germans especially, the students, unfortunately it isn't a phenomenon widely discussed, there are some things that simply cannot be discussed, no I cannot share in your loathing for Berlin, I think you are being unnecessarily harsh, of course we all need a recovery period from it, back in the States, but we are devoted to Berlin it is a very special city it is a phenomenon unparalleled in diplomatic history a stateless city a "Western" city in "East Europe" under our protection you must recall John F. Kennedy's famous words *I am a Berliner* in the very geography of totalitarianism the glittering city survives the jewel afloat upon the sea of darkness survives and flourishes under our protection for it will not be attacked by the Enemy an armed attack on Berlin is *precisely the same* as an armed attack on Chicago or New York or Washington. . . . But of course we have not forgotten your brother.

Night, and morning, and the comforting beat of the streets, a marvelous sexual urgency to the displays, the surface, bright bold plastic colors, festive crowds, nothing to fear. Berlin was reduced to rubble and rubble has no memory so you cannot expect a poignant sense of history: and in any case does history exist? Everyone appears to have been born after 30 April 1945. If not, if they are older folk, they certainly served courageously in the Resistance; they may have been wounded, imprisoned, tortured—the usual. They are Americans at heart. They are patriotic. If they want the two Germanys united it is only in the interest of world peace, a bulwark, as the saying goes, against the Enemy.

My ticket has been secured for the flight to Frankfurt at 13.00 hours. Everything is in readiness except what does it mean, Rudi at the Flash Point wriggling his hips, and placing a forefinger against his smiling lips, and then against mine. *Nein! Not a word! No more, mein Herr! Not to me!*

Hitler is forever, my doomed brother wrote, on the flyleaf of his German-English dictionary—*he has made the rest of us fiction.*

At the Checkpoint it is remarkably easy to *cross over*: one is simply a tourist, an interested and sympathetic traveler, the passport is all, the passport is indispensable, one travels from West to East with agreeable ease, machine guns are doubtless manned in those tall deserted buildings, but one feels little apprehension: look at the pots of pansies arranged prettily along the curb, the usual pansy-hues, sweet little imperturbable faces, a welcome treat for the eye amidst all the gray concrete and barbed wire.

I shall not cross over, however. They are waiting for me to do so: hence, I shall disappoint them. (It seems I have an engagement elsewhere—with both Brigit and Heike, at the *Salon Mandy*.)

Overnight the Wall has become all walls.
The explanation is—the Wall.
I need not repeat my brother's *exact procedure*, to comprehend this self-evident fact.

===

The logic of the groin, the wordless satisfactions of the groin, bill-board nudes iridescent and fleshy as if alive. Baby giantesses, un-dulating in the night sky. Consider the eternal wisdom of the groin which opposes that of the Wall: for the Wall is Death.

No mein Herr, I believe you are mistaken: the Wall is Life.

For, consider: while it appears to be nothing but tiresome con-crete, and electrified wire, guarded by bored young soldiers and German shepherd attack dogs (top of the breed, needless to say), while it appears to be merely a political expediency *required by both sides*, it is, in fact, Life. Like Gretel, like Rudi, like that "Herr" at the Salon who was in truth eine "Dame," like many another, too numerous to list. For, as one approaches the Wall, even from the "Western" sector, through one of those amazing rubble-lots off Friedrichstrasse—note how the pulse helplessly quickens, no mat-ter how the mind intones *you are safe on this side, they have no reason to fire upon you coming from this side*, note how the heart grows tumes-cent, how vision is sharpened, the very air rings with delight.

The Wall is forever; but the rest of the world—a fiction.

Tell me a riddle, Heike, a fairytale, a German legend, slim-thighed Hans, buttocks so neatly cupped in American blue jeans, what do you know of the Wall we can't know, until we draw proof in the form of blood, scratching and clawing at the concrete—?

The Wall offers the felicity of an object that is, yet is not, a meta-phor.

The Wall offers the felicity of a metaphor that is, yet is not, an object.

The Wall is finitude. An absolute end. The headboard of the crib, against which your baby skull pressed. And the foot of the crib. The railings. The blankets. The smooth white porcelain walls of the tub, too steep for you to scale. The floorboards, the rocky earth, the coffin: finitude: a way of making an end.

The Wall is, by the sleight-of-hand of logic, all walls. Especially when you are drunk, or euphoric, or too depressed to raise your head. *Why did he die* matters less now than *how precisely did he die* but if they imagine (for certainly they are watching) I am going to re-peat his performance as 17 June advances they are mistaken. His-tory cannot imitate itself without human participation.

===

Mid-June. Nearing the solstice.

N.B. In certain areas tall wire-mesh fences have been erected as well, in front of the (concrete) Wall; and these fences are topped with barbed wire through which Death silently and secretly and ceaselessly pulses. One touch—! One touch.

A way of making an end.

Once upon a time, in the remote days of the Holy Roman Empire, there was a cruel landowner, a nobleman of immense wealth, who built a great castle in the Bavarian Alps, and instituted so terrifying a means of punishing wrong-doers amongst his peasants that, for many centuries, his name was associated with a certain species of tyranny: dreaded, and yet respected. And known throughout the land.

His ingenious method was: the wrongdoer was locked in a high tower in the remotest wing of the castle, and the promise made, under God, that he would not be put to death, nor even tortured; and that the nobleman, who was a Christian, would see that he was fed never less than once daily, for the re-mainder of his natural life. The prisoner could never hope to taste freedom again: for, even should a civil war bring about the fall of the castle, or should a younger and weaker (which is to say, less punitive) heir come into power, the prisoner would be summarily executed by the keeper of the dungeon. Thus it was, a covenant was forged: and the criminal was granted the privilege, most unusual in those barbaric times, of knowing that the nobleman was bound to his pledge; and that the future, in a manner of speaking, was assured. Never freedom: but a natural span of life. In a manner of speaking.

The tower dungeon measured some fifteen feet in diameter, and its ceiling was perhaps twenty feet high. It was windowless, save for a single aperture, a hole struck through the stone wall, some eighteen inches across, at the level of the floor. Through this crude opening light shone, and "fresh air" circu-lated. The opening offered, as well, an apparent means of escape.

Now, it happened that the prisoner could not see what lay directly below the hole in the wall, unless he managed to force his shoulders through, and to squirm partway free, into the daylight: for the tower wall was some five feet thick, and the opening itself constituted a kind of tunnel, to be burrowed into, if the prisoner's strength was great enough. Once the prisoner made this bid for freedom, however, it was unlikely that he could retreat back into the dun-geon. (Indeed, there are no recorded instances of such a feat.)

Without exception, prisoners became obsessed with the aperture in the wall, and spent all their waking hours (and, doubtless, their sleeping hours as well) in contemplation of it. Gradations of sunlight, or dusk, or dark: the faint luminous aura of the moon: mist, or rain, or pelting sleet, or snow: how wonderfully various, the elements of the world beyond the aperture! Many a prisoner lay directly before it; others crouched against the farther wall, staring in fascination until they were nearly blind; or they squatted with fists pressed against their eyes, that they might see nothing, and be tempted by nothing. They soon forgot to pray because their apprehension of the opening was in itself a ceaseless prayer.

Now, through the crude "window" they could breathe the unmistakable odor of ripened, rotting flesh; but they could also breathe, when the wind was exactly right, the bright fresh magnificent air of high meadows, and steppes, and snow-ridged mountains—and sometimes even the odors of home: the comforting smell of woodsmoke, and familiar food being prepared by solicitous hands. (It did not distress the prisoners, that, in their villages, in their own former homes, life continued as usual. For life is for the living, is it not?—and nothing is served, by foolish mourning.)

The curious thing was, though these prisoners were, as we have seen, treated with considerable mercy, being provided with food, clothing, shelter, and protection from injury, through their lives, it nonetheless transpired— sometimes within the space of a scant day or two!—that they would go berserk and choose "freedom," and force themselves through the narrow hole in the wall, no matter the physical pain involved, and their ignorance of what lay outside. Unhappy wretches! Foolish peasants! They abandoned the guarantee of undisturbed animal existence for the possibility—no, the probability—of non-existence: so displaying, it might be said, the very same willfulness, and rebelliousness, and lack of discretion, that angered their lord in the first place, and brought them to the tower.

(For how could they, granted even their madness, close their senses against the blatant fact of rotting corpses, whose stench was wafted to them on every breeze, save when freezing temperatures locked all decaying phenomena in place; and how could they fail to comprehend the screams of scavenger birds, and the circling and darting shadows that so often brushed against the mouth of the aperture?)

Yet the old legend would have it, and, indeed, our knowledge of human nature concurs, that the perversity of even the most ignorant peasant was such, that "freedom" (though also Death) exerted its ineluctable attraction over imprisonment (though also Life) through many and many a year.

Such is the folk wisdom my tireless research daily yields. Unless Rudi, or one of the others, is telling me lies. Unless they are confusing me with someone else.

DÉTENTE

It was a time of platitudes, brisk handshakes, faces creased with
smiling, wise folk sayings. So many wise folk sayings. " 'Nothing is
more distant than that which is thought to be close,'—a Russian
folk saying, very old. Very wise, yes?" The chairman of the Soviet
delegation, Yury Ilyin, spoke in impeccable English with a lazy
sort of irony that appealed to the Americans even as it chilled
them. He was tall, silver-haired, patrician, a former ambassador to
the Court of St. James, a former dean of the Gorky Institute, an old
and highly respected friend (and rival) of the Soviet President . . .
so very courtly with the few women at the conference, Antonia in
particular, that one might have thought him, well, mocking certain bourgeois customs. And no one among the Americans had
known how to interpret his toast, offered at their first luncheon:
champagne glass held high, smile measured to show a very few
slightly discolored teeth, eyes cold, hard, mirthful, expressing the
gratitude of the Soviet delegation at being invited to the Falkstone
Conference, yet warning that "brotherhood" cannot be achieved
too quickly, by mere physical proximity: for (as the wise old peasants knew) *nothing is more distant than that which is thought to be close.*
   At the crowded cocktail reception on the evening before the con-

ference officially began, Yury Ilyin had shaken Antonia's hand vig-
orously, and studied her name-tag (encased in plastic, neatly
typed, it gave to Antonia's haphazard sense of herself a certain
agreeable focus), and inquired politely if she was related to the es-
sayist, or was he a journalist?—Haas? It took Antonia an awkward
little pocket of time to come to the conclusion that Ilyin actually
meant her. A number of her essays and articles had been translated
into Russian, nothing of her fiction, so if she was "known" to the
Soviets it must be in those terms; but Ilyin had confused Antonia
with . . . was it a ghostly male analogue to herself? "You're confusing me with myself," she said, a little sharply, "I *am* Haas."

Ilyin was so practiced a diplomat, so skilled a navigator of
murky international waters, he laughed, and apologized, and
adroitly changed the subject. How very generous the wealthy
Falkstone had been, to bequeath this magnificent property to charity . . . did not Antonia agree?

All of life is real enough, Antonia often thought. But it isn't evenly
convincing.

There are incalculable blocks of time, days and even weeks,
months, that pass in a sort of buzzing silence; you find yourself
sleepwalking through your life. A voice responds to other voices,
the voice is yours but not, somehow, significant; not convincing. A
body moves among bodies, requiring a certain space, known by a
certain name (hers seemed to be "Antonia Haas," for life) but,
again, it isn't very significant or convincing. Then the fog lifts—
sometimes abruptly, rudely. You didn't quite realize you were
sleepwalking until you're wakened and the sunshine suddenly
hurts your eyes, the voices hurt your ears, you find yourself astonished by what stands before you. The buzzing silence gives way to
sharp emotion.

Antonia felt it, regarding one of the members of the Soviet crew.
His name was Vassily Zurov: she liked the sound of it, the sibilants,
the authority of the "v" and the "z." She liked his public manner,
his habit of speaking passionately, jabbing at the air, not ashamed
to press his hand against his heart, speaking so rapidly at times
that Yury Ilyin felt required to signal him to slow down, out of
consideration for the translator. A tall slope-shouldered man of
about forty-five, lean, cautious, less given to nervous smiles than

certain of his Soviet colleagues; and not at all fawning. When he spoke he had a habit of widening his eyes so that the whites showed above the dark iris, fierce and glowering. His metal-rimmed glasses were often askew on his long bony nose. A lank strand of hair (dark, graying, silver-streaked) fell across his furrowed forehead. . . . He looked, Antonia thought critically, like a divinity student out of a Russian novel; one of the demons of Dostoyevsky's *The Possessed*, perhaps. If she had not been told at last week's briefing session that all of the members of the Soviet delegation were probably members in good standing of the Communist Party, she would have thought nonetheless: A fanatic of some sort, look at those eyes, look at that pale twisted mouth.

Unfortunately Vassily Zurov knew very little English; if Antonia wanted to talk with him it would have to be through a third party.

Antonia found herself quite entranced by spoken Russian. A barrage of sounds, utterly alien; a virtual windstorm; poetry in motion. It seemed to her a language of giants, of legendary folk. And the gestures that accompanied it were outsized, shamelessly dramatic, fierce . . . so unlike the rather timid gestures to which she was accustomed. She was a woman of some linguistic ability, she could speak fairly fluent French and Italian, could manage German, but though she had tried to learn some elementary Russian in preparation for the conference she seemed to have already lost most of it: the slow stumbling childlike words, the faintly preposterous sounds, the nervous refuge in *Da, da*. Not only was she forgetting much of what she had laboriously memorized, she didn't seem capable of remembering from one hour to the next how to pronounce the Soviet delegates' names. (She supposed they must be sensitive to such slights, such inadvertent insults.)

Vassily Zurov spoke; and the simultaneous translator—hidden at the far end of the room in a glass-fronted booth—made a spirited effort to keep pace with him, and even to mimic his rich florid style: *What is the function of art? From what does it spring in our hearts? Why do a people treasure certain works, which they transmit to the generations that follow? What significance does this have? Is it a human instinct? Is there a hunger for it, like a hunger for food, love, and community? Without the continuity of tradition, what meaning is there in life? As our Chinese comrades discovered to their chagrin, after having tried to erase their entire heritage—*

But this was the translator's voice, another man's voice; and Antonia was having trouble with her headphones. . . . *the writer's mission in our two great nations? Is there a historical destiny that.* . . . Zurov lacked Ilyin's diplomatic aplomb. He was clearly nervous, excited. This was his first visit to the States—he had been invited to a previous conference but hadn't been allowed to come. Antonia remembered from the briefing session that Zurov (novelist, translator, teacher) had been in trouble from time to time with the authorities, having been associated with a "liberal" magazine (whose editor was expelled from the Writers' Union and sent away to a labor camp in the North); his personal history wasn't available; none of his work was translated into English. His awards were surely impressive in that other sphere—*The Order of the Red Banner, Two Lenin Orders, Medal for Valiant Labor*, medals for prose fiction, 1978, 1981. Contributor to the journal *Literaturnoye Obozreniye*. Born in Novgorod in 1939, a resident now of Moscow.

Zurov was clearly one of the stars of the Russian delegation, though his books were not available in the States, and only the Soviet specialists knew of his reputation. His appeal to the Americans lay in his warmth and evident guilelessness; perhaps he struck them (so Antonia thought) as the quintessential Russian—peasant-turned-divinity-student-turned-revolutionary. He directed that morning's somewhat quixotic subject ("What Are the Humanistic Values of Present-Day Literature?") away from specific authors and titles and into an abstract, inchoate, heated region of ideas. Such speculations about life, art, and the meaning of the universe had fascinated Antonia in her late adolescence; listening to Zurov she felt herself powerfully moved. It was all so childlike, so naively appealing. Almost alone among the conferees Zurov spoke with the urgency of an artist who wants desperately to communicate with his fellow artists. Antonia's earphones picked up static as he came to the end of his speech—*Art is political always, art is apolitical always?*—and she couldn't quite decipher his meaning.

In eager faltering English he said, gripping his microphone: "Thank you, that is all I wish to say."

From her third-floor room in the Falkstone Institute Antonia telephoned friends, a married couple, in Chicago. They asked how she was enjoying the Adirondacks, wasn't it rather early (it was June) for the mountains, and how did she feel: her health, her nerves, her stamina? She heard her voice responding to their voices and it sounded normal enough, even rather composed. She told them she was feeling fine—there was nothing like one's public self to eclipse, even to make irrelevant, the private self.

After a few awkward minutes they began to speak of Antonia's husband, who had been behaving badly, though not entirely unpredictably, for the past several weeks. In fact he had disappeared from Antonia's life, more or less. "Well—he doesn't seem to be in Chicago," Vivian said apologetically. "At least he hasn't called."

Antonia, who had been fairly certain her husband was headed for Chicago, said nothing. She was pouring an inch or two of cognac into a plastic cup. Vivian went on: ". . . know how Whit sometimes exaggerates, teases. He has such a . . . he has such a surrealistic sense of humor."

"I wasn't aware of that," Antonia said in a lightly ironic voice.

Antonia sipped experimentally at the cognac, which was very strong. It was a gift—a rather premature one, surely—from a red-faced, gregarious Ukrainian who had been gaily attentive to her the previous evening. *All the way to my homeland*, he said, in cautious English, presenting Antonia with the unwrapped bottle. (According to the Soviet biographical sheet he was a poet, a writer of sketches, and a member of the board of the Soviet Writers' Union; according to the American delegates' briefing he was an "infamous" Party hack.)

Both Martin and Vivian were on the line, asking about Antonia's impressions of the Russians, and whether some international event of the other day (Antonia scarcely listened) would have a deleterious effect upon the conference; they ended by asking if they should give Whit Antonia's number if he called. "He has the number," Antonia said.

"How long has he been gone?" Martin asked carefully.

"Six days," said Antonia.

"Did he take many clothes, or much money . . . ?"

"Not that I know of," Antonia said. "But then he never does."

Of course it wasn't true that Antonia was Haas; or that Haas was exclusively Antonia. There was a husband, of sorts. They had been married seven years. Though he wasn't a writer—he was in fact a rather aggressive non-writer—he had been "Haas" far longer than Antonia.

These are problems that arise from a bourgeois existence, Antonia might tell Vassily Zurov. He would understand, he would be sympathetic. We are obliged to think about something in order to fill up time . . . so we think of sex and death, of loss, of symbolic gestures, failed connections . . . romantic love in all its guises.

Antonia Haas was in temporary retreat from her own life, which she might, or might not, explain to Zurov. There would be after all the problem of their lacking a common language. So far they had smiled at each other over glasses of sherry, and talked through one of the several interpreters—You are a poet? No? A writer of prose? Ah yes—essays and journalism? No? Not just? Novels as well? Not yet translated into Russian?

When her personal life began to unravel Antonia reached out for her public life. It was, oddly enough, far more stable; predictable. She gave talks, lectures, readings; she taught courses for a pittance in and around New York City; she traveled masquerading as herself. A year ago she would have declined the offer to participate in a four-day meeting of Soviet and American "cultural representatives" (writers, critics, translators, publishers, professors of literature, etc.) at the Falkstone Institute but this spring she was grateful to be a part of it. There were the usual promising words, she liked them well enough to half-believe in them, *unity, cooperation, universal understanding, East and West, friendship, sympathy, common plight, peace, hope for the future.* At the opening session the Soviet chairman had spoken in his faultless but rather mocking English of the need for both Soviets and Americans to resist "our common enemy who seeks to divide us." (Who was this common enemy? What did Ilyin mean? The American delegates' rapporteur, a Harvard man named Lunt, advised that they believe nothing of what Ilyin said: it was a kind of elegant static. But Antonia couldn't help thinking that Ilyin must mean something. And wasn't Vassily Zurov nodding along with him . . . ?)

Antonia was small, slender, thirty-six years old. She thought of herself as disguised: she could not quite connect with her outer being (pale green eyes always a little damp, dead white skin, chestnut-red hair) and wondered that others did not recoil from it, suspecting deceit. She was particularly disturbed when people "complimented" her on her youthful appearance in one way or another. On the first morning of the Falkstone conference, for instance, a young woman journalist told Antonia with a beaming smile that she'd always pictured her as much older—elderly in fact. Once, in Whit's company, a middle-aged woman told Antonia half-accusingly that she had "always" thought Antonia Haas was dead. Since it was difficult to reply to such statements Antonia said nothing, and was beginning to acquire a minor reputation for being cold and aloof.

Antonia Haas thought of herself as a novelist, primarily—she had published two novels and had been working on a third for many years. Her ostensible subject was the upper-middle-class Catholic milieu of her girlhood in Boston. Obliquely autobiographical, taking in what might be called a "wide scope" of society, the two published novels were admired by the few critics who cared to review them, but were not commercially successful, and were reprinted in paperback only after Antonia had achieved a somewhat controversial eminence for other work—essays on literature, art, and culture in general. For the most part the essays were appreciative; they were certainly methodical, models of unobtrusive research and scholarship. (In fact, as Antonia and her closest friends well knew, the essays—particularly the most critical and iconoclastic—were substitutes for the novel she couldn't quite write: little explosions of emotion that should have been transposed into fiction but, failing that, were put to pragmatic use elsewhere. She had become a public success by way of systematic private failings.)

So it happened that Antonia was constantly meeting distorted images of herself—visions of "Antonia Haas" that struck her as possibly more real, more authentic, than the Antonia she knew. Though she was fairly shy, at least given to long periods of not speaking (while others not only spoke but chattered, hummed, buzzed, glowed with conversation) she had somehow acquired a reputation for being shrill and argumentative. She was believed to be, even admired for being, cruel. Her admirers thought of her as brilliantly malicious, her detractors as simply malicious. In the past ten years she had published lengthy interpretive essays on John Cage, Octavio Paz, Rebecca West, contemporary German

films, contemporary versions of Wagner, but it was for her rather
brutal analyses of various prominent persons (Tennessee Williams,
Robert Motherwell, Tom Wolfe, Iris Murdoch) that she seemed to
be known. If six review-essays were appreciative and generally positive, and a seventh was sarcastically negative, it was only the seventh that drew comment; acquaintances telephoned her to
congratulate her for "speaking honestly," strangers sent her post-
cards, her husband praised her for being a "fighter." (Antonia
complained to him that popular culture seems to push individuals
toward what is most aggressive, most combative, and least valuable, but Whit accused her of being disingenuous. "At heart you're
really competitive, you're really hostile," he said. "You may as well
own up to your fundamental nature. Stop pretending. Stop posing
as a *lady*.")

Meanings, identities, hung on her like loose clothing. In fact her
own clothing, these days, hung on her loosely.

She would tell Zurov, if he inquired, that she was not only an
estranged but an abandoned wife. Did it show? Or was it yet another unconvincing pose?

Is it so, a plump affable young Russian, Yury Ilyin's secretary,
asked Antonia and several other Americans at one of the cocktail
receptions, that each year in the United States there are between
700,000 and 1,000,000 children who run away from home . . . ?
"We find this difficult to comprehend," the young man said, regarding them through his thick glasses, "and must ask if the figure
is not inaccurate. *Where do all the children go?*"

The Soviet visitors had been briefed with odd snippets of information, statistics that did often sound inaccurate, improbable, but
might well be authentic, so far as the Americans knew. "Facts"
about venereal disease, child-prostitution, muggings, rapes, mur-
ders, arson—the lot. *Where do all the children go?* lingered in Antonia's mind. But she was thinking of adults. She was thinking of
marriages. Not simply where her husband had gone this time but
where, in a more general sense, he and she were going; whether
they had any control over their modes of travel, let alone their the-
oretical destinations. Of course, adults do not *run away*, they simply
leave, with or without explanations.

Whit had left her several times before, always abruptly, angrily, following a disagreement. He'd abandoned her in a motel in Arizona once—taking his suitcase, his share of the toiletries, and the car. He had walked out on her at a party celebrating the wedding anniversary of the couple who were their oldest friends. And hadn't there been another time? . . . a quarrel about a penned-up ocelot in the old Central Park zoo, whether Antonia should complain about the creature's ill-treatment (it was wailing, shrieking, "piteously" as she said) or whether they should go to lunch as they had planned. Whit had walked away that time. And hadn't looked back. And was gone for twelve days.

Talking at lunch with a group of Soviet delegates, among them Vassily Zurov, Antonia had adroitly deflected a polite question about her marital status by saying that such questions were not relevant—they were meeting together as persons, were they not, with a common interest? One of the Russians translated for the others, who listened intently, smiling, nodding, staring at Antonia. His translation struck Antonia as far longer and more florid than her own remark warranted; when he finished the Russians laughed and nodded in agreement. Had she been witty, in Russian? Zurov was inspired to try out his cautious, heavily accented English with her. "Yes, it is so, it is of course so," he said emphatically, "what you tell us."

Vassily Zurov began to sit beside her in the Institute dining room, and to hover close by at the cocktail gatherings. During the long and sometimes soporific sessions (speeches, speechifying, "spontaneous" questions and answers) he frequently smiled in her direction, as if they were suffering to approximately the same degree; his hair was bunched and spiky, disheveled by the earphones. Once, when a stout, swarthy, and resolutely gregarious Soviet delegate from Georgia told a lengthy anecdote about Stalin (Stalin gruff and kindly as someone's old eccentric uncle) Vassily drew her aside with a look of embarrassed amusement and asked if she would like to take a walk around the lake before dinner.

Antonia agreed. She was appalled by the Soviets' apparent attitude toward Stalin—*did* they remember him as gruff, kindly, someone's old uncle?—but thought it best not to ask her friend. In any case she hadn't the language in which to ask him.

So they walked out, quickly, with an air of mutual relief. Yes the

Falkstone Institute was situated in a beautiful part of the world, yes they should all be supremely grateful to be there. Halfway around the lake, as they stood on a grassy knoll looking at the glittering water and the Institute's fieldstone buildings on the opposite shore, Vassily took Antonia's arm gently, experimentally, and slipped it through his. Antonia did not resist and thought herself quite daring. Was this Russian behavior?—might it mean more than it indicated, or less?

"You are very nice. Beautiful. And *very* nice," Vassily said, choosing his words with painful care. He was obviously quite excited: Antonia saw a gratifying flush on his throat, working its way unevenly to his face.

(At the initial briefing session Antonia and her colleagues were told by Soviet experts that the Soviet delegation was under strict control. No matter how friendly and even rebellious they might seem they were "on a tight rein," and "under the iron glove" of the formidable Ilyin, who was himself described variously as a "Machiavellian," a "butcher," an "old Communist hack." They would at all times be observing one another closely, spying, informing. Above all they would be intimidated by Ilyin and his aides. But now it seemed to Antonia that Vassily Zurov was his own man; so far as she could judge he was no more subservient to his chairman than the American delegates were to theirs. Perhaps it was all exaggerated, inflated, made into a sort of melodrama, Antonia thought, the mutual suspicion of East and West; Communists and Americans; the outmoded vocabulary of the Cold War; the strain, the tension, the self-conscious gestures of brotherhood; the ballet of détente. . . .)

Walking with Vassily, she felt only a sense of freedom and elation, as if she, and she alone, were on the brink of a revelation. It had political overtones but its primary nature was personal—immediate and individual. After all she could not resist being delighted with his presence and (perhaps) flattered by his interest in her.

It seemed to her, too, that he was rapidly becoming more proficient in English.

At breakfast the next morning they sat together at a far table, alone. Antonia asked him about his novels: might they be suitable

for translation into English? Were they primarily political? Or—?
Smiling, frowning, he asked her to repeat the question.

She did; and he seemed to understand. Leaning forward, gesturing broadly, staring fixedly at her as he spoke, he labored to reply in English: "My books are political . . . as all art."

Antonia too leaned forward. "All art? Did you say all *art?* . . . But all art isn't political." She spoke too rapidly and was obliged to repeat what she'd said. "Art isn't political in its essence."

Vassily was staring at her, smiling, not quite comprehending. But perhaps he did comprehend. He adjusted his glasses as if preparing for a debate. Antonia tried to explain, to elaborate. "Of course some forms of art are political. Some writers are basically political writers. But in its essence art isn't political, it's above politics, it refers only to itself. You understand, surely. You agree. I'm sure you agree. Politics necessitates choosing sides, it excludes too much of life, life's nuances and subtleties; art can't be subservient to any dogma, it insists upon its own freedom. Political people are always superficial when you come to know them. Most of us can't be forced to choose sides—it's brutal, blunt, it isn't even altogether human—"

He was listening with painful intensity. It would have been difficult for Antonia to determine precisely what it was in him that attracted her so powerfully. He was not an inordinately handsome man; his mannerisms sometimes annoyed her; he had a tendency to play the clown, to regress to childish gestures and expressions, when baffled by English. For some time, too, she had stopped thinking of men as men, she had stopped thinking of herself as a woman in terms of men, the whole enterprise seemed so futile, so upsetting. Adultery had appealed intermittently, it was true, but only as a way of revenging herself upon her husband; and as her love for Whit ebbed her desire for revenge ebbed as well. There was, still, the incontestable value of adultery as a means of getting through the day (or the night); it was an activity charged with enough feeling, enough fundamental recklessness, to absorb thought and to dissipate anxiety about other things. Some of her friends had made it into a vocation; others cultivated it as a hobby; others, the more seasoned, avoided it not on principle but out of lethargy. If Antonia allowed herself to be touched by a man . . . if she leaned forward to brush her lips against a man's lips . . . or to "allow"' a man to kiss her ... she would, for a few minutes, be spared the vexing din in her head. (Whit. Whit's whereabouts. Whit's plans for the future. Her own plans, which involved not only her marriage but her not-entirely-defined career. And there were the shopworn but still glamorous, and, yes, exciting questions of her adolescence: What is the meaning of life? Is happiness possible? Are we born only to die? Is art a means of achieving immortality?—is it *really*? Does God, in whatever form you wish to imagine Him, or It, exist? Antonia knew that the Russians, Vassily Zurov in particular, would not have jeered at such questions. She believed that he might even have one or two answers.)

Now he was attempting a spirited reply. Half in English, half in—was it French?—he was instructing her that art *is* political. He gestured broadly, he jabbed the air with his forefinger, he spoke at length and then repeated himself. "Everything. Yes, Antonia, you can agree," he said. He lifted a water goblet and gestured in her direction as if offering a toast; he took a sip; extended the glass to Antonia as if he wanted her to drink from it as well—but she declined the odd gesture, pretending not to understand. Why was he so demonstrative, so noisy? "Everything," he said eagerly, "—is political. You see, the water in the thing I have here. Glass, is it? Cup? Everything."

Antonia shook her head irritably to show that she didn't understand. And now that several of Vassily's comrades were coming to join them—now that their edgily flirtatious conversation was going to be interrupted—she rather wished she were somewhere else; with her American colleagues, for instance.

Vassily greeted the others in exuberant Russian; he pulled the only English-speaking Soviet into the chair beside him so that the man could help with his conversation with Antonia. She looked from one to the other, smiling a strained polite smile, as Vassily spoke in rapid Russian, watching her cagily.

The translator—listed as a poet in the dossier but identified as an *apparatchik*, a party hack—beamed at Antonia and translated in heavily accented but correct English: "Mr. Zurov inquires—you do not think that art is political? But it is always political. It seeks to alter human consciousness, hence it is a political act. He says also that a mere glass of water is an occasion for politics. He is saying—but you see, Miss Haas, many of us spoke of this last night,

perhaps you did not read the local newspaper?—no?—he is refer-
ring to an article about the poisons that have drained into the
mountain lakes in this area, 'acid rain' it is called. And the Canadi-
ans, your neighbors to the north, have complained. Yes? This is familiar to you? Through the winter, evidently, rain and snow have
been blown into the mountains from somewhere to the west where
there are coal and oil combustion plants, and nitric and sulfuric
oxides have been concentrated in the snow, which has now melted
in spring—so Vassily is repeating—and there are now toxins in the
lakes—and the fish, the trout, have died in great numbers. And
so—"

Vassily interrupted him excitedly, watching Antonia's face as he
spoke. His friend then translated: "He does not wish to distress you
on so beautiful a day when we are all happy and begs now to be
forgiven. He only means to say that perhaps you did not know how
the simple act of drinking a glass of water can be related to politics
and to history, if only you know the context in which it is performed and the quality of the water; but of course if you are ignorant and do not know or choose not to know, you will imagine
yourself above politics and 'untouched.' " The translator paused,
and smiled yet more deeply at Antonia, and said: "Indeed you
must forgive Vassily, now he worries that he has offended you, and
it is only his nature, Miss Haas—he is blunt and speaks his mind,
he is known for this, I am afraid, at home."

Antonia sat stunned, looking at Vassily's anxious face. She could
not have said why she was so astonished, so oddly demoralized.
Had Vassily really said those things?—Vassily who seemed so
childlike, so puppyish? She realized that she had underestimated
him, had been rather condescending to him, and could not now
determine whether she resented Vassily, or her own ignorance, for
the error in judgment.

A long, a very long, day of speeches. "Allow me to speak, I shall be
brief," said an editor of the Soviet journal *The Universe* (was that
title accurately translated?—Antonia wondered) before speaking
for an hour. The discussions grew abrasive, even churlish. Several
of the Soviet delegates had begun to appear, suddenly, less charming; less gallant; less deferential to their American hosts. The questions were rhetorical and had the air of being not altogether

spontaneous: Why do United States citizens know so little of Soviet literature?—why is there so much racist and pornographic material for sale in your country?—why do you allow a "free market" for the peddling of such trash? Why are the only Soviets you read and teach in your university those who have betrayed their homeland and boast of themselves as "dissidents"?

And of course the American delegates, Antonia among them, were moved to reply along predictable, though unrehearsed lines: First Amendment to the Constitution . . . tradition of freedom of the press . . . human rights . . . democracy . . . distrust of censorship in any form . . . and so forth. (Though the American replies had not been prepared beforehand they sounded, to Antonia's critical ear, rather contrived. Suddenly she and her fellow delegates were caught up in a high school debate and they had forgotten the handy old clichés and platitudes.) As for the dissidents—it seemed to be the case that their work exerted a certain appeal, whether literary or commercial, that, unfortunately, most Soviet writers' work did not. American publishers, privately financed, published as they wished.

This final statement quite angered Yury Ilyin, who said in his cold flawless English that the issue of the dissidents was not, in his eyes, a literary or humanistic issue at all; it had to do with overt illegal activities in the Soviet Union, and the right of a sovereign state to deal with its criminals. "I would think that you Americans are interested in legitimate Soviet writers," he said, his gaze moving evenly about the table, sparing no one, "—otherwise why did the Falkstone Institute extend its invitation to our group to visit the States?—why not assemble your much-acclaimed dissidents, and allow them to preach to you their falsehoods and slanders?"

It was an awkward, really very disagreeable moment. Antonia, steeling herself not to shrink from Ilyin's eyes, noted that Vassily was sitting hunched over, his glasses off, peering short-sightedly at his clasped hands. With his spiky rumpled hair he looked like a man surprised in his sleep. His pale mouth worked, his forehead was deeply furrowed. Antonia had the idea he was about to interrupt his chairman. He had been at one time, hadn't he?—a dissident of sorts himself; at any rate he had gotten into trouble with Party officials. (The rapporteur from Harvard hadn't been able to find out much about Vassily Zurov, he was one of the "mysterious" members of the Soviet delegation, virtually unknown in the West.)

The "great" Mayakovsky was frequently cited; the concept of "socialist realism" elaborated upon; Marxist metaphysics was presented briskly by a youngish Moscow writer who was First Secretary of his Writers' Union and evidently a rising Communist star *. . . we have first matter, and later comes spirit, and then comes "spirituality" (unfortunately there is no exact word for that concept in Russian) which is the activity of highly organized matter.* Antonia made a vague gesture toward taking notes, but were the man's words really worth it? *The activity of highly organized matter*: what in God's name did that mean? She wondered, not for the first time, if the simultaneous translator was muddling the Russians' remarks.

And on, and on. Maxim Gorky, the "father of Soviet literature." Lenin, who "stated clearly" that the function of the printed word is organizational. Jack London . . . Theodore Dreiser . . . Stephen Crane . . . Steinbeck (in his early and "most vigorous" career). Dostoyevsky was, it turned out, lately being "re-examined." When Vassily spoke he was less oratorical than the previous day, and made some interesting (though, Antonia supposed, fairly self-evident) points about "your great American poets Walt Whitman and William Carlos Williams." Antonia herself spoke in turn for twenty minutes of the "post-modern" novel and its movement inward toward lyricism and poetry, away from the statistical world, the objectively historical or political world. . . . She twisted the top of her pen uneasily as the Soviets gazed at her with immense interest. (Were they musing along Dr. Johnson's lines, that the mere spectacle of a woman speaking in public was extraordinary, like a dog walking on its hind legs? Or was it Antonia Haas's fate to be simply the most attractive woman at the conference?) When she finished her presentation a few questions were asked, not abrasively as she had feared, but rather courteously: were not such novels doomed to "decadence," to being unread by the "masses," and soon forgotten . . . ? Antonia found herself defending a mode of literature she didn't in truth greatly care for, or practice; her own fiction was solidly set in a place and a time—the Boston of her girlhood years, the America more generally of her parents. But the Soviets, who had read nothing of her fiction, could not know this; nor would they, perhaps, have greatly cared. It occurred to Antonia after she finished that she had no idea how her words were being translated. She had no idea what the Soviet gentlemen, staring at her with such intensity, believed she had said.

Antonia watched Vassily, wondered what he was thinking, why he had not glanced at her for some time. She wondered what the man had endured ... whether he had been harshly punished, frightened, coerced into adopting at least the outward gestures of non-rebellion. The Americans had been told not to mention certain things to the Soviets, even in private: under no circumstances should they inquire about certain books, written by Soviets but published outside the country; nor should they inquire about dissidents whose work they might know. Labor camps, prisons, mental asylums—don't bring the subjects up, don't arouse grief or antagonism. Antonia had read that during Stalin's reign several hundred poets, playwrights, and prose writers were murdered by the secret police, in addition to the other millions of "enemies." ... In the Sixties there was the highly-publicized case of Joseph Brodsky, put on trial for being an "idler" and a "parasite" without any socially useful work, and sentenced originally to five years of forced labor in the North; more recently, the joint trial of Siniavsky and Yuli Daniel, who dared claim "artistic freedom," the right to follow wherever one's imagination led. ... The men were both sentenced to several years' hard labor in a "severe regime" camp. There was the example too of a young man named Galanskov, the editor of a Moscow literary magazine of "experimental tendencies," first sentenced to a mental institution, then to a brutal concentration camp where he was allowed to die. Should she ask Vassily about these men, or remain silent? Perhaps he would like very much to speak with her ... it was highly possible after all that he'd known Galanskov well.

When Antonia thought of how little she and her fellow Americans risked in publishing whatever they chose, she felt stricken with a sense of guilt. And yet they too were filled with complaints, they too claimed to feel unjustly treated. ...

Antonia's head began to ache suddenly.

The chairman of the American delegation was speaking slowly (Christ, how very slowly) on the "humanistic tradition" in the West. Yury Ilyin then countered with remarks on the "humanistic tradition" in *his* country. Antonia, who rarely suffered from headaches, was seized with a wracking pain. It seemed to have something to do with the earphones . . . with the phenomenon of hearing Russian spoken and then, immediately, its English equivalent. The translator was so quick he sometimes began speaking before the Russian was entirely concluded so that, for a confused moment or two, Russian and English overlapped.

Ilyin was to have the final word on what he called this morning's "very fruitful" discussion. *Brotherhood, universal understanding, hope for global peace*—these expressions issued from his thin smiling lips like packets of noxious gas. Antonia regarded the man with awe. It must have been her weakened state—she saw the appeal of the bully, the murderer. If he could send enemies to prison camps, could he not elevate friends, disciples? Oh yes. One must believe. Ilyin was an anti-Semite, it was said. A neo-Stalinist. He detested the English in particular because he had lived among them for years in London; except of course it was the Chinese he detested— he had visited *them* many times. Now it seemed to be the Americans he detested, judging from the gravely ceremonial nature of his mockery. And he seemed only mildly tolerant of most of the members of his own delegation, who clearly belonged to a social class lower than his own. Vassily, and Boris, and Grigory, and Vitaly, and a younger beetle-browed Yury. . . .

Ilyin's words were being taped for rebroadcast. He spoke slowly, expansively, in near-perfect English, expressing the "fervent wish" that the United States would soon come to the "enlightened realization" that total freedom, in the arts as in any other sphere of life, is an ignorant, one might almost say a primitive, condition. "Our great peoples aspire to the level of civilized man, is it not true?— and to do this," Ilyin said, smiling around the table, "—one must leave the barbaric behind."

In Antonia's room up on the third floor she was saying, too rapidly, to Vassily: "I'm out of my element here. I don't belong. I'm a writer, not a diplomat—not a skilled hypocrite. I don't have the stamina, the nerves, for this sort of thing—"

Vassily, like any suitor, had come to bring her gifts: a bottle of vodka, a box of chocolates with a reproduction of the Ural Mountains (pink, gray, pale blue) on its cover, a copy of one of his novels. Now he stood perplexed and uncomprehending. "You are angry? You are—not hoping to leave?" he asked.

Antonia was saying that she had come to the conference to talk about literature, not to debate politics. She saw now that Ilyin had prepared a script, a sort of scenario, back in Moscow; it was his strategy to lead the Americans by the nose, to make fools of them, intimidate and harass—an old Communist tactic, but shouldn't he be ashamed of himself, to practice it among friends? "Isn't the aim of this conference friendship?" Antonia asked angrily. "Why are we here, otherwise?"

Vassily seized her hands and stared urgently at her.

"You are not leaving—?"

He kissed her hands lavishly. Antonia stared at the top of his head, at the thinning hair at the crown, feeling a sensation of . . . a wave of . . . something like love, strong affection, sheer undefined emotion. He was so romantic, so passionate, unafraid of making a fool of himself, or being rejected—an anachronism in her own world, and doubly precious. She could understand nothing of what he said—he spoke excitedly in Russian—but there was no mistaking the earnest, rather anguished look in his eyes. Antonia felt a pleasurable sensation of vertigo, as if she were standing at a great height with nothing to prevent her from falling.

In an impulsive gesture, not thinking what she did, Antonia reached out to embrace him, to bring his head against her breasts. She was suffused with warmth, tenderness, desire. She felt the man's sudden trembling; to her amazement he seemed to be crying. ". . . so sweet, so kind and good," Antonia murmured, as if to comfort him, hardly knowing what she said, ". . . I love you, I wish I could keep you here, I wish I could do something for you . . . save you . . . I wish we could go away somewhere and hide . . . I wish there were just the two of us . . . I've never met a man so kind, so tender. . . ." Vassily was gripping her hard, perhaps desperately. She could feel his hot breath; he seemed to be trying to burrow into her, to hide his face in her. "I know you've suffered," Antonia said softly, stroking his hair and the back of his warm neck, ". . . I know your life has been hard . . . I wish I could help you . . . I wish you could stay here with me. . . ."

They would become lovers, Antonia thought in triumph. Her own breath came fast, warm, shallow. Perhaps she would return to Moscow with him. Perhaps she would have a baby: it wasn't too late, she was only thirty-six, *was* it too late—? Stroking Vassily's neck and shoulders, embracing him clumsily (Antonia was thrown off balance by the way they were standing—it was not a posture either might have chosen) she felt her eyes flood with tears, she was on the verge of sobbing uncontrollably. Love. A lover. A Communist lover. A divinity student revolutionary.... Her husband would be stricken, demoralized. He would accuse her of recklessness. Of having rejected *him*. How could she be so deluded?—she couldn't possibly love this man since she didn't know him; she couldn't possibly love him since she was incapable of loving anyone....

Antonia's whispered words were confused, half-sobbed. She was saying that they were all homesick—Americans as well as Soviets—they were all lonely, so very lonely—

Vassily straightened to kiss her, and at that moment the telephone rang; and it was over. Like a frightened child he jumped away from her—she stepped guiltily away from him—as the phone rang close by, loud and jeering. Who could it be!—who knew about them!—Antonia thought, quite rattled.

Disheveled, flush-faced, Vassily backed out of her room, muttering words of apology, or love, Antonia could not understand.

The two of them, fortunately or unfortunately, were never to be alone together again.

The next morning, enlivened by a spirit of adventure, she and Vassily and one of the interpreters went for a rowboat ride before the nine o'clock session. The wind was chilly, Antonia regretted not having worn her heavy sweater and scarf, but wasn't it June?—nearly summer?—and wasn't she adored? She had passed a delirium of a night, sleeping in fits and starts, thinking of *him*; seeing his face in the morning she judged that he had spent a similar night, thinking of *her*. But even before the accident (was it an "accident," really, or the consequence of their own stupidity?) she found her suitor's exuberant Russian manner jarring. His white shirt was partly unbuttoned, showing graying kinky hair; he stared at her too earnestly, too openly, with a fond broad smile that seemed both anxious and proprietary. It must have been clear to anyone who saw them that Vassily was in love with her; the interpreter (First Secretary of the Leningrad Writers' Union, genial, grinning, swarthy-skinned) laughed and shook his head and even waved a warning finger at Vassily, declining to translate for Antonia *all* he said.

Antonia was the queen, the adored one, seated in the prow of the boat; the interpreter was seated at the rear; Vassily commanded the oars with extravagant gestures, splashing a good deal of water, and laughing gaily. Indeed there was much laughter, a highly charged sort of gaiety, a sense, even, of the daring and the outlaw—for as Antonia recalled there was a notice in the Institute lobby warning against "unauthorized" boat rides on the lake. She wondered, suddenly worried, whether they would be late for the session; a schoolgirl sort of alarm arose . . . might the three of them be scolded for their little adventure?

"We should head for shore now," Antonia said several times, brushing her hair out of her eyes. She spoke to Vassily, who must have understood, yet continued rowing with broad uncoordinated strokes, splashing water onto her ankles and legs, smiling at her. "Tell him, please," she said to the interpreter in the rear, "to head back. It's getting late."

The interpreter spoke earnestly to Vassily, who replied with a shrug of his shoulders and a torrent of Russian; his words were translated, somewhat apologetically, for Antonia—"Vassily says we are all running away—an escape into the mountains—into the woods. He says to tell you that he is very fond of you, perhaps you are aware of the fact, it is no secret, previous to this he has traveled in Northern Africa but not Northern America and it is all so splendid he is drunk with love . . . he does not want the days to end." The interpreter leaned stoutly forward and said with an air of confidentiality: "Vassily is famous for his high humor, you must know. It is a joke, running away into the mountains. Perhaps you have noted it, how Vassily is understood. It is a joke—playful. Very much to laugh."

Then Antonia saw that her feet and ankles were wet because the boat was leaking.

Alarm, frightened laughter, much agitation on Vassily's part—though never any actual panic, for how could three adults drown, so close to shore, and in full view of the Institute? The water, however, was freezing. The boat was leaking badly. Antonia half-sobbed with frustration and shame. The absurdity of her situation!—she was sure everyone at the conference must be watching them, through the broad plate-glass window of the dining hall.

Despite Vassily's spirited rowing they did not quite make it back to the dock: they were forced to abandon the sinking rowboat in about three feet of water, less than ten feet from safety. "I will save you— No danger— I will save—" Vassily cried, his teeth chattering from the cold. He tried to make a joke of it, though he was clearly chagrined. The interpreter cursed in Russian, his face gone hard and vicious, his skin dark with blood.

Vassily did help Antonia to shore, and insisted upon taking off his shirt to drape over her shoulders. A number of their colleagues came out to help. There were offers of sweaters, a jacket, even a blanket. But the three truants insisted, laughing, that they were all right—all they had to do was change their clothes.

Antonia, stricken with embarrassment, noticed a photographer on the veranda of the main lodge, his camera aimed in their direction. Whether he was an American or one of the Russians she couldn't tell—she pulled away from Vassily irritably, and said: "I'm all right *really*—please don't fuss."

By two-thirty, when the conference officially ended, Antonia's romance with Vassily Zurov ended as well.

The final session was a curious combination of strain and ennui. Old issues resurfaced, old resentments. . . . A member of the Soviet delegation insisted upon replying to a statement of the previous day concerning freedom of speech and of the marketplace; he harangued them for thirty impassioned minutes ("One could package and sell human flesh, no doubt there would be eager consumers, if you hold to a marketplace ideology where everything is for sale, everything is to be peddled, if you believe that in a 'democracy' it is valuable to know what people want, why *not* package and sell human flesh, what is to prevent . . .") Another, identified as a scholar and professor at Moscow University, spoke in a dramatic voice of the "racist" propaganda in the American press, on all levels of society: he had discovered on a previous visit to the States anti-Negro propaganda published openly and subsidized by leading capitalists; and what of the amazing instance of the American Nazis who were defended by many persons not long ago, and written up admiringly in the press (". . . you have not suffered a war, it is your ignorance masked as innocence, you do not know what Russians know, victims of the madman Hitler! . . . when every family, yes, no family without exception, suffered tragedy! . . . and we do not forget so simply as Americans can").

A fierce little debate arose next, over the issue of the dissident writers, the Soviets-in-exile: the American view being that they were writers primarily, the Soviet view that they were not writers at all but enemies of the state who "used" writing as a tool. Ilyin rose majestically to beat them all down. He spoke of Soviet anger at the insult that the American President always surrounded himself with Soviet "authorities" who were in fact anti-Soviet; and of the insult that the leading American universities—indeed, all American colleges and universities—pretended that Soviet literature might be represented by such writers as Solzhenitsyn and Brodsky, traitors to their homeland and no longer citizens, and Nabokov, who was an American ("Yes he is American, a citizen, American to the bone with his lust for the marketplace"). Equally outrageous was the fact that American sympathy was now being stirred for the mentally unbalanced Sokolov and the criminal Siniavsky, and others whose works were worthless . . . mere trash. There can be no genuine brotherhood between Soviets and Americans, Ilyin lectured, or such insults would not be permitted. "Those who are called by you dissidents are criminals and nothing more. They are ordinary criminals. Indeed, why are such matters a concern of the United States, where criminals are dealt with harshly enough, if they are of the appropriate color or class? It is none of your business how we govern," Ilyin said calmly. Antonia saw that all the Soviets were sitting silent, their eyes hooded. Vassily himself had taken off his glasses and sat hunched forward, staring at his clasped hands, expressionless. Now he will protest, Antonia thought—now he will get to his feet and speak: poor Vassily! Even as the elated thought ran through her mind she knew he would not rise to his feet, he would not speak, he would sit mute like the others.

"Problems of human rights remain the problems of sovereign states," Ilyin said, "not to be interfered with by outsiders. You would think that the Americans, priding themselves on their freedoms, would be wise enough to allow other states theirs. Why do you imagine," he said, gazing at them with an air of aristocratic contempt, his voice beautifully modulated to express an incredulity that was in fact mere mockery, "—why do you imagine that your views of human rights and freedom must be ours? Why do you even wish to think so . . . ? The tragic misconceptions of even the most intelligent of Americans never cease to astonish us."

And Vassily and the others sat mute, looking down. But then, as Antonia thought afterward, so did she.

While she was packing the telephone rang, and when she picked it up she could hear Whit's voice—he seemed to be arguing with an operator, the line buzzed with static—and very quietly, discreetly, Antonia put the receiver back. When the telephone rang again in a minute or two she let it ring. That seemed the easiest solution, somehow—the coward's solution, the diplomat's.

Despite her dark glasses the bright sunshine hurt her eyes; her headache had started up again. Yet Antonia managed to say goodbye to everyone. She was determined to be warm, friendly, courteous, shaking hands even with Yury Ilyin, who promised her that her books would find "ready translators" in his country from now on; he would see to it. Books were exchanged though there was little likelihood of their being read, bottles of cognac and vodka were passed out, and boxes of candy in gaily-colored tins. For the several American women involved in the conference there were hand-carved brooches made of walrus tusks. (Antonia, examining hers, thanking the Soviets with a smile, wondered if she had heard correctly—walrus tusks? The brooch, though large, weighed lightly in the hand and might well have been made of white plastic.)

The limousines were waiting. A small contingent to take the Soviet delegation to New York City; two airport limousines to take Antonia and her companions away; but it was inevitable that everyone say goodbye yet again, and promise to keep in touch, to write, to visit, to translate. . . . Vassily stood near, smiling at Antonia, though no longer with that ardent hopeful gaze; his expression had gone resigned, a trifle bitter. He knew how she judged him and the others. Certainly he knew. He wasn't a fool, perhaps he wasn't even the amiable well-meaning romantic figure he had seemed to Antonia, but another person altogether, a Soviet writer who had not only managed to survive but who had been allowed to visit the United States. Antonia smiled at him as she smiled at the others. Though she knew very well that she had no right to blame Vassily Zurov for her own disappointment in him—though she knew very well, in fact, that she was hardly in a position to pass judgment on anyone, East or West—she felt her anger backing up everywhere in her, throbbing throughout her body, beating cruelly behind her eyes.

Vassily squeezed her hand roughly, kissed it, leaned close. "You will visit us someday soon?" he asked. "You will be a guest of my government, a week, a month—?"

"Perhaps," said Antonia, avoiding his gaze. She was smiling her bright American smile but the corners of her mouth had begun to weaken.

"A month, two months?—in good weather? As a guest of my government?" Vassily repeated. He still held her hand but she slipped it away discreetly.

Already things were shifting into episodes, acquiring anecdotal perspective. Vassily Zurov, a Soviet novelist, a resident of Moscow, born 1939, had visited her in her hotel room at the Falkstone Institute and had embraced her, pressed his face against her, very likely declared his love for her; and Antonia had felt, hadn't she, such immediate, such extraordinary affection . . . of a kind she would not have believed herself capable of feeling any longer. And then . . .

Vassily took hold of her hand again, rather hard. It was clear that he wanted to kiss her—but of course he didn't dare. Instead he awkwardly pursued the subject of her coming to Russia to give lectures, to meet with fellow writers?—yes?—would she consent? She saw that Vassily chose to interpret her disdain as feminine shyness, or timidity; she understood that he would not release her until she gave him the answer he required, that his companions might overhear. So she smiled, she smiled broadly, and murmured that helpful word, *"Da."*

MY
WARSZAWA:
1980

In room 371 of the Hotel Europejski in Warsaw a bellboy in a tight-fitting uniform is asking Carl Walser a question in English. But it is not an English Carl or Judith can comprehend—like Polish it slips and hisses, plunges too rapidly forward, comes too abruptly to a full stop. Does he want a larger tip? Judith thinks, puzzled, slightly angry (for she has brought to this beleaguered country hazy but stubborn ideas about the "people" and their integrity), is he offering them a service of some dubious sort—? She thinks of, but immediately rejects, two or three unpleasant possibilities.

The bellboy isn't of course a boy, he is perhaps thirty years old, smiling a strained unconvincing smile as if in the presence of fools or children, his nicotine-stained fingers making a prayerlike impatient gesture. As he repeats his question to Carl—only to Carl, he ignores Judith—Judith cannot stop from observing that his skin is remarkably oily, his teeth are gray and crooked, his eyes slightly crossed. (She has been noticing teeth in this part of Europe. East Europe. She suspects that her penchant for noticing details, for being struck in the face by details, will soon become a curse, and is in any case a symptom of her Western frame of mind—a hyperesthesia of the soul.)

"Yes? What? I can't quite—" Carl is saying, cupping his ear. His high spirits at simply being here, in Poland, in Warsaw, in this "representative" hotel, in this very room, have become strained by the bellboy's persistence; Judith notices a slight trembling of his jaw. "If you could repeat more slowly—"

"—Dollar," says the bellboy, grinning, now looking nervously from Carl to Judith as if seeking her aid. He has given the word an odd intonation but Judith certainly recognizes it. "Dollar—zloty—change—money change?" In his outgrown costume—short green jacket, red collar and cuffs, small tarnished brass buttons—he strikes a note both comic and sinister.

Finally Carl understands. He says at once: "No thank you. Thank you but *no*. And please get out of this room."

Judith is surprised at his sudden vehemence but the bellboy, sweating and smiling, appears not to understand. "Dollar, zloty?" he says, gesturing with all his fingers, "—please money change?"

"Thank you, no," says Carl. "Will you leave—?"

The bellboy retreats, grinning and twitching, his gaze hopelessly out of focus. If Judith knew which eye to engage she would signal the poor man a look of courteous regret, sympathetic disapproval, something adequate to the occasion; but the exchange has taken place rapidly. And she is a little intimidated by her lover's high moral tone.

The incident of the *"agent provocateur"*—as they will call it afterward—leads at once into their first serious quarrel since leaving New York. "Why were you so rude," Judith hears herself saying, so upset she cannot unpack her suitcase, "—why did you treat him like that? You can imagine how poor, how desperate he was—how we must appear to them—" So the words spill out, righteous, quavering, though Judith has vowed not to argue on this trip; though she has promised herself that her behavior in Carl Walser's presence must accurately represent her feeling for him.

Carl is hanging things in the closet methodically. Without troubling to glance at her he says that she's being foolish, sentimental—they've been warned against money changers a dozen times, *agents provocateurs* who can get them arrested. "You *don't* think that poor silly man was a police agent, do you?" Judith says incredulously. "That's ridiculous." Carl does not reply. (The official rate of exchange is 33 cents American currency to one zloty; on the black market, however, it is $1.50. And the German mark is even stronger.) "You don't *really* think so, you're just being cruel," Judith says.

As he sets his small portable typewriter on the bureau Carl says mildly, in the voice he knows will provoke Judith Horne into an outburst of indignant anger: "For all I know, for all *you* know, everyone we meet on this visit might be working for the police."

Formidable Judith Horne, enviable, much-photographed: today she is wearing a black suede jump suit with innumerable zippers, slantwise across each breast, at her thighs, at each knee—one horizontal, the other vertical. Kidskin boots, gloves. (Warsaw is cold in May.) She is striking to the eye, aggressively casual; the Poles will not know how to interpret her. A woman, yes—but a *womanly* woman? She is wearing jewelry—three rings on her right hand, two rings on her left; and several necklaces—beautiful sullen-heavy silver that looks, and is, very expensive. Her gray eyes are wide-set in her strong (slightly Slavic?) face, her mouth in repose sometimes appears tremulous; but that, surely, is a misconception since Judith Horne thrives on combat, her profession as writer is almost exclusively combative, analytical, severe, resolutely unsentimental. Or so her reputation would have it.

Olive-dark skin, not yet visibly lined, clean of makeup; strong cheekbones; a strong squarish jaw; dark brown slightly coarse hair worn, for the European tour, in a braid that falls between her thin shoulder blades—a fashion stylish enough in the West but which might strike East European eyes (Judith isn't innocent of the possible confusion) as in some way, well, *peasant.* Her fingers are long and slender and restless; her mannerisms are abrupt. In public her voice is clear and dauntless as a bell. Her intelligence is bright, brittle, rarely in question, and then only by persons—almost always men—bitterly jealous of her reputation. (Judith Horne is clearly the most important member of the American delegation to this First International Conference on American Culture, for instance. Though only a few of her essays have been translated into Polish, and not one of her books is available here, the intellectual Poles seem to be agreeably familiar with her work, or at least with its dominant ideas.) She is a successful American—which is to say, simply, an *American*. With her passport she can travel anywhere. Her curiosity, her blunt questions, her skepticism, will never get her into official trouble: it's sobering to realize that Judith Horne, and Carl Walser, and Robert Sargent, and the other Americans "of literary distinction" who have come to Warsaw for the conference, can *never* get themselves into trouble . . . for anything they might say or write. Their defiance of their government might be published in foot-high headlines, or engraved in stone, and they will never be arrested or imprisoned or executed or even interrogated. So they appear formidable in their brazenness, their eerie invulnerability, like mythic creatures, demi-gods, or golems not quite possessed of souls. It is never clear how they are to be interpreted but it is always a possibility that they can prove helpful.

About Judith Horne there are two mysteries, not related. The first is spurious—*Is* she female in the classic sense of the word? The black jump suit armored with its zippers; the expensive but unpolished boots; the squarish combative jaw and the mouth that tightens rather than relaxes into a smile. . . . And her famous strong will. . . . Yet, there is the journalist Carl Walser, with whom she appears to be traveling. They are lovers, surely; though probably not married. But what precisely *is* the nature of their love? —A trivial mystery but one which engages some murmured speculation. Even in East Europe the private life is hardly over.

The second mystery: her background.

Horne is an English name, a nullity of a name. But Judith. *Judith*. Biblical, Semitic. . . .

And consider the woman's dark somewhat kinky hair, and her dark uneasy eyes; the edginess of her imagination. Her American fame too, with its New York City base. (Her Polish hosts have generously exaggerated all this, but no matter.) All of which suggests—the Biblical Judith, the Hebrew Judith.

(Judith intends to keep her background to herself, which seems to her nothing more than discretion in this part of the world. She sees no reason to burden her well-intentioned hosts with the dreary and possibly too-familiar recitation of facts—another American with Polish-Jewish ancestors, Polish-Jewish victims, come at last to visit Poland. And Judith thinks of herself as only obliquely Jewish anyway: she has some Jewish "blood," no more—remote aunts and uncles, cousins, who lived in a farming village northeast of Warsaw and who were shipped away (yes, all were shipped away) to die at Oświęcim; that is, Auschwitz. But Judith does not care to bring up the subject. Judith is not going to bring up the subject.)

Thirty-three thousand feet above the earth, traveling eastward in defiance of the sun, Judith found herself mesmerized by the cloud tundra above which the plane moved with so little apparent effort. In transit, in motion. America behind, Poland ahead. A fictitious sort of balance, Judith thinks: in size America is a continent, a complete world; in size Poland is New Mexico.

Beside her Carl Walser sits comfortably with his lightweight typewriter on his knees, recording notes, ideas, suggestions to himself. He will write—perhaps he has already begun to write—a story on the "atmosphere" of Poland; after Poland he will spend two weeks in West Germany, interviewing German citizens. What are their feelings about the presence of American GI's in their country—how do they feel about the recent arrests of drug dealers, the recent scandal involving so many GI's: heroin, hashish, cocaine, marijuana being sold to Germans, many of them teenagers. It will make a provocative story. It will stir questions, denials, outbursts. So Carl works steadily, with no mind for the extraordinary cloud landscape beyond the plane's broad wing. He has seen it all before.

Nor will Judith annoy him by calling his attention to it: they are not newlyweds, after all; they are not obliged to share every sensation.

The Awkward Age lies opened but unread in Judith's lap. A tragedy with the tone and pace of a comedy, or was it a comedy with the pretension of tragedy. . . . Since Judith Horne takes her reading very seriously there is a logic to the choice of Henry James vis-à-vis Communist Poland but at the moment she is too distracted to recall her motives. Thirty-three thousand feet above the earth it is sometimes difficult to recall any past intentions, any past self, at all.

Do you think you should risk it? Carl asked some weeks before. Meaning the visit to Warsaw. Of all places, Warsaw.

Judith was offended. You don't know me very well *yet*, do you, she said quietly.

As if she were Jewish—a Jewess!—*she*, Judith Horne.

═══

She takes care not to think about that Jewish "blood" (whatever "blood" means); she takes care not to think, not to brood upon, Carl Walser, whom she loves with an emotion that is incalculable. Perhaps it is humiliating, demeaning, even futile; perhaps it is exhilarating; in any case it seems necessary. Carl Walser who is her friend before he is her lover, Carl Walser who is assuredly not "her" husband. . . . She argues with him about the issue of Jewishness, blood, ancestry, guilt. After all she is more directly, more *significantly*, English: the Hornes are from Manchester, her father and mother married young, it all took place a very long time ago, before 1935. They married in New York City and Judith was born in New York City and has lived there all her life, she isn't religious, she certainly isn't sentimental about the past. . . .

Are we arguing, Carl might ask. And Judith hears herself say— No, of course not. There is no issue about which we might argue.

Bound for Poland Judith found herself sleepless in the hours after takeoff, as uneasy as if she'd never flown before. She was the plane's only witness (so she imagined) to the 2 A.M. sunrise with its marvels of light. Carl slept heavily beside her and could not be nudged into waking.

One moment there was only dark—that "blackness ten times black"—and then, abruptly, the light appeared. The sun did not rise, it simply appeared, *And then there was light.* A rosy bronze deepening in the plane's massive wing . . . the sea of cloud gradually defining itelf. The darkness dissolved, they were being hurtled east, plunging through time. It is an extraordinary experience no matter how often one lives through it. . . . Judith stared at the lunar landscape, the rivulets and gullies, the ravines, the abysses, and felt both elation (for it *was* sunrise, this *was* beauty) and a curious impersonal dread. What did human claims mean, after all, at such a height—what did "time" and "history" mean? The minuteness of personality, wisps of vapor contained precariously in human skulls—? Thirty-three thousand feet in the air it was possible to speculate that neither "Judith Horne" nor "Carl Walser" existed: and that "human love" was sheer vapor, the most illusory of cloud-formations.

Judith's sporadic reading in philosophy and Eastern religion allowed her to know that the very inhumanity of the universe is a consolation. But she felt no consolation, she felt only a bone-chilling loneliness. While her lover slept beside her, his breath arrhythmic and moist, one of his strong hands lying against her thigh. Other passengers, stirring from sleep, must have been annoyed by the dawn—they began to pull down their opaque shades. Of all the consolations, Judith thought, pulling down shades must be the most pragmatic.

Smoke, coils of smoke, airless air heavy with smoke: in every Pole's fingers a burning cigarette: meeting rooms, restaurants, even on the street. A smoke-haze that stings Judith's eyes, permeates her clothing, makes her hair, her very skin smell. Even Carl, who smokes himself, is annoyed. "No ventilation, that's the problem," he says, "of course they can't afford such luxuries. . . ." Layers of smoke-cloud in the shabby coffee shop of the Europejski Hotel, drifting layers of smoke-cloud at the luncheon hosted by the Polish Writers' Union and *Literatura na Swiecie*. Even at the ambassador's residence, at the jammed cocktail reception. Ten o'clock in the morning, cigarettes and coils of smoke, vodka served in cylindrical glasses, the polished wood of meeting tables, tea served Russian style: a glass set on a silver holder, wedges of lemon; and always, in the background, tiptoeing, old Polish women carrying trays . . . carrying trays . . . meant to be subservient and unobtrusive but in fact extremely obtrusive . . . interrupting the flow of remarks with their profferings of tea and cream and sugar, vodka, cognac, warm mineral water; taking away ashtrays to empty them, bringing ashtrays back, fussy, vaguely maternal, *always* on hand. And in every Pole's fingers a burning cigarette.

"What do you make of it," Judith asks Robert Sargent, an American poet here for the conference, a slight but old acquaintance, sweet and mandarin and ostensibly apolitical (the only other conference Robert has been invited to, he claims, was a "Festival of the Arts" organized by the sister of the Shah of Iran some years ago—Robert accepted the invitation immediately, without question; attended the festival without precisely absorbing the climate of opinion surrounding Iran at that time; came away admirably innocent); "what do you make of the compulsive smoking, the drinking?" Judith asks.

Robert considers her question, frowning. His eyes are a pale frank childlike blue behind the round schoolboyish lenses of his glasses. His expression is contemplative, even fastidious. Then he says, sighing, that since the takeoff from Kennedy he has been in a peculiar state of consciousness and isn't altogether certain *what* he thinks about anything. Flying so terrifies him, Robert says, he takes three or four Valium; and on the plane he quickly has one or two—well, several—drinks; and after that he slides into—a rocky but uninterrupted oblivion. The change of time zones has certainly affected him too, he feels both inappropriately elated and sick, "high" and exhausted. No, he tells Judith, he hasn't been aware of smoke in Warsaw since fresh air, being drafty, often irritates his nostrils and provokes sneezing fits. "In a way I feel I am in my own element here," Robert says. "The delightful hotel like something out of an old film—the secret cocktail bar in the basement—don't you and Carl even *know* about it?—it isn't advertised, of course—and the Stalinist architecture, the shabby people, the long queues—the sense of time having stopped in the early Fifties, or, I suppose, in 1944; something in it appeals to me."

"You don't think the smoke is a political gesture?" Judith asks, nettled by Robert's dreamy calm.

"A political gesture . . . ?" says Robert, blinking, as if he has never heard of such a thing. He gives off an agreeable odor of alcohol and talcum powder. The tiny white lines radiating from his eyes suggest his age—forty-eight, fifty—but do not detract from his rapt boyish air. He repeats, savoring the words: "A *political* gesture . . ."

It is said of Judith Horne by her most severe critics that she lacks consciousness of herself: she pursues intellectual notions to the point of, say, the absurd, without knowing—or is it simply caring?—what she does. In truth Judith long ago decided to be merciless toward what might be called her social, her "womanly," self. She will not be waylaid by Robert Sargent's ingenuousness. "Yes, political," she says. "Smoking and drinking compulsively. In the Soviet Union it's said to be even worse. Here, it's smoking and drinking and religion. Haven't you noticed, Robert, our hosts are all *Catholic*?"

"All Catholic?"

"Catholic."

"Ah—*Roman* Catholic," says Robert. "The religion. Yes—very nice—quaint—I've been attracted to it myself off and on."

Judith waves away a cloud of smoke. Her throat constricts in anger. She says passionately: "The smoke-haze of Warsaw is no less political than the smoke-haze of their religion. This is a *tragic* nation."

"It is?" Robert says, startled.

Weeks ago Carl said to Judith in her apartment on Eleventh Street as they sat drinking coffee with their lives in snarls and knots about them, as usual: "Do you really think you should risk it, Judith?"

"Risk what?" Judith asked irritably. "Please don't speak in riddles."

"The Polish tour," he said. "Ten days in Warsaw."

His voice was uncharacteristically light, his manner uncharacteristically gallant. Judith perceived that her lover's normal ironic tone was now in suspension; which meant that he was being careful with her. He was being *nice*. "Yes?" she said. "What about it? Do you prefer to go alone?"

"That isn't what I mean, Judith."

"Then what do you mean?"

Carl was a former foreign service officer—he'd quit both because of the Vietnam War and because the State Department was going to ship him to Reykjavík, Iceland—who knew a great deal about international politics and had a way, sometimes charming, sometimes not, of hinting that he knew much more. So that his pretense that night of being vaguely baffled was all the more suspect. "What do I *mean* . . . ? Or what have I *said*. . . ."

Rain was drumming on Judith's window. *Her* window, *her* apartment—they had experimented with living together on several occasions, but none had been a success; Judith appeared capable of making the effort—the sacrifice—of having no real private sanctuary in her life, but Carl, who had lived alone for too long and who cherished his loneliness, evidently could not. Though he protested that he loved her—he *really* did love her. It was invariably Carl who wanted to try again.

Do you think you should risk it, he asks casually. As if he doesn't know Judith at all.

Because she is silent he continues, as if arguing, quietly, calmly:

"You've sometimes been upset by circumstances, haven't you. And this Warsaw conference—Poland—your family background—"

"You're provoking me," Judith says carefully.

"I'm preparing you. Preparing us."

She refuses to look at him. At such moments the anxiety of her love for him—for his remorseless authority—is so keen, she believes that the slightest touch of his hand would cause her to burst into angry tears. Rigid she sits apart, rigid she holds her head high. A swan's graceful neck—so an interviewer once noted, apparently without irony. Does she compel Carl Walser with her beauty? Or is her beauty entirely fictitious? (Lovers, Judith knows very well, flatter each other innocently and shamelessly. But when love is withdrawn the flattery too is withdrawn: You aren't *really* so exceptional. So beautiful, so graceful, so wise. You aren't *really* going to live forever.)

". . . has a tragic history, I think we can agree on that," Carl is saying reasonably. "I've been in Warsaw several times—it's a somber place. Something is clearly going to happen to them soon and whatever it is, it won't be pleasant, it won't be *Polish* as they might wish it. And over their shoulders is the Uprising. They can't forget. The wounds are that fresh. It's all very real—they loathe and are terrified of Germans. To hear them talk you'd imagine that anti-Semitism is an invention of Germans and Russians exclusively. Unless of course you know something about Polish history."

"I think you exaggerate my weakness," Judith says.

"You are hardly a weak woman," Carl says.

"My sensitivity, then. My 'femininity.' "

"East Europe is a strain on anyone's nerves," Carl tells her. "The more sensitive you are, the more strain. Furthermore—"

Judith cannot resist interrupting. "Do you know, Carl, there was a pogrom in my family's village outside Warsaw, in 1946."

Carl sips at his coffee, wincing.

"1946," Judith says.

Carl sets down his cup, makes a whistling sound, as if it were expected of him. "In *1946*? For Christ's sake why?"

"Not why—we know why," Judith says. She is trembling with dignity, control. "We always know why. The question here isn't *why* but *how*."

==

Judith, late for a meeting with the Polish Writers' Union, is striding toward a glass door, a double door. In her stylish jump suit,
chains about her neck, she is hurrying, staring at the pavement, her
brain jammed with shards of thought. And Polish words. Polish
syllables. That dizzying cascade of Polish *sounds*—a mountain
stream breaking and crashing about her head, scintillating, teasing, utterly unintelligible. Though one of her guides has been trying patiently to teach her a few elementary expressions she seems
incapable of remembering from one day to the next. For one who
lives so intensely in language, with such customary control, it is
unnerving to journey into a country whose language is so very foreign. Not a word, not a phrase, is familiar; even the hand gestures—lavish, stylized—confuse her. If she were in France, or Italy,
or Spain—if she were in Germany—she would feel immediately at
home.

   She strides along the dirty pavement, her leather shoulder bag
swinging at her side. The morning is cold; damply cold; melancholy. She is acquiring a reputation for always being late for meetings, luncheons, dinners. Precisely why she cannot say: elsewhere
Judith Horne is known for being punctual. But there are so *many*
meetings and luncheons and dinners. . . . Always, it seems, she is
hurrying; always, she is about to be late. Toweling her long thick
hair dry in the hotel room, in the dismal bathroom, dressing hurriedly while Carl waits, rattling the oversized keys to the room.
"They're going to misunderstand," he says, "—they'll think you're
being disrespectful. Why can't you get ready on time?"—a husbandly question, of course; and quite reasonable.

   Judith cannot explain. She does not know why she isn't herself
here, in this particular place, when she has traveled widely since
the age of twenty—when she has boasted of being most comfortable while traveling, in motion. She doesn't know why she feels so
edgy here, so obsessed by melancholy thoughts. The architecture
(which should interest her) depresses her; the smoky air (to which
she should have become accustomed by now) makes her sick; the
odor of fried onions, the sight of Pepsi-Cola bottles everywhere,
displayed on banquet tables like bottles of French wine, the half-
fearful half-brazen references to Soviet Russia ("The light doesn't
always shine from the East!"—the boldest statement she has heard
a Pole utter), the shabby hotel room in the shabby hotel, the very

look of the overcast sky. . . . Judith cannot tell him that she feels
unreal; a fiction; an impostor; shaking so many strangers' hands,
smiling and being smiled at in return. She feels weak. She feels
Jewish at last. And womanly—in the very worst sense of the word.

A Jew, a woman, a victim—can it be?

"Robert is later than I am most of the time," she says sullenly, as
if reporting on a favored brother. "And that woman from the State
Department—"

"Marianne Beecher? But I don't think it's the State Department
exactly. Some education foundation—"

"She's always late. She's always begging so very prettily to be
forgiven."

"Judith, the issue isn't Marianne but you," Carl says.

The very equanimity of his remark infuriates her. She tells him
she can't help it. She hurries—but she's late. It's like a stereotypical
dream situation in which she hurries in order to be late. She can't
sleep until four in the morning—is awakened at six—tries to sleep
again—falls into a light groggy sleep beset by violent dreams—
then he shakes her awake and it's almost nine o'clock and they're
late again, late *again.* Yes it's her fault but she doesn't know why
unless she is breaking down.

Carl gives her a look both censorious and fearful. For what if she
does break down . . . ?

She strides toward the glass door, ten minutes late for whatever
has been scheduled for 10:30 A.M. The door is an automatic door
which will open, must open, when she breaks a certain invisible
force-field. She is late but she means no disrespect (should she
apologize?—or maintain her dignity?); she is late but she isn't precisely ill. Impossible to blame her hotel, or Poland itself. . . . Her
amiable guides Tadeusz and Miroslav are parking the car up the
street. They have just brought her from the modest office of her
Polish publishers where she received, with some ceremony, her Polish royalties, held in trust for her in Warsaw these many years.
(Several "classic" essays of Judith's have been translated for an-
thologies of American writing of the Sixties and Seventies.) Six
thousand four hundred and twenty-three zlotys!—which must be
spent before she leaves Poland.

Judith naively believed that the money was worth far more than
it actually was. The senior editor of the publishing house, and an

elderly female clerk, and Tadeusz, and Miroslav, and one or two others—all stood watching as she signed papers in triplicate, as if this were a significant (an historic?) moment. Six thousand four hundred and twenty-three zlotys paid to the author Judith Horne: how will she spend it?—what will she do, suddenly wealthy? She must give gifts to them all, she must treat people to dinners, gaily she will spend the zlotys, but how much, precisely, are they worth? Though she knows vaguely of the rate of exchange something childlike and hopeful in her leaps at the very thought of so much . . . cash.

She glances up to see her hurrying reflection in the door. Tadeusz is calling out: "Miss Horne!"

She had been about to walk head-on into the door.

She had been about to walk into it, thinking (but why?) that it is a seeing-eye door, that it would open automatically with her approach.

"Thank you, Tadeusz," she says, her face burning, "I was distracted, I—I wasn't thinking."

She pushes the door open. As if nothing were unusual. As if she hadn't come within a hair's breadth of crashing into plate glass and seriously injuring herself.

A droll little incident to report to Carl, she thinks.

Unless of course she had better not report it to Carl.

Here is the Old Town District, restored since the devastation of 1944; here is Castle Square; Market Square; the Adam Mickiewicz Museum (where Judith and the other smiling Americans are presented with a bilingual edition of Mickiewicz's *Complete Poems.*) Weatherstained monuments, churches, cathedrals. Rococo statues of the Virgin, a stone effigy of the head of St. John the Baptist. Medieval alleyways, a Gothic guardhouse, nineteenth-century street lamps, plaster facades, vaulted gates, forged iron doorcases, barrel-organs. All very beautiful, Judith thinks, staring, deeply moved in a way she cannot recall having been moved before; not knowing in which direction her emotions might rush next. Her Polish guides are young and enthusiastic and rather shy; she suspects they feel extremely vulnerable—for what if their "distinguished" American visitors don't praise this rebuilt district?—what if they murmur only a few courteous pleasantries, and move on? Judith reads a plaque aloud, in its heroic entirety: Market Square of the Old Town Monument of National Culture and Revolutionary Struggle of the People of Warsaw Turned to Ruins by Fascist Occupants in 1944 Raised from Ruins and Returned to the Nation by the Government of People's Poland in the Years 1951–1953.

They pass by the Jesuit Church, so jammed with worshippers at this hour of the evening (8 P.M.) that people are standing out on the cobblestone street, in a light cold drizzle. Judith and Carl try to listen to the priest, who is giving an impassioned sermon—in Polish of course—his words amplified by a loudspeaker. How young he sounds, and his voice so melodious, and intelligent, and reasonable!—Judith listens with her head bowed. There is such passion in the young Jesuit's voice, such urgency, she halfway feels that, at any moment, the language will yield its mystery to her: she will understand, and her life will be transformed.

But their religion, Judith thinks, what of their religion—the Roman Catholic Church. The Church of bigotry, racism, pogroms.

It puzzles and alarms her that all their guides—these wonderful bright young literary people—declare themselves Catholic. Tadeusz and Miroslav and Andrzej and Jerzy and Maria and Elizbieta. They are proudly, defiantly Catholic.

"Aren't there any Communists in Poland?" Carl joked at a small dinner at the ZZPK Club honoring the Americans. But no one laughed. After a moment Jerzy said, squinting through a cloud of smoke: "No, Mr. Walser, but there are many police."

Tadeusz is working on a doctoral degree in linguistics at Warsaw University; Miroslav, the recent father of a baby girl, does nightschool teaching—Polish, English, French—and freelance translations. Andrzej and his wife are both high school teachers who live with Andrzej's parents in one of the crowded high-rise apartment buildings in the suburbs; they have been waiting for an apartment of their own for—eleven years. Jerzy is a junior editor in a textbook publishing house; Maria, one of Judith's favorites, is an American studies scholar, a graduate student who has visited the States (she spent a year at the University of Iowa). Elizbieta, who looks so very young, is married, has a four-year-old son, teaches whenever she can get a course and does freelance translations too; she is highly

enthusiastic about a project she hopes to begin as soon as the conference is over—the translation of Jane Austen's *Emma* into Polish.
Please don't ask if they would like to study abroad, in the States for
instance, the embassy people cautioned Judith and the other delegates, you'll only arouse their hopes . . . of course they would like to
leave Poland.

Nevertheless, talk drifts in that direction. Perhaps the young
Poles initiate it themselves.

Travel abroad, to United States . . . England . . . Sweden . . .
Italy.

To be awarded a fellowship for study abroad, to be invited to
the West for a semester or a year—the young people agree quietly
that this would be wonderful for them, for their careers and their
lives.

But the competition is very strong, Miroslav murmurs. The
awards go to professors, important editors. Older men.

Tadeusz agrees that there isn't much chance for people like
them. "We must be realistic," he says, sighing, coughing as he
smokes, "—my brother, for instance—he defected to Stockholm on
his year away—so it would be impossible for me to get a visa now;
forever, I am afraid, it will be impossible."

Discreetly, the Americans query the Poles about the Communist
Party—that is, the Polish United Workers Party—and about the
Soviet Union. What of censorship, repression, arrests . . . ? But the
Poles are reluctant to speak. And Judith quite understands: Carl
has been saying since their arrival that there are certainly police
spies involved in the conference, and that their guides, however
friendly they appear to be, will be interrogated afterward. "I suppose they might even inform upon one another," Judith said
slowly, as if such a thing were really impossible and Carl would refute her at once. But he said nothing. He may have laughed.

No, Judith thinks, watching their faces—Tadeusz, and Miroslav, and Maria, and Andrzej, and Jerzy, and Elizbieta—no, these
young people are genuine, these young people are *ours*.

"*Aren't* there any Communists in Poland?" Robert Sargent asks,
slightly drunk, disappointed, "—I was anticipating all sorts of at-
tacks, like the kind I get back home—you know, that I and my art
are degenerate—hermetic—Mannerist. But no one here has read

my poetry, it seems. And everyone likes me!" He smiles his marvelous dazed smile and blinks at Judith through his schoolboy lenses.
"When I said that the United States is an imperialist nation—we
are, aren't we?—sweet little Miroslav shrugged his shoulders and
said, Who is better? And they are all Catholic, Judith, as you
saw—it's so wonderfully *bizarre*."

Judith tells him soberly: "Their religion is all they have, Robert.
When one can't move horizontally, one must move vertically."

Church bells are forever ringing across the city, young priests stride
along the narrow streets, Masses are always overflowing out onto
the sidewalks. Judith tries not to think: censorship, repression,
contempt for women, anti-Semitism, pogroms. Yes there have always been pogroms and today the nation is (as an official inadver-
tently bragged) 97% pure.

The young people absorb nothing of their guests' bewilderment
at all this religion, this conspicuous faith. In fact they are eager to
know—What do Americans think of the Pope? Pretty blond
Marianne from the arts foundation in Washington, far more
skilled at diplomacy than her face and her clothes and her finish-
ing-school manners suggest, elects to speak quickly for the American contingent, before anyone else can reply. The Pope is very
popular of course. Intelligent, remarkable, world leader, international stature, extraordinary. A force for morality and justice and
freedom in the world. A force for good.

With a shy smile Jerzy points out that there are millions of Poles
in the States, which might account for his popularity there. And
Marianne says at once, "Not at all—certainly not—Americans all
admire the Pope immensely. He *is* an extraordinary man."

Judith considers saying a few words. She has been uncharacteristically silent for hours. Moody, disoriented, not "quite
right"—a consequence perhaps of the transatlantic flight, loss of
sleep. But if she begins speaking she might not be able to stop.
What of the Church and Polish history, Jews, discrimination, mass
graves, death. . . .

(Carl senses her agitation. He has told her, as if she required
telling, that religion for the Poles means *Poland*. *Poland* and not
Russia. Their own history and their own language—it's as simple as
that. "A church of hatred—of rot," Judith says. "Yes," says Carl.
"But their own.")

Still, consider the young priests in their ankle-length black skirts, fresh-shaven, handsome, swinging along the streets—isn't there something engaging about them, something fascinating? Judith stares, stares. At one point, in a group including Robert Sargent, the two of them happen to exchange a glance; and she realizes that she has been looking upon these young men with the startled appreciation of a male homosexual.

They are shown madonnas everywhere—in niches, in courtyards, on pedestals. And the Soviet-built Palace of Culture in the center of the city—a rainstreaked monstrosity with Byzantine spires and domes—Stalinist chic—a dingy wedding cake about to collapse. "You can see why people fall in love with East Europe," Carl says expansively, "—everything is so sad here, even the jokes and the laughter are sad, people want *uplifting*. They want us. Westerners on the streets milling about in the lobbies of hotels, eager to change hard currency into zlotys. . . . They like us well-heeled Americans almost as much as they like the well-heeled Germans."

"That's an absurd thing to say," Judith says.

"I thought it was a vicious thing to say," Carl laughs.

The smoke-haze, cigarettes burning in fingers, slanted between lips, everywhere. The odor of fried onions. The tolling church bells, worshippers hurrying again to Mass, in a shabby courtyard off a side street near the University an extraordinary sight: a sooty-skinned madonna and child in a niche about eight feet above the pavement, both plastic flowers and real tulips—red tulips—arranged before it. Elizbieta explains, "The Virgin—she is protecting the people who live here, especially. I mean—they believe in *her*, in her power. To protect them."

"I see," Judith says.

"They are perhaps slightly superstitious," the young woman says, smiling, looking from Judith to Carl as if to gauge their feelings. "I mean—in this district. But it is something they believe strongly in, the statue."

"Yes," says Carl, "but why is the Virgin black?—she *is* black, isn't she?"

Elizbieta considers the question. The Madonna is dusky-skinned but not otherwise Negroid; and the infant in the crook of her arm is clearly a northern European—a Polish?—baby. Judith finds herself moved by the ugly plastic flowers, the red tulips wilted and brown, the shadowy dirt of the little niche, the impoverishment of the tenement building. If she draws a deep breath—which she will not—she will smell the perpetual odors of grease, potatoes, onions, damp. She is moved too by young Elizbieta's shy smile in which there is a margin, however subtle, of pride.

"Oh I would say . . . I would think the people found this statue . . . somewhere or other, like a store with old things, you know . . . maybe in rubble, debris. You question because she is black?—yes, but probably this is the only statue of the Virgin and Child they could get. The people who live here, I mean. They are very specially devoted to her, you see."

"Are they?" Judith says, staring at the Virgin's dark chipped eyes.

"Yes," says Elizbieta. "All of us. For she does protect."

In the elegant drawing room of the residence of the United States deputy chief of mission the American conferees are being introduced at last to a number of Polish dissident writers. Judith notes that all eight are men—are there no dissident women?

Her question results in a mumbled reply, an air of vague irritation, that does not inspire her to ask it again.

She finds herself in a spirited conversation with a tall sad-eyed man of middle age who publishes translations under a pseudonym. He will not tell her, but she has learned beforehand that he was fired from his teaching position at the University, and can no longer publish under his own name, as a consequence of his criticism of the government. Nor will he tell her that he lives in a single room—a hovel, really—in a crowded tenement building. Instead they talk of the Soviets, the Polish "people," recent events in West Germany.

She is introduced to Wladislaw, Witold, Andrzej. The enormous drawing room has begun to fill up with smoke. There is vodka, there is cognac, there is strong black tea. A servant appears and disappears, discreetly; a man whose expression is totally neutral. Judith, drinking her third cup of tea, notes that her saucer and teacup rattle—are her hands trembling that badly?

She resists watching her lover at such times, in crowded social gatherings. Of course he is eloquent, wise, warm, funny, argumentative, even a little bullying. She loves him and is humiliated by

her love for him and will not observe him at such times, any more
than he pauses to observe her. Explain to me about Werblan, Judith says to one of the Poles: Werblan, a notorious high-ranking
Communist. And what of Khoyetzki. And Konwicki, whose fiction, translated, she has read with great admiration. . . .

Robert Sargent, cheeks flushed with drink, draws Judith over to
another corner. He and a young American documentary film-
maker named Brock have become involved in a noisy general conversation with three Poles and a member of the U.S. embassy—the
cultural attaché, in fact, who has arranged this important meeting.
Unfortunately the Poles know only rudimentary English; everything must be translated. Judith, whose natural speaking voice is
rapid, has to force herself to speak slowly . . . slowly. Is the situation
worsening, or does it remain static? she asks, squinting against the
smoke. Is there any logic to it? Is it true you're forbidden to own
duplicating machines?—you can't even print up wedding or funeral announcements without the censor's seal of approval? And
will there be—here Judith draws a deep breath, then decides, yes,
she will ask—"Will there ever be open rebellion?"

The talk shifts to Brodsky, that envied hero. What of Günter
Grass, what of Bienkowski. Judith nods, speaks animatedly, tries to
absorb not only all that is being said but all that is being indicated.
She shakes hands. She is being touched on the elbow, turned another way, introduced, drawn into another discussion. She tries not
to note how, in any conversational group, the dissidents direct
their questions primarily to the American men—any men at all—
even the junior staff members of the embassy. She will save up for
retelling back in the States, when the anger is safely subsided, an
anecdote about being questioned by one of the dissidents about
her relationship to the conference—she is Mr. Sargent's secretary,
perhaps? She is Carl Walser's assistant?

"No," Judith said flatly, and refused to elaborate.

"No? *Not?*"

"No."

A "discharged" editor of a philological journal, a "discharged"
professor of economics, a white-haired gentleman (a poet) who has
been arrested eleven times in the past several years: the U.S. embassy people seem quite keen on him. Judith is led forward to meet
a prominent culture critic, the editor of the country's leading

Catholic journal. His handshake is strong, vigorous, and Judith's is
no less forthright.

They talk for a while of Miroslav Khoyetzki, who became famous for having been arrested for the twenty-first time a few weeks
previously. By applying different articles of the criminal code the
police were able to legally take from his apartment: tins of meat, a
jar of curry sauce, a pair of scissors, blank paper, a typewriter, jazz
recordings, scientific journals. He is charged with publishing ille-
gally—bringing out books banned by the censor. Is he in jail now,
Judith asks. What will happen to him?

Judith excuses herself, the smoke is so thick. In the bathroom—
which is modern, elegant, very clean, "American"—she studies her
face in the mirror without affection and decides that her sallow
skin and the shadows beneath her eyes emphasize her Semitic
blood. I know your position on censorship by the Communists, she
will ask the dissidents—but what is your position on censorship by
the Church?

She returns to the room but does not ask the question. Nearby,
Carl is talking animatedly with a frizzy-haired youngish Pole, one
of the translators, and close beside him stands Marianne Beecher,
of whom it is whispered that she is a spy—she travels about East
Europe spying on foreign service people for their mutual employer,
the State Department. But her official identity has to do with a science foundation—or is it education—or the arts—and Judith must
not underestimate the woman's intelligence simply because she is
so very beautiful. That madonna's face, that air of half-surprised
wonder, that exquisite blond hair. She is wearing a linen suit, deep
pink; a pale gray silk blouse; gold earrings; fingernail polish; high
heels; her legs are lovely, slender. And it's clear that she has done
her homework before attending this party.

Judith observes to an American diplomat that Poland doesn't
seem to be a Communist country at all—it's an occupied country.

He agrees. The very air is poisoned, isn't it?

Isn't it!—now Judith knows why she has been feeling ill for days.

They speak together in an undertone, like conspirators. He says:
"Even when these people talk openly, as they are now, you can
sense the contamination, the fear. They can't really trust anyone—not even one another."

Judith sees the sad pouched eyes, the bracketed mouths. Courageous, stubborn men. But they too can be broken, as history has shown. "Tragic" Poland. The Uprising of 1944, Hitler's command that Warsaw must be completely destroyed, razed to the ground. How could any Pole forget? How *dare* any Pole forget? Even the younger people—born as late as the very Sixties—refer to 1944 as if it had taken place only a few years ago.

And in our country, Judith thinks, history is something that happened only a few weeks ago—or didn't happen.

The reception continues. One reception blends into the next: vodka, cognac, cherry cheesecake, a second trip to the bathroom (Judith's nose is oily, her eyes bloodshot from the smoky air, her nerves strung tight), a convoluted tale about the Polish P.E.N. which "discriminates" against its own young people. The translators, it seems, never cooperate with one another; they're jealous, suspicious, selfish; often they won't even reveal what their projects are. "Sad," agrees Marianne Beecher, glancing at her jeweled little watch.

It is said of Marianne Beecher that she has a Ph.D. in art history, other degrees in psychology and economics, she has traveled virtually everywhere for the State Department. In this room of dour hangdog men in ill-fitting suits the vision of Marianne is almost disconcerting. (That morning in the Europejski coffee shop she entertained a table of fellow Americans with tales of how she is continually mistaken for a Polish prostitute. "It's my hair," she said, laughing irritably, "—and the fact that I'm usually without an escort." She told of a Japanese businessman in the hotel who seated himself near her in the lobby the other morning and pushed a fifty-dollar bill, an American bill, in her direction. When she failed to respond he added another fifty. Finally she got up, walked away, too furious to speak. "What I should have done was take his money," Marianne said, "—just put it in my purse and walk away. That arrogant little bastard!")

Now Marianne and the cultural attaché draw Judith into a conversation about current party leadership in Poland. The word Stalinist is used. Allusions to Czechoslovakia, Hungary . . . remember the uprising of 1956. . . . Judith says impulsively: "Please, is there anything we can do to help? I mean we Americans—could we form a committee, could we write about your situation and publicize it—more than it has been publicized—could we finance trips to the States, or Sweden?—England?" The cultural attaché is pleased at Judith's remarks but cautions her in an aside: these particular men, after all, cannot get visas to the West.

"Yes," says Judith, embarrassed. "Of course not. I realize that."

The Poles are listening intently, hungrily. It is the first time they have looked at Judith Horne as she is accustomed to being looked at, in her own sphere—as if she had significance, as if she possessed power. The cultural attaché is saying: ". . . anything you might do back home, of course . . . you might work directly with P.E.N. . . . you might donate some money to the Index on Censorship in London, and get your friends to donate too. . . . In fact I can deliver mail to certain individuals if you send it to me in care of the embassy," he says. "Our post office box is New York City. I'll give you my card."

"Yes," says Judith. "Thank you. I want to do whatever I can."

The dissidents continue to stare at her as her words are translated. Judith smiles, smiles. She has never smiled so much. Finally they smile at her in return, offer to shake her hand again. "I want to do whatever I can," she hears herself say.

Waiting for Carl, propped up in bed, reading *The Awkward Age*.

Twice this evening the telephone has rung—the bell jingles, twitters, but no one is calling. Carl is away at a meeting of Polish filmmakers which Judith, unsteady on her feet, decided to miss. Now she is alone, and rather lonely. Now she has time in which to contemplate her predicament.

The "awkward age" in James's novel is an entire era, an entire swath of idle English society; it also refers specifically to the age of a young woman—no longer a girl—as she steps into the adult world, not very prepared. She has no vocation, no fate, no life except marriage. Nanda *must* marry.

And must I? Judith thinks.

Except for the fact that she has outlived her girlhood by many years. She has outlived—defiantly, bravely—the period of her availability.

A number of men have loved her and she has loved them, or some of them, in return. (There have even been one or two women—but never mind.) Now, in love with Carl Walser, her vanity is pricked by the fact that she is not loved in return quite so much as she loves: not pound for pound, ounce for ounce. Her passion must be greater than Carl's because her ferocity is far greater. Consequently she hates him and often fantasizes his death.

Lately she thinks of herself as a mourner—lamenting her youth, her nearly forgotten Jewish blood, the sick sad futile sentiment of being *female*. She has wanted only to be a woman of independent means—a woman secure in a public career, a formidable public reputation—a woman whose name is comfortably *known*: and all this she has, and more. Her books and articles bring her a steady income, she tours the United States each spring giving lectures (and her fee is not modest), she has only to pick up a telephone or write a letter or make inquiries and an academic appointment would be offered her at once . . . at least as a visiting professor. She is a thoroughly successful woman in a bitterly competitive field yet now, lately, her thoughts have fastened helplessly upon Carl Walser. Does she want only a life shared with him, *conventional* in every sense of the word . . . ?

Fortunately, she thinks ironically, I'm almost too old to have children. *That* temptation is nearly past.

Again the telephone almost rings, and again no one is on the line.

"Yes? Who is it? What do you want—?" Judith cries.

It is twelve-thirty and Carl is late returning from the meeting. Carl is very late: hadn't he said he'd be back by eleven?

Earlier today Judith gave a highly successful lecture at the University. Three hundred students had crowded into a tiered auditorium to hear her. There were professors, a gratifying contingent from the U.S. Embassy, there were newspaper and magazine reporters. Judith Horne the distinguished American writer. Judith Horne the distinguished American cultural critic. A handsome dark-haired woman in a gray corduroy jacket and gray slacks, a white turtleneck sweater, hiding her nervousness by walking briskly to the podium, exchanging light laughing remarks with her Polish hosts. She felt exhilarated, elated—a sign of panic, perhaps—and her cheeks were flushed, her eyes bright. She was no longer precisely a beautiful woman but she was certainly striking. *The distinguished American woman of letters Judith Horne. . . .*

Carl couldn't attend, he'd been elsewhere, interviewing two

Poles involved in the "Flying University"—an informal and indeed illegal organization that offered courses late at night on subjects forbidden by the official universities. These days, in any case, Carl was being patient with her—watchful, cautious.

Having an audience was a marvelous tonic for Judith. She spoke with her customary passion and authority, she knew she was doing well, being admired, her words taking root. The topic was broad enough—Contemporary American Culture—but Judith chose to surprise her listeners by talking about censorship in America, church-inspired, state-inspired, marketplace-inspired. It did not escape her notice that her Polish audience was *very* interested.

Yes, there was censorship in the States. But it was oblique, informal, indirect.

Making her points Judith felt her voice gain strength, she felt how forcefully she was convincing her audience. And afterward the applause was gratifying—really, rather overwhelming. Even the embassy people clapped. (For Judith Horne had the reputation of being quirky, provocative, provoking—there was no telling what she might say. It wasn't until hours later that Judith realized she had totally forgotten to speak of censorship by the Roman Catholic Church. . . .)

"I hear it went beautifully," Carl said, rummaging in his suitcase for something. "I hear everyone was impressed. Why did you worry?"

"Did I worry?—I don't remember worrying," Judith said.

She ran both hands roughly through her hair, which needed shampooing again. The air of Warsaw was so polluted, so filthy . . . but she loathed the shabby little bathroom.

"I hope you weren't disappointed that I couldn't make it," Carl said.

"Of course not."

Idly, Judith took the bouquet of flowers from the bureau—six red roses, baby's breath, daisies, carnations—and dropped it into the wastebasket, container and all.

"Why did you do that?" Carl asked, staring.

"I don't like flowers," Judith said.

"What do you mean?—of course you like them."

"I don't deserve them."

Carl stood with his hands on his hips, staring at Judith as if he'd never seen her before. There was a tiny red nick on the underside of his jaw—he'd shaved for the second time that day.

Judith went on, not quite coherently. "I don't like flowers, I don't like the assumption behind them—a woman is presented publicly with a bouquet—a woman is obliged to be grateful—" She paused and made a wriggling gesture with her fingers. "It's such a masquerade."

After a moment Carl turned back to his suitcase. He rarely troubled to unpack his suitcases of small items—underwear, socks—even when he was staying in one hotel room for a week or more. Consequently he was always rooting about, rummaging impatiently.

". . . I don't feel I deserve them," Judith said.

"Well, all right. But you're being ridiculous."

"I don't *want* them."

Carl found what he was looking for and went into the bathroom and closed the door.

Now the telephone is ringing, full-throated. Judith pushes aside *The Awkward Age*, picks up the receiver, says quickly, "Carl?— hello?" But of course it isn't Carl. A man, a stranger, is speaking in a language she cannot comprehend. She tries to explain that he must have the wrong number but of course he can't understand, he persists, seems to be trying to argue. "You have the wrong number," Judith says, suddenly furious. *"Please leave me alone."*

Long lines in Centrum and in the other downtown stores. Futile for Judith to shop there, simply to spend her zlotys, and in any case the goods look second-rate, shoddy. Long queues at fruit stands: withered lemons, small shriveled apples in outdoor bins. The ugly Palace of Culture dominates the skyline. SMAK bars, SPOOTEM restaurants, signs for Pepsi-Cola and Coke and Hot Dogs. Church steeples with graceful Moorish lines. (Which is the church in which Chopin's heart is said to be buried—Judith must visit it.) Red trolley cars, red buses, hurtling along the streets, emitting their poisonous exhaust. Crowds, noise, rain in the morning and sunshine at noon, a pervasive chill. Cobblestone streets. Monuments. The elegant Park Lazienkowski. The Palace Marszatkowska.

—How many Jews live in Warsaw at the present time? Judith asks, and her guide Tadeusz replies, There are no statistics.

Driven from place to place, from meeting to meeting, in a handy Boy Scout sort of van owned by the U.S. Embassy, or in Soviet-built Fiats—perky little vehicles possessing the size and grace of tin bathtubs. (Judith's teeth rattle, the cobblestone streets are not easy to navigate.) Where was the Jewish ghetto? Judith asks, and one day, finally, she and Robert Sargent are driven to it—but there's nothing to see except pavement, high-rise apartment buildings, a monument. "When you say that Warsaw was completely rebuilt," Judith tells the Poles, "you don't of course mean *completely*—the ghetto wasn't rebuilt."

The monument to the Warsaw ghetto is rectangular, made of a lightless tearstained stone. Five prominent figures, all male; heroic; "noble"; with muscular chests and arms; *very* male. (A female in the background, emerging feebly from stone. Judith recognizes the figure as female because it is equipped with breasts and carries a terrified baby.) It hardly needs to be pointed out that the heroic stone figures boast a craggy Aryan look—not a Jew in their midst.

Robert Sargent tries, and fails, to take a picture of the monument; but the film is jammed in his camera. Judith can't make it work either. "Mechanical things lose their ability to function in my hands," Robert tells her, "—I don't think it has anything to do with this place."

Judith makes other, persistent inquiries about the number of Jews in Warsaw, and this time the answer is more helpful: Maybe seven . . . hundred? . . . seven hundred fifty? . . . but very few children. Perhaps no children.

Her teeth rattling in the Soviet-built cars, her senses stung by something acrid in the air. *Is* there a poison here?—but what is it?—where? Judith doesn't care to be morbid or sentimental; she really isn't the kind of person who feeds personal hungers with grandiose "historical" notions. That is cheap, that is unworthy of her intelligence. Warsaw is a city that was destroyed by the Nazis but rebuilt itself—almost completely. Look at Old Town, they are justified in being proud of Old Town. Judith and Carl stroll through it in the early evening, grateful to be alone after a day of meetings, receptions, speeches, handshakes, smoke-filled rooms, cognac, tea with lemon, smiles disclosing sad stained teeth . . . grateful for the open cobblestone square, the freedom from traffic and exhaust. The facades of the buildings on the market square are almost *too* perfect. Less absurdly ostentatious than the Grand Place of Brussels, but touristy nonetheless—almost "quaint"—handsome olive greens and pale russets and gray and brown and subdued red brick: all very clean, very neat. Too bad the Soviets are bleeding these people white, Carl observes. They could fix up the rest of Warsaw.

Hills, cobblestone streets. Rozbrat, Krakowskie Przedmieścic, Wybrzeze, Gdanskie, Bolésce, Rybaki, Kozia. The same damp chill. Polish spring. Money changers approaching them on the street, quite openly, even insolently, like panhandlers in New York: "Change—? Money change—? Dollar, zloty—?" Following after them with hands extended. No thank you! Judith says angrily. She is ashamed for her Polish friends.

Warsaw is an occupied city, an occupied zone, Judith thinks, waking, staring at herself in the dim bathroom mirror—and something is happening to her here. *Is* there a subtle poison in the air? While her lover dresses in the other room, whistling under his breath. He was out very late last night. He too has his secrets, his malaise. (Judith has decided to forgive him his most recent infidelity. She tells herself she hasn't any curiosity about the woman though she wonders . . . was she an American, a Pole?)

No time to think, to brood. She has thousands of zlotys to spend, must buy gifts, books, take everyone out to dinner, perhaps on the last evening of the conference. If this won't strike the young Poles as too blatantly "American" a gesture of charity, condescension, good will.

No time to meditate upon subtleties. Not here. Driven about in the embassy van, in one of the Fiats, Robert Sargent jostled against her, smelling of shaving lotion. Judith must fight her almost physical distress at the sound of Polish—the frustrating tumble of words, melodic, inaccessible, the structure of the compound sentence with its many variations: the subordinate clauses, the coordinate clauses: which Judith can hear (or so it seems) without being able to understand.

My Warszawa, she thinks. The place of my undoing.

The language remains inaccessible in its beauty. And Carl, what of Carl?—she forgives him his infidelity (his most recent infidelity) but cannot forgive him the fact that he lied to her and expected her to believe it.

No time to herself, shaking hands, squinting against the smoke, accepting another glass of tea Russian style. No time to brood about that monument to the "martyrs" of the ghetto, the Jewish resistance; it seems curiously beside the point to be bitter or even uncommonly interested at this point in history—for 1944 *was* a long time ago. And should Judith Horne take the entire Polish delegation out to dinner, perhaps at the famous (and expensive) Crocodile Restaurant on the square? Or will they sneer at her behind her back? Or do they genuinely like her, admire her, as they appear to? (There have been several floral bouquets so far. She hasn't been able to bring herself to throw them all away.)

There isn't time, they are being herded into the embassy van, Judith is listening with enormous interest to an anecdote told by the American cultural attaché whose last post, evidently a perversely cherished post, was in Saudi Arabia: 130-degree heat, damp heat, public stonings, yes, but worse, far worse punishments, and sanitary conditions, and sickness, and of course women *there* don't exist—really don't exist. Judith is concerned with her digestion, her bowels. She has come to dread the very look, the odor, of the bathroom in her hotel room. The oilcloth shower curtain with its faded floral design. The stained sink, the stained tile floor. The enormous crazy roaring splash when the toilet is flushed. ("I thought my toilet was attacking me!" Robert Sargent said with a shudder.) Judith's eyes water, her head reels; she must concentrate on a not quite coherent but possibly hostile charge being made by a red-bearded young playwright: they are both on a five-member panel organized by P.E.N. to discuss the "problem" of translating. The young man's English has a distinct Scots accent, acquired from his two years abroad. Other accents are British and Midwestern (the University of Iowa, to be specific). Judith assiduously inquires after names and addresses, accepts printed cards, if only there were time to think . . . she wants to help the Poles get translated into English, published in the States . . . and she knows of exchange-student programs, she can inquire about grants for study, Iowa, Columbia, Stanford, Michigan, she will write letters of recommendation, make telephone calls. Back in New York she intends to form a committee to help the Polish dissidents who have lost their jobs and are "nonpersons"—she will make contact with Polish dissidents in exile in the States—she will donate money to the Index on Censorship in London. Exhaustion rings her eyes, her hands tremble, she fears she is losing her energy, her faith in herself. Does anything we say or write or publish *matter*, she thinks, when we risk nothing?—we who are free.

But there isn't time to puzzle over the situation, the embassy van is idling at the curb, Tadeusz is waiting, Marianne Beecher is wearing soft flannel trousers and a casual suede jacket as if in imitation of Judith Horne's style, there will be a television interview at 2 P.M., Carl has been attentive all morning, Tadeusz smiles his shy, exquisitely courteous smile and corrects—but very gently—her pronunciation of Mickiewicz for the second or third time.

Groggy with sleep, leaden-boweled, Judith turns from him as if to hide in the bedclothes. Carl is trying to wake her. Down on the street the morning traffic has begun, in the corridor outside the room workmen are moving furniture, there are maids with vacuum cleaners, the same chill pale light suffuses the room: *Warszawa*. Judith must wake once again to her city.

Carl asks is she ill?—otherwise they must hurry.

Perhaps he hasn't been unfaithful to her, she thinks, her eyes shut, perhaps Carl always tells the truth and it is she who distorts everything. Quick to see meanings, significance, even in the wallpaper, heraldic designs too faint to engage a more robust eye.

"That woman journalist who has been asking to interview you, Marta something, she's probably downstairs in the coffee shop waiting," Carl says, stooping to peer at himself in the bureau mirror, combing his hair, "—I think you'll like her: she's quick, sharp, intelligent, knows English quite well."

"Marta who?" Judith says. "I don't remember any Marta."

". . . met her the other evening, she has read most of your essays she *says*, she's of course very eager to meet you. . . . Are you all right, Judith? Why don't you get up?"

"I don't remember any Marta," Judith says. "I don't remember any appointment for an interview."

"I have the woman's card here," Carl says. Judith does not look in his direction. "—You asked me to take it, write down the details, don't you remember?"

Judith does not reply.

Carl goes into the bathroom. Running water, the straining noise of the old plumbing, the roar of the flushed toilet.

Today Judith is going to be taken at last to the Jewish cemetery. She has declined to tell Carl (who is busy with engagements of his own) because she knows that he will disapprove. Do you really think you should . . . ? he will ask. Though perhaps he will say nothing at all.

Carl reappears, Judith is up, brushing her hair impatiently. Stroke after stroke. Curly kinky dark-but-graying hairs in the hairbrush.

He asks her about *The Awkward Age*, and she says it isn't a Polish sort of story, and he says, Yes, but how do you find it? and she says, Very slow, very rich, very dull, very profound—in fact heartbreaking. He says that James always is, if you read him correctly; and Judith says, I make an effort to read most books "correctly."

Carl rummages through his suitcase. He says, as if casually: "Of course you do, Judith. You're the star of the conference, after all. The queen, the A+ student, the one with the most style, the only one the Poles want to interview. . . . What are we arguing about? Are we arguing?"

"I don't know," Judith says evenly, "—are we arguing?"

Carl doesn't reply. Judith continues her rapid compulsive brushing.

After a moment, in a slightly different voice, Carl says: "They were asking me yesterday about the NATO thing."

"The NATO 'thing'—?" Judith asks.

"In Norway. You must have read about it. They've decided to install five hundred seventy-two new missiles, some sort of five-year plan."

"Because of the Soviets?"

Carl lets the lid of his suitcase fall and says irritably: "The joke of it is that NATO is begging the Soviets this week to negotiate an arms control agreement but the Soviets won't negotiate unless NATO abandons its plan. Does that make sense?"

"What has Norway to do with it?"

"The meeting took place there. I don't know. Norway has nothing to do with it—no more than any of these countries."

Judith drops the hairbrush on the bed. "Yes I know about that," she says, the leaden sensation in her bowels growing heavier, "—or something exactly like it. I read it in the embassy bulletin the other day."

"Well—this is newer news."

"It's all the same news."

"Our Poles were asking me about it yesterday at lunch," Carl says. "Not exactly—as you know—*asking*. Because of course they don't really know what's going on in the world. They know that their government censors the news but they don't know if they can trust Western reports and of course we don't either."

"They don't even know their own history," Judith says.

"Does anyone?"

"Don't be flippant: *yes*. Yes, some of us do know."

"We know what we've been told, what we read."

"Yes, and we make it our business to be told and to read a great deal."

Carl says, sighing: "West Germany is quite willing to go along with the NATO plan, for obvious reasons. England and Italy have fallen into line too."

"But the Soviets have missiles too," Judith says, frowning. "Why are we arguing?"

"We're *not* arguing," Carl says. "I agree with you. The Soviets have thousands of missiles—they've been manufacturing one a week. Most are aimed at West Europe but some are aimed at China."

"Yes," says Judith. "We know. And North America."

"It isn't new news, you're right. It's exactly the same old news."

Judith is now hunting through her suitcase, through her leather bag. Passport, notebook, wallet, crumpled Kleenex, a loose ballpoint pen. A much-folded street map of Warsaw. Why am I here, she thinks, staring at something in her hand—why in this room, in this city, with this stranger?

She stares at the item in her hand and eventually it becomes a plastic toiletries case.

Carl says abruptly, touching her arm: "Judith, I feel that I'm confronting an adversary in you. It's gotten much worse this past week. The tension, the continual strain—"

"An adversary in *me*, or an adversary *in* me?" Judith asks absently, not turning. After a moment, when he fails to respond, she says lightly: "Maybe you just feel guilty."

"Why should I feel guilty?" Carl laughs, backing away. "I'll meet you downstairs."

Now things rush head-on, a cascade of minor epiphanies.

The mystical interpretation of the universe, Judith thinks, is probably correct: each day is precisely *the* day, each hour and each moment is an eternal present, immutable. Thus Pascal might argue, thus Spinoza, and all the Oriental mystics, and ... The world is awash in visions yes I fully realize. But to explain to melancholy Robert Sargent on the way to the Gezia Cemetery as the poor man recites his litany of bad luck (his malfunctioning camera was "lost" somewhere in the Europejski; this morning he didn't wake until ten-thirty already late for the opening session of the day, lying in a pool of harsh sunlight on the carpet of his room *fully clothed*; he was paralyzed, stricken, unable to remember clearly whether he was back home on Thirteenth Street or still in Warsaw or was it Paris?—how very long he has been traveling! His soulmate, as he calls him, has surely betrayed him by now, back on Thirteenth Street; surely he has broken into the forbidden liquor cabinet as well, being a creature incapable of delaying gratification, let alone fidelity in the usual sense of the word: so he awoke this morning, did Robert, a vile taste in his mouth, his eyes unfocused, saliva drooling in a thread down his chest, Robert Sargent the unassuming though much-acclaimed post-modernist poet who has quietly confessed in interviews that, yes, he *is* related to John Singer Sargent that extraordinary genius but what good does it do him!—he who is merely *Robert* Sargent!—he awoke to the stench of vomit not his own and the certitude that his traveler's checks were gone and all his zlotys and hard currency as well, and personal papers, notes scribbled over with firsts drafts of poems; and after ten minutes of this soul-paralysis he managed to crawl to a chair and hoist himself to his feet and yes everything *was* gone—stolen—everything except the notes for poems, and of course the handful of zlotys for who would want *zlotys?*—has Judith ever heard anything so piteous?) ... sitting beside Judith in a Fiat driven by a young Polish editor named Bruno ... sitting shivering in a tweedy sports jacket baggy at the shoulders and worn at the elbows, a true poet's costume, appealing to Judith for aid or advice or sympathy or simply shared amusement at his predicament. Is it the human predicament, Robert wonders?

"The cultural attaché has been very kind," Robert says in an undertone to Judith, "I mean he didn't scold. If he felt disgust he was kindly enough not to betray it. He promised to cable home for money for me, thank God he knows exactly what to do, I was sick with dread of going to the police, you know I'd never do such a thing, the young man—a blond, a poet too or so he claimed—the young man was very, very naughty to have run off with my things but I can't really blame him, I mean after all I *am* an American, we're all fair game so to speak, don't you think? In any case I couldn't possibly have described him, my glasses had fallen off . . . my vision has deteriorated badly in my left eye since my arrival in Warsaw, in fact. . . . Oh Judith we've been here so long!—away from home so long! You *won't* laugh at me back home, will you, dear, and spread tales . . . ?"

Judith laughs uncomfortably and pats Robert's arm.

The world is awash with visions, she thinks, and today, the day of her visit to Gezia Cemetery, is the only day that matters; the day of salvation or damnation; this hour, this very moment. But Judith is not a religious person. She is not inclined to mysticism, however comforting or terrifying. She cannot really believe in the blood—in the rich dark unconscious current of being—whatever it might be called—whatever arcane expression: she cannot believe. And the trouble with epiphanies is that they fall from the air all too frequently.

Nevertheless Gezia Cemetery affects her profoundly, leaves her rocky and exhausted and scant of breath. Spring is still withheld, suspended; here birds call to one another with a wintry plaintiveness; the atmosphere is rural and timeless, distant from the city of Warsaw which in fact surrounds it on all sides. A chill greeny-damp tranquility, hundreds of startlingly white birch trees, grave after grave. . . . In such places one realizes that the earth belongs not to the living but the dead, who populate it in such incalculable numbers.

Robert Sargent is similarly subdued as well, staring, as Judith does, at the city of graves. His childlike blue eyes are widened, his hands are thrust into the pockets of his oversized tweed coat.

The elderly caretaker Pinchas leads Judith and Robert and their tall young Polish guide. A wide pathway of cracked pavement, beneath overhanging tree branches, between rows of graves. Pinchas is gnomelike and droll and quietly assured. No American visitors intimidate him—he has had so many. Ceaselessly, tirelessly he speaks, pointing out graves, identifying the dead with a careless fond familiarity. Judith notes his leathery expressionless face, his sunken Slavic eyes, protruding ears. Kafka in caricature—grown old and sallow. He wears a shirt and tie and a soiled coat. He appears very much at home in this beautiful desolate place as if he has lived here all his life. "Is Pinchas a first or a last name?" Robert inquires, but when Bruno translates the question the caretaker does not answer. Perhaps he is deaf? His monologue continues almost uninterrupted—now he is pointing out a ruined mausoleum, speaking in low rapid Polish.

"A wealthy manufacturer," Bruno translates. "One of the class of Jews who made Warsaw a center of commerce for all of Europe. . . ."

The little procession continues. Judith is wearing only the suede jump suit, her head is bare, she is never quite prepared for the chilly May wind. Robert Sargent stoops to read inscriptions but of course the inscriptions are unreadable. "It's frightening to realize that Latin too can be of no help," Robert murmurs. Five hundred thousand graves. Monuments of all sizes: some as high as fifteen feet, some low and squat, some mere markers half-covered by grass. Judith, always alert to details, asks about materials: that is Swedish granite (the black stone); Polish granite (pink-gray); sandstone; marble. Pinchas points out with melancholy pride a gravesite elaborately ornamental (pansies and petunias in bloom, protected by iron grillwork), the father of a millionaire now living in Miami Beach, "the wife sends a check twice a year to cover all expenses," Bruno translates, Pinchas leads them on, pointing out a small brick tower in another large fenced-off plot, "here the great Mendelssohn, great in his day, secretary to Marx. Very fine people, very wealthy."

Judith and Robert see a swastika scratched on a granite monument nearby.

The cemetery is actually a forest, Judith thinks, in which graves are tolerated. Everywhere are lovely trees—birch, maple—just beginning to leaf. Pale cold green, almost translucent. Now Pinchas is pointing out the graves of famous Jews—poets, writers, musicians—famous men—Bruno translates with a quiet courtesy, as if he has been this way before and has heard Pinchas's monologue many times.

These, after all, are the fortunate Jews—the Jews who died natural deaths and were buried in their own soil.

Epiphanies cancel one another out, Judith thinks, wiping her eyes roughly with the back of her hand. Robert notices but discreetly turns aside. After a moment he says, as if to comfort her: "Once, years ago, I was fighting my way across a street in Rome, I was a young man then, and absurdly vulnerable, and something about the crowd of *handsome people*—for Romans are all handsome, or nearly—something about the crowd pierced my heart. *This is a lonely predicament,* I thought. I never understood the sentiment but I think it applies to today."

Judith neither agrees nor disagrees.

At the cemetery gate she gives the caretaker a twenty-dollar bill—hard currency—and notes how the old man's deep-sunk eyes fairly glow. He is moved, agitated, repeats his thanks in Polish several times, shakes her hand until Judith, embarrassed, half-ashamed, edges away.

Driving back to the Europejski Judith senses Bruno's disapproval. Robert Sargent says: "You made old Pinchas's day, my dear. In fact you've probably made his year."

Carl says quietly: "It's simply that I feel I am confronting an adversary in you."

Judith says: "I don't understand."

Carl says: "I mean an adversary *in* you—inside you—a rival of mine. He's inside you and the two of us are struggling for you."

Judith laughs sharply. Her lover's tone is so humorless and flat, and his words are so ridiculous. "But is the struggle worth it?" she can't resist asking.

Carl is sitting on the edge of the rumpled bed, a newspaper on his knees, sheets of notebook paper scattered across the bedclothes. His eyes are threaded with blood, his skin sallow. It is past nine o'clock and he hasn't shaved and the lower half of his face looks malevolent. There is something weary and husbandly about him and Judith thinks, He is going to ask for a divorce.

Each woke before dawn. Traffic noises, plumbing. Judith woke to her low-grade Warsaw anxiety as if surfacing through a few feet of gray soapy water—no depth to it, but enough to drown in.

Last night, if she remembers clearly, they had tried to make love for the first time in many days. Carl was tender, desperate. "Is it men you hate," he whispered, "—or the entire species?"

Judith prides herself on being a woman who believes in the body, in the life of the body. "Sensuality"—as a philosophical principle at least—means a great deal to her. So she could not reply. She turned away, sobbing, burying her wet face in the pillow.

Now it is morning and she is in control. She says: "You make such pronouncements as a way of not saying other things."

"Such as—?" Carl asks, watching her.

"*I love you, I hate you,*" Judith says lightly. "The usual things that people say, or so we're led to believe."

"I'm not in the habit of making formal pronouncements regarding my emotions," Carl says. "You must be confusing me with someone else."

"Of course," Judith says. "That must be the problem."

". . . This adversary I spoke of," Carl says, assembling the newspaper, frowning at his ink-stained fingers, "this adversary is *your* emotion. A kind of shadow, a reflection. It isn't precisely you—Judith—but it inhabits you. I can see it dimly at times, at other times it eludes me—it's too cunning. It occupies you and crowds me out, it's a rival, I think it's winning."

Judith says slowly, beginning to be frightened: "I don't understand."

Carl sighs, tosses the newspaper away. "You're not a happy woman," he says.

"Is that an accusation?"

"A man feels a certain challenge with a woman like you—your intelligence, your quality. Your style. There aren't many women I can talk with as an equal—no I *won't* apologize for that remark, I haven't time for hypocrisy right now—and I think you must know how I value our friendship?—of course you know. But this struggle with—with whatever—this adversary—*you* becomes exhausting."

Judith stares at him. For a long moment neither speaks. Then she hears herself say in a soft, rot-soft voice: "But I don't understand, I love you."

"Oh yes, do you?" Carl says at once, as if fearful of allowing the words any resonance. *"Do* you?"

"I love you."

Carl smiles coldly at her, or in her direction. He is sitting, still, on the edge of the bed, his shoulders slightly hunched, a man of young middle age, dark chest hair shadowy inside his white undershirt. Ten years, Judith thinks, panicked. Twelve. My lifetime. And now in Warszawa.

(The other day, walking through Old Town, they stopped to examine a display of "carved" Christs in an outdoor booth. The Christs were all on the cross but there were several close-ups, the head and shoulders, the crown of horns, lurid droplets of paint-bright blood. The figures had the slick stamped-out look of manufactured goods though they were advertised as handmade, which Judith found both amusing and depressing. Dying-eyed Jesus Christ in cartoon colors. "Shall I buy you one, Judith," Carl asked, "as a souvenir of Poland?" Judith drew away, suddenly angry. Mockery was inappropriate here—mockery was beside the point. The market square, the cobblestones, horse-drawn buggies hauling tourists, melodic incomprehensible Polish spoken on all sides, heavy shutters on the buildings, eighteenth-century facades on all sides. . . . Except of course they were not legitimately eighteenth-century because everything was post-war, arisen from rubble. Judith thought: I never felt Jewish before. Before Warsaw.)

Now Carl is winding his wristwatch, not quite impatiently. In his weary husband's voice he says: "Well. We should go downstairs, our guides are waiting."

But Judith stands staring at him. "I don't understand," she repeats stubbornly. *"You* seem to want nothing I offer. Nothing that's deep, that's genuine or permanent. When I'm happy, you're indifferent or jealous. When things go well with my public life, my career—you draw away, you *are* jealous. *Don't deny it.* Yet you were attracted to me because I have a public career. Only when I'm miserable are you sympathetic, only when things go wrong—then you say absurd things, things I can't understand. The sort of thing you've been saying this morning."

Carl rises abruptly to his feet, is about to go to the closet, but Judith grabs hold of his arm. She hears herself saying the most remarkable words: ". . . You don't love me. You don't give a damn about me. Nothing is genuine or . . ."

Carl tries to quiet her but she cannot be quieted. Now she is half-whispering, sobbing: "I can't bear this—boxed up in this wretched room with you—do you think I want to be here, do you think I'm enjoying this? I hate you! Your cruelty, your condescension—"

"Judith, for Christ's sake—"

"I want a normal life with you!" Judith says, her voice rising. "I believe in mutual respect—honesty—fidelity—I've been willing to wait—I've been willing to sacrifice my pride—but I won't demean myself for nothing!—for you!"

She has become hysterical suddenly. Carl tries to hold her; she pushes him away; she strikes out with her fists, sobbing like a child. It is all very amazing. It is not really happening and Judith cannot accept responsibility.

A hysterical woman, no longer young, screaming with such rage that her face is distorted . . . her throat scraped raw with words she cannot believe she hears: "You don't love me! You never have!"

Afterward, an oasis of calm. Frightened tenderness.

"Of course I'm sorry," Carl says, shaken by the scene. "Of course I love you. But I'm not always certain that . . . that I know you."

"You know me well enough," Judith says.

She is lying on the unmade bed, exhausted. Her voice is flat and dull; her head feels hollow. Loathing for herself, for the absurd creature Judith Horne, has acquired a sharp tangible taste, like vomit.

"It's this place, we've been poisoned by this place," Carl says slowly. He might be echoing Judith's own words, speaking in her own cadences. ". . . An occupied zone after all."

"Yes," says Judith flatly. "An occupied zone."

Is it Napoleon, there in the wall?—in a faded mural of curlicues and clouds? Judith, bored by the soporific ceremony in the museum, no longer quite so fascinated by the sound of Polish and not at all fascinated by the English into which it is being translated, seeks out diversions in the ceiling, in the floor, in the wall. The air is thick with smoke, no windows have been opened, vodka is being served in tiny glasses, tea Russian style, an old woman servant tiptoes officiously about. Judith notes with envy that Carl is writing something quickly in his notebook. A bell is ringing in the steeple of the Jesuit Church, a high cold clear sound. They will be leaving Poland at the end of the week. Soon. But perhaps it is too late.

Judith studies the mural of Napoleon. A portly cherub captured by an adoring painter in the moment of—can it be?—his ascent to Heaven.

(For Napoleon is a savior to the Poles, having promised them "freedom." His armies are consequently awaited with enormous hope.) Judith notes the laurel leaves in his hair, the way in which his eyes turn upward in an ecstasy of heroic innocence. He wears a freshly starched white waistcoat, a short green jacket with red collar and cuffs and smart little brass buttons. It seems to Judith that she has seen this Napoleon somewhere else in Warsaw, but she cannot remember where.

The Americans are taken to visit a collective farm outside the city, and then to the village of Zelazowa Wola, Chopin's birthplace. Judith tries to read Mickiewicz and decides the translation must be inadequate. She studies publications the Poles have given her and notes the recurring words, the inescapable words—*collapse, subjugated peoples, revolutionary fervor, sacrifice, betrayal, tyrants, annihilation, survival, partition, national independence, clandestine organizations, secret police, Uprising, oppressed peoples, despot, oppressor, suffering, struggle.* It is too painful for her to read again about the Uprising of 1944 and the Nazi attack.

At lunch an earnest young university instructor tells them passionately that Soviet Russia is not a nation like any other. "Democracy is too weak to deal with such people," he says, exhaling a cloud of smoke. "If it was not the case of the many Jews in Washington, in your country, there would be an invasion tomorrow— the next day!—you would see. But their influence is strong, very strong, and never friendly to Poland."

Judith takes Tadeusz to dinner, alone. She would prefer to ask him questions about himself but he insists upon asking her questions: in fact he is interviewing her for a Polish literary journal, as it turns out. Her theory of literature . . . her judgment of her contemporaries ("You have formed an opinion of Jerzy Kosinski?") . . . her aspirations for the future. They dine on rump of boar, duck Cracow style with mushrooms, cabbage with nuts, mizeria (cucumber salad), date mazurek, saffron baba. Very sweet wine. Very strong coffee in small cups. Tadeusz is profuse, blushing, in his gratitude.

(Seven months later Judith will receive a translation of the interview, sent to her courtesy the U.S. Embassy. She will be stunned, in fact incredulous, at the hostility of the interviewer and the distortions of her remarks. *Judith Horne pretends a wide awareness of Polish culture but betrays herself by ignorance of . . . Judith Horne like her compatriots boasts smug superiority to U.S. writers like Saroyan, Sinclair Lewis, and Jack London, whose works are prized above hers . . . Judith Horne manifested dislike of her hotel accommodations, Polish food and customs, the busy streets . . . the very air itself which she claimed to find unclean.*)

"Well—the Jewish ghetto wasn't much of a loss architecturally," Judith hears one of the Poles say to one of the American delegates; but it takes her too long to absorb the meaning—by then the conversation has shifted, moved on. In any case she is too demoralized to speak. In any case she is intent upon threading her way through the crowd and finding the women's restroom.

Gossip that might interest Judith and Carl: it was in this very house—the U.S.-owned residence of the deputy chief of mission—that Mary McCarthy wrote *The Group*. Does she, Judith, admire that novel? Is it much read and respected in the States at the present time?

Robert Sargent drifts into the coffee shop forty-five minutes late, so freshly shaven his fair skin gleams, so sleep-befuddled his eyes appear half their normal size. "Judith—Carl—it's the most bizarre thing—my toenails are growing wildly here in East Europe, I've had to clip them back twice this week, is the same thing happening to you?"

Since Gezia Cemetery Robert has been particularly edgy, antic, bright, insouciant in her presence. Judith has stopped smiling at his remarks, which only provokes him all the more.

"*My* toenails," says Carl, yawning, "—have atrophied."

Hoping to avoid the furniture-congested corridor that leads to the hotel's central staircase—a kind of grand spiral with a solid crim-

son carpet—Judith seeks out the back stairs, the fire exit, and de-
scends floor after floor in the half-dark, trying doorknobs (the
doors are all locked), her heart in a flurry. Is it possible she'll be
trapped in the stairwell?—it isn't possible because she can always
scream, pound on the doors, perhaps there is a fire alarm. Unfortunately the floors are not marked. Unfortunately the air is very close
and warm, vaguely feculent.

Finally Judith is in the basement—she can go no further—turning a doorknob, throwing herself against the door, hearing a few
yards away the voices and laughter of strangers. It is extremely
warm here, and quite dark. "Hello," says Judith, "—is someone
there? Can you let me out? The door is locked—"

But no one hears. In a panic she runs up to the next floor—
which is, perhaps, the ground floor of the hotel—and tries the door
but of course the door is locked. "Hello," she calls out calmly, "is
anyone there? Can anyone hear me? I seem to be locked in. . . ."
An odor of fried onions, grease. No sound. Nothing. So she hurries
up to the next floor, her heart now thudding, and then to the next,
and the next. . . . But the doors are all locked. The doors are all
locked.

Suddenly she is pounding on a door, shouting for help, desperate, shameless. A pulse beats wild in her head. "Help me—
please—I'm trapped—please, isn't anyone around?—oh God
please—"

Then it happens, marvelously, that a door is opened *on the floor
below*, as if in response to Judith's cry. She hurries downstairs,
shouting. Two men are backing through the doorway, carrying a
stepladder. Judith rushes upon them, manic with relief and gratitude: "Oh for God's sake *thank you*—oh please don't let the door
close—"

She hurries past them, past their astonished faces, and finds herself at the far end of the very corridor that leads to room 371.

An amusing anecdote to tell Carl, someday. Or her friends back
home.

Then again, perhaps not.

Judith jots down names, and addresses, in her notebook. Yes she
knows someone at the University of Iowa—yes she has a friend at
Stanford—certainly she will make inquiries about exchange fel-

lowships. She is introduced to the hearty bearded Secretary of the
International Committee for Unification of Terminological Neolo-
gisms. He shakes her hand hard, tells her that he is also a translator,
under contract to translate one of her books—though he would
prefer to do a book not yet published in the States. "Not yet published? But how would that be possible?" Judith asks, puzzled. The
young man leans close to her, smiles nervously, insolently, says: "It
will be that I must work closely with you, Miss Horne, confer with
you over the manuscript itself . . . spend three–four weeks at the
least in New York City collaborating. . . ." Judith draws away and
says: "I don't think that's feasible." He says, smiling: "Then I must
convince you!—only make me the opportunity."

Judith is appalled at the tiny worms of dirt that roll beneath her
fingertips. Between her breasts, across her thighs, her belly. She has
taken only the briefest, most perfunctory showers in Warsaw.

She rubs her skin hard with a washcloth. A white washcloth in
which the ubiquitous word *Orbis* is stitched. Layers of grime, flakes,
near-invisible bits of dirt. Her feet are especially afflicted. It takes
her twenty minutes to get clean; her skin is reddened in ugly
swaths, smarting.

I'm turning into mere flesh, Judith thinks. A beast.

Two members of the American delegation are leaving early, having come to Warsaw from Budapest. They are on a six-week tour of
East Europe for the State Department, as "cultural emissaries,"
and Judith admires their stamina. "We've absorbed firsthand the
tragic history of Poland," one says, "—and the tragic history of
Hungary. Before that—the tragic history of Bulgaria, Yugoslavia,
and Czechoslovakia. Do you know where we're headed next?—
East Germany."

Carl is typing out the first draft of a story on the political atmosphere of Poland that will eventually wind up in the *New York
Times Magazine*. In fact Carl Walser will get the cover that week.
Now he glances up irritably at Judith who wants his advice:
Should she buy gifts for their Polish hosts?—all of them, or only
the ones they've become acquainted with? Or should she treat the
whole group to a dinner in Old Town? (It falls to Judith Horne to

be bountiful because she is the one with all the zlotys—neither Carl nor Robert Sargent received any Polish royalties at all.)

"Or do you think I should give the money in person to one of the dissidents?" she asks. "I mean—the one who needs it most."

"Who the hell would that be?" Carl asks.

"I have his name written down," Judith says, searching through her purse, "—the one with the beard, Wladislaw something. Elizbieta told me about him, he's a member of the Social Defense Committee who's been arrested a dozen times, he's penniless, I remember thinking I felt a particular kinship with him—"

"Who the fuck *is* the man?" Carl asks impatiently. "A face, a handshake?—a pair of melancholy watery eyes? Just because the man can't speak English and he's been arrested a few times you want to give him money."

Judith turns her purse upside down. Scraps of paper fall out, much-folded notebook pages. "Elizbieta said he'd been in Sweden for a few years publishing Polish writing but he got so homesick he had to return, despite the danger. Now he can't get a visa and he's unemployed—you must remember him—you and Marianne were talking with him too."

"You've become unbalanced here," Carl says.

"Because I feel sorry for these people? Because I feel sympathy?—I want to help?" Judith says angrily.

"You don't *know* them. A dissident isn't by definition a saint—there are anti-Semites who are dissidents—look at Solzhenitsyn. You're being ridiculous, this is another form of hysteria."

"I don't think of Solzhenitsyn as an anti-Semite," Judith says.

"He's a Russian, isn't he."

"Is he an anti-Semite?" Judith asks, staring at Carl.

"He admires Nixon. He admires stability. What do you think?"

Judith says nothing, staring. She is breathing quickly and shallowly. Carl says, trying to take her hand: "For Christ's sake sit down, you look exhausted. *You can't save the world.*"

Judith draws away. "I'm not at all exhausted," she says. "I feel the strongest I've felt in days."

"Fortunately we're leaving tomorrow."

"I'm not ready to leave, I want to *do something* for these people."

"Sit down. Come here."

Judith has located a scrap of paper, her finger shaking. "Here it is—Barańczak—is that the name? I'm probably not pronouncing it correctly—"

"Barańczak," said Carl doubtfully, "isn't that another man? The philology professor with the bad eyes?"

The embassy van is being routed down a side street. On the boulevard is a royal procession—or what appears to be a royal procession—limousines, army vehicles, police on horseback, many soldiers. The sidewalks, however, are totally empty.

Brezniew, it is explained to the Americans—Brezniew back in town, the Warsaw Pact discussions, twice in a single month.

"Suppose he's assassinated," Robert Sargent says with an exquisite shiver. "Wouldn't we be in a fix then!"

Marta, her short dark hair frizzed about her face, her dark eyes bright, smoking cigarette after cigarette, flattering Judith Horne with her spirited admiration. Of all the American writers "of the highest rank". . . . Of all the American writers who have visited Poland. . . . "And of course," Marta insists, making an emphatic gesture that Judith has come to recognize as specifically Polish—a kind of restrained jab with the flat of the hand against the air, accompanied by a look of fastidious pain—"of course it is pleasing to me as a woman, I mean that *you* are a woman too, though your writing is superior to—is that the expression?—the feminist ideas of the elementary level—"

Judith murmurs an assent, or a question; but Marta continues speaking. She is pert and argumentative and almost ugly, then again she *is* attractive, her features mobile, her eyes narrowing and widening with intensity. Ah, how delighted she is to be interviewing, at last, the distinguished American writer Judith Horne! For days she has been begging for an interview, leaving messages at the Europejski desk, trying to make requests through the U.S. Embassy people, and now . . . now there is *so much* to ask. . . .

Judith squints against the smoke, begins to gnaw on a sore thumbnail. She always dislikes flatterers, however guileless, but there is something about Marta that offends her in any case.

Marta is Jewish, of course. No doubt about it. The eyes, the nose, the mouth, the frizzy-kinky hair—doesn't she resemble Judith herself, in a smaller pushed-together version? But she is wearing a small gold cross around her neck. Small but prominent.

Defiant. It tides the hollow at the base of her throat, moves with her breath, her voice. Judith finds herself staring at it as Marta "interviews" her—fires long paragraphs of questions that contain their own answers; recites critical judgments of Judith's work on which Judith is asked, please, to comment; asks once again, as so many Poles have asked, what are Judith's firsthand impressions of Poland?

Judith interrupts. "That thing you're wearing—are you Catholic?"

Marta draws back. The reaction is almost mechanical; it seems to Judith not quite unpremeditated. Marta says with an air of surprised gravity: "Yes of course I am a Catholic." After a pause she adds: "I am a convert."

"A convert," says Judith. "When were you converted?—is that the correct expression, *were* converted?—how old were you?"

"At the age of sixteen," Marta says uneasily, "—but we have not much time, Miss Horne, we must concentrate on you."

"I asked you to call me Judith."

"Yes—but it is so difficult, you see!—for you are famous—and we have not much time if you must all leave tomorrow—so soon!" Marta tries to smile engagingly. "In fact my next question is, Miss Horne, when will you return to our country?—and stay for a longer time?"

"Was your entire family converted," Judith asks, "or just you?—I'm not clear about these procedures."

"I made my own decision," Marta says, again with that air of dignified surprise, "—my beliefs are my own, you see, coming from within."

"What about your family?"

"My family," Marta says slowly, carefully, "is scattered . . . not in Warsaw." She sucks on her cigarette, exhales smoke. Judith irritably waves it away.

"Scattered—?"

"Scattered, living in different parts," Marta says with a shrug of her shoulders, "some are, you know, dead—missing." After a pause she adds in an undertone: "My family was very wealthy. Aristocrats. My grandfather and his uncles—they had an export firm. They did business, Miss Horne, in London, Paris, Berlin, Vienna—everywhere. Leather exports of the finest quality."

"I see," says Judith. "Aristocrats."

Marta pauses long enough to allow a young waitress to pass by their table, then leans forward, her expression keen, shrewd, her voice lowered. "The Jews—the other Jews—I mean the Jews of Warsaw, of the ghetto—they could have saved themselves if they made the effort," Marta says. "Also the villagers. You see, Miss Horne, they were very slow—very ignorant—filled with superstition—lazy." Marta shakes her head, half-sorrowfully, half-repulsed. That look again of fastidious pain. "They could have saved themselves, the ones who ended up in Oświęcim. But they did not try."

"They did not try," Judith says slowly.

"It is difficult to explain to an American," Marta says, "but you must know—they were peasants—mainly peasants. Very ignorant."

"Mainly peasants," says Judith quietly. "I see."

There is a long uneasy pause. Judith stares at the tea glasses on the table, at the lemon wedges. The coffee shop is noisy, smoky, bustling, cheery even in the dimness, not a place for significant gestures.

"Now, Miss Horne, to continue," says Marta, "—I have here an important question—"

In one version Judith suddenly slaps the cigarette from Marta's fingers: it falls to the table, rolls to the floor. In another version Judith simply rises from her chair so abruptly that her interviewer is startled, jerks back, drops her cigarette. It falls to the table, rolls to the floor. . . .

Carl follows Judith upstairs, comes into their room some thirty seconds after her. He appears to be more bewildered than angry. "What the hell happened down there?" he asks.

Judith, trembling, standing at the window, does not reply.

"—I wasn't watching, myself—a few of us happened to be having coffee—I saw you and Marta come in and you seemed to be getting along well—I *told* you she was nice—the next thing I knew you were on your way out and the poor woman was calling after you."

"Was she," Judith says. "I didn't hear."

Judith and Carl excuse themselves from the evening's program to have dinner alone, though both of them—as they explain to the conference director—would have liked very much to see the Poznan Dance Theater at the Opera House. "Next time we visit Warsaw," Carl promises.

They leave the Europejski and cross the wide windy square to the Victoria Hotel, the single "international" hotel, for an expensive meal. Polish cuisine, of course—but in quiet, elegant surroundings. (The tablecloths are white linen, there are single long-stemmed roses at each table, a pretty young woman in a filmy white dress is playing a harp, the lighting is discreet, flattering.) "I don't know why we're doing this," Judith says guiltily. "I really *don't* like pretentious overpriced restaurants."

"Maybe you do," says Carl, "*really.*"

Judith hears the mild contempt in his voice but refuses to respond. They have quarreled so much in Warsaw, emotion of any kind now strikes her as futile. Rage and tears and hatred followed by embraces, comforting, forgiveness. The gestures of "love." Even when she is denouncing her lover a part of her stands aside, skeptical, doubting the very authenticity of the moment. Is Judith responding to Carl Walser in himself, or is she only fulfilling a role?—saying lines not her own, lines that belong simply to Woman.

Self-loathing has swollen in her, she thinks, like a fetus.

Carl orders a bottle of wine though Judith isn't drinking. Mineral water with ice will be fine. (*Ice.* Neither of them has had an iced drink for days except at the residence of the deputy chief of mission: what luxury!) Carl decides upon a shrimp cocktail though Judith warns him that the shrimp very likely won't be fresh; after all, Warsaw. He orders the shrimp cocktail anyway and Judith orders borscht. Her choice should have been a wise one but the borscht is simply liquid, very sweet; she takes only a few sips and puts down her spoon. Carl's shrimp are tiny and rubbery. "Maybe they *are* rubber—rubber shrimp for tourists," he says. Judith says: "I told you not to order shrimp."

"Yes," says Carl, "right, you did."

The doomed meal continues. Stringy roast beef, duck roasted so long it has become impossibly dry. Judith watches her lover, thinking, I hate this man—if we were married I would leave him. But she cannot help noticing his handsome flushed face (anger becomes him, even his eyes appear darker, shrewder), his movements which are no less graceful for being irritably self-conscious. If we

were married I would leave him, Judith thinks. But we are not
married.

The dining room is fairly crowded, unlike the sepulchral dining
room of the old Europejski. Here, guests are extremely well
dressed, the atmosphere is gracious and restrained, the young
woman harpist is really quite talented so far as Judith can judge.
(She is playing a dreamy version of "Clair de Lune.") At a table to
Judith's right German is being spoken, briskly and loudly; at a
smaller table behind Carl two older women sit, talking in what
seems to be Swedish. There is a French table, there is another German table. No Polish? Carl's eyes move restlessly about. "What do
you think," Judith asks in an undertone, "—the Germans? Surely
they aren't East Germans, here?" Carl tries to overhear the conversation, sitting very still. After a minute or so he says: "I think
you're right. *West* German."

He and Judith exchange an amused, baffled, startled look. . . .
Remarkable that West German tourists should come to Warsaw,
of all places: unless of course it isn't at all remarkable, it has become customary, no one except Judith and Carl is surprised.

"Well," says Carl in the flippant tone Judith has come to dread,
"—*we're* here, after all."

The statement is illogical, senseless, not even witty; but Judith
does not wish to question it. At times there is a childhood spirit
between her and Carl, childhood in the least agreeable sense: you
said that, I did not, you *said* that and got it wrong, no I did *not*, I
hate you, I hate you too, I *hate* you I wish you were dead.

The check for the meal is slow in coming. Carl drums his fingernails on the table, Judith yawns behind her hand. Such fatigue,
she thinks, could crack the high ornate ceiling of the dining room,
could crack the very surface of the earth. "I'll wait for you in the
lobby," Judith says, "I can't stand your restlessness," and she rises
abruptly from the table and strides away, her face flushed, her
leather bag swinging. No other woman in the dining room of the
Victoria Hotel is wearing trousers tonight, let alone so defiantly
sporty a costume as a suede jump suit with a half-dozen oversized
zippers. But then no other woman in the room has the presence of
the American Judith Horne.

She waits for her lover in the lobby. Examining advertisements for hotels elsewhere in Europe—Prague, Budapest. Handsome high-rise hotels with "every modern convenience." She yawns again. In another day they will be leaving Warsaw—in another day they will be gone. They will fly out of Poland to Frankfurt, to the West; immediately they will recognize their home territory. Posters of left-wing *Terroristen* are prominently displayed in the Frankfurt Airport—sad sullen intelligent faces, the eyes rather like Judith's own—and young German guards stroll about in pairs, their submachine guns cradled casually in their arms. A journalist friend of Judith's who once interviewed West German soldiers reported that the young men had never heard of Auschwitz, Belsen, Dachau . . . they'd never even heard the names.

Along with standard signs for restaurants, restrooms, telephones, and first aid there will be, in the Frankfurt Airport, signs for sex shops: cartoon drawings of the female figure. Home territory, the West.

Judith rouses herself from her reverie to see Carl approaching, through the plate glass door. He is walking quickly as usual; his expression is irritable, sullen, as if he knows she is watching and refuses to raise his eyes to hers. Impatiently he puts bills in his wallet, his head lowered. Judith watches him without love and thinks, I don't know the man who is going to walk head-on into that glass door, I have never seen him before in my life.

And then, incredibly, it does happen: Carl walks into the door: his head, slightly bowed, slams against the glass with a thud that reverberates through the lobby. People glance around. A woman exclaims in English—"Oh that poor man!" And Judith has not moved. She has watched her lover walk into a glass door and she has not moved, she has not spoken, she stands rooted to the spot, staring like any stranger.

Blaring American rock music on the plane, announcements in Polish and Russian, box lunches of cheese, cold cuts, rye bread, Pepsi-Cola (warm) in small plastic cups. The stewardesses are Russian but their stylish self-conscious chic is international: blue suits with white turtleneck blouses, very red lips, rouged cheeks, long shining hair braided and fixed at the back of the head with silver barrettes. We have already left Poland, Judith thinks, climbing into the Soviet plane.

"Are you all right. . . ?" she asks Carl hesitantly. The ugly swell-
ing on his forehead doesn't hurt, he has assured her. But she saw
him swallowing aspirin back in the hotel, two and three at a time.

"You could have injured yourself seriously," Judith murmurs.
Her eyes flood with tears at the memory, the image: Carl walking
so confidently into that glass door. Before Judith had time to call
out a warning.

"An idiotic accident," Carl says, shrugging. "It serves me right.
Expecting a door to open automatically in Warsaw. . . ."

In the hotel room they packed quickly, carelessly. The room was
in great disorder. Judith threw things in her suitcase without taking the time to fold them, she made a fumbling attempt to sort
through her many papers—the farrago of names and addresses on
slips of paper, notes to herself, booklets, maps, pamphlets printed
by the state and pamphlets printed by illegal presses—while Carl
said, "Never mind all that, come on, the limousine is waiting,
throw it all in the suitcase or throw it all in the wastebasket, we're
late."

Judith didn't have room for everything in her suitcase yet how
could she sort through her things with Carl waiting, watching,
pacing about . . . ? "Please don't make me nervous, damn you," she
said, and Carl said, "for Christ's sake come *on*," and finally Judith
threw nearly everything away—except three or four printed cards;
these she secured in one of her pockets. "Here," said Carl, stooping
to pick up *The Awkward Age* from the floor, "this too, let's go. We
are not going to miss that plane."

Handshakes at the airport, farewells that might have been farewells between old friends, old comrades. All is rushed, precarious,
poignant. Judith is touched by Tadeusz's shy smile—that look of
genuine loss, of stricken comprehension—the essence, she thinks, of
Polish melancholy. "Thank you so much for your kindness, your
generosity," Judith says, shaking his hand hard, shaking Miroslav's
hand, embracing Elizbieta who is, she discovers, terribly frail, "I
have your names and addresses, I will write, we'll see one another
again someday, thank you all very much. . . ." Carl too shakes
hands, smiling. Judith has noticed that he is blinking frequently
and that his right eye is awash with tears. The bump on his forehead is ugly and, even with its ridge of dried blood, slightly
comic—a blind but glaring third eye. (The young Poles asked dis-

creetly what had happened and Carl said, embarrassed, trying to laugh, "Nothing, an accident—entirely my fault.")

The plane taxis along the runway, exactly on time. Judith grips her lover's hand for comfort, for strength, thinking as always at such moments *The plane crashed within seconds of takeoff, killing all passengers and crew,* but nothing happens, nothing has ever happened, the plane simply rises, riding the air. Below there are squares and rectangles and long narrow strips of farmland . . . railroad tracks . . . highways . . . the long building of a collective farm. My Warszawa, Judith thinks, blinking tears from her eyes, recognizing nothing.

The plane ascends, banks to the left, moves into a blazing white mist. Now all is routine, mechanical. "There's the collective farm they took us to," Judith tells Carl, who is studying a glossy booklet printed in Cyrillic—he can read Russian, up to a point—and he looks over, peers out the window, frowns, says: "No I don't think so, I think the farm we saw is in another direction, miles away."

OLD
BUDAPEST

On her second morning in Budapest, Marianne Beecher incon-
spicuously left the conference headquarters in a Soviet-built Fiat
driven by a Hungarian editor who wanted, as he said, very much
to show her the city from Gellért Hill, above the Danube—"otherwise, Miss Beecher, you will not see anything; you must have a car,
and you must be driven up into the hills, or the city is too crowded
to be seen."

His motive in taking her, Marianne reasoned, was either sexual
or political: experience suggested that it would probably not be
both.

Since there was no speed limit within the city, traffic presented
some very interesting problems of negotiation, which, Marianne
noted, her companion executed with skill, and even a kind of flam-
boyant charm. The Buda streets were hilly and curving; cobblestones made the feisty little car rattle, and jarred Marianne's teeth;
there was an air—greatly enhanced by the sudden May sunshine,
and the odor of lilacs, and the Hungarian's ebullient chatter—of
festivity, celebration, the suspension of ordinary law. She might
have been slightly embarrassed by the fact, which he gaily insisted

upon, that they had met two years previously, at a similar conference in Warsaw ("Where, Miss Beecher, you and your happy colleagues stayed at the Victoria; and I, unfortunately, and my colleagues, at the Europejski—so very *Polish* a hotel"): embarrassed not because he remembered her, and she did not remember him, but because she had no way of knowing whether she had been introduced, at that time, as an "administrative assistant" for the National Science Education Foundation, or an employee of the State Department, or a private citizen—a teacher, perhaps—with a particular interest in science education, and in East Europe. (For, after all, Marianne's maternal grandparents were of Lithuanian and Hungarian extraction; and the pronounced slant of her cheekbones might be said to be Slav. She even knew a few words of Czech, as a consequence of a brief though intense love affair with an avant-garde Czech playwright, expelled from his country in the early Seventies, and resident, for an indeterminate period of time, in Washington.)

The Hungarian's name was Ottó; he edited a journal for one of the institutes, having to do with both "science" and "culture." Unfortunately it was only in Hungarian, and not translated into English, so that Marianne couldn't read it.

"My particular field," Ottó said, "was geology—I mean, when I was in school. Now, journalism; and music; and other kinds of writing. And you?" Marianne judged him to be in his late twenties, though his thinning brown hair, and furrowed brow, and a certain fussiness in his manner made him seem older. He wasn't tall—only an inch or two taller than Marianne herself—and his narrow shoulders were slightly stooped, in an attitude of deference Marianne supposed was misleading. (She had happened to overhear him speaking to one of the desk clerks in the hotel, in rapid and belligerent Hungarian.) His eyes were very dark, and deep set in his face; his smile was charming, though somewhat insistent; she felt herself responding to him as if he were an attractive man, and their interest in each other only personal. She saw that he was wearing a wedding band, and that his fingernails were agreeably clean. And his dark flannel suit, though by no means Western in cut, struck her as superior in some indefinable way to the clothes worn by most of his compatriots.

"My field?" said Marianne. "Education."

In truth, she had a master's degree in biology; and she had taken a number of courses, in her late twenties, in art history, sociology, and international law. She was a very beautiful woman and she enjoyed her extreme visibility, in East Europe in particular: but she shied away from discussing herself at length, less out of a feminine fear of being intimidating to men, than out of a habitual need to misrepresent herself—for Marianne had known, even as a young girl, that there is a measure of power in how much factual evidence one withholds. Because she was a blond, and impeccably groomed, and wore a half-dozen rings and bracelets, and high-heeled shoes with thin straps, it was always assumed, by men and women both, that she could not be of more than average intelligence. And this assumption she judged to be to her advantage.

"You are a teacher? An editor?" Ottó asked curiously.

"A traveler," Marianne said.

His laughter was warmly responsive, but she could not tell if it was genuine or forced; nor had she any idea, whether he commonly maneuvered the little Fiat with such offhand, cavalier skill, or whether her presence, and her lily-scented perfume, distracted him. And why did he keep glancing at her? She doubted that he truly found her so absorbing—perhaps he had the notion that she expected it of him.

But he was really quite congenial, as he chattered: and his English was no hardship to hear.

He told her that she was fortunate—she and all her associates—that the weather had changed, only the week before, for winters in Budapest were depressing; as she might know, the air was now seriously polluted, and almost suffocating on overcast days. One cannot know, Ottó said with a dry barking laugh, if one is sick from natural causes, from the "inside," or if the malaise comes from the outside, falling from the sky.

Marianne did not pursue this, but said, again, that she found the city remarkably beautiful, and even uncanny. The church spires, the narrow streets, the friezes and iron grillwork, the lilacs everywhere in bloom, the gate towers and Gothic arches and ornate facades of buildings, and the tile roofs that rose so steeply they reminded her of—she didn't know how to express it—fairytales, or dream landscapes, or illustrations in children's books. "A more beautiful city even than Warsaw," Marianne said judiciously.

"Ah, well—Warsaw," Ottó said, with a melancholy shrug of his shoulders. "But then there is Prague, most beautiful of all: I mean, I suppose, Prague as it used to be. Perhaps it is already too late, for a traveler like yourself, Miss Beecher, to visit Prague."

Marianne had been to Prague not long before, and it was quite true, she had come too late: that shabby, litter-strewn, demoralized city could not possibly have been the legendary Prague.

Ottó continued, his voice dripping with irony: "Budapest is still—Budapest. As you see. Old Budapest picturesque and accessible. A jewel of a city, in recent years at least. Very pleasing to the eye. Historic buildings, restored 'points of interest,' Roman artifacts, Turkish, and all the rest—some slight Russian influence as well. You haven't come too late for Budapest, Miss Beecher."

On Gellért Hill Ottó pointed out to Marianne the Buda hills, and Pest, and the Parliament building, and Margaret Island, and the Fisherman's Bastion, and the dome of the Coronation Church, and the amazing Hilton Inn—its great windows blazing bronze in the sunshine. "One of our new wonders, quite supplanting the old," he said with a bitter smile. The wind whipped Marianne's hair and her eyes filled involuntarily with tears. "You are a most unusual American, I must say, to prefer to stay elsewhere, in one of our own hotels," he added, with an embarrassed smile.

He then pointed out the enormous statue of the Soviet "Liberator." "It is a considerable artistic achievement, is it not?—making its impact so powerfully upon the senses, and then upon the soul. But they say that the statue of Lenin, in East Berlin, is even more magnificent."

His pronunciation of "magnificent" was so exotic, Marianne did not recognize the word at first.

Ottó continued: "But Lenin of course is a god, and must be built to scale. This liberator is only a commoner—hence his modest proportions."

He laughed, and his laughter turned into a painful spasm of coughing, and Marianne waited patiently until he recovered. His mirth wasn't altogether convincing, though the coughing was.

It was always the same: East European laughter disoriented Marianne because she never knew how to interpret it.

After this, Ottó's manner changed, and within a few minutes Marianne knew what he wanted of her.

Would she take a forty-page "analysis" of contemporary culture back to the States with her?—a soiled, dog-eared manuscript, in Hungarian, with a pseudonym on the title page. "You have only to mail it to the Index on Censorship," Ottó said quietly. "Or—if it wouldn't be an inconvenience—you might show it to some of your friends, in Washington and New York. A New York agent. . . ."

Marianne took the manuscript from Ottó, and weighed it in her hand. Despite the somewhat chill wind, that seemed to be blowing at her from all sides, her cheeks felt unpleasantly warm; she judged that, from the surprising degree of her chagrin, she must have been anticipating a sexual interest after all.

"I don't think I can," she said.

But he didn't seem to hear. He kept talking, and smiling, and leaning close, and stooping slightly, to peer into her face. His eyes were so dark as to appear black; the whites seemed unnaturally white.

He talked, he talked rapidly, and then again more calmly, daring to touch Marianne's arm, smiling and winking close to her face. He was part Jewish, Marianne must know that it was very, very hard, to be Jewish, in this part of Europe, his grandparents and other relatives had been shipped "to Germany" in March 1944 and not one survived. Now the Germans—that is to say, the West Germans—the former Nazis—were not only allowed to visit Hungary as tourists, but positively welcomed for their hard currency: which was the hardest currency in Europe. The Deutsch mark was prized even above the American dollar, did Marianne know the outrage that there were places in Budapest where Hungarian currency wasn't accepted!—and the old Nazis were driven about in their black Mercedes and the Hungarian lackeys bowed low hoping for tips in hard currency, the old Nazis even dined in splendor in the very best restaurants in the city, beautiful restaurants Ottó had never stepped into, did Marianne know the comedy that some of these restaurants were in buildings formerly used for German fortifications and Gestapo headquarters!—oh it was very amusing, it was very funny, Ottó agreed that one must laugh.

Before Marianne could express her sympathy, or commiserate with him, Ottó adroitly leapt away from that subject and began to denounce the Russians: who liked to pretend, in this part of the world, that the Germans had invented anti-Semitism. And what of the pathos of Poland, and East Germany, and Czechoslovakia.

And Rumania. Did Marianne know, the Rumanians were so frightened of "foreigners," that when he, Ottó, telephoned an old acquaintance in Bucharest, the man hung up immediately when he heard a "foreign" voice—! This had happened only the week before.

Yet the Hungarians were not much better, Ottó said. Now his olive-dark skin was suffused with blood, and there were flecks of saliva on his lips. The Hungarians—the Hungarians!—always at one another's throats—unable to agree—to unify—did Marianne know that during those weeks in 1956 there were more than fifty groups opposing the Russians! A tragic history, Ottó said angrily, a maddening history, the Turks, the Germans, the Russians, Hungarians, and Poles understand one another perfectly but it is an understanding of shame—a kinship of shame—

And now, Ottó said, for no reason, his visa had been refused to Japan, though he had visited Japan before, and England too, and Sweden, but not yet the States, he had no idea why his visa had been refused unless it had to do with his brother-in-law who was outspoken and troublesome and perhaps mentally disturbed, but how could that be Ottó's fault?—for they knew nothing of Ottó's secret thoughts, his secret "analysis," on which he had worked late at night for years, for five or six years, very late at night, his wife had no idea, his wife believed he was copyediting manuscripts for the journal, but no one knew, it was absolutely private, and a very crucial work, pertaining to the current situation in Hungary, and exposing the betrayals and corruption and outright crime, not just among the leaders but among the professional classes as well, and Ottó's own associates, did Marianne know how strange it was, how unbalancing, never to exactly know the degree of truth, of what was being said: mistaking truth for lies, and lies for truth, and misreading, and misinterpreting, in school Ottó had thought it was just school, but then the university was the same, and now his work, and his marriage! "It is very strange," he said, with a small twitching smile, "it is—a pavement always tilted, the floor of a room always at a slant, so that things roll off the table but you cannot quite see why—you stare and stare, but you cannot see—you too are standing off-balance—crooked—but then you ask yourself, is it a malady of the inner ear, the mechanism that controls balance, and therefore your own fault?—but you cannot know—and if a kindly person whispers the truth to you, how can you know that it is the truth—for you have so little practice! All your energy is drained, in not going mad!"

He had been planning this impassioned outburst, Marianne reasoned, since the first minute of their conversation the evening before. (They had been introduced by one of the embassy officials, at a crowded reception at the American ambassador's palatial residence in the Buda hills.) Yet, knowing now that Ottó desired her as nothing more than a function, a kind of conduit, Marianne felt a perverse belated interest in him as a man; as a physical presence. His moist dark eyes, his flushed skin, his overbearing manner, the heat of his breath, even his disheveled hair—which had, earlier, been combed across his head with a touching precision— appealed to her. And the fact too that he was married, and a few years younger than she, and conceived of himself in such desperate terms. . . .

The romance of East Europe, Marianne thought. The tacky, seedy, despairing glamour of lost causes; the air of the fantastical and the drab; the queer elation of the American, in striding through this world, as through a twilit world beyond the looking-glass. That Ottó desperately needed her, or someone with her privileges—that he attributed to her the power of working a perceptible difference in history—that he had not so much rebuffed her as a woman, as deified her, in another, less personal way: all this was enormously appealing.

Yes, Marianne said softly, backing away (for it was late: she had a luncheon engagement: her mind sped onward to a late-afternoon gathering at the residence of the deputy chief of mission whose wife, rumor had it, had left abruptly for the States, and with whom might she have dinner if she was very very fortunate, and careful?—and there was the peripheral hope, really a little girl's hope, that someone would rescue her from the shabby local hotel her *per diem* necessitated, and bring her across the Danube to the city's sole international hotel, the Hilton; for she hardly shared her companion's contempt for it, and in any case her excellent clothes, and her meticulously groomed beauty, demanded a more reasonable setting): yes, she murmured nervously, slipping the bulky manuscript into her bag, I understand, I know, it's very difficult for you, for people in your position, I'll do what I can, we are all very sympathetic in America, please don't worry, please don't be so upset, I'm deeply moved that you should trust me and of course I will guard your—

Ottó seized her hands and kissed them warmly. He too was so moved that, for several embarrassing seconds, he seemed unable to speak. Then he said: "You are so kind, Miss Beecher—so generous, so beautiful, so kind—I knew you would be—Americans are so kind—to help a person like myself—who is no one, who is nothing!—who can never hope to repay you as you deserve—"

Later, he gave her his card, and cautioned her against attaching it to the manuscript.

"Of course I wouldn't do that," Marianne said, somewhat offended.

On the long transatlantic flight from New York to Frankfurt Marianne had spent some hours trying to read a "classic" novella of the early nineteenth century, set in eastern Hungary: the queer, lush, slow-moving *Brigitta* by a German gothicist named Adalbert Stifter, of whom Marianne had never heard. (She had been encouraged to read this "beautiful" novella by an acquaintance who taught at Georgetown: It will help you to understand the Hungarian soul, he said.)

But Marianne found the prose all but unreadable.

The Hungarian landscape was described in painstaking detail—it seemed, in its vast outsized spaces and extraordinary terrain, *other-worldly*: a fairytale landscape. And the Hungarian characters were giants, in the extravagance of their emotions. Marianne, who judged herself skillful in the art of reading people, could not read *these* people; and felt some resentment. For why should anyone have imagined that she, Marianne Beecher, would care to read a German wanderer's overwrought impressions of the vast Hungarian steppes, and his tedious recounting of a visit to a castle improbably named Uwar?—and how could she take seriously a man's passion for a heroine who was not only no longer young, but so interminably *good*?

When she came to the story's climactic passage, the hero's *I had to go through the whole world until I learned that beauty lies in the heart and that I had left beauty at home within a heart* she shut the book irritably, and tossed it aside.

She wondered if, once one ventured out into the countryside, away from Budapest, the Hungarian people were still so primitive.

In her hotel room, waiting for the telephone to ring, she glanced hurriedly through Ottó's manuscript. Of course it was unreadable, it was in Hungarian. Marianne knew no more than a half-dozen words in Hungarian and she was always mispronouncing them. . . . The manuscript was dog-eared, and soiled, and inexpertly typed, on a machine whose i's and p's were breaking. The poor man had been touchingly naive, Marianne thought, to imagine that anyone could interest a "New York agent" in such a document, not even translated into English. But she could very easily mail it to the Index on Censorship, in London; she would ask someone at the embassy in Bonn to mail it out next week.

(Unless of course the customs officials discovered her with the manuscript on her way out of Hungary. She couldn't recall whether they had been lenient with her last time; or was she confusing Hungary with Czechoslovakia . . . ?)

She supposed that Ottó exaggerated the danger of his situation, as a means of exaggerating his significance. In this part of the world such self-deceptions were not unusual. All your energies are drained in not going mad, as he had said; or had that been another Hungarian . . . ?

The telephone rang and Marianne set the manuscript aside, and took care to place Ottó's card elsewhere—atop the cluttered bureau top with her cosmetics and a half-dozen other cards, given to her by Hungarians since her arrival. The cards were all of an identical size and texture, as if printed by the same press.

"The Red Army keeps peace in Europe."

The Embassy's director of public relations spoke with such a measured air of audacity that Marianne understood he frequently made this remark, and was frequently challenged on it. "Without the Russians," he continued, "—these absurd little countries would be at one another's throats, every border in dispute, every language group set against its neighbors. Hungarians—Rumanians—Czechs—Slovaks—Serbs—Yugoslavs—and all the rest. We know very well what would happen because it has happened so many times in the past. Subjugated peoples aren't saints," he con-

cluded, leaning gracefully over to fill Marianne's glass with white
wine, "—just ask the Jews."

If he had anticipated some lively opposition from the five or six
guests seated in the elegant living room of the residence of the deputy chief of mission, he must have been disappointed. No one dis-
puted his remark about the Red Army; and Marianne's friend
Tommy said, laughing, "Because the Jews are a subjugated people, or because the Jews aren't themselves saints—?"

They talked about anti-Semitism in Hungary, and in Poland
("Isn't Poland the very worst?"); and in Soviet Russia ("No—Soviet Russia is the worst"); and back in the States, on Long Island,
for instance, and in Washington. The director of public relations,
whose last post had been in Canada, told a lengthy and rather
nasty anecdote about anti-Semitism in Ottawa; and Tommy, who
was with the North American Studies Institute, and a guest at the
four-day conference Marianne was attending, told an equally
nasty anecdote about anti-Semitism in Paris. ("In some ways the
French are the worst," he said.)

"No, certainly not: Russia is the worst," said the deputy chief of
mission, who had been a journalist stationed in Moscow, for *News-
week*, before entering the foreign service. "I'm Jewish, and I know."

Naturally they deferred to him, because it was his house; and his
was the highest rank present.

"Yes, Russia is a sobering fact of life, or of history," the cultural
attaché granted, "—but we mustn't slight Germany. There is always Germany. As Stalin said—'Dictators come and go, but the
German people remain the same.' "

Everyone laughed heartily. The deputy chief of mission offered
Marianne a cigarette, and asked *her* opinion; but Marianne de-
murred, saying that the only Russians she had met—foreign service people, visiting writers and professors—had seemed quite
congenial.

"Oh yes, certainly, to *you*," the deputy chief of mission said with
a mirthless laugh.

Their conversation shifted to the conference, which had not yet
acquired any clear political overtones; and to a recent suicide off
Liberty Bridge, just below Gellért Hill, which would of course remain unreported. The suicide rate in Hungary was high as always;
also madness and alcoholism; but statistics were difficult to come

by. . . . They talked animatedly of the latest decline in the value of
the American dollar, in terms of the Deutsch mark; and to the *Her-
ald Tribune*'s "masochistic" coverage of the arrests of several American G.I.'s (all of them black), in Mainz, West Germany, as a
consequence of a drug raid by German police. "The Army does
need some action," one of the men said irritably.

Gathered for drinks were several embassy people, all men; and
an economist from Harvard, also male; and a Belgian named
Johan, a correspondent for *Le Soir*, who was assigned to cover the
conference but was finding it predictably dull. And there was
Tommy Cole, thirty-five, divorced, a specialist in Central European history; and Michel, an economist in his early forties associated with Credit Suisse. And the silent smiling Indonesian wife of
the director of public relations, a beautiful olive-skinned young
woman whose black hair was arranged in a stylish chignon, and
whose darkly bright gaze moved from man to man, never alighting
upon Marianne: the director's second wife, of course. (She had
doubtless set out to improve her life-style, as the saying went, by
way of sexual adventurism, while employed at the American embassy in Djakarta. Marianne knew without being told what had
happened: the supplanting of the old wife, the triumph of the new.
It was a familiar story. No one in this group would disapprove; and
Marianne was forced to grant the young woman a measure of respect, since director of public relations was a fairly decent rank.)

They talked for a while of serious things. Did they know, the
deputy chief of mission said, lowering his voice, that there was a
mass graveyard in one of the Budapest suburbs—probably in
Rákoskeresztur—"the prisoners' cemetery"—guarded by soldiers
and surrounded by barbed wire? In it were buried men and
women who were executed after the Soviets invaded, in November
of 1956; but none of the families of the executed is ever allowed to
visit the cemetery, and, in fact, the existence of the cemetery itself
is a state secret.

A few of the guests knew, the others didn't. Marianne said that
she hadn't known (though she remembered, dimly, having been
told of the cemetery once before); but it didn't surprise her.

"The Hungarians are such tragic people," she said.

Everyone concurred; they sipped their drinks in silence.

Then the conversation shifted, brightened. They spoke of the
Ambassador's brother, who had managed an excellent deal on a

Mercedes ($24,000 in cash, paid on the line in Stuttgart); they spoke of the reception at the Institute for Cultural Exchange, across the river in Pest (at which they would soon be due—was it already 4:30?); and how the new NATO meetings were being reported in Budapest; and whose wife had flown abruptly back home from an African post. ("Oh, *her*—poor Gladys—this is the second or third time she's cracked up," the cultural attaché said.) What was the latest news of the American hostages (businessmen, not foreign service) in that hijacked airliner in Nepal? And how did Marianne and Tommy like the Visegrád, where they had been taken for a very long lunch by several Hungarian cultural officers . . . ? (Lurid and glamorous, the judgment on the Visegrád was. But if you sought old Budapest, the Visegrád with its marble cupids, and gurgling fountains, and red plush settees, and liveried waiters, and gilt mirrors, and ubiquitous sinister plants was not to be missed.)

"How long will you be staying in Budapest, Marianne?" the deputy chief of mission asked casually. "A few days beyond the conference, I hope?"

"My hotel room is only booked until Tuesday," Marianne said.

The deputy chief of mission laughed, as if she had given a charmingly ambiguous answer.

Marianne's cheeks were slightly flushed from the wine. Her aureole of frizzed blond hair; her black silk blouse and beige suit, of fine light wool; her thin-strapped black shoes that showed her slender ankles to great advantage; her jewelry, her posture: everything about her was striking, really quite perfect. She was at the height of her beauty if not precisely (so she told herself) at the height of her life. (Many years ago, in another phase of that life, Marianne had been chosen May Queen in a competition that involved numerous beautiful and "talented" young women in several Midwestern states, including her home state of Missouri. Miss Marianne Beecher, Queen of the May, in an old-fashioned white chiffon gown with full rustling skirts, and tiny shoulder straps, and a bodice cut low enough to show the pale tops of her breasts, yet not so low as to be indecorous, unmaidenly. She would not win such a competition now, she knew, but she retained still, years later, a just perceptible air of the queenly and the romantic, which men often imagined no one else had ever discovered.)

"You really should stay a few days beyond the conference," the deputy chief of mission said, "—just to relax and see Budapest."

"Yes, certainly," Tommy said at once. "I'll be happy to take you around if I can stay myself."

Their conversation, warmed by the wine, stimulated by the smell of lilac, drifted onto various subjects. Everyone complimented the deputy chief of mission on his beautiful residence: the house was eighteenth century, with neoclassical ornamentation, and stately high ceilings and windows, and gleaming parquetry, and marble fixtures. The furniture was starkly white and modern, selected in Paris by the chief's wife, but property of the United States Government. ("Where has his wife gone?" Marianne asked the cultural attaché earlier; he said curtly, "Back to the States— she's a nice woman." Marianne did not want to inquire further. She would have heard, she supposed, if a divorce was imminent. The deputy chief of mission was an exceedingly handsome man in his early fifties, gray-haired, eager to laugh, and, it seemed, somewhat lonely; it would be a very foolish wife, Marianne thought, who stayed away too long.)

Tommy observed that one of the embassy drivers, a young Hungarian who knew virtually no English, and was completely oblivious to the chatter of his American passengers, wore cowboy boots with two-inch heels and a tight denim outfit with *Texas* stitched in back; and sported a long greasy quilled hairstyle of the sort that American boys, of a certain class, had worn in the Fifties. The Harvard economist asked about local help, domestic servants, wages, Catholic beliefs, superstitions; did it seem to them that "intellectual" Catholics in this part of Europe were serious about their faith, or simply making a defiant gesture vis-à-vis the Russians . . . ? Marianne said that the Hungarians weren't nearly so religious as the Poles; in any case she thought that perhaps religion might be both genuine, and an act of rebellion. "And it blends in seamlessly with anti-Semitism," she said—earning herself some surprised and admiring laughter from the men.

The cultural attaché worried that it was getting late, shouldn't they be starting out for the reception across the river?—but his superior, the deputy chief of mission, asked if anyone would like a last drink, maybe something stronger; he wouldn't mind a martini himself; it had been a long day. The rather mysterious gentleman named Michel (Was he French? English? Russian?) examined his

watch—and a handsome watch it was—and said lazily that they
had plenty of time; the Institute would be unpleasantly crowded,
the usual assortment of Communist hacks and hangers-on, why
should *they* hurry? "Far more comfortable where we are," he said.

Marianne asked the men generally whether things were tight in
Budapest—Were people being followed and harassed, visas refused, that sort of thing?—and the public relations man said he
didn't *think* so, Budapest was still the favored city, the most Western of the cities; consider all the business the Hilton was doing,
after all. (The Hilton, in Budapest!—and in partnership with the
Hungarian government, of all remarkable coups.) Plenty of foreign
currency pouring in, including the Deutsch mark. . . . They talked
of various currencies. The American dollar, and the English
pound, and the French franc, and the Hungarian forint, and the
Polish zloty ("now *there's* a sick Polish joke," one of them said). The
Harvard economist mentioned that he had once attended a conference in Warsaw, and one of his hosts, a professor at the University
of Warsaw, had asked him if he might take a manuscript of his out
of the country and try to get it published in the United States: all
very awkward, of course, and embarrassing, because though he
had wanted to help the man (of course) he was quite frankly afraid
of being apprehended. "What did you do, finally?" the deputy
chief of mission asked; but the economist's shoulder shrug was ambiguous.

India was mentioned. The cultural attaché said he'd been stationed at Nepal for three years, and virtually everyone he encoun-
tered wanted help of some kind—visas to the States, jobs in the
States, favors from the States, you name it. "A nation of beggars,"
he said contemptuously. Marianne thought she saw the Indonesian
woman's expression shift subtly; but she couldn't be sure. The cultural attaché was saying that India's "higher consciousness" was a
lot of crap: he knew of young brides who were burned to death by
their husbands and mothers-in-law for failing to supply, say, a
scooter or an extra television set, as part of the post-dowry.

The deputy chief of mission agreed vehemently. He thought of
India as a nation of wood ticks; you had simply to walk carelessly
about, and they swarmed up your legs.

Everyone laughed. The deputy chief of mission asked again if
anyone wanted a martini: there were lemons in the refrigerator as

far as he knew. Unfortunately his housekeeper was off for the afternoon; and his wife—well, his wife was visiting her family in Virginia. But he could make a first-rate martini, certainly, wouldn't anyone care to join him? The cultural attaché said yes; the Harvard economist said yes; and Michel; and Tommy. And Marianne rose gracefully to her feet in her precarious high-heeled shoes, and volunteered to slice lemons: why didn't the deputy chief of mission make the drinks and she would prepare the lemons . . . ? She felt domestic, even wifely. She felt, suddenly, wonderfully romantic.

Through the high arched doorway, along the corridor, Marianne could hear the men talking. A familiar but always intriguing subject: which posts were now desirable, which were not. Moscow was dull and depressing though in the giddy days of Khrushchev it had been quite otherwise (so the deputy chief of mission said, with a bemused headshake: he'd been a reporter at the time, and loved it). Berlin was claustrophobic; the Wall could make sensitive people ill; and East Germany was unspeakable. Stockholm would be a marvelous city except for all those dark freezing months. And security was tight, very tight. (The West German Embassy, next door to the U.S. Embassy, had been terrorized a few years before, and everyone was still jittery. In Sweden Americans had "guilty" consciences regarding Chile, Argentina, Guatemala, Salvador. . . .) Attractive posts, like Rome, could be dangerous; safe posts, like Bali, Canada, Iceland, were maddeningly dull. Who could bear to push papers in Brussels, or in Geneva, or in Bonn . . . ? There was a considerable blow to the ego in coming from, for instance, East Germany to London, despite London's richness, for in England nothing one did mattered greatly while in East Germany virtually anything one did, no matter how small, how casual, could matter immensely. ("You can change someone's life by making a telephone call," the director of public relations said, licking his lips. "You can save people. You can punish them.")

Ah, the nostalgia for those hardship posts!—the fond memories! Evacuated from Baghdad (the U.S. flag carefully folded and carried beneath one's arm); evacuated from Cambodia . . . Iran . . . Lebanon. Threatened by Red terrorists in Rome; carried up the Amazon in a skiff; assigned to a Georgian outpost with a wife and infant in the dead of a Russian winter. . . . Many were the tales, delicious the recalled adventures, often centering upon a marriage: its breakup or its strengthening. Marianne was intrigued by these stories though she had heard most of them before.

In the kitchen Marianne found several lemons in the refrigerator—not entirely fresh, but sufficient for her purposes.

The residence dated back to the eighteenth century but its kitchen had been remodeled along smartly conventional American lines: Formica and textured plastic and an olive-green stove and refrigerator to match, a glossy page out of a General Electric brochure. Through the half-open window Marianne saw a clump of rich dark lilacs and a fifteen-foot-high stone fence with spikes and scattered shards of glass along its top.

Wine-warmed, her coordination was slightly off, but she managed to locate a fairly sharp paring knife and a bread board, and set industriously to work. She hummed to herself, thinking of Tommy (who was not yet her lover though he behaved with such excited gallantry toward her, perhaps the others thought he was); and of the deputy chief of mission with his inkwell eyes crinkled in good humor and his sweet boyish smile (though the smile surely was misleading: he was known in the service as ambitious if not ruthless); and the attractive Belgian journalist (whose name she seemed to have forgotten); and the yet more attractive Michel who had stared almost rudely at her through his amber-tinted glasses (Michel whose accentless English might be said to be—odd). And there was a Fulbright fellow resident spending the year in Budapest whom she had met the evening before, who had wanted to see her again; and someone from the *Times* whose by-line she recalled; and that youthful Japanese businessman who was staying at the Hilton, who had paid her such lavish, rather silly compliments. Suddenly she thought of Ottó: had she remembered to bring along his card, so that she might ask one of the embassy men about him . . . ? Perhaps it was risky to have left his manuscript in her hotel room but it was too heavy to carry with her.

She imagined a conversation with the deputy chief of mission on the subject of Ottó and a manuscript to be smuggled out of Hungary by Marianne Beecher of Washington, D.C. How did she know the man wasn't a Communist bent upon entrapping her, do you want to get us all into trouble?—and Marianne's faltering stubborn reply, But Ottó is different, he really *is* different, I would stake my reputation on it. Something about the man's eyes. . . .

She heard laughter from the other room.

She was ready to return with her various lemon slices when someone entered the kitchen behind her. She heard the floorboards gently creaking; but no one spoke. It might be Tommy playfully tiptoeing up behind her . . . it might be the deputy chief of mission come to see what was taking her so long . . . it might be the cultural attaché on an errand, sent to fetch more Brazil nuts (the men had been eating them rather gluttonously) or cocktail napkins. Marianne didn't turn but she saw a tall ghostly reflection in an aluminum door to one of the cupboards: tall: which (fortunately) ruled out the director of public relations who was hardly more than her height. She couldn't identify the man but she chose not to turn in surprise; instead she pretended to be cutting a final lemon slice, nervously aware of her pretty small-boned hands . . . and her perfect fingernails which were painted a pale frosted pink . . . and her numerous rings and bracelets (perhaps she wore too many but she loved them all: each item of jewelry was distinctive, each represented a certain pinnacle of achievement, gifts from admirers, gifts from Marianne to herself, the exquisite white-gold Swiss watch with diamonds for numerals . . . the opal ring edged with sapphires . . . the antique pearl ring . . . and the rest). She continued to hum to herself as the anonymous man approached her from behind. He was making no effort to walk softly, he wasn't trying to alarm or surprise her, it might be said to be a romantic gesture, gracefully executed.

The first kiss would be delicate as a bone-china teacup of the kind one might unwittingly crush between his fingers, holding it too tight.

The man slid his arm lightly across her shoulders. And may have murmured a question. Marianne shivered with pleasure at the very casualness of his touch. She might have been a wife, he might have been a husband, how fragrant the lilacs blooming in the sunshine just outside the window, how tart, how bracing, the smell of fresh-cut lemon, and her hands *were* beautiful, and her rings and bracelets and her black silk blouse and designer suits. . . . Marianne drew a breath of sheer exhilaration that she was the very person she was: Marianne Beecher and no one else.

Perhaps it was only Tommy after all, Marianne thought as she lay the paring knife carefully down, and wiped her fingers on a napkin. (He had playfully nuzzled her neck in the back of the embassy limousine while they were being driven here, after their long giddy lunch; but they were not yet lovers, he was being presumptuous, from Marianne's pragmatic point of view it wasn't completely settled that they would become lovers.) It might well be the deputy chief of mission, whose kitchen this was, after all, and whose rank was very high: just below Ambassador. Yet what if it was the mysterious Michel with his curt clipped manner and his reluctant smile. . . . She hoped it was not the cultural attaché who was clearly a very nice bright hard-working man but too earnest for Marianne's taste, and of a rank she found difficult to take seriously.

He gripped her shoulder; Marianne instinctively closed her eyes, and rested her head back against him as they kissed; and immediately she felt a splendid rush of emotion, hazy, sweet, familiar, she was sixteen years old, she was fourteen, even thirteen, being kissed in a doorway . . . being kissed surreptitiously at a party . . . breathless in a corner, her heart beating hard, her eyes shut. . . . She might have been even younger, ten or eleven, practicing kisses against the mirror in her bedroom, secret and daring.

It was a gentle kiss, experimental, improvised. Marianne responded with a small frisson of surprise, a semblance of surprise. She was touching his arm lightly, she hoped she had wiped off the lemon juice, how sweet to be approached with such tact and delicacy, in so gentlemanly a fashion, she thought suddenly of the Hungarian editor and herself walking on Gellért Hill, and along the Danube, the warm moist sunshine heavy with the smell of lilacs, so many romantic couples, lovers, the young ones amorous as puppies, but there were middle-aged lovers too, Marianne was embarrassed to see a man and a woman in their fifties, pressed close together on a stone bench, kissing with such frank and impassioned energy that they must have been oblivious of their surroundings . . . and Ottó said in an undertone, Romance is desperation and we are a desperate people—we laugh a great deal too.

Now she felt the kiss deepen, and a feathery-light sensation ran through her body, her belly, her loins, a sensation familiar enough but always in a way new, and reassuring, and impersonal; and in another second or two the tenor of the kiss would change and become more serious: the man would part her lips, his tongue would prod at hers, his teeth grind lightly against hers, they would still be smiling but the kiss would have become serious, and Marianne's plans for the rest of the day—was this Saturday?—might have to be substantially altered.

She had come to Washington, D.C., at the age of twenty-three, and had not been so romantically-minded, at that time. She had been ambitious, though no more ambitious than the young or youngish or middle-aged men with whom she had had friendships; and once—after her twenty-ninth birthday—she had calculated on marriage, with a Justice Department official of high rank whose marriage had been deteriorating, rather publicly, for years: but Marianne's calculation alarmed her, for being so wrong. And the emotion she had squandered after the break-up—some three or four months of angry tears, and insomnia, and periods of depression as capricious and unpredictable as a windblown spring sky—had alarmed her too, for being so profitless.

So she changed her job, acquiring through a valuable connection (who owed her a favor or two, for her discretion as much as for her amiability) an excellent position with the National Science Education Foundation, East Europe division, so many blocks from her former job that all the restaurants, cocktail lounges, and pubs were different; and nearly all the faces new.

In her early thirties Marianne discovered in herself a limitless capacity for romance. It might have had something to do with her frequent travels; and the charming gifts pressed upon her, as "samples" or "souvenirs" or "mementos"; and her wonderfully intense, and interrupted, friendships with her fellow citizens abroad who were, like Marianne Beecher, more or less in constant motion. (The foreign service employees were never assigned to any country for more than three years and, though their frequent moves disturbed them initially, they soon came to be a source of stimulation and even reassurance: for nothing mattered, or in any case mattered greatly.) Sometimes Marianne complained with an air of melancholy sincerity that her life moved too quickly, the pace was vertiginous, and all the more accelerated by the fact that others' lives, similarly paced, intersected constantly with hers; sometimes she even declined a tour abroad, and stayed home for as long as six

months, before becoming restless. But what was quite like the
queer intoxicating air of suspension, of a journey behind the "Iron
Curtain"?—the term itself, corny and endearing, evocative of romance? She loved the embassy limousines driven by handsome
"native" drivers in uniform; she loved the crowded receptions in
ambassadors' residences that had been, not many years ago, palatial Fascist headquarters; and the lavish bouquets awaiting her, in
her hotels; and the long luncheons, the innumerable toasts at dinner, the secret meetings with dissidents—pouchy-eyed gentlemen
in ill-fitting suits, living in furnished rooms, subsisting on translators' fees, in exile in their own countries.

The air of seedy intrigue, in the second-rate local hotels, did not
displease her; nor did the antiquated elevators, the cavernous dining rooms in which no one ate, the frayed velvet settees, the badly
worn carpets, the waitresses with their tight-curled hair and lip-
sticked lips and cheap high heels. Bellboys who offered to change
money with the breathless air of offering an illicit pleasure—telephones that rang and jangled during the night, with an exuberant
life of their own—desk clerks who stared with startled lust—Party
members who made a show of behaving like commoners—university people and translators and editors and scientists and writers
and "humanists" of every variety who knew nothing first-hand of
the United States except that it was paradise, for all its lurid failings, and nearly as hard to enter. And there were, too, upon occasion, in these very cities, extraordinary international hotels where
German and English were briskly spoken, where every room contained a compact refrigerator well-stocked with drink, and room
service could be relied upon for caviar of the kind Marianne had
developed a taste for, and excellent pâtés, and champagne, and
eggs benedict prepared at midnight. If, gazing down from her
hotel room in one of these resplendent towers, Marianne could see
queues of drab-clothed women waiting for stores to open, or if it
suddenly occurred to her, seeing very young or very old cleaning
maids pushing carts piled high with linens and towels and food-
encrusted plates, that the great hotels were staffed by slave labor,
she did not fail to absorb the pathos of the situation: for her imagination had become nervously sensitive with the passage of years.
That she was nearly always under surveillance by the secret police,
or could imagine herself so, rarely upset her, for, with her visa, she

was never in any real danger of arrest unless the political situation changed abruptly; but there was, nonetheless, a certain indefinable melancholy associated with such visits, which afflicted Marianne with the force of nostalgia. How can you bear to travel in those tragic countries, acquaintances asked, isn't it frightening, isn't it depressing?—and Marianne gravely replied: But someone must do it, after all we can't abandon those people to the Russians.

It had taken Marianne only a few years to discover that love affairs, however gratifying in other respects, were "romantic" only at the very start. With the air of an experienced theoretician she had come to see that the first sexual union, though passionate, and desired, and usually pleasurable, already marked the end of the romantic phase, and initiated the participants into another, marked by physical compulsions of various degrees of intensity. Erotic sensation, fixed so obviously in the body, shared the body's fate, of succumbing to necessity; and necessity was always tiresome.

It was the first kiss, the first irrevocable gesture of intimacy, and proprietary claim, that constituted, in a sense, the climax of romance; and the first kiss that had acquired, over the years, in Marianne's imagination, a somewhat numinous and even sacred value. It was innocent, it was astonishingly bold, it was warm and tactile and yet hardly more than symbolic!—and it could not be too highly prized. Or was it, Marianne sometimes wondered, the first significant *gaze* that passed between her and a man, heavy with erotic meaning, almost intolerably exciting in all that it promised, or hinted at, or threatened?—this gaze, this exchange of looks, that constituted the pinnacle of romance: for she had experienced looks from men that penetrated her to the very marrow of her being, and left her dazed, and baffled, and weak, and, in a sense, obliterated. And stricken by the realization that no physical gesture, following such promise, could be equal to it. (It sometimes happened that Marianne accepted cards from men, and slips of paper with their names and telephone numbers on them, and, at the end of a crowded day, back in her room, she would arrange everything on her bed, to deliberate over whom to telephone at once, whom to forestall, whom to flatter while eluding, whom to erase from consideration altogether. Pondering such possibilities, examining the names and trying to match them with faces, Marianne amused herself by wondering if, perhaps, in a manner of speaking, the secret height of romance hadn't already been passed—and a more predictable phase begun. For what, after all, was the range of experience left to her?)

Warm and playfully chaste at the start, the kiss had suddenly become more forceful: a man's kiss, a proprietary kiss, leaving both participants breathless, and Marianne's slender neck somewhat strained. Of course it was the deputy chief of mission, of course it would be this gentleman, and none of the others, for Marianne stood in his kitchen, in his house, and his rank was estimable, and he must be very lonely with his wife back in the States, and no hostess to oversee his household.

"Hello," he said, "I thought I'd come out to help," and Marianne said, "I'm very happy that you did," and he said, "I was afraid you wouldn't know where to find things, in a strange kitchen," and Marianne said, laughing, "I don't have any trouble finding things—and it's a very American kitchen."

"When did he give it to you?"

"The other day—no, it was this morning."

"Let me see it."

"It's in Hungarian. It's all in Hungarian."

"I can read a little Hungarian."

"I don't think I can, I mean I don't think I should give it to you: I told him I would keep this all secret."

"He shouldn't have asked you to smuggle it out. He knows better."

"He seemed desperate."

"Marianne, they're *all* desperate," the deputy chief of mission said impatiently, "—or want to give that impression to foreigners like you."

He was standing naked in Marianne's hotel room, near the bureau, glancing through Ottó's manuscript and unwittingly blocking Marianne's passage to the bathroom. Unclothed, he was shorter, more firmly fleshed, than Marianne might have predicted.

"I'm sure he was sincere," Marianne said. "I'm sure the manuscript is authentic. In any case the Hungarian authorities aren't terribly suspicious, are they?—I shouldn't have any difficulty—"

"What is the man's name? Isn't it on the manuscript?"

"No, of course not. He isn't that foolish."

"What's his name?"

"I can't tell you."

"I might very well know him, I know most of the dissidents."

"I don't think he's known as a dissident. He has been working on the manuscript late at night, he told me, and even his wife doesn't know, and—"

"Marianne, what is his name?"

"I can't tell you!—that would be betraying him."

"He might very well be an *agent provocateur*—have you thought of that?"

"Of course I've thought of that; but he certainly isn't."

"How the hell do you know?"

"I *know*. The way he spoke with me, his voice . . . his eyes. . . ."

The deputy chief of mission snorted with laughter. But he didn't appear to be smiling. He said: "I suppose he kissed your hand and assured you he didn't at all resent you for being an American—not at all."

"He didn't kiss my hand," Marianne said, her face reddening. (She couldn't recall if he had: probably so, her hand had been liberally kissed in recent days.) "I can vouch for his sincerity, really. . . ."

"Is he at the University?—is he with one of the foundations?—is he an editor?—a translator?"

Marianne hesitated. "He's an editor," she said.

"Yes, and what is his name?"

"I think it's Ottó—Ottó something. I can't pronounce the family name."

"Do you have his card?"

"No, I don't think so."

"Of course you have his card—he must have given it to you."

"I don't really think he *did*. . . ."

The deputy chief of mission ignored her and began to search through the clutter of cards Marianne had accumulated. She thought his behavior impertinent—outrageous. He was saying: "You should either give this manuscript to me, or dispose of it very carefully. I certainly can't advise you to smuggle it out of Hungary."

"But I promised the poor man. . . ."

"A professional woman like yourself!—taking the risk of being caught, arrested. I wouldn't be at all surprised if the man was a police agent."

"I'm sure he *isn't*. He's simply a very troubled man, there seems to be something wrong with his marriage as well, he's Jewish and that's probably part of the problem here in Budapest," Marianne said quickly. "Look, please, those are my private things: what are you doing?"

"Suppose the manuscript did get translated, and published?" the deputy chief of mission said vaguely, pawing through Marianne's papers, "—Who do you think would trouble to read it? Hungary hasn't any riveting news for us, a quarter-century after 1956. Is this his card? Lotz Ottó?"

"Lotz *Ottó*?"

"The name is reversed in Hungarian. —Yes, this must be his card."

"Put it back, please," Marianne said, laughing angrily. "You really have no right. . . ."

He turned to her, smiling, exasperated. "I'm only thinking of you, dear Marianne," he said softly. He let the card fall to the bureau top. "I want to stop you from making a most unprofessional blunder."

"But if you met Ottó you'd feel differently!" Marianne said. Her own words stirred her: she even clasped her hands in a gesture of entreaty. "He isn't any more than twenty-eight or -nine years old and already he's turning gray—his shoulders are stooped—he has such beautiful eyes but there are deep creases in his forehead—"

"Ottó Lotz. I don't really think I know the name."

"I simply can't betray him," Marianne said. "I feel that I've already betrayed him. . . ."

"How? By telling me his name? *I'm* certainly not going to turn him in," the deputy chief of mission said, staring. "My only concern is for you. And for the embassy of course—since you're associated with us."

"But I'm not in your employ, am I."

"It might be argued that we're both in the same employ."

"I *can't* betray him—"

"All I advise, Marianne, is that you dispose of the manuscript carefully. Detach the pages, throw them away in various spots, rip

them up but not too conspicuously—would you like me to take it
to the office, to feed into the shredder?"

"Would he really be in such danger if the manuscript was discovered?" Marianne said doubtfully. "This is Hungary, after all.
Not Russia."

"Don't tell *me* where we are!" the deputy chief of mission said,
laughing, trying to take Marianne's hands in his. He leaned
forward to kiss her. "I'm thinking of you, dear. Not Ottó what's-
his-name."

Marianne did not respond to the kiss but did not shrink from it
either. She said sullenly: "Please don't be solicitous about me—you
hardly know me."

"All I suggest is that you dispose of the manuscript discreetly;
and forget about your Hungarian friend with the beautiful eyes."

"I can't do that," Marianne said. "I can't forget him."

"Can't you?—really?—an experienced woman like yourself?"

After this exchange Marianne decided that she liked the deputy
chief of mission considerably less than she had anticipated. She
caught the knowing, slightly hectoring tone of his last remark; and
though he was naturally eager to see her again, that very evening,
in fact, she suspected that the peak of romance was already past.

In any case the telephone was ringing. It began to ring ten minutes after the deputy chief of mission left, just as Marianne stepped
out of the shower.

It was Michel, who insisted upon taking her to a Mass at Coronation Church, close to the Hilton; it was an experience no visitor to
Budapest should miss, he said.

In the enormous, rather airless church Marianne felt a mild and
not altogether unpleasant sense of vertigo. She slipped her arm
through Michel's, she gripped it tight, looking about with widened
admiring eyes. The high vaulted ceiling . . . the ornately carved
altars . . . the baroque fussiness of the colorful designs (zigzag,
curling, twisting, spiraling patterns in reds, golds, greens, blues)
that covered virtually every square inch of the walls. . . . It was a
dream city, a nightmare of sorts, an illustration in an old-fashioned
children's book. . . . She stared, trying to absorb as much as possible. Here were fifteen-foot-high candles; here the air was heavy,

giddy, with incense; giant pillars supported the ceiling high above; a remarkable glowering light shone from the rose window; all was enchanted . . . but at the same time noisy, crowded, confused. There were too many people in the church. The air was stale, stifling. Despite the fact that the service was well under way tourists—German, it seemed—continued to talk without lowering their voices; they even pushed aggressively against the *Turist Stop* sign in the center aisle.

Marianne tried to listen closely to the elderly priest's sermon, incomprehensible as it was. What a torrent of Hungarian!—and how very queer, his quavering singsong voice! She thought his vestments magnificent, if slightly ludicrous: he wore a robe fashioned for a much larger man, stiff with gold ornamentation and trimmed in a very bright crimson; and a tall hat similarly trimmed in gold, perched atop his swaying head. His movements were slow and pompous; perhaps arthritic. His voice was droning, singing, soporific—an elderly child's voice.

Michel grew restless after a few minutes but Marianne ignored him; she wanted to immerse herself in the service, in the experience of attending Mass at the famous Coronation Church . . . she *was* an American after all, she *was* a tourist of sorts, why should she be cheated of this opportunity? But there was much that distracted. Not only the puppetlike motions of the costumed old man, but the grotesque red velvet canopy over the pulpit (which must have been ten feet high); and the carved pulpit itself, so profusely decorated with geometric designs of various shapes (diamonds, squares, rectangles, distorted triangles, elongated circles) that she felt her vision begin to blotch, as if she were being hypnotized. She tried to keep awake, alert; felt some perverse gratitude for all the milling about, the mutterings, whisperings, intrusions; tried to focus on the painted statues, which must have been centuries old—a Virgin Mary, a plump Christ Child, a bluish-skinned Jesus Christ on the cross, arrested in a moment of anguish, eyeballs turned up (Marianne did not want to think *comically*) in his head. The spectacle was barbaric, extravagant, incomprehensible—a feast for the eye if not for the mind.

Marianne grew drowsy and saw the massive pulpit floating like a gondola, a jeweled throne, rising above the congregation. It might have contained a king of legend, even a god, and not an el-

Joyce Carol Oates

derly Hungarian man with a high-pitched and slightly peevish voice.

Afterward Marianne asked Michel what the sermon had been about, but Michel shrugged his narrow shoulders and said he didn't know. He had picked up a word here and there—he knew some Hungarian, not much—but he hadn't been able to fit the words together. The name of the Virgin had been mentioned numerous times, if that was any hint.

Marianne thought it very rude of the tourists to prowl about in the aisles like that, taking pictures and not troubling to lower their voices. She had heard Americans as well as Germans. Again Michel shrugged and said: "It's the tourists, actually, who keep Coronation Church open and functioning, didn't you see the signs begging for contributions?"

In a polished ebony-black taxi Michel carried Marianne and her several pieces of luggage across the Danube, from her somber Hungarian hotel in Pest to the magnificent Hilton above the river. It was one of the wonders of New Budapest—an American hotel built in and upon the ruins of a medieval monastery, whose massive plate-glass windows were tinted bronze, mirroring the sun. You could look out of the Hilton at the Hungarian parliament buildings across the river but the illusion was that no one could look in.

Very close by was the historic Coronation Church, of course; and, even closer, the historic Fisherman's Bastion. In a nearby square, King Stephen in a manly pose on horseback; and a large, rather busy memorial to victims of the bubonic plague of a bygone century. There were many colorful gypsy restaurants, there were outdoor cafés. The Hilton boasted several boutiques that sold "authentic" peasant costumes.

Michel's reservation at the Hilton extended through the next week, prepaid, courtesy of Credit Suisse. Unfortunately he had to leave early Monday morning; but he hoped Marianne would stay on for a few days, using his room, and charging anything—well, virtually anything—she wished.

"I'll be discreet," Marianne said, laughing. "Don't worry."

"I don't worry," Michel said.

Marianne thought it puzzling that Michel's last name was Holland and that he traveled with a British passport. His English was accentless, uninflected. Yet she couldn't quite believe in him as a British citizen; during their first evening together she made the tactical blunder of saying that he spoke English flawlessly . . . and he said, leaning forward to kiss her, "And so do you, Miss Beecher."

He dressed with care and taste in suits custom-made in London; his style was conservative, with small touches of fashion—a floral necktie, a pastel striped shirt. He owned several pairs of amber-tinted glasses with differing frames: tortoise shell, aluminum, black plastic. He gave Marianne the impression of being a man of leisure but in fact he was traveling constantly—twelve months of the year, as he said, with satisfacton—and it suited him. He told her that he too felt very much at home in East Europe. "So long, of course, as one travels on a British passport."

Though Michel was a British citizen his home, so to speak, seemed to be in Geneva at the present time. He had once worked for the World Bank . . . he had once been involved in OPEC nego-tiations . . . many years ago (he happened to mention) he had studied at the London School of Economics. He may even have married, he may even have had children, Marianne didn't press for answers. (Answers were always problematic; one might be de-luded into accepting them at face value. And, in any case, they often provoked questions in return.)

Marianne amused herself thinking he was Soviet-trained, hence his precise and rather mechanical English. He was with the K.G.B., most likely, not on a mission but returning from one.

But it was too extreme a fantasy, too romantic. And K.G.B. agents, in Marianne's limited experience, were never so urbane and attractive as Michel Holland.

Marianne herself was looking exceptionally good these days. Her blond hair, her flawless skin, her beauty queen style. . . . Simply having moved across the wide Danube from noisy Pest to scenic Buda, a bouquet of lilacs in her arms, had heightened her spirits considerably.

With certain Americans, an admiring Pole had once told Marianne, the happiness of the soul floods directly into the face.

Michel didn't trouble to compliment Marianne on the beauty of her face or her body, as if assuming she knew very well who, or what, she was. He himself was tall, trim, vigorous, with hard wiry muscles in his shoulders and thighs in particular. Marianne noted that his right arm was slightly larger than his left—from playing squash, she assumed. "All the men I know play squash, in Washington and at their posts," she said. "It's touching what fanatics American men are, in their sports."

"Yes," said Michel. "They must have some constants in their lives." A moment later he said, lazily: "That *is* the word, isn't it?—'constants'? Or 'constant?' "

In bed, guilty as children and laughing quite a bit, they talked of the conference across the river; the usual Communist hacks and informers; and here and there—yes, they *did* exist—a "real" Hungarian, just as there were "real" Poles, "real" Czechs. They talked of the deputy chief of mission who was in line (so scuttlebutt would have it: Michel had heard the rumor in Bonn) for an important Ambassadorship, assuming nothing disruptive happened in Budapest. Michel said that he hoped there would not be "awkward feelings" between them, as a consequence of his and Marianne's "sudden friendship"—the three of them would be meeting now and then, in Europe and elsewhere.

Marianne observed that the deputy chief of mission was married, after all. In any case he was a thoroughly professional man.

Later, they were awakened by a maniacal tolling of bells from the Coronation Church nearby. And all the other bells of the city, it seemed, joined in. Exuberant—gay—childlike—clamorous— wildly triumphant: Marianne had never heard anything quite like it.

She asked Michel why bells rang so loudly every day at noon, was something special being celebrated?—and he told her that the Hungarians were honoring the most recent military victory their army had had, many centuries ago, in their defeat of the Turkish army.

In the luxurious fluorescent-lit bathroom with its tiled walls and its fixtures of simulated marble, Marianne took the opportunity of glancing through her friend's passport as he slept. She saw, to her surprise, that he *was* a British citizen . . . born 1936, in London. He had newly stamped visas for Czechoslovakia, Bulgaria, Yugoslavia,

Rumania, and East Germany, as well as for Hungary and Poland. The photograph showed his likeness, stern about the mouth, unsmiling. *Michel Louis Holland, brown hair, brown eyes, six feet three inches tall, weighing one hundred eighty-five pounds, required to wear corrective lenses. . . .*

Though Marianne was extremely careful about the bathroom light as she left, and didn't even risk closing the door, she had the idea that Michel was awake and watching her through partly closed eyes. She had the idea, even, that he might well expect her to acknowledge the situation—for Marianne was, after all, a much-traveled young woman, hardly an amateur. But she chose to say nothing until morning. Then, after they had made love, she laughed, and showed her perfect teeth, and said: "You have a beautiful passport, Michel, it does you credit."

"Yours is beautiful too," Michel said.

Only by accident did Ottó's dog-eared manuscript become a topic of conversation between them. Michel happened upon it while searching through Marianne's smallest suitcase, for a jar of face cream. (Marianne was taking a luxurious bath, immersed in lavender-scented bath beads provided by the Hilton; she had asked Michel to bring her the jar, having forgotten about the manuscript.)

"What is this, dear Marianne?—'The Bringer of the End: A New Analysis'—and no name attached. *Very* weighty, and very badly typed: the author is perhaps a friend of yours?" Michel asked, amused. "A Hungarian comrade, perhaps?"

He was standing in the doorway, glancing through the manuscript. Marianne's breasts were hidden by clumps of tiny frothy bubbles but she felt shy nonetheless. She also felt a small thrill of alarm—could Michel read Hungarian? But no one could read Hungarian.

Afterward, when Marianne was dressed, she asked him, casually: " 'The Bringer of the End,' did you say?—is that the title? But what does it mean? Do you read Hungarian?"

"Hardly," Michel said.

"But what does the title mean?"

"I haven't any idea," Michel said. He was combing his hair carefully, regarding himself in the enormous bureau mirror. "Who gave you the manuscript?"

"Oh—someone. No one. A man I met at the conference."

"A scientist of some kind?—works for one of the science journals?"

"I really don't know," Marianne said. "He took me up to Gellért Hill to show me the city, he seems to be a very troubled person, I felt sorry for him, I wanted to help him . . . want to help him." She paused, and laughed, and said: "He told me I might show it to a New York literary agent."

Michel laughed too. He showed no further interest in the manuscript, which he had returned to Marianne's suitcase, exactly as he'd found it.

He hugged her about the hips, almost too hard. "A handsome young Hungarian, yes? Most likely a Jew? Was he a satisfactory lover, or were you bored? Dear Marianne, I suspect you are easily bored."

"Not at all," Marianne said.

"Yes, I suspect your mind drifts—wanders—moves along to the next city, ponders over the accommodations. Unless someone pays scrupulous attention to you. Extremely scrupulous attention."

Marianne laughed breathlessly, steeling herself against whatever the man would do to her—as a lover he was remarkably inventive, tireless, rather without mercy.

"*Extremely* scrupulous attention," he said, smiling.

He took her to a gypsy restaurant called Mátyás Cellar, where they had rich Hungarian food, and drank a good deal of Hungarian wine. He took her to the Ferenc Erkel Theatre in Republic Square, where, though they greatly admired the dancing (a modern dance with lively "peasant" influences) they chose not to return after the first intermission. In a somber-lit café in Pest they kissed, and drank Hungarian beer, and, from time to time Michel slipped his fingers through Marianne's so that she felt, with both surprise and pleasure, how unusually strong his fingers were.

There was a sweetly melancholy mood about them since Michel had to fly out to Prague on Monday morning. Prague, that most melancholy of cities. And Marianne was on her way to Bonn. She said: "I'll miss you, Budapest will be terribly empty without you."

Michel laughed almost loudly. He doubted, he said, that she would be lonely since there were always telephone messages in the mailbox for their room . . . appearing as if by magic on the very day Marianne moved to the Hilton. (The deputy chief of mission had called several times, of course, asking Marianne to call him back. And there was "T," and "D," and someone named Carl whom she couldn't place: surely not Carl Walser to whom she had finally been forced to be rude, back in Warsaw . . . ? And there was that funny little Japanese businessman, his accent so peculiar, his manner so intense, Marianne hadn't quite grasped the nature of his business: oil, or education?—finances? By chance his hotel room was only a few doors down from hers and Michel's, on the sixth floor of the Hilton.)

"Well—I'll miss you too," Michel conceded, squeezing her fingers in his.

Marianne couldn't resist asking him again what "The Bringer of the End" might mean.

So, the afternoon before he left, Michel took her to the Nemzeti Múzeum to show her a crude statue of the hooded dwarf Telesphorus. He was a mythological creature of Roman origin whose mission it was to escort the dead to the underworld. He has an ugly little puss, Marianne said, touching his pug nose. Telesphorus crouched atop a red marble sarcophagus, of a badly faded and crumbled stone. It was difficult to take him or his function seriously in the bright clinical glare of the room, amidst schoolchildren and camera-toting tourists.

"So you see, Marianne," Michel said, "—your nameless friend imagines himself a very dangerous fellow indeed. He writes in the 'last days' of an era. He means to usher in the end."

Michel left the Hilton early on Monday morning and Marianne slept late, with the drapes drawn, until, at eleven-fifteen, the telephone began ringing. It was Tommy, down in the lobby, could he come up?—was she free?—but Marianne told him irritably that she already had a luncheon engagement. She would probably be busy all that afternoon and the evening too but he might call in the morning if he liked.

The Japanese businessman had hired a car to drive them out to the historic village of Szentendre, where they had lunch in an attractive inn. The man's name sounded like—might it be Kiyoaki?—Marianne had no idea how it might be spelled. It was difficult to understand him at first but Marianne grew more accustomed to his accent as they talked. He had, he said, spent many periods of time in the States and liked San Francisco very much, and New York City of course; but the "inside" of the continent puzzled him. It seemed so large, and wasn't it more or less uninhabited . . . ? The desire of most Americans was to live in California or New York, was that true . . . ?

The Japanese businessman was perhaps over forty but he looked a great deal younger, with his very black shining hair, and his black eyes, and quick delighted smile. He was a vegetarian, he said, but it pleased him to watch a woman of Marianne's beauty and slenderness eat meat "with appetite." (Marianne was disappointed in the quality of the beef she had been served, but she ate it nonetheless, and rather hungrily.) He admired her stylish frizzed hair, her fair coloring, her several rings, her topaz-and-jade necklace; he inquired more than once if she was an actress, or an "American beauty queen"; might he visit her the next time he flew to the States?

Marianne gave him one of her little packet of cards—

MARIANNE BEECHER
National Science Education Foundation
(East Europe Division)
Washington, D.C. 20036

He wanted to give her a six-ounce bottle of Jean Patou perfume; and an evening purse of lamb suede lightly quilted (made in Finland); and a Swiss wristwatch with a small black square-cut face and stylized numerals. "I'm sorry, I can't accept such expensive gifts," Marianne said firmly. "The watch especially—it's clearly very expensive."

She spoke gently in order not to hurt Kiyoaki's feelings; but he insisted that the gifts were merely samples—"with no expense to anyone, I can assure you, Miss Beecher."

Marianne said she couldn't accept them anyway.

"It isn't done," she explained.

In the end, Marianne too decided to fly out from Budapest before the week was over. She was restless, bored with the Hilton, ready for the next city.

While packing she discovered that Ottó's manuscript was missing.

She searched for it everywhere—in the bureau drawers, beneath the bed, on the window sill behind the heavy drapes, in her own suitcases. She cursed under her breath; she was nearly weeping with frustration. It seemed to her (though she couldn't be sure about this) that several of her Hungarian cards were missing as well. "Oh damn it, what can I do . . . ?" she said aloud. The bell-boy was already knocking discreetly.

Though she always vowed to leave herself enough time Marianne's departure from a city was invariably rushed, uncoordinated. She was so late in getting started (her plane was scheduled to leave in forty-five minutes) that she wasn't able to leave a telephone message for the deputy chief of mission over at the embassy: she dreaded having irrevocably offended him.

As for "The Bringer of the End"—it was nowhere in the room. And she *had* no more time to waste.

By a stroke of luck—Marianne had almost begun to count upon her luck—she didn't have to resort to hiring a Hungarian cab to drive her to the airport. She was invited to ride along with a Munich businessman in his hired car—a luxurious black Mercedes, air-conditioned, deeply cushioned, with a glass partition separating the front and back seats. Sheer fortuitousness: Marianne and the German businessman happened to be going through the Hilton's revolving doors at nearly the same moment.

His name was Hans, he was a youthful fifty or so, with sandy graying hair and a forthright smile; his English was sharply accented but charming nonetheless. He had many direct questions to ask of Marianne: Was she acquainted with the "head man" (by which he meant the deputy chief of mission, and not the Ambassador, at the U.S. Embassy: the Ambassador was a political appointee); what was her "uncensored" opinion of the Hungarians; did she think they were a cagey lot, not to be trusted, or were these only the Hungarian Jews that stuck out . . . ? Had she been as surprised as he at the meager continental breakfast the Hilton served?

Along the slow, slow Pest road to the airport Marianne showed Hans the Swiss wristwatch, explaining that, since she had no use for it (yes it was very beautiful but she already had a fine watch

of her own) she wondered if anyone in his family might appreciate
it . . . ?

He exclaimed over its beauty. He gave it a hard little shake, and
held it to his ear, watching Marianne with the equanimity of a
man of taste. Marianne said again that she loved the watch but she
simply hadn't any use for it, was there anyone in his family he
might wish to give it to, as a surprise gift from Hungary?

After some spirited bargaining they arrived at a satisfactory
transaction; Marianne's cheeks grew prettily warm, and Hans interrupted himself with barks of delighted laughter. She handed
over the delicate little watch and received for it a gratifying quan-
tity of Deutsch marks, the hardest currency in Europe.

LAMB OF
ABYSSALIA

So great was my joy at being home that I could not sleep. Not the first night, not the second, not the third. I lay awake in my comfortable bed and could not sleep. The room's fixtures were not familiar. Perhaps darkness distorted them. I scrambled to the top of a hill but the parched, cracked earth beneath my feet would not support me and at the very brink of triumph—at the very brink—I lost my balance and fell backward with a scream.

A small landslide was loosed: rocks, pebbles, chunks of mud.

There were screams. They were not familiar screams. *Lamb of Abyssalia,* the voices pleaded. *Lamb of Abyssalia have mercy on us.*

Quietly I made my way through the sleeping house.

No one heard, no one knew. Everyone was asleep. It was necessary to walk quietly, stealthily. During my eight-months' absence I often thought of home, especially those last several weeks when I was very tired. I thought of myself tiptoeing through the house, silent and invisible, poking my head into every room, checking to see that everyone was safe. I love you, I whispered in my feverish sleep, I will protect you. Now that I was home it seemed that I might encounter myself on the stairs or around a corner—a tall, thin, smiling, featureless person with a slight limp. I love you. I will protect you. But don't wake: don't stir in your sleep. Isn't it enough to know that I am home and that I will never leave you again?

In their rooms, in their beds, my children slept. When I heard their soft, feathery breaths I felt as if I might swoon. How I loved them—! I would never leave them again. The danger was too great.

I drew near to their beds, trembling. Of course they had forgiven me for being away—they knew no better than to forgive me. My children. My dear ones. Quietly I leaned over to kiss the youngest one's forehead. He stirred in his sleep, he sighed, his breath was sweet. I wiped a thin thread of saliva from his chin. . . . The eldest did not wake when I approached his bed but he began to grind his teeth suddenly, as if the landscape of his dream had unaccountably turned threatening. But only for a moment: only for a moment. Not wishing to wake him I did not risk brushing my lips against his forehead, I merely stared at him in silence, I blessed him in silence, and then backed away. In my daughter's room I stood for some time, motionless, in awe of her beauty. The fair down of her cheeks and arms, the dimple near her mouth, the small snub nose: her beauty frightened me. Her seventh birthday came and went while I was in Abyssalia, in the night-half of the world.

I could not sleep so I slipped from my bed and went downstairs to my study. I thought it prudent to begin work. I had been home now for nearly a week and I had not begun to work.

You will accomplish very important things, my elders told me. One of them shook my hand, covering it with his other hand: I believe there were tears in his eyes. (And he was by no means a sentimental man.) I smiled and stammered my gratitude as always. You will go farther than any of us, my elders said with their bright hopeful smiles. They were not jealous, there was no need for jealousy; they knew how I revered them.

Their prophecies have turned out to be, for the most part, true.

———

Once I flew against the sun—eastward against the sun's motion—and I passed beneath the sun and in that way overtook the sun. On my return flight I flew westward beneath the sun and the sun's rays stung and I was drawn by the magnificent tug of the sun westward and it appeared that once again I overtook the sun as I passed beneath the sun but perhaps this was an illusion, like many: perhaps I did not overtake the sun on either flight.

There are eight notebooks, a duffel bag and a knapsack filled with three-by-five cards, and several piles of papers—some of them are rumpled letterheads from the Hotel Bru'jaila, some are merely slips of paper. Twists and bits of paper. I spend my hours smoothing papers with the flat of my hand. The halo of light that falls atop my desk is very intense. I am fearful of insects—fearful that they will flock to the light and hit against the shade and against my face—but I keep on with my work.

On the fourteenth floor of the Hotel Bru'jaila the hoarse-voiced Minister of Finance and Development introduced me to a very curious, very strong but also very sweet—stingingly sweet—drink called Ā-sā. Ā-sā? I am not sure of its pronunciation. It is a brownish purple-red, a claret red. In certain lights. In other lights it is very dark. When I tasted it two wires leapt into life, running up my nostrils and back into my brain. What is Ā-sā made of, I asked the Minister when I was able to speak. He ignored my question; perhaps he did not understand it. You try more, you like, he said flatly, unquestioningly. You will enjoy. He watched as I sipped at the tall iced sugar-rimmed glass on the fourteenth floor of the Hotel Bru'jaila.

On the banks of the River of Blossoms, and the River of Faith, and the Blessed River of Forgetfulness. Squatting creatures with human characteristics: their great dark bruised eyes, their brain-damaged eyes, seizing me and releasing me in the same instant. I adjusted my sunglasses. I moistened my lips.

The white man is considered by the Abyssalians to be a kind of ghost or "trick" person. A "trick" shadow. Moving my hands slowly before their eyes, this way and that, I noted that their gaze did not follow the movement of my hands.

Certain insects buzzed angrily about my face.

Lamb of Abyssalia pray for us. Lamb of Abyssalia have mercy on us.

I stooped and kissed the child's forehead. Perhaps it was my imagination but his skin felt feverish. I drew my cool fingers across his forehead; I brushed a strand of hair away, noting its silkiness. I forgive you, the child whispered. I love you and I forgive you but you must never leave me again—you must never leave your family again. We wept together. Our cheeks were hot with tears. I was a giant creature crouched over his bed, my face must have been terrifying, so contorted with sorrow, yet the child found it in his heart to forgive me. But you must never leave your family again, he said.

Abyssalia. Bounded by Equatorial Guinea, the Republics of Rambu and Nazaire, and the French Territory of the Barrantes. Area: 114,000 sq. mi. Pop. (1976 est.): 2,800,000. Cap. and largest city: Bru'jaila (pop. 1976 est., 174,000). Language: Abyssalian, Bantu dialects, French. Religion: animist approximately 70%; Muslim and Christian minorities.

You like, you will enjoy. You will learn.

The Lamb of Abyssalia is led from hut to hut, and at each dwelling bits of its fleece are plucked. The hill people are tall and very dark and their cheekbones appear to be pushing through their skin. Their eyes appear to be growing back into their skulls. It is said (and I had no way of confirming) that from 5%–8% of the population lives to be more than 110 years of age.

Infant mortality, however, is high. Very high.

The Lamb of Abyssalia is led in a great circle and is brought back to the little altar before the priest's hut. The Lamb is always a male; it is a very choice lamb, never more than one month old. Music of a sort—gourds, drums, a fife-like pipe—accompanies the Lamb's passage.

I crouched over the narrow bed, I brushed a strand of hair out of the child's eyes. My God I am so frightened. So frightened. But the child slept his deep innocent sleep. My fingers trembled: I pulled a single strand of hair out of his scalp: I yanked it free.

I began to sort the note-cards. Twelve separate piles. And the slips of paper—some of them no more than an inch square. Scrawls in ballpoint and in pencil. Some words illegible. Snips and bits of paper. Magic utterances. Twists of words. Syllables missing: I sweated through my clothes there in Abyssalia and my wisdom is therefore fragmentary.

As far as the eye can see, a wave of bodies: a sea of bodies.

Making their way along the banks of the River of Blossoms. So many! I held my sunglasses in place for fear they would fly off.

Why are there so many, I asked, seeing the caved-in eyes, the swollen stomachs, the knobby bones. Where are they going, I asked.

A religious procession, I was told.

One crumpled bit of paper speaks of those gaily colored rags.

Another speaks of the heat, and of course the odor.

Another speaks of the noises: the groans, the grunts, the random shrieks, the occasional outbursts of song. And of laughter? I am not sure.

Still another note, much-folded, speaks of a wraith-like mask hovering above a bright orange rag. *It appeared to be a mask,* the scrawl declared hesitantly. How curious, a kind of death's-head, the eyes, nose, and mouth darkest, as if shaded in by crayon or charcoal. How curious, that it should be trembling. Quivering. Pulsing. I came closer and saw that it was something living: a swarm of dark-glinting insects. Mosquitos. I came closer still and saw that it was a child's face but the face was covered with insects, and the insects were most crowded, most dense, on the eyes and nose and mouth. (I began to shout. I began to scream. I clapped my hands and some of the mosquitos rose from the child, sluggish and heavy with blood, not very disturbed. I could not stop shouting. Perhaps I was screaming. Someone touched my shoulder and drew me away. Stop, they said, you must stop. You'll have sunstroke. You'll be very, very ill. I was still screaming. Insects darted against my face; something had bitten me on the right cheekbone. There was a terrible stench. The child's face was swollen and bleeding and very ugly. Perhaps it was not a child. It wore a twisted orange rag. Come away, they said gently, the mother has abandoned him and death is inevitable. Why do you tire yourself in this heat?)

=

A detailed description of the Hotel Bru'jaila: its waterfall, its pot-
ted trees and flowers, its velvet couches, its marble floors, its marvelous air-conditioning. (Some of the women wore sweaters, in fact.
One wore a lynx stole.) The Minister of Finance and Development,
the President of the University of Abyssalia, a smiling young black
man named Robert, and I, on the fourteenth floor of the hotel,
eating native dishes, listening to a combo playing breezy tunes
from the American Forties. You'll be very, very ill. In the distance
the hills evaporated into a sullen heat-haze the color of sand. Isn't
the fourteenth floor of any hotel really the thirteenth floor, I inquired, my breath hot from the Ā-sā I had drunk too quickly. Only
Robert caught my meaning. He had played tennis at Harvard
with Neville Hughes's son: did I know Neville Hughes? He had
done so much for the cause of Abyssalia, for its liberation. In 1957.
Surely I knew him? I was joking, surely, to say I did not know him?

I shielded my eyes against the sun but it did no good. Everything
caught fire, everything was seared with heat. During the afternoon
the sun shook itself like a giant, bumbling, good-natured dog and
descended from the sky and dwelt among us and caused us to swim
through him—it—*him*. I lay on my cot in my tent, in bedclothes
soaked in the River of Faith. Insects threw themselves against the
netting. Something burrowed beneath my fingernails, into my
armpits, into my left ear. O help me. O God help me. I drank in
the evenings, writing in my notebook. The book would grow, the
book would blossom, I would rise when my name was called and
come to the podium where the President of the Academy of
American Letters would shake my hand and present me with a
scroll. I would clear my throat nervously. I would give my brief
prepared speech. My lips would part in a grateful smile as I stared
into the audience, row upon row of applauding individuals. I am
very happy, I would say, I am very grateful, I am humble, I am
surprised and pleased, I am ill. You must excuse me but I am very,
very ill.

The applause would continue, however.

===

Applause, applause.

Murmurings, shouts, outbursts of song or laughter or—? Rage,
perhaps. Terror. Millions upon millions of creatures with human

characteristics, swarming upon a river-bank, splashing in the bright green fetid water, their rags catching fire in the sunshine. Such fine gay brightly dyed colors! The glinting movement of their wings, the fixed precision of their eyes. Swarming. I waved my hands violently, I cried out, but no one listened. Had my foot slipped I would have fallen among them. Beneath them. Had my foot slipped, had the plane's propellers failed to start, I would never have returned home.

Where my joy is so intense that I crouch above the little girl's bed, my face swollen big as the ceiling. O look! A cloud dark with thunder! In my own dreams I run shrieking up a hill, my feet scrambling beneath me, and in utter silence I don't—quite—don't quite— Someone's tiny soft hand reaches out blindly. Someone's fingers tweak my nose. Daddy? Daddy? Look at funny Daddy! I am convulsed with a joy that cannot quite translate itself into laughter and when I wake I am not in my bed, not in any of my beds: I am standing, still, above the child's bed, my back stiff and my neck taut with pain. My cheeks glisten in the pale moonlight. My eyes are awash with a stranger's tears.

Lamb of Abyssalia, my lips plead, have mercy on us, pray for us, have mercy. . . .

No one may witness the sacred ceremony, they told me gravely.

It is death to witness the sacred ceremony.

So they told me in Bru'jaila but they turned out to be misinformed—which was so often the case. (They knew less about their own history and the details of their tradition than I; but of course I kept such knowledge to myself.)

We camped on the bank of the River of Blossoms, and then again on the bank of the River of Faith. The Blessed River of Forgetfulness excited my curiosity until I saw it—a squalid muddy stream not much larger than an irrigation ditch, curling through the vegetation. I wished to dip my hand into it, thinking perhaps that I would be blessed with forgetfulness, and as I stooped my hat fell off—did not fall so much as leap—or perhaps it was tugged off by an impish river demon—and though I lunged for it immediately it was lost.

I tied a piece of cloth about my forehead as I had in the days of my youth, running long-distance in the sun.

A bright red rag about my forehead to keep sweat from my eyes.

I grew gay, talkative, spirited. A single swallow of wine was enough to inflate me like a balloon—my eyes fairly bulging with elation. At first the others laughed with me. They grinned and shook their heads from side to side, signifying now *yes*, now *no*, sometimes a noncommital *Yes?* that had no human meaning at all. Afterward they grew silent. Then sullen. Then fearful.

What can be done, I asked, having witnessed the Sacrifice of the Lamb at last, my head awash, my lips rubbery with grinning. What can be done?—who will do it?—what will salvation consist of?—who will be the savior?—will we survive the summer?—will we get back to the capital?—will we be devoured like the Lamb, hairs plucked from our heads and bodies, our eyeballs chewed, our blood splashed on the lovely blank foreheads of children who would rather be somewhere else playing?—our sacred organs anointed with oil, our bones ground down fine for fertilizer?—will we acquiesce to the sacrifice, or will we go berserk at the last moment and fight?—and will we fight bravely, or hopelessly, thrashing about like children? What can be done, I cried, unable to sleep for the fourth night, what can be done and who will do it? *Who will do it?*

I spoke of the Blood of the Lamb and though my eyes were glittering with tears and my throat constricted with the desperate need not to cry and my voice trembled foolishly, the audience forgave me or did not know. They were waiting merely to applaud. They were waiting for the presentation ceremony to end. Afterward there would be conversation, drinks, high spirits—a release from my voice and the queer wet blank stare I fixed upon them. They waited merely to applaud. They were not restless—it was a very courteous and civilized audience.

I would praise them all, I would bless them. I would kiss their parched foreheads. An immense face floating above a crib, lips puckered for a kiss: a ticklish kiss! The child dreams of a swarthy face, a creature from the dark side of the earth; the child groans and twists from side to side. The fetid smell of the river is in the room with us. Why are the windows closed, why have I forgotten to open them?—or are they open?—is the wind blowing from the wrong direction? As far as the eye can see there are bodies. Bodies heaped upon bodies. Some are alive, crawling upon the dead. Some have been devoured by flame and are now ashes that float past us on the sacred stream. As far as the eye can see: the swarming of dark, oil-slick bodies. My foot slips, I am falling, I clutch at the sides of the crib but cannot break my fall, the air is rich with the odor of decaying flesh and excrement and something sweet, achingly sweet, like sugar cane; in the distance the holy bells are clamoring. Wait, I cry, what can be done, who will do it—

The audience begins to applaud at last.

Come away, someone says, touching my arm. Come away.

I would resist but I don't want to disturb the boy. I allow myself to be led quietly out of the room.

Can't you sleep? But why? Why can't you sleep? Have you really tried? How many nights has it been? Won't you try a sleeping pill? Won't you see a doctor? How long can this go on? What can I do? What can be done?

Her voice is too soft, the harsh crazy clamor of the holy bells drowns it out. Why don't the bells ring in unison, I asked, surely they are not in competition with one another—? But they are ringing in unison, I was told. They *are* ringing in unison.

I'm so afraid, she says. Staring at me. She too is sleepless though she would deny it if I inquired. She is sleepless because she spies on me, listening to my footsteps, following in her mind's eye my passage through the house. Though I walk on tiptoe and have no more weight than a dream-wraith, she can hear me: her eyes are wide with fear. She *knows*.

And yet she can't possibly know.

You're frightening the children, she whispers. You're frightening me. Sometimes I think—

That's ridiculous, I tell her, smiling.

I think you might harm one of us—

Ridiculous.

A very choice lamb it was, a male no more than four weeks old. Led past the excited villagers by an old man who scolded it fondly, tugging at the length of twine tied about its neck, making of its squealing terror a kind of joke. Yes yes yes yes yes! Such foolishness! Such a baby! Bits of its wool were plucked by greedy fingers.

And stuck in hair, behind ears, in ears, even up nostrils. There was music, there was singing. Everything was gay, noisy, cacophonous. Children screamed with excitement. Women rocked from side to side, clutching their breasts. I stood to the side, staring. I was invisible: no one saw.

I kept a careful journal.

At last the lamb was dragged to the little stone altar at the center of the village and killed with an ordinary knife about the size of a fishing knife: blood was sprinkled liberally in all directions by the old man: and then the villagers were anointed, one by one, on their foreheads and collarbones: and then most of the lamb was devoured raw. (Afterward the lamb's skull was fixed to a tree in a grove of trees outside the village. There were skulls or parts of skulls on most of the trees.)

The people were so happy afterward, I whisper.

She does not hear. She leads me along the darkened hallway, her hand closed tight about mine. As far as the eye can see there are bodies—some with heads balanced precariously upon skeletal necks, their eyes dark and bruised and sightless; some with swollen bellies; some with no bellies at all. I will save you, I tell them. Have faith in me. But my wife leads me past them, stepping daintily around them. We are both barefoot. We are both frightened. If the stench of the bodies sickens my wife, however, she gives no sign.

You must sleep and then you'll be well again, she says. Then you'll be yourself again.

I stoop and kiss the child's forehead. Is he feverish? Is his face swollen?

The people were so happy afterward, so *happy.* I try to explain. There is no fear, no pain, no sorrow, no possibility of being lost—not even in that vast wilderness. Have faith in me. Don't doubt me. My dear one, my love, sweet mouse, sweet baby. Do you hear?

OUR
WALL

Long before many of us were born, The Wall *was*.

It is difficult for even the most imaginative and reckless of us to posit a time when The Wall *was not*.

Of course there are people—older people—who claim to remember not only the construction of The Wall (which, in its earliest stages, was rather primitive: primarily barbed wire, guarded by sentries and dogs) but a time when The Wall did not in any form *exist*.

Could one go freely into the Forbidden Zone then? We children never tire of asking, faintly scandalized and ready to burst into nervous laughter as if in the presence of something obscene. But the elderly tell us that there was no Forbidden Zone then, in the days of their youth.

No Forbidden Zone?—we are incredulous.

No Forbidden Zone?—we are somewhat frightened.

The shrewdest child among us, who is always asking bold, impudent questions, says brightly: If there was no Forbidden Zone then, why was The Wall constructed?

But no one understands his question. He repeats it insolently: *If there was no Forbidden Zone then, why was The Wall constructed?*

No one, not even our oldest citizen, understands. Each of the boy's words, taken singly, is comprehensible; but the question in its entirety is incomprehensible. . . . *Why was The Wall constructed?*
It is far easier—most of us find it easier—to assume that The Wall is eternal, that it ever was and ever shall be. And that the Forbidden Zone (which of course none of us has ever seen) is eternal too.

Several times a year, though never on predictable dates, our leaders declare a Day of Grace. Which means that citizens of our country above the age of eighteen who are free of debt, familial responsibilities, and other private or civic handicaps, may attempt to scale The Wall without fear of punishment or reprisal. On a Day of Grace all explosives buried in the earth are inoperative; the current flowing through the barbed wire is shut off; the watchdogs are tied fast with chains; the sentries in their sentry boxes, hidden from sight, do not poke the muzzles of their submachine guns out and fire. It is said that on each Day of Grace a number of citizens do run across the burnt-out section of earth before The Wall (in some parts of the city it is no more than thirty feet wide, in others it is at least one hundred feet wide and represents, as one can well imagine, a formidable expanse!)—a number of citizens do run to The Wall and scale it and disappear on the other side. And are not stopped, not even scolded. So it is said.
And what becomes of them, on the other side? No one knows.
Of course we are only human, and rumors fly from house to house, wild improbable tales are told and repeated and embellished, no one knows what to believe. It may be claimed that a Day of Grace has been announced for a certain area—a privileged area—and not for another; or that the Day will begin on the first stroke of noon instead of on the last, or on the first stroke of midnight instead of on the last; or that there will be no restrictions at all regarding age, financial status, etc. As one might well imagine such cruel rumors result in butchery: the unstable rush forward too soon, or too late, or on the wrong day entirely, and before the horrified eyes of hundreds of witnesses (for there are always witnesses along The Wall) are shot down, or blown quite literally to bits by landmines, or savagely mauled by dogs. For we are, despite our history, a hopeful people.
Nevertheless each Day of Grace is eagerly awaited. Speculation on

the exact date is widespread; we are all acquainted with certain obsessed and rather pathetic individuals who can speak of nothing else (though—of course!—these are the very individuals who would never dream of trying to scale The Wall). Even those who have never in their lifetimes witnessed a single successful escape (for sometimes the slang expression "escape" is used openly)—people who have been passive onlookers, for decades, at many a spectacular and heartrending slaughter—continue to have faith. One would think that their number might gradually dwindle, but the contrary happens to be true. For we are, as our historians have noted, a hopeful people.

The Wall appears to be about twenty-five feet high, though some theoreticians claim that it is considerably higher, while others believe that it may be lower. Measurements are imprecise since they must be made—if at all—at a distance from The Wall, and under cover of darkness. It is a commonplace belief that The Wall is made of fairly smooth concrete, an ordinary enough material, and in itself not particularly fearful. The top has been rounded for aesthetic and security reasons: it is more attractive that way, and presents more difficulties for those who try to scramble over the wall using their bare hands. (Barbed grappling hooks are said to be necessary for a successful escape, but such grappling hooks are forbidden by law. Indeed, there are those of us who have never seen a grappling hook, not even a picture of one: yet we whisper the words "grappling hook" amongst ourselves quite freely.) Our elders claim that The Wall did not always have a rounded top, but it is difficult for most of the population under a certain age—about forty—to remember any other kind of top.

In heavily populated areas of the city there are two additional "walls" or barriers. One is a wire-mesh fence with barbed wire at the top, which is (evidently) electrified; another is a row of anti-tank obstacles placed at five- or six-foot intervals. The obstacles, like The Wall itself, are painted a uniform dove-gray, and are quite attractive. Beds of yellow and purple pansies lend a cheerful touch: nothing extravagant, but welcome to the eye.

In less populated areas The Wall stands majestically alone, and in the burnt-out space before it landmines have been buried so carefully that (so it is rumored) not even the shrewdest eye can detect them. Nocturnal hares, poor creatures, frequently detonate these explosives. They know no better. We are often awakened from our sleep by the sharp cracking thunder of an explosion: is it near, or far? At such times we lie awake, not caring to speak, for what is there to say?—the hares know no better, they are poor ignorant beasts, and nuisances at that.

Two nights ago there was an explosion. Difficult to judge its distance. To the east, to the west?—difficult to judge. Did you hear that noise, one of us asks another softly, and the other says, Did I hear what? or perhaps does not reply at all. What is there to say? Nocturnal hares, nuisances.

The Wall is considered a work of art by some citizens, and an abomination by others. The largest percentage of the population, however, does not "see" the wall at all—that is, literally. Consequently The Wall elicits no emotion and, indeed, the term "The Wall" is rarely used. The expression *over there* is fairly frequent, as in (to a naughty child): If you don't behave I'll send you *over there*. (Over where? I once asked my mother boldly. Over *where*? *Where*?—You'll see over where, my mother said, slapping my face. Her breath came quick and hard; her own cheeks were burning.)

And do you know that children's bones are buried in The Wall?—in the foundation of The Wall? Children of exceptional beauty or talent—children who were orphans, or in some way unprotected—too high-spirited for their own good and for the good of the community. On dark wet nights when the wind blows from The Wall you can hear their querulous chatter.

Of course these are silly tales, in which none of us believes. In our district we have eradicated superstition. The Wall is The Wall and (so we believe) it is made of ordinary material. It is *not* haunted: its great strength has nothing to do with children's corpses. Sometimes, late at night, you can hear their faint high voices. Where are we, what year is it, what has happened . . . ?

But no: there are no voices: there are no spirits. The Wall is only (*only!*) The Wall.

One of the voices is my brother's voice.

Do you hear him, I asked my parents, but they did not hear a thing. Only the wind, the wind. Rain drumming on the roof, on the windows. Streaming down the windowpanes.

I burrowed beneath the bedclothes to the foot of the bed and lay very still. My thumb and then two fingers stuck in my mouth. The wind, the wind from The Wall, rain drumming on the roof all night, his voice, his crying for help, I could see him dragging himself on the stubbled grass and his uplifted face glistening with blood: and the half-circle of witnesses. For there are always witnesses—silent witnesses—along the many miles of The Wall.

Toward morning, when the wind died down, I fell asleep. And did not dream at all.

It is only a coincidence, but according to reliable sources the next Day of Grace will fall *on my eighteenth birthday*. Which is to say, at the very end of the interminable month of August.

The Wall: which stretches out forever. Mesmerizing and boring and beautiful, so beautiful! You can't know. You can't know unless you crouch here with me in my secret place, my hiding place, in a stand of scrub birch hundreds of yards from the nearest house. Underfoot are shards of glass, fragments of board, rubble from The War (which took place long before I was born, before even the building of The Wall—if the old people can be trusted to tell the truth). I crouch here for long minutes at a time, staring at The Wall, letting its gray uniformity flood into my brain. Mesmerizing and boring, so boring, and so beautiful, our Wall!—long minutes, long unrecorded hours at a time, my back aching, my face beaded with sweat. I want nothing from The Wall, I am content merely to gaze upon it. Knowing that it is there. That it exists. That one cannot move *in that direction*. That there is a *Forbidden Zone* which has been explicitly marked, and from which we are to be protected forever. How was it possible for human beings in my country to live, to endure their lives, before the construction of The Wall?— when they might have *freely* moved in any direction, even in the direction of that which is forbidden? (The thought fills me with anxiety. Tears begin to sting in my eyes, and threaten to roll down my warm cheeks. To move *freely* in any direction, what horror!)

Gray concrete. Miles. Years. A lifetime. An eternity. So boring. At peace. So beautiful my heart plunges. In the midday sun, in the

late afternoon sun, in a fine light drizzle that obliterates all out-
lines . . . The Wall is absolutely motionless . . . one cannot imagine
a time when it was not . . . and the sentries' boxes every two hundred yards or so . . . the border guards (chosen for both their skill as
soldiers and their loyalty to the State) hidden from view, even the
muzzles of their submachine guns hidden. As a young boy I
wanted to be one of them. But then the shame of my brother, the
fuss, the black mark. . . . I want to be one of them now. I want to sit
for long empty mesmerizing hours inside a sentry box, a submachine gun in my hands, always ready, always ready to fire.
Ugly things are told about some of the border guards.
—They shoot *at will* if they choose. If a face offends them, or a ges-
    ture. If they are bored. If nothing exciting has happened in a
    long time.
—They themselves are frequently defectors. (Which is, of course,
    logical. For no one has such opportunity to escape as they do.
    Enviable men! I hate them, as everyone in my district does.)
—They have no more loyalty to the State than the next person,
    but enjoy the power of the sentry box and the feel, the weight, of
    the submachine gun in their hands.
I crouch in my hiding place for hours. Sometimes it seems that
years have passed. I am not a child now. I am waiting.
Beyond The Wall the sky is a feathery blue, or a turbulent rippled
gray. Sometimes it rains. Sometimes the sun glares. I am at peace,
gazing at The Wall. Its wonderful sameness, its mysterious
strength . . . while human beings change . . . grow old, weak, unre-
liable. I am at peace here. If I hear gunfire in the distance, or the
barking of dogs, I am never agitated. For I do not intend to make a
run for it like the others. I am content to live my life *on this side*.

What, precisely, is the Forbidden Zone, from which the citizens of
my country must be protected?
Absolute truth is impossible to come by, since anyone who climbs
The Wall successfully disappears from our world and never returns; and anyone who climbs The Wall unsuccessfully is killed on
the spot. However, here are the most popular theories:
—There is a paradise beyond The Wall in which men and women
    live "freely." (Though of course they must be bound—how
    could they fail to be?—by The Wall, just as we are. Perhaps it is
    somehow worse for them because our Wall surrounds them.)

—There are dangerous, diseased, psychotic people beyond The Wall. A race not unlike ours, but degenerate. A brother-race? But degenerate. At one point in history (evidently during the life-spans of some who are still living) all of us constituted a single race, from which the population of the Forbidden Zone fell away.

—There is nothing but a graveyard beyond The Wall: a mere dumping ground for the dead. The bleak truth of The Wall is that it protects the living from the dead (the noxious gases of the cemetery); or, as the more subtle among us reason, it protects us from our own future.

—There is an ordinary world beyond The Wall—our own world, in fact—but it is a mirror-image, a reversal. None of us could survive in it.

My own theory? I have none. I think only of The Wall. The fact of The Wall, which settles so massively in the mind. The Wall exists to be scaled, like all walls: it is the most exquisite of temptations. The Wall poses the question—*How long can you resist?*

I am a good runner, I can run for miles, my heart beats large and steady in my chest, my pulses race, my muscular body grows sweat-slick, I am pitiless toward my legs and feet; and my hands are strong. These are mere facts. They point toward nothing beyond themselves.

"Traitors"—"criminals"—"subversives"—"degenerates"—"enemies of the People"—"victims of aberration": these are the official terms for those who defect from our side of The Wall. A formal death sentence is passed upon them in absentia, and their families are subjected to harsh penalties. (Though in fact it frequently happens that the families, having publicly exhibited their shame and grief, and having publicly vowed their love for and loyalty to the State, escape the most severe penalties and even enjoy a curious sort of celebrity. For humiliation, if it is properly absorbed, can be a sacred experience.)

Yet I would not abandon my family. My mother and father who lie to me, as they lie to each other; but out of necessity; out of love. I would not abandon them as others have.

I have never seen The Wall desecrated.

I have never been a witness.

Except: I was among that crowd of schoolchildren who gawked at the dying boy at the foot of The Wall one weekday morning. He had tried to escape during the night and had actually scaled The Wall—he was strong and supple, he must have prepared for his "escape" for many months in secret—but of course the guards shot him down, as they always do: who could elude them? They shot him during the night but did not kill him and so he lay for hours, for many hours, into the dawn, the morning, the mid-morning, bleeding to death in a field of stubbled grass, and calling for help. A high faint voice. An incredulous voice. Not a voice I recognized.

Sunday, the last Sunday of the month, is to be a Day of Grace. My eighteenth birthday. The official proclamation has not been made but rumors fly freely from house to house.

The Wall, in the midday sun, appears to show a certain *benevolent* aspect. If you stare for a very long time, your eyes held open wide, this *benevolence* becomes obvious. Yet why has no one remarked upon it, to my knowledge?

So few of my fellow citizens "see" The Wall at all.

Wasn't that your brother who was shot down in the field, people asked.

I don't have a brother, I said angrily.

Wasn't that your brother?—the one they shot down? schoolchildren teased.

My brother? Whose brother? I don't have a brother.

They jeered and threw stones at me. Chanted: He deserved it, he deserved it, the traitor, he deserved every bullet they gave him! *I don't have any brother,* I shouted.

It is said, and if you climb high enough you can ascertain for yourself, that The Wall zigzags and curves back upon itself, by no means describing a perfect circle around the Forbidden Zone. Strange. Hard to comprehend. Unless the workers who built it were drunk, or playful. Or subversive.

To caress—just once—the blank face of The Wall. To get that close. To lay your hands upon it. Just once! In dreams, the most shameful and turbulent of dreams, where one is clambering up

The Wall—*and* being riddled by the guards' bullets at the same time (for death too, at such a time, in such a manner, would be exquisite): in dreams we scale The Wall nightly, and keep our secrets to ourselves.

The Wall, where small yellow butterflies impale themselves upon the barbed wire. A great fist in my chest. Broken glass beneath my feet. A delirium that must be love. . . . Of course there are lurid tales: men and even women shot down and dragged away and never heard of again, and never spoken of again. Because they stared too hard at The Wall. Might have seemed to be studying it, memorizing it. Adoring it. (Do I know anyone who has disappeared? I know no one. "Disappearing" carries with it the obliteration of memory, after all. *Everything* connected with a traitor is lost.)
A very strange tale, too wild to be credible, about a family in a balloon who drifted across The Wall. Seven people including a baby. Romantic but implausible. . . . Wouldn't a large balloon make an irresistible target?

(Someday, it is whispered, we *will* overcome The Wall. And mate with those men and women on the 'other side.' As we are destined to do. As we had done in history. We will breed a race of giants once again, we will conquer the world. . . . The Wall, one must assume, has been erected solely to prevent this, the fulfillment of our destiny: The Wall is an invention of our enemies and must be surmounted.)

But now, today, this sunny morning, what of today?—my eighteenth birthday? A helmeted guard has poked his head out of his sentry box and is waving to me in my hiding place. Yes? Yes? Perhaps he knows it is my birthday? I stand slowly, blinking. The sunlight is fierce. The guard has taken pity on me, perhaps, and is waving me forward. Come stand in the shadow of The Wall. Come press your overheated cheek against The Wall's cool side. . . . For the first time I can see fine cracks in The Wall, and weeds growing lavishly at its base. (I have never been so close before.) Come closer, have no fear, long before you were born The Wall was, and forever will The Wall endure.